A novel

Eva Marie Everson

FIREFLY
SOUTHERN FICTION
LIGHTHOUSE PUBLISHING OF THE CAROLINAS

Firefly Southern Fiction is an imprint of LPCBooks
a division of Iron Stream Media
100 Missionary Ridge, Birmingham, AL 35242
ShopLPC.com

Cover design by Elaina Lee

Library of Congress Control Number: 2021930332

ISBN-13: 978-1-64526-309-8
E-book ISBN: 978-1-64526-310-4

PRAISE FOR *DUST*

From the first word to the last I was enthralled with this story. Everson's love-story-through-time will appeal to every reader who cheers when love triumphs. This is Everson at her best.

~Rachel Hauck
New York Times bestselling author of *The Wedding Dress*

Author Eva Marie Everson's characters in *Dust* are flawed, their choices, both good and bad, intersecting and influencing each other's lives. Everson's layered southern family drama reveals the complexities of relationships and the unexpected and sometimes painful consequences of our choices. While we might regret how what we say and do affects others, with every turn of the page Everson reminds readers of a vital truth: life doesn't have to be perfect to be good.

~Beth K. Vogt
Christy award-winning author of the Thatcher Sisters series

What is one life worth? Eva Marie Everson's *Dust* takes the readers on a slow, Southern, and yes, dusty journey through several decades as we watch the lives of her characters intermingle amidst the little and big tragedies, heartaches, and celebrations of life. With breathtaking, sometimes sensual prose, Everson explores romantic love in all its passion and brokenness as the characters make choices whose consequences bleed into other lives for generations. A thought-provoking and soul-stirring story.

~Elizabeth Musser
author of The Swan House Series

Allison meets Westley as a callow girl and enters their marriage on the wings of starry-eyed optimism. It is the 1970's, and Westley has kept a secret that impacts the years to come. In a web of memorable characters who intersect profoundly, *Dust* is a novel of exquisite breadth and width, a soulful story of a woman coming into her own that shows us it is the seemingly ordinary life that is, in fact, extraordinary.

~Claire Fullerton
award-winning Author of *Little Tea*

Fans of Eva Marie Everson will rush to purchase her latest novel, *Dust*. A complex story line moves the story at a rapid pace which makes readers fall headlong into this page-turner. The characters remain with you long after the ending and you will find yourself thinking about them long after the final page. In *Dust*, Everson secures her place at the top of women's fiction.

~**Renea Winchester**
award-winning author of *Outbound Train*

Eva Marie Everson's novel *Dust* is a poignant story about family, not simply family defined by DNA. but the struggles, joys, and disappointments that bond us. These characters face challenges that ultimately determine who we really are and how we love one another.

~**Christa Allen**
award-winning author of *Since You've Been Gone*

Dust invites readers to dwell inside a story of hearts so vivid, one cannot help but smell the vintage-era scene in which they breathe. Eva Marie Everson sculpts each scene with emotional and relational authenticity. Every character rises with such profound realism from the pages, tears well for the fates of both hero and antihero. Everson deepens our compassion for those on various sides of life's dramatic struggles. Yet she also carries us from realistic pain points to address the ultimate existential question: meaning. As a therapist, I see the reflections of living souls in the eyes of Everson's characters. My only challenge in endorsing *Dust* lies in offering a recommendation with eloquence worthy of this author's extraordinary talent.

~**Tina Yeager**
LMHC, Award-winning author, Speaker
Flourish-Meant Podcast Host, Life Coach

I didn't write today. I read—all day. I didn't cook today. I read—all day. I didn't eat today. I read—all day. *Dust*, by Eva Marie Everson is an epic story. I loved it as much as I loved *A Woman of Substance* by Barbara Taylor Bradford. This is Everson's best book ever!

~**Ane Mulligan**
bestselling author of *Chapel Springs Revival*

"How is it that our lives can be so affected by the decisions of othe. A question asked in Eva Marie Everson's book, *Dust*. Her amazin character development will make you wonder if you've met some of these people in your life. She takes you on a journey of love, loss, and everything in between. A must read and maybe even more than once.

~**Edwina Perkins**
Managing Editor, Harambee Press

Everson, at her page-turning, keep-you-reading-all-night best brings *Dust* to the world. She has penned a novel that intrigues, shell shocks, and keeps you guessing. She peels back and exposes the beauty and tragedy of everyday life. She draws in-depth psychological characters that pop in and out, leaving you reading until wee hours seeking them.

~**Merilyn Howton Marriott, M.S., LPC**
Award-winning author of *The Children of Main Street*

This is Eva Marie Everson's opus. I have read her books for years and this one takes story to a new level. Filled with characters whose personalities are so vivid, you feel as though you are peering over their shoulders, Everson wraps you tight in the drama of a family and how, even with good intentions, things can go awry. Everson's descriptions of the era make you long for the time you may have walked there. *Dust* is memorable. *Dust* is endearing. *Dust* cannot be wiped out of your mind at the end of the day. This book will remain with me forever.

~**Cindy K. Sproles**
bestselling author of *What Momma Left Behind*

In *Dust*, Everson commands a rich Southern setting and a wide cast of characters with a deft hand and an evocative voice. Perfect for book clubs and women's groups, *Dust* brings to life the questions of every woman who has wrestled with marriage and motherhood, while understanding that, sometimes, we live not only with the choices we make, but the ones that are made for us.

~**Lindsey Brackett**
award-winning author of *Still Waters*

ACKNOWLEDGMENTS

Anyone who knows anything about classic rock knows that "Dust in the Wind" was released as a single in January 1978 by the progressive American rock band, Kansas. Written by Kerry Livgren, the song became a track on the group's 1977 album *Point of Know Return.* The song was haunting. Beautiful. One of my favorite all-time pieces of music from my young adult years. The inspiration, it has been reported, came to Livgren from biblical scriptures (Ecclesiastes 1:14, 3:20; Genesis 3:19) but the song itself was composed only as exercises for the guitar (to learn fingerpicking). Chances are, "Dust in the Wind" wasn't played on the radio until late January 1978. I took the creative liberty of giving it airtime for Allison and Westley in October 1977. And that's okay. I am a writer; I can do that.

So, allow me to begin by thanking Kerry Livgren for such an amazing piece of lyrical literature. When I heard the song on Pandora a few years ago, the idea for *Dust* formed, then took on new meaning as I focused not on our being *dust in the wind* but in where that Wind carries us. I will also admit that Michelle's misunderstanding of "Carry On Wayward Son" was originally, well, mine.

There are so many others to thank: my Page 6 group from Word Weavers International who read the bits and pieces of the manuscript for over two-and-a-half years; Ramona Richards, my critique partner; Jessica Everson, who said she didn't understand the quandary women found themselves in in the late 1970s and so inspired me to go back and "fix things;" Tina Yeager who said, "Who will victimize Cindie next?" and so opened up a whole new world and character in Patterson Thacker; Merilyn Marriott who helped me understand the nature of the self-sabotaging beast; my agent, Jonathan Clements, who encouraged me, even after some time had gone by, to keep at the writing of the story; my husband who left me alone while I sequestered in my office for hours upon hours only to emerge a tad moody; my street team who gave me so many high-fives and who, by and large, taught me that "I have all idea" must be a colloquialism known only to the Southern region of my birth (so I removed it from the dialogue); Ann Tatlock, my editor (I am still so excited!); Lucie Winbourne for her proofreading talents; and to all those who prayed me through an incredible difficult time in which the writing of this book took place.

Finally, "thank you and I love you beyond measure" to the Lord God Almighty whose Word tells me that although my bones may one day return to dust, I have a purpose, and that, no matter how great or how small, that purpose matters.

Eva Marie Everson

Dedication

To my Little Bro ...
... who loved Jesus ...
... and classic rock ...
I miss you more than I have words.
And I love you to bits.
Big Sis

Before...

Patterson
June 5, 1965

Atlanta wasn't just steaming hot; Atlanta was practically on fire. And so was Patterson Thacker, who stood at the Groom's Room window, blinking toward the church's parking lot three stories below. He breathed slow and steady as words repeated in his head. His heart. *He could do this.* He could marry Mary Helen and be true to her. To her and to the children they would someday have. He wanted this. Had chosen this ... more or less.

He took another breath. Tugged at the bow tie his father had tied a bit too tight. Watched steam rise from the asphalt to form ghostly mists. Again, for the hundredth—no, the millionth—time that day, he willed his nerves—and his expectations—not to get the better of him. Because he knew, he knew he had to be careful. His unadulterated passion for the woman who, somewhere in this building of cold stone and stained glass and stretching spires, was as hot as the day. This day. Their wedding day.

Of all days ...

He grimaced. Mary Helen had worked herself into a lather planning the perfect date. A date that, she'd told him when she'd settled on it, would occur early enough to keep their guests from walking through the outskirts of hell to reach the church doors. One that meant their outdoor reception at the country club could be—and would be— enjoyed by all.

But her meticulous planning had come to naught; Atlanta was smack dab in the middle of a heatwave unlike anything they'd experienced that century—or so the weatherman declared only nights before during the five o'clock news.

Of course, Mary Helen had been fit to be tied. She couldn't believe it, she said. Absolutely couldn't believe that God in his mercy would do this to her ... to *her* of all people, good Christian that she was.

Patterson had tried to calm her. Tried to tell her that, no matter what—heat or cold, rain or shine, if the flowers stood glorious in their vases or wilted like Grandma's lettuce—they'd be married soon. Husband and wife, off to live the best life any two people ever had. And wasn't that the whole point of the day, he'd asked, his fingertips traveling the length of her arm in some hopeful way of easing her frustrations.

But she'd slapped his hand away, which—with all their years together—hadn't surprised him. She'd pretty much been slapping his hand away since the night seven years ago when a high school football game slated them for the state championship. A night when he'd noticed her—really noticed her—for the first time, cheering from the stands for the team. From that night on, they'd been an item— "Patterson Thacker and Mary Helen Robinson"—the golden couple, the couple most likely to ...

But she'd kept him on a tight physical leash from night one. Sticking to group dating and closed-mouth kisses and hands kept at safe distances. A fact, he convinced himself, in keeping with the standards of her being "the kind of girl a man brings home to Mother."

"The ones you bring to your bed," his father had informed him in one of the rare moments when they spoke of such things, "and the ones you bring home to Mother are not the same girls."

Time had proven his father's sage words—advice, perhaps—to be true. There had been a girl during his first three years at Princeton—a flower-child-hippie-type named Dani—who'd fit the first bill just fine. He would have *never* brought Dani home to Mother. Or to Atlanta for that matter.

Fun while it lasted, but once he'd proposed to Mary Helen, he kissed Dani goodbye.

So to speak.

He sighed deeply now, thinking of her ... wondering where she was and how she was and if she ever thought of him fondly. The heat through the window—or was it the memory of Dani tangled in threadbare sheets—warmed him enough that he tugged again at the collar of the overly starched tuxedo shirt. And, again, the blindingly white bow tie resisted the insert of his index finger as though its ulterior motive—and perhaps Mary Helen's—was more to strangle him than to make him look debonair.

"A sign of things to come," his best friend—and best man—said from behind. Patterson turned to smile at Dexter Holloway, who stood peeling his tux jacket off. "Goodness, man. Could Mary Helen have picked a hotter day? Even the air conditioner can't keep up."

"Don't start," he answered. "She got so emotional after the weather report the other night, I thought she was going to have a meltdown that would make every Southern woman worth her salt stand up and take notice." He stepped away from the window. "I mean it, Dex, if it weren't for all those gifts at her mama and daddy's house, she probably would have cancelled the whole thing." He grinned to lighten the notion. "You know Mary Helen can't resist a good china pattern. And the thought of returning all that Limoges ..."

Dexter slid the cuff of his shirt over his watch. "Son, you've got about ten minutes before the reverend comes in here to get us." He looked up with a grin. "Run now and I'll provide cover."

"Come on. After seven years, you think I'm about to run off now?"

Dexter nodded, bringing his hands to rest on his narrow hips. "Seven years and counting. Son, I cannot believe you two held out this long."

"Wasn't my idea."

"But tonight's the night."

Heat—different than before—slid over Patterson, and he smiled. "Let's certainly hope so." He looked at Dexter then, a man who'd been married two years now. A man whose wife was about to pop, ready to bring his baby into the world. "Ever hear of a woman balking on her wedding night?"

"I'm sure some woman somewhere..."

Patterson raised his brow in jest. "But Mary Helen will be worth the wait."

Dexter laughed. "Oh, I'm sure ..."

Patterson paced the room then, the thick red carpet soft beneath shoes that had been polished to such a shine he could see his reflection in them. When he stopped at the window again, he tapped the toe of one to the beat of a rhythm only he could hear. One that came out of nowhere. One with lyrics he whispered under his breath.

"What's that?" Dexter asked.

Patterson looked up. "Nothing," he said with a shrug. "For some reason I'm singing 'Subterranean Homesick Blues.' I got the album last week and—other than when Mary Helen's had me at this function or that—I've listened to it nonstop."

"I read somewhere that Dylan's recording another one soon."

"Oh, yeah? That would be cool." He paused, thinking. "Man, I love Dylan..."

Dexter plopped down onto a charcoal-gray sculptural sofa that appeared to have been dropped onto one too many times by one too many groomsmen. "This waiting ..."

Patterson found the nearest chair, unbuttoned the tux jacket, and eased down. "You think you're anxious. What about me?"

"Different reasons," Dexter teased, which made Patterson chuckle.

"This time tomorrow..."

"... the wait will be over."

The door slid open bringing both men to their feet, turning to see Reverend Pinkerton peering around it. "Patterson," he said, entering with his hand extended. "You ready, my boy?"

Patterson looked at Dexter and winked. The reverend meant one thing, but the two of them were thinking another. "Yes, sir," he answered, taking the pastor's hand and giving it a firm shake.

"Well, then," Reverend Pinkerton drawled. "Just to let you know, I stopped by the Bride's Room a moment ago, and Mary Helen is as pretty a picture as you could ever imagine."

Patterson's smile grew, his cheeks growing taut at the thought of her both in and out of her wedding gown. She'd told him all about it, but of course he'd yet to see it. Tradition prohibited and, God knew, Mary Helen was a woman of tradition. But she'd talked about the lace and the satin and the fullness of the skirt brought about by layers of netting and the veil and her shoes and her bouquet and even the bridesmaids' gowns and shoes and bouquets until he wondered if she were marrying him because she loved him to the ends of the earth the way he loved her or because she loved a good wedding.

"I imagine she is," Patterson said as Dexter slapped him on his shoulder as if to congratulate him for marrying a girl such as Mary Helen. The way his father had after securing the bow tie too tight. And, for a moment, the picture of Dani rushed over him again, the feel of her in his arms almost tangible until he shook it away.

"Well, then," Reverend Pinkerton repeated. "Let's go get you two married, shall we?"

"Yes, sir," Patterson said. He followed the old cleric through long hallways filled with reflective color from stained glass windows, then down two sets of narrow staircases that led to the door where countless grooms before him had entered the opulent glory of the sanctuary. Where they'd stood at the altar, hands clasped low and in front, waiting ... ticking away the minutes until the ringbearer and the flower girl and the long parade of bridesmaids escorted by groomsmen came to their stations ... until Wagner's "Bridal Chorus" swelled from the organ's pipes and, finally, a man caught sight of the woman who walked in his fiancée but would walk out his wife.

One hour, Patterson told himself as Reverend Pinkerton jerked the old door open. Less than one hour, really. In a short while, Mary Helen and he would walk up the aisle she'd walked down, this time to the pulse of Felix Mendelssohn's "Wedding March." He would endure the reception and the cutting of the cake and the first dance and the photographs and the well-wishes of every friend and family member Mary Helen ever thought to know or have. And then, they'd be off ... off to their honeymoon and their first night as man and wife. Off to a new life.

A *good* life where he'd provide for her on a college professor's salary and she'd rear their children to be among Atlanta's finest.

Yes. Finally. Mary Helen Robinson would be his and life would be the proverbial piece of cake.

Chapter One

Allison
October 1977

When I think back on it, I realize I never received a formal proposal of marriage. Not really, anyway. He never got down on one knee, never presented me with a diamond ring sparkling above a blanket of black velvet, prisms shooting out in the moonlight. There was no sweet scent of honeysuckle wafting from my mother's garden. No violins playing in a quiet Italian restaurant while candles flickered atop checkered tablecloths. He never said the words women—especially those reared in the South—dream of. Never said, "Will you marry me" or "Will you make me the happiest man in the world and be my bride" or "my wife" or any of the phrases that accompany dreams.

He never promised me a perfect life. He never promised me forever.

What he said—if I remember the words clearly after all these years—was, "Well, that sounds good."

And, I suppose, it was.

We had been alone in his parents' home that afternoon in 1977, the two of us, neither one having to go to work that day. I don't remember why. Maybe it was a holiday—Columbus Day, perhaps, what with it being the middle of October. His parents had gone to the grocery store—fabulous cooks that they were. Gone to pick up necessary items for the dinner they'd whip up in the oversized farmhouse-style kitchen where miles of Formica countertops stretched over and under tall white cabinets.

I'd been invited to stay.

I may have driven out there earlier in my '65 Mustang (already a classic) or Westley may have made the forty-five-minute drive in his '74 Pinto to pick me up. Again, these are the things I cannot remember. Not that it made any difference to the end results.

The day was warm, and Westley had gone outside to pull a few weeds from his mother's flower garden while I stayed indoors to watch Match Game '77. I'd always been a sucker for television game shows. My youth had been spent watching *Password* and *Concentration*. *Let's Make a Deal* (with the lovely Carol Merrill). *General Hospital* and *Peyton Place*. The latter two, of course, not being game shows but television dramas my mother didn't mind me watching.

For the life of me, as I write this, I don't know why not. Her sole goal in life when it came to me, I often thought, was to protect me. To save me from any form of scandal, whether real or perceived.

So, there I sat, watching Gene Rayburn in the comfortable but overly decorated home of my boyfriend while he worked outside on a day I cannot recall, and while his parents shopped at the local A&P for a meal I cannot remember. At some point, during commercials, I took my own break and wandered around the rambling house, which I found as easy to do as wearing a pair of old house slippers. I had no fear of being "found out," although I should have. I'd only been dating Westley six months and was hardly a member of the family.

But I'd imagined it. The first time I came to his home for dinner and saw the long formal dining room table draped in linen and adorned in crystal and silver and the most stunning pattern of Noritake china I'd ever seen, I knew *this* was the family for me. *This* was the family my father and especially my mother would happily approve their youngest daughter leaving their fold for. Not going to college for. In fact, my mother would be downright giddy at the prospect, especially considering the bum—and a religious one at that—my sister had married.

I walked to the front of the house where the formal living room—Victorian and polished—sat dark and lonely, drapes pulled to keep the sunlight from fading the velvet. I ventured to guess that—other than me and the weekly maid—people rarely came into this room with its low ceiling and thickly carpeted floor. A baby grand piano sat in the far-left corner, draped with a fringed silk scarf and topped by a satin-and-lace hurricane lamp that, when turned on, cast faint light on a cluster of silver-framed photos of family members long ago dead and buried. Women in high-neck collared dresses and men with the hook of a walking cane draped over one arm. Babies, sporting button noses and Cupid's-bow lips, and donned in flowing white christening gowns. I touched the ornate corners lightly, wondering who they may have been and thinking to ask Westley when he returned inside. Or ... someday.

Across a narrow foyer, the room Westley's father used as a study and office beckoned me to enter. I stood then at the wide doorway and looked in, taking in the antique rolltop desk, counting the nooks and crannies and tiny drawers filled with who knows what. A tall stack of books sat willy-nilly to the right while papers and files and pens and pencils scattered across the top blocked every inch of the oak grain beneath.

Against the back wall, a floor-to-ceiling bookcase rose and yawned, its shelves nearly buckling from the weight of volumes of tomes. I wondered if Dr. Houser had read them all. Or any at all.

I stepped across the hardwood floor to the front window to peer out, to see if Westley was anywhere around, then caught sight of him ambling from the mailbox at the end of the lane leading to the white clapboard house, correspondence held tightly in one hand. He was a handsome man—an odd sort of cross between Barry and Robin Gibb minus the beard, which I still find hard to explain really. It was as if he had been cut from the same mold but had somehow been lost in the transfer from heaven to earth and, instead of landing in England, found himself in a crib along the coastline of Georgia. Now nearly twenty-eight years of age—almost nine older than me—he was tall and well-built, with soft brown curls he meticulously styled, and a thick moustache that tickled my nose when he kissed me, which was often and well.

The voice of Gene Rayburn called me back to the family room, so I scurried in, more than anything not wanting to be caught prying. I had barely gotten back to the sofa and crossed my arms and legs in an "I wasn't doing anything" fashion when Westley stepped in from the door leading to the kitchen.

"Hey there," he said, smiling. "I should have changed to jeans and a tee."

He wore a pair of tan corduroy bell-bottomed pants that fit him scrumptiously. He had unbuttoned the cuffs of his shirt—polyester and quite stylish for the time—and was already at work on the mother-of-pearl snaps going down the front. I averted my eyes, allowing myself only to look at Charles Nelson Riley, who quipped a line toward Gene Rayburn. Safer there by a mile.

I'd seen Westley bare-chested, of course. We'd spent hours upon hours soaking up sun on Tybee Island that summer. But the oddness of his coming out of his shirt in the privacy and sanctity of his parents' home—while altogether acceptable at the beach—struck me. After all, we were innocent in our relationship. Innocent and *alone* ...

"Hey yourself," I said. The contestant with the Farrah Fawcett hairstyle kissed Richard Dawson for his role in her win of $500 in prize money as Westley flicked off his shirt.

I glanced over, noting as quickly as possible the tan of his skin, the flat of his belly, the pink of his nipples, and a small tuft of hair between them that formed a V. "It's hotter out there than I thought it would be," he said. "I'm going to take a quick shower and change into something a little cooler."

A new contestant came on the show and Gene Rayburn announced that they'd return after a word from their sponsor. I cast my eyes toward Westley's, careful to stay focused on the green of them. "Yeah. Okay," I said. My leg—the one crossed on top—began a furious pump of its own accord.

He chuckled, then plopped beside me. "Excuse the sweat," he said before reaching over to kiss my ear. Down my throat. Back up again.

"Westley," I breathed. "Your parents ..."

He ignored me. Instead of going for the shower—awkward as that would have been with him down the hall splashing around naked as the day he was born—he slid his arm around my shoulder, cupped my chin and kissed me so soundly I felt as though I had been dropped into a tunnel. Although common sense shouted otherwise, I allowed myself to sink into the rough fibers of the sofa, keeping my palms flat on my thighs, all the while allowing him to press harder while kaleidoscope colors exploded behind my eyes.

Westley had that effect on me.

And then ...

"Westley Houser!"

I jumped, wiping my swollen lips with the back of my hand, blinking furiously to clear my vision and to assess the situation. I was in the Houser family room ... Match Game '77 ... the show had gone to commercial. Westley had taken off his shirt ... tuft of hair ... kiss from heaven ... and now ... his father stood in the doorway holding a brown paper bag full of groceries, his face aghast while mine blushed furiously.

But not Westley. He only grinned and said, "*Allison* Houser," combining our names so seamlessly as to suggest I'd always been known as such.

I sucked in as much air as the room held, my chest exploding from the pressure.

And that's when it happened. Westley looked from his father. To me. Said, "Well, that sounds good" and beamed back up at his father. "What do you think, Dad? Should I make an honest woman out of her?"

An *honest* woman? "I-I—never—" I stammered. "Dr. Houser, we've not—I've never—"

"Better get used to calling him *Dad*," Westley said, standing. He displayed his shirt to his father. "I was about to shower. Pulled those weeds like I told Mom I would and got a little warm ..." He winked in my direction. "Then a little sidetracked." He smiled at his father. "Isn't she adorable, sitting there all red and flustered?" He didn't wait for an answer. Instead, he started for the dining room, which led to the hallway, the bedrooms, and baths. Then, halfway into the dining room, he added, "Oh, and the mail is on the kitchen table," then disappeared into the hallway.

But not before I noted the envelope jutting out from his back pocket.

And just like that, I was engaged.

Westley's father leaned over, the paper bag crunching, kissed my cheek, his horn-rimmed glasses pressing into my flesh, and said, "Welcome to the family. I hope you can do something to tame that son of mine," before calling out, "Mom, we're going to have a new addition to our family."

Westley's mother entered the room, her hair the same wispy curls she'd passed on to her son, her eyes just as bright. Just as kind. She'd been a slender woman once. I'd seen the photos the night I had my first meal with the family. That night when I saw the linen and crystal and silver and Noritake china and determined I wanted to become a part of this family. That night when, after dinner, his mother entertained me with stories of Westley's youth while showing me photo after photo of her firstborn son.

"He was the daredevil," she told me as she pointed to another black-and-white photo. "See him on that bicycle? I don't care what it was, he'd jump it. Never feared a thing."

"Not Paul," Dr. Houser said of Westley's younger brother, only fourteen months his junior. "Paul was more sensitive. A reader. A thinker. Westley never met an obstacle."

A "baby sister" named Heather, now away at college, born years after Westley (she and I were only a few weeks apart in birth and, so far, got along famously), rounded out the family and, in the process according to the photos, his mother's frame. Not fat or flabby by any means, but when she hugged me, I felt as though I'd wrapped my arms around a bowl of warm pudding. Smooth and sweet, like vanilla. She also smelled of powdery perfume; it lingered on my clothes long after her embrace and drifted through her home like a friendly ghost.

Now, she stood in the doorway, her purse in her hand as though she'd been about to deposit it somewhere, staring at her husband—bespectacled and amused—and asking, "Who on earth are you talking about?"

Dr. Houser nodded toward me. "Allison. Westley asked her to marry him."

Mrs. Houser threw her hands up in the air, the purse hitting her bosom, and expelled a shrill I suspect was as much shock as joy. "Well, if anyone can tame him, it's you, my darling," she said, reaching for me.

I realized then I hadn't moved from the sofa since *the kiss* but had instead practically grown roots in the tweedy fibers. I hugged my future mother-in-law, being careful of the purse she continued to dangle. I breathed in the scent of her, thinking I could die in this woman's arms right then and there, completely unmarried, still as much a virgin as the day I was born, and I'd be all right.

Perhaps it was then I realized I would soon marry not a man, but a family. Well if I didn't realize it then, I certainly did later.

More than that, I was also about to marry a challenge.

Tame him, my foot.

Chapter Two

My father traveled most weekdays with his work—leaving Monday morning and arriving home sometime Friday afternoon—so Daddy was gone the day Westley proposed. I didn't want him finding out about my upcoming nuptials over a late-night phone call with my mother, and I thought it best not to tell him without a lot of preparation first. I had always been Daddy's baby girl. The notion of marrying versus going to college next year would need to be approached gently. With care and tact. Perhaps with prayer and fasting.

So, after a lot of talking it over and a little begging on my part, Westley agreed not to say anything about the engagement until after Daddy returned from wherever he happened to be that week. "But I'll be there Friday night. Seven thirty on the dot. Ready to ask for your hand in marriage." He waggled his brows as if he would actually consider doing such a thing.

I returned home after dinner, stepped through the back door of the ranch-style house we called home, and said goodnight to my mother who sat knitting another of her remarkably complex afghans while watching one of her programs. "Well, wait," she said. "How was dinner?"

"It was good," I said. I raised the Tupperware container I carried and added, "Mrs. Houser made a delicious autumn squash soup. She sent you some for your lunch tomorrow."

Mama beamed as though she'd been invited to the meal. "Well, that was nice of her."

"She's a nice lady." I raised the container higher. "I'll put this in the fridge."

Which I did, then went on to bed as though nothing new or exciting had occurred in my life that day beyond a dinner date with Westley and his parents. But once I slid beneath the thick bedcovers, I held up my left hand, staring at it in the faint light from a streetlamp that cloaked the room in a washed-out gray, and wondered what type of ring Westley would one day slip on my finger.

I turned to my left side and reached with my right hand for the portable radio on my bedside table, permanently tuned to WBBQ out of Augusta. I flipped the power to "on," then turned the volume knob until the song playing came in loud enough for me to hear but low enough not to keep me awake. Within minutes the unmistakable voice of Harry Nilsson lulled me to sleep, holding me there until morning.

I had planned to wait until Westley arrived to say something definitive. To talk casually during Friday night's supper about *not* going to college—no, not even next year. About one day leaving home … having a family of my own … that kind of thing. I'd planned, for goodness sake, to break my upcoming nuptials to my parents gently. With Westley next to me on the sofa.

Instead, two seconds after Daddy said grace, I raised my bowed head and blurted, "By the way, Westley and I are getting married."

Unlike Westley's parents, who ate the last meal of the day in the dining room, we had supper at the kitchen table. That night, our everyday china plates were full of fried pork chops and mashed potatoes cradling a spoonful of gravy and resting beside a mound of English peas. And when I made my announcement, both parents left their concentrated efforts on eating to look up at me; working mouths suddenly stopping mid-chew. My mother reached for her seafoam-green Tupperware tumbler of sweet iced tea, took a gulp, and swallowed hard. I looked from her to my father, who did the same, and waited.

When they said nothing, I continued. "It's no big deal really."

My mother blinked then. "What do you mean? How can getting married *not* be a big deal?"

"I mean the proposal."

My father found his voice. "How did he—what did he—" He took another drink from his powder-blue tumbler before adding, "I don't remember him coming to me about this."

"Daddy," I said with a shaky smile, then placed my fork and knife against the plate and reached for his hand, pale like the rest of him. "I don't know that men do that anymore."

"Well, I think they should," Mama said. And then, as if we were now ready to move on to the next subject, "But never mind. When is the wedding?"

"I haven't approved this—"

"Of course you have," Mama said, her words passing in front of me as if I had no bearing on the weight of them. "He's Westley Houser, for crying out loud."

"We haven't set a date," I interjected. "Like I said, it was no big deal."

Mama stood, walked to the sink, rinsed out the dishcloth, and began to wipe countertops already spotless. "How can you say that? How can you say that the words a young woman hopes to hear—how can you say ..." She turned to face us then, crossing her arms, the dishcloth dripping water to the linoleum at her Keds-shod feet.

I laughed. I had to do something. I was so nervous and giddy and scared, so I laughed. "His father caught us—" I paused, feeling heat rise in me, then thinking I should hurry and finish my sentence lest my father think the absolute worse of his chaste daughter, I said, "—kissing."

"Kissing?" My father boomed, then laughed so heartily, the table shook under the heaviness of his forearms resting against the edge. "Well, thank you, God, for small favors."

The heat inside intensified, so I picked up the fork and knife and went to work on slicing a bite of pork chop. "Anyway ... he caught us kissing and he said Westley's name and then Westley said my name, only he added his name to the end of it."

"Allison Westley?" Mama laid the dishcloth over the faucet and returned to the table.

I raised my brow at her. "No, Mama. Allison Houser."

My father chuckled again. "That's original." Daddy turned his attention back to his supper. "When will Westley be here?" He raised a teasing brow toward me. "I will need to talk to that boy."

"Tonight," I said. "I told him you were coming home this afternoon and—this should make you happy—he insisted that he—we—talk to you ... both ... tonight." I glanced at the round acrylic clock hanging high over the kitchen sink. "He'll be here around seven thirty."

"An hour," Mama said. "That hardly gives me time."

"For what?" I asked. "It's just Westley. The same man who came over last Sunday to watch the game with Daddy. The same man who arrives every Friday night at seven thirty on the nose."

"But this time he'll come as your fiancé," Mama said, then looked at Daddy with pleading brown eyes. "Explain it to her, Darryl."

I looked at Daddy, whose square-shaped face registered the same surprise I'd felt after realizing I had become engaged. "Explain it to *her*?" he asked. "Why don't you explain it to *me*?"

Mama stood from the table, this time with a grunt of frustration. "I'm going to get ready," she said before leaving the room. "So much to do ... *so* much to do ..." Her voice faded the farther into the house she went.

I looked at Daddy, who now ran a hand over his close-cut white hair. His blue eyes danced a little as he said, "Darlin' ... that mama of yours ..." as though the brevity of words were some form of explanation.

I squared my shoulders. "Well, a wedding should keep her occupied for a while," I said. "I think now that I'm grown and working and what with you gone so much of the time, Mama needs a project. You know, other than knitting and circle meetings."

Daddy pushed his plate an inch away from where it rested. "Ah, but what will she do *after* the wedding?"

"Probably run over every morning to wherever Westley and I live to make sure I've mitered the corners of the bedsheets."

Daddy laughed again. "Look here," he said directly. He placed his warm hand over mine, which I'm sure was ice cold at the thought of what I'd just said. "Give Mama some space, you hear?"

"Yes, sir."

"And get this kitchen cleaned up for her, will you? Lord knows what she's doing back there in our bedroom but putting on the dog is probably at the head of it."

"Yes, sir." I stood and began to gather the plates.

Westley arrived at exactly seven thirty, which was his way. Everything about Westley was calculated. In the short period I'd known him, I'd come to realize that right up front.

We'd met only six months earlier—which in retrospect meant that we had no business getting married or even becoming engaged. The day we met, I'd come down with a sore throat, called our family doctor who, in turn, told me he'd call in a prescription to the local Rexall. "I betcha it's nothing more than the weather causing your throat to hurt," he said. "Weather these days doesn't know if it wants to turn loose for spring or hang on for winter."

"That and what with all the flowers beginning to bloom," I said as though I had a clue.

"Yes, yes," he said. "All right, my dear. The prescription will be waiting on you when you get there."

"I'll go over during my lunch hour."

I'd graduated high school the year before. After my sister married the bum, my parents had placed all their hope for a college grad in the family on me. Then, as graduation crept closer and closer, and much to my parents' disapproval, I made the monumental decision not to go to college right away, but to give myself a year off from the world of academics. I'd spent my senior year in a job program the high school offered. Every weekday, instead of staying until three, I walked out after lunch, threw what few books I now lugged onto the backseat of my car, and then drove three miles to a local printing company located on a downtown side street. There I learned the trade of "office work." There wasn't a whole lot to it, but I got along well with the owners and the customers. Within weeks I could take job orders like a pro, had learned the art of upselling, and had—as my employer Mr. Foster said—organized the storeroom and filing cabinets into something manageable.

Before I'd come to work there, the whole operation was a nightmare. Mr. Foster—sixty if he was a day—and his wife innately knew where everything went, but to the rest of the employees (in other words, me), the storeroom seemed a web of confusion.

Then, as I neared graduation, Mrs. Foster had to have some type of life-altering surgery and Mr. Foster asked if I'd like to stay on during the summer with an increase in hours "until you go on off to school."

I explained to Mr. Foster that I had given myself a year off and so staying on wouldn't be a problem.

"But why?" he asked, as if I'd told him no. "Why wouldn't you want to grab your education by the throat as soon as you can?"

The question jarred me. "I—uh—well, to be honest, Mr. Foster, I don't have a clue what I want to do with the rest of my life—no idea at all—and I thought that—maybe with a little time—"

Mr. Foster removed his readers and dropped them into one of the pockets of the dark-green bib apron he wore at work. "All you'll do the first year or so is take the basic classes. May as well get them out of the way while you're deciding."

I frowned. "Have you been talking with my parents, Mr. Foster?"

Mr. Foster's jawline went slack. "Why, no. I just think that—you young people today don't know how lucky you are to get to go off to college. Back in my day it wasn't as easy. It was a different America."

I smiled now. "I've heard." If not from my teachers, from my parents. And if not from my parents, from my grandmother, who I called "Grand," because—oh, she just *was*.

"Southern women are strong by nature," she'd once told me. "We are the true Scarlett O'Haras. We raise our radishes into the air and declare that as God is my witness, we shall never go hungry again."

She squared her eyes with mine. "Remember that when life tries to kick you down."

"So, I mean, if you'd like," I now said to Mr. Foster, "I can stay on as long as you need."

"I suppose," he agreed with a nod, "that your decision—bad as I think it may be—is a good thing for Mrs. Foster and me."

He wasn't kidding. Turned out, Mrs. Foster's surgery didn't go as well as the doctors had hoped. She decided time spent "on her feet" had come to an end, which meant that Mr. Foster gratefully offered me full-time employment. He increased my pay to $2.35 an hour, which, in those days of six-cent postage stamps, was akin to making me rich beyond my wildest dreams. Especially if I continued to live at home with Mama and Daddy. And I remained careful of frivolity.

I disconnected my call with Dr. Carter that afternoon, managed to wait the good half hour until noon, then let Mr. Foster know I was going to run up to the drugstore.

"You sick?" he asked, looking up from his desk by peering over the readers perched on the tip of a too-thick nose.

I smiled to keep him from worrying. "No sir. Not really." I touched my throat. "Just a tickle, but Dr. Carter has called in—"

"Pick me up some lozenges," he said, his eyes dropping back to the work scattered on the metal desk. "In case I start to feel it, too." He smiled without looking at me. "Can't have both of us feeling puny."

I nodded, then turned to leave, but not before he added, "And tell Gladys to put it on my bill."

"Yes, sir," I hollered, then opened the rattling old glass-and-wood door, closed it behind me, and headed a block up and around to where the drugstore sat wedged between a hunting supply store and a shop where all young brides and mothers-to-be registered for pricey gifts. I opened one of the double doors leading into the store and breathed in the scent of candles and incense—something new Miss Gladys had introduced along with a line of American Greetings cards that had nothing to do with birthdays or anniversaries, sympathy or sick days, and thin books of select poetry by Rod McKuen. "Trying to keep up with the times," she'd told me the last time I'd gone in and studied one of them. She then showed me a new collection of inspirational cards boasting the poetry of Helen Steiner Rice. I ended up purchasing one for Mama, one that spoke of the beautiful yet complex relationship between mothers and their daughters.

On the day of my sore throat, however, I found Gladys Howard standing in the aisle that offered women's products on one side and baby items on the other, something I'd always found to be a bit of an oxymoron. "Hey, Miss Gladys," I said to her.

"Allison Middleton," she said. Gladys Howard always greeted the young men and women of our town by their first and last names.

Miss Gladys was a wonder to me. Her husband of only a few years had been killed early on in Vietnam, leaving her to raise twin towheaded boys. Her parents owned the drugstore, so she went to work for them and had managed it as far back as I could remember. Although a strikingly beautiful woman, she'd never married again—never dated that I'd heard of—but instead dedicated herself to her sons, her community, and the drugstore.

Thinking back on it now, Gladys Howard had not even hit forty the day I walked into the store for a prescription and some lozenges, but her elegance and life-wisdom made her seem at least a decade older. She was also a woman I *wanted* to be like, which was why I sought her out each time I came in, hoping maybe a little of her would rub off.

She straightened an item on the shelf, then turned to me. "How's your mama? I missed church last week, so I haven't seen her in a week or so."

"Mama's fine," I told her. Miss Gladys and Mama were in the same church circle and occasionally met in each other's homes for coffee and planning. "Are *you* all right?"

"Oh, yes. Yes. I don't know what happened Sunday. I completely overslept, and the boys were at a friend's so ..." She smiled broadly then. "Did you hear that the boys have both been accepted to Southern? Thank the good Lord they took after their daddy in the smarts department. So ... I guess in the not-too-distant future, I'll be rambling around in that house all by myself." She spoke the words as if this were a fate worse than death, but the pride in her voice brought a smile nonetheless.

"What will they major in?" I asked.

She laughed lightly as she crossed her arms. "Oh ... girls probably." Then she cleared her throat and said, "I'm just thankful neither of them wanted to follow in Dan's footsteps and join up."

Awkwardness settled around us. I wasn't a child anymore, but I wasn't a grown woman either. I had no idea what it meant to love someone and then lose them, especially to something that made no sense. "Well," I said, pointing to the back. "I'm here to pick up a prescription."

Life returned to her eyes and she asked, "Are you sick?"

I touched my throat as I'd done earlier and said, "No, ma'am. Just a tickle, but Dr. Carter ..."

Miss Gladys touched my arm lightly as she leaned in and half-whispered, "Honey, wait till you see what we've brought to town."

"Ma'am?"

"He's charming. He's not too bad on the eyes. *And* he's single."

I looked toward the back of the store, then again at Miss Gladys. "Ma'am?"

"His name is Westley. Spelled with a 't' in the middle. Westley Houser. He's our new pharmacist. Graduate of the University of Georgia, but his daddy is a provost over at Southern."

I furrowed my brow. "Where do they live?" I asked because I'd never heard of the Houser family. And living in our little town meant knowing everyone in it. And most of their business.

"Over in Stoneham," she said, jutting her head back a little toward the south end of town to indicate a community forty-five minutes on the way to Savannah. "I don't know how we managed to snag him *here*, but I reckon he wanted to stay close to home. Of course, there's nothing in Stoneham, so ..."

That much was for certain. A few grand old houses, a couple of stores, and a tiny post office. Two churches with a cemetery each to house their dead, headstones leaning against time behind each one. "Well," I said, taking a step toward the back. "I'll just have to check him out."

"You do that," she said with a conspiratorial grin.

In the end I don't know who checked out whom, but from the moment we set eyes on each other, life stopped long enough to draw us together as if it had always intended to do just that.

That evening, right after supper and the washing and drying of the dishes, the phone rang. My father answered as he always did when at home. A second or so later, he called me to the phone and said, "Some young man for you," then extended the handset in my direction, his expression matching my confusion.

"It's Westley," my caller said after I'd said hello. "Westley Houser."

I opened my mouth to say something, but words refused to come. After a few seconds he added, "Are you there?"

"Yes," I said finally. "Yes … but how did you get …"

"Your phone number is part of your records at the store."

"Oh."

"Not that I couldn't have looked you up in the phone book. By the way, did you know you're the only Middleton in Bynum … or the whole county for that matter?"

"I—yes."

"Hey, I know it's last minute, but can I interest you in a bite to eat? I just finished up here and I'm starving."

I looked around the room, my whole being now completely out of sorts and my sore throat nothing more than a vague memory. My father stared at the television. My mother had picked up her knitting and, feet tucked under her, sat on the sofa. She worked the needles furiously and by instinct. I stood behind Daddy's chair, aware that even though they were not staring *at* me, they heard every word being said and would drill me as soon as I got off the phone. Not too many *young men* called the house. Once upon a time, they called for my sister Julie, yes. Before she met the bum.

But not me.

"Sure," I said. "Do you know how to get—"

"I'll figure it out."

And he had. He'd figured it out at least twice, sometimes three times a week since. And, he'd become my every waking thought. The breath in my lungs. The period at the end of my sentence. From the absolute beginning, I knew—instinctively I knew—that one day he and I would marry. That I would never go to college—at least not anytime soon. That he'd be the father of my children. The reason I'd wake up in the morning and go to bed at night and move through the hours between. Westley Houser was all of life rolled into a big red rubber ball and tied off with a wide ribbon, able to bounce higher than all the others in the bin.

And—even though *my* ball was a little low on air—I believed that, with him, I'd soar above the rest.

Chapter Three

On my third Christmas, Santa managed to get a swing set from Sears & Roebuck into his sleigh and deposit it—red bow and all— to the backyard of our home. He even positioned it so my mother could stand at the kitchen window and watch my sister and me pump our little legs, forcing the cold metal swings higher and higher. Over the years, until I was too large to fit on its narrow seat, I spent the better part of my thinking hours there. This was where I dreamed. Where I created situations and circumstances I called "my stories." This is where, when I'd reached the end of them, I'd leap, arching above the green earth, arms flung wide, until I landed flat on my feet with a jarring bound.

I had turned thirteen or possibly fourteen when Daddy finally removed the rusted chains and unused swings and the two-seated glider, replacing them all with a wooden patio swing. He painted the frame and the swing in a soothing shade of forest green. Now, my actions upon it were different, but I still had a renewed place to think. To contemplate. To write in my diary uninterrupted. And to sit with friends on warm summer evenings, waiting for the sun to dip behind the line of tall, dark pines until the lightning bugs emerged. Waiting for the blue of the sky to turn to gray and then to black and the stars to come out. Waiting to lean my head back and look up and say, "There's the Big Dipper ..."—the only constellation I clearly recognized in the summer months.

Orion being the one in fall and winter. But that came later. With Michelle.

The evening Westley came over to talk to my parents—my father in particular—and after all the hand-shaking and after my mother had written down his mother's phone number in the little address book she kept in a kitchen drawer so they "could talk," Westley and I slipped out of the back door. We walked hand in hand around the front of the house to the far-right side where the swing had been moved, then dropped onto it. Night's cloak had already been donned and a distinct chill hung in the air. I shivered as I snuggled into Westley's arm, draped across the back of the swing. "Cold?" he asked as he removed his jacket without waiting for an answer.

I shook my head to indicate I would be fine, but he had me wrapped and tucked before I could say the words. I laid my head on his shoulder then, feeling the safety of being with him. Of knowing that—soon enough—he'd be my husband. I, his wife. And that we could do this forever.

He kissed the top of my head, leaving his lips at the crown until I looked up and found him smiling at me. "I thought we were going to tell them together," he said.

I kissed him lightly. "I couldn't wait."

He cocked a brow at my words as though he was about to reprimand me, but when I smiled, he smiled back and asked, "Do you want to talk about dates?" I returned to my original position, then threw my legs over his so I fit like a child against an adult. Westley adjusted me to his liking, then said, "Hmm?"

"I hadn't really thought about it."

His finger traced a line along my shoulder. "How does May sound to you?"

I calculated the time. "I thought most brides had a year to plan," I said, suddenly feeling a little sleepy ... and a little too comfortable scrunched up against him.

Westley tipped my chin up and kissed me in the same way he had the day of the proposal, leaving me wanting so much more than we *should* do ... or possibly *could* do ... especially considering our current location. "Do you *want* to wait a year?" he asked when the kiss ended.

"No," I croaked.

"Me either."

"But I *do* want to wait," I said, shifting the meaning.

He ran his index finger down my nose. "I understand that ..." He kissed me again, just as passionately as he had a moment before. Then, "How about December? You can be a Christmas bride."

I leaned back, the wood beneath me becoming like bricks. "I couldn't possibly get everything done in two months, Wes—"

He kissed me again. "Valentine's Day?" he asked when we came up for air and my whole body wished to ignite.

I threw my legs to the ground and bounded up. His coat puddled at my feet. "Hold on," I shouted as I sprinted toward the house on al dente spaghetti legs and the swing creaked and shook behind me.

"What are you—" Westley called out.

"Just hold on," I hollered like a fishwife, now at the front door. I sailed through it, nearly colliding with my mother who passed through the living room toward the back of the house. Or, I assumed such; she could have been standing at the wide picture window overlooking the front lawn, keeping watch over her virginal child.

"What's wrong?" she asked, her face drained of its natural tan.

"Nothing," I said as though "what could be?" and then hurried toward the kitchen. "I need a calendar."

Mama was on my heels. "Are y'all planning a date?"

"Yes."

"Let me get the '78 calendar that came in the mail the other day." She turned toward her bedroom.

"Yeah—okay—sure," I said while snatching the '77 calendar from the same drawer where Mama kept her address book ... pens ... a few pencils ... some paper clips ... a pair of paper-cutting scissors ... and a pack of emery boards. I shoved the drawer shut, met her back in the living room, took the calendar from her extended hand, and said, "Thanks, Mama."

"Why do you have—"

"For comparison," I lied easily, then stepped back into the chill of the air.

I made my way to Westley, who sat languidly, a cigarette hanging casually between his fingers. The night had closed in so that I barely made him out until I reached him and slid back into my place beside him. He readjusted his jacket around me, then took one more draw before flicking what was left of the cigarette to the ground and slowly blowing the smoke from between his lips. I opened the '77 calendar and frowned. "I can't see a blessed thing."

Westley dipped his hand into the pocket of his polyester pants, brought out a lighter, and "flicked" it. "Don't overexaggerate, Allison."

I prickled. "I'm not."

He kissed my temple. "What is this?" he asked, looking down with a smirk. "December, you say?"

I pointed to the square marking the Saturday before Christmas. "I must be out of my mind," I said. "But if we set the wedding for December seventeenth, the church will already be decorated, which will cut down on a large part of the … you know … stuff to do."

"Flowers and such."

"Yes. The Chrismon tree will be up and the poinsettias people always give in honor of or in memory of someone are always placed around the altar. I imagine that would look pretty nice."

Westley took the calendar from my hand. "I say, let's keep it simple. What about you?"

I stared up at him again, lost for a moment in his eyes and the twinkle that outshone the stars already popping out overhead. "The simpler the better."

"Who needs the nonsense?"

I drew closer to him, intoxicated by the Jovan Musk cologne and the faint hint of tobacco still lingering from his occasional indulgence. "Who indeed," I murmured, my voice dropping low and uncharacteristically sexy. What I knew about the art of seduction I had drawn from the movies I'd seen that included a modicum of forbidden or saucy romance—*Romeo and Juliet,* for one. *Love Story,* for another.

Westley cupped my chin, halting me. "Little girl, if you don't want to embarrass you and me both on this swing, we'd best get inside and tell your mama and daddy that we've settled on a date." His voice carried both a half-tease and a warning.

Heat rose in me, furiously slapping me from the inside out. "You're right. Of course." I stood abruptly. The calendars dropped to my feet and Westley reached for them as he unfolded himself from the swing, then took my hand in his free one.

"I must be out of my mind," I repeated.

"Two months," he said, then tugged me toward the front door.

My grandmother—my mother's mother—showed up the following afternoon after church and Sunday dinner, and the dishes had been washed, dried, and put away. My sister and her bum husband had driven over from Statesboro as they always did, both acting deliriously happy and in total denial of my parents' feelings toward *him.* They left shortly after cleanup, which was my cue to head back to my bedroom for a much-needed nap. I'm not sure how long I'd slept before my mother tapped lightly on the door before entering. I spent a good five seconds blinking to figure out where I was. "Mama ..." I frowned at her, my eyes scrunched in protest.

"Grand is here."

My grandmother was a marvelous woman—short in stature but commanding the attention of army generals. Despite the fact she scared me spitless at times, she was among my favorite people in the whole wide world.

"What's this I hear?" she asked when I found her in the kitchen. "Paulina tells me that our girl is getting married?"

"Grand," I said with a blush, then bent over to wrap her in a hug. "I am."

My grandmother had been a widow longer than she'd ever been

a wife, her husband—my grandfather—dying after being struck down by a drunk driver while walking down an old country road. My grandfather, my mother often told me, enjoyed long walks on Sunday afternoons down the dirt roads near their farm. That day had been no different. Church, followed by dinner, followed by Grand and the kids lying down for the Sunday afternoon nap, and my grandfather meandering out the front door. But by that evening, Mama said, when her father had not returned, Grand went out in search for him, finding him lying in a twisted knot, the life already gone from him.

"Something rose up in your grandmother that day," Mama told me time and again. "Something strong and powerful. She's never lost it." Pride welled up in my mother's voice when she spoke of her father's death and of the effects it had on her mother. But she never spoke of how it had affected her. She'd been only eleven at the time. Two years younger than her sister Pearl and three years older than "the twins," Meryl and Melvin. She never said a word about growing up during those hard years without a father … of her mother having to "go into town for work," or of her mother eventually selling the farm and the whole family moving away from the only home they'd ever known. She never mentioned how it had been that she married Daddy without her father there to give her away, a thought that now struck me nearly off my feet.

But I'd heard the stories, mostly from Aunt Pearl, who Mama said could talk the ears off a mule, and a little from Daddy who used them to help "explain Mama" to me.

Several years back, Grand settled into a small house on Georgia Avenue, one that may have been at one time a starter for some sweet couple back in the 1940s but was now a "last home" for her. Almost a shotgun-style house, but not quite. Still, by standing at the front door one could see clear to the back door and, if it was open, into the backyard, which was twice as large as the house. There was a sitting room full of overstuffed old furniture, a dining room not big enough for a proper table and china cabinet (but Grand managed to squeeze them in anyhow), two bedrooms connected by a single bath, and a kitchen stretching wide against the back of the house. It often smelled of cinnamon and rich coffee grounds and reminded me of small plates topped with fat brownies and tall glasses of cold milk on hot summer days. I adored visiting her there and slept over enough that a few of my clothes hung in the front bedroom closet along with at least two pairs of shoes tossed willy-nilly on its floor.

"Well then," Grand now said as she rolled up the sleeves of her blouse, "we have a lot of work to do, don't we." It wasn't a question. Very few things with Grand ever were.

"What do you mean?" I asked, completely unsure.

"Cooking. Cleaning." She looked pointedly at me. Me who had never so much as fried an egg or done a load of laundry. My mother had always done that ... wasn't that *her* purpose? "Let's start with the basics, shall we?"

Mama smiled lightly as she patted my shoulder. "I'll leave you two to this. Your daddy and I are going to watch a little television in the den."

I knew my mouth hung open like the entrance to a cave and my eyes moved wildly between the two women who meant the most to me in my life. "Mama," I whispered as Grand began rattling around under one of the cabinets where stainless steel pots and pans were stored.

Mama patted my shoulder again. "Have fun," she mouthed back as Grand suddenly popped up, her hand gripping a pot handle.

"Now then," Grand said, turning to me like a drill sergeant. "Do you know how to boil an egg?"

Chapter Four

Elaine Singletary had been my best friend since as far back as I could remember, our mothers being the same. Mama and Mrs. Singletary had become close after Grand moved herself and her children to town, Mama often saying that Rose Warren Singletary had been her lifesaver during those awful days of change and upset.

I felt the same about Elaine. She was my rock. Or at least she had been until Westley came along and then he took that role. She was also the kind of girl who flitted wherever the wind took her—and for now, it had taken her to college to study nursing. After that, she told me, she had no plans other than to bask on the beaches of Tybee for a while.

Elaine took the '70s seriously, making note of every fashion-labeled, glossy-covered magazine with slick ads deemed stylish. She parted her long copper-penny hair straight down the middle; it fell thick to her waist, swaying back and forth when she walked. She wore all the right clothes and, being the petite thing she was, looked sensational in every style. I was by no means a large girl, but next to Elaine I felt positively monstrous.

On that Sunday afternoon, after Grand left—and after I'd not only learned how to boil an egg, but how to crack six of them into the mixture that would become my first pound cake—I called Elaine on the phone to see if she'd already left for the university.

She hadn't. "Hey," I exclaimed, relieved. "You're still there."

"Yeah," she drawled, her voice whispery soft and intellectual. "I don't have to be in class until later tomorrow afternoon, so I'll drive back to Statesboro sometime in the morning."

Elaine had attended Georgia Southern since fall term after our senior year. "I'd like to come by and see you, if that's okay," I said. "I've got something to talk to you about."

"That sounds ominous. Sure. Come on."

I darted into my bedroom, retrieved my keys and purse, and then let Mama and Daddy know where I was going.

Mama stood in the middle of the den, arms crossed, and eyes wide. "Well—what—what . . ."

"Spit it out, Paulina," Daddy said from his chair. I noted a dessert plate with telltale signs of my pound cake sitting on the occasional table next to him.

"What if Westley comes over?" Mama finally sputtered.

"He won't be here until later. Besides, his church was having some kind of function today and his mother and father really wanted him to hang out afterward." I shrugged. "I don't know what, really. I just know he said he wouldn't be here until later on." I looked to my father. "How was the cake, Daddy?"

Daddy smiled in approval. "Not bad," he said, rubbing his belly. "Especially seeing as that was your first go at it. Westley will gain twenty pounds the first year of marriage, I'll betcha."

Mama crossed over to me then and her hands fluffed my hair, which fell in dull brown waves to my shoulders. "We really need to talk about your hair."

I pulled away. "What about it?"

"Leave her alone, Paulina," Daddy said, his eyes fixed on the television.

"We have to think about how she'll wear it for the wedding." She looked at me sympathetically. "You got my sister's hair, God bless it."

"Pearl has beautiful hair," Daddy said, his head still not moving.

Mama huffed. "Not Pearl. You act like Pearl is the only sister I have. I'm talking about Meryl."

I started for the door. "Mama, we'll talk about my hair later. Right now, I really need to get to Elaine's." I flashed a smile her way to soften the moment. "I'm going to ask her to be my maid of honor."

"Oh," Mama said, suddenly brightening at the thought that I was doing something toward my impending nuptials. "She doesn't know yet?"

I shook my head. "No. I wanted to tell her in person and this weekend has been so busy." I glanced at my wristwatch. "I really need to go so I can get back before Westley arrives."

Mama shooed me toward the back door. "If he gets here before you, I'll make sure to cut him a slice of cake."

I drove to my best friend's house—a rectangular brick structure situated in the middle of a street that V'd off from downtown's main street—in less than ten minutes. Not that in a town the size of Bynum it took much longer than that to get *anywhere*. Unless, of course, one traveled by bike, which Elaine and I had certainly done enough in our younger days. There wasn't a Saturday or weekday of the summer months I could remember that hadn't involved meeting halfway and then riding most of the day away, up one road and down another, finding our way downtown, pedaling between storefront buildings. Making our way to the local five-and-dime for a candy bar and an orange Nehi. At some point we'd find our way back to her home or mine where we'd eat a sandwich and a handful of chips. Tummies filled, we'd change into our swimsuits, then pedal to the county recreation department where we swam for hours, our bodies coated in coconut-scented lotion and the overpowering odor of chlorine.

We'd spent our youth tanned and toned and blissfully happy.

There was also nothing I didn't know about her and little she didn't know about me, even though her fairly recent decision to go to school and mine to stay in Bynum meant we talked less as the weeks and months slipped by. Especially as my relationship with Westley deepened.

I couldn't help but wonder what kind of reaction I'd get from Elaine; she hadn't quite forgiven me for not going away to college together. Being dormmates. Sorority sisters and all that. I imagined that, by Elaine's way of thinking, my marriage to Westley was nothing more than me throwing my life away on the first man to pay me the tiniest smidgen of attention.

But I hoped for better.

When I pulled into her driveway, I found her standing on the side lawn, bent over, garden hose in hand, wrapping it into a circle on the ground near the azalea bushes. She flung her hair over her shoulder as she glanced at me. "Hey, there," she said.

"What are you doing?" I asked, crossing the grass, brown mostly but, like a balding man who refused to shave the few hairs crossing over his head, still sporting green patches.

"I washed my car earlier," she said, now straightening. "Told Daddy I'd put everything back where I found it, so I am." She ran her hands along her jeans to dry them, then reached to hug me.

"I've got news," I told her straight up.

"Let me guess. Westley asked you to marry him." Then she laughed. "I'm just kidding. I know you two haven't dated long enough for that."

"Uh—"

The color drained from Elaine's face, leaving a sprinkling of freckles prominent across her nose. "Oh, gosh. No. Seriously? *Seriously?*"

I nodded. "Seriously."

She grabbed my left hand and yanked it toward her. "I don't see a ring."

"I don't want one. I mean, an engagement ring." I laughed lightly. "Actually, we haven't talked about a ring. I assume we'll buy matching wedding bands or something equally as silly and romantic as that."

Elaine pulled me toward the front door. "Come on in. Oh, my gosh. *Seriously?* But you haven't dated that long and—oh, my gosh! *When?*"

"A few days ago ..."

"No, goofball. When's the wedding?"

"Oh. December. Seventeenth."

We stepped into the nearly dark living room, one I knew as well as my own. Each piece of furniture. Each framed photo. Each piece of artwork hanging too high on the walls. "Mama," Elaine called out, closing the door behind us.

I opened my mouth to quiet her, but her mother stepped into the room as though on cue before I could say a word. "Well, hey, Sugar Foot. Elaine said you were coming over."

"Hey, Miss Rose," I said to the woman whose name fit her, her face flowerlike, her features soft and tiny.

"Guess what," Elaine said, still holding on to my left hand. "Guess who's getting married."

Miss Rose had the decency to ask, "Who?" Then, turning to me, said, "You?"

I nodded. "I came over to ask Miss Blabbermouth if she'll be my maid of honor." I swallowed. "I've asked my sister and Westley's— Heather—I've asked them to be bridesmaids."

"Well, my goodness. When is the wedding?" Miss Rose asked, guiding Elaine and me over to the sofa while she eased herself into an occasional chair covered by soft fabric that boasted peonies in varying shades of pink.

"December seventeenth," I answered as she reached over to switch on a rose-tinted table lamp. "One week before Christmas."

"So soon?"

"You're not pregnant, are you?" Elaine asked.

"*Elaine,*" I said and jumped an inch.

"Really, Elaine," Miss Rose said with a sigh. "Pay her no mind, Allison."

My gawking eyes met Miss Rose's. "I've tried that. It doesn't work."

"Well, I mean," Elaine began in defense of her statement, "why so soon if you're not pregnant?"

Heat rushed to my face. "If you must know," I said through clenched teeth, "We are *waiting* until we get married and ... well—well—we are getting married on the seventeenth of December."

"Best to marry than to burn with lust," Miss Rose said, and Elaine and I turned to her, our mouths fell open. "Or something like that."

"What?" Confusion etched along the lines of Elaine's voice.

"It's in the Bible," I told her. "If you'd paid more attention to the sermons and less to Danny Simmons every Sunday morning when you *used* to attend ..."

"I couldn't help it," Elaine said coolly. "He was adorable."

"I wonder whatever happened to him."

"He moved to Raleigh, remember? Right after junior year."

"Oh." I shook my head to clear it of the boy Elaine had drooled over from junior high until he disappeared from the class roster. Even while dating other boys, Elaine's heart belonged to Danny Simmons. If only Danny Simmons had realized it. "Anyway ... you'll be my maid of honor?"

"I think you're crazy. You are *crazy* to get married so soon." Her eyes filled with sudden knowledge—or at least what she would have called knowledge. Maybe even wisdom. "You know what this is," she said. "This is you not dating enough in high school. I've been studying this kind of thing in my psych class. You should have had more boyfriends. If you had, you wouldn't be jumping at the first man who came along."

Not dating in high school—or not dating much—was true enough. I'd barely gotten a date for prom, much less had a steady. Not that I was horribly unattractive, because I don't believe I was—or am—but more that I tended to lean to the shy side. Elaine said I was afraid of my own shadow, which bordered on some level of truth. Regardless, I knew—no, I *believed*—that Westley was more than simply the first man to come along. Westley was ... well, *Westley.*

"I really wish you'd come to Southern with me," Elaine continued, nearly bouncing in place. "You still can, you know. Think about it. Put the wedding off for a year and—"

I gazed into the deep green of her eyes. "I'm in love with Westley Houser and I'm going to marry him." My brow lifted. "So, please? Be my maid of honor?"

"Oh, for the love of everything," she said in defeat. "What do I have to do?"

"Get fitted for a dress you'll wear once, show up at a few showers if you can, and be at the church on the evening of the sixteenth and the afternoon of the seventeenth."

Elaine pulled her hair over her shoulder and twisted it until it looked like a rope then let it go. "I can do that," she said as though she'd considered saying no. "But, if you change your mind between now and then, you and I can get an apartment together and you can get your fanny into school." Her shoulders sagged. "I mean, do you really even know this guy?"

I looked again to Miss Rose for help. "Like I said, Allison. Pay her no mind. She gets fixated on something and that's that. I knew her daddy was the man I was supposed to marry not five minutes after we met, and we've been together ever since."

I turned back to Elaine. "I know it's soon, but I *do* know him. And if you'd had the chance to spend a little more time with him, you'd see. He's wonderful, Elaine. And I love him like mad."

Elaine sighed then, relinquishing all debate within her. "All right. I'll be there."

I made it back home with five minutes to spare before Westley arrived. It goes without saying that my mother had managed to work herself into a tizzy by then. "Dear Lord in heaven," she said as soon as I entered the house. "Do you have any notion what time it is?"

I did and I told her so. "Mama, for heaven's sake, please calm down. You act like he's Prince—what's his name? Prince Charles, or something."

Mama shooed me down the hall all the while muttering, "Well, he's practically the Prince of the county. Now, go change into something else before he gets here."

I stopped at my bedroom door and turned to face the woman

whose voice would be the one inside my head and heart for as long as I drew breath ... whether I liked it or not. "What's wrong with what I'm wearing?" I asked, looking down then to my favorite pair of slacks and its matching floral peasant top.

"You've had that on since you got home from church." She turned me and nudged me into my room. "Why not put on a dress for a change."

"Mama," I laughed. "Westley will think I want to go to church or something ..."

"You'll be a married woman soon," she continued. "You'll want to start looking the part of a grownup and not some child."

"Mama," I continued in my protest. "Grownup women wear slacks and blouses." I pointed to her, moving my finger up and down to prove my point.

Mama walked past me to open my closet door. "I was thinking this would be nice," she said, reaching so quickly and easily for a wrap-around dress of geometrical shapes in dark tones I knew she'd stood in front of my closet earlier to choose the perfect frock.

"All right, all right," I said, taking it from her. "Give me five minutes of peace so I can change, please."

Mama made it nearly to the door before reminding me, "We'll need to go shopping soon for a dress you know."

"I know," I said, waving the backs of my hands at her, indicating she needed to move along.

"And your trousseau."

"Mama—"

"Have you decided where you're going—"

"*Mama* ..." A flash of light from beyond the sheers of my bedroom window indicated that Westley had arrived, his car gliding down our driveway.

"Oh, there he is," she breathed as if he'd arrived in a golden carriage pulled by six white horses.

In less than five minutes, I managed to get into the dress, run a brush through my hair, and apply a touch of spearmint-flavored lip gloss. As I walked toward the voices coming from the den, I heard Westley say, "—thought I'd talk to her about it tonight, but wanted to clear it first with you, sir."

Daddy cleared his throat to answer as I stepped into the room. "Clear what?" I asked.

Westley smiled broadly and stood, then walked over to me and kissed my cheek. "You look incredible," he said.

I felt Mama's smile clear across the room; I hardly had to look to see the gloat on her face. But I gave her a wink to ease the tension. "Mama insisted on a dress," I said. Then, "So, what were you talking about?"

Westley took my hand in his and returned us to sit on the opposite end of the sofa from where Mama perched. "My brother and his wife have invited us to their place in Baxter next weekend." His eyes found mine, drawing me into a desire I thought would slay me on the spot and right there in front of my mama and daddy. My breath became so ragged I wondered if they were aware of the sheer discomfort pushing its way through me, especially with them occupying the same room.

It seemed to me that since Westley had proposed I'd felt a greater desire to be his wife than I ever imagined. And, at that moment, it also seemed that December seventeenth was a million years away.

"For what?" I finally said.

A smile as warm as liquid sunshine danced between us. "I think they just want to get to know you better."

I looked at my father, waiting for his reaction. "What are their names again?" he asked.

"My brother is Paul, sir. His wife is DiAnn. You'll meet them, of course, at the wedding."

The thought of meeting my future brother- and sister-in-law in five short days tightened my stomach. What I knew of them was vague. From what Westley had told me, they both had cushy jobs and lived in a lakefront house. They owned a boat, which they enjoyed taking out on the water most weekends and during the long summer evenings. Paul and DiAnn had been cut from the same cloth, he'd said.

Both enjoyed the out-of-doors as much as they loved being inside curled in front of a crackling fire, reading a good book. They were both college-grad smart, but laughed easily at the silliest of things, never making those not nearly as smart feel inadequate. A thought that relieved me to no end. "You'll really like them," he'd told me, and I believed it because Westley had said it and I took his every word as gospel.

"I don't know them," I said to my parents then, as if that settled everything. "But Westley—"

"Baxter is about four hours from here," Daddy noted. "What are your plans, then?"

Westley released my hand, leaned forward, and placed his elbows on his knees. "Well, sir ... I thought we'd drive over on Friday after work—maybe get off a little early if we can—" He glanced at me, then back to my father. "Paul and DiAnn have a large home, sir. Plenty of room." Westley's chuckle fell more inward than out and came without the good sense to blush in the slightest. "What I'm saying is, Ali will have her own room. Her virtue is safe with me, sir. I can assure you of that."

Ali. A name he'd never called me previously, but one by which he'd refer to me from that moment on. A name that lent itself to an intimacy far more exquisite and frightening than we'd experienced on any level up until that moment.

I blinked until my gaze settled on my shoes, a clunky pair of platforms I'd purchased the same day as the dress, their colors complementing each other.

"And you'll be back Sunday?"

"Yes, sir," Westley answered. I looked to where my father sat, seemingly relaxed under the notion of his virgin child taking a cross-state trip with her fiancé.

"Mama?" he said then, looking at my mother as though her opinion mattered, even while we all knew that Daddy had the final say in moments like these.

"I'm sure we can trust them," she said. "After all, they'll be married soon."

"Well then," Daddy concluded. "I don't see why not."

And with those words, I unknowingly headed into the rest of my life.

Chapter Five

Sometime after my thirteenth birthday, my father's parents moved from Georgia to Florida. I never completely understood why—something about my grandmother's oldest sister's husband dying and them needing to be closer to her.

Until then, once a month, my parents, sister, and I piled into Daddy's sedan and drove an hour and a half to their farmhouse. Julie and I spent our time in the backseat drawing an imaginary line and then daring the other to cross it. "*This* is your half," Julie said to me. "*This* is mine. Do not enter into my half."

Then Julie looked out the window to the world beyond while I dove headfirst into the first in a pile of books that took up most of my foot room.

Being at my grandparents' was an adventure. A vacation from life as I knew it. The rooms of the old farmhouse wrapped around one another. There were secret nooks and crannies and a two-sided wrap-around front porch decked out with a wooden swing at one end, a wrought iron glider at the other, and plenty of rockers in between. My grandparents were retired tobacco farmers, so ashtrays on stands stood in wait between several of them, typically filled with scrunched cigarette butts and graying ashes. The front porch always smelled of old tobacco and roses, my grandmother's favorite flower. In the spring and summer months the sweet taste of gardenias lay over them both, which made me nearly intoxicated.

My grandmother—whom we called Granny—had placed an outdoor chaise lounge in the corner of the porch where one side met the other. It boasted blue floral vinyl cushions Granny could wash down with soap and water after rain showers left their muddy and dusty remains. If ever I had a favorite place in the world, this was it. Shaded by the overgrown azaleas, my back to the world, stretched out, a sweating Coca-Cola bottle wedged between my thighs, and with a good book in my hands. And if a decent breeze happened by, I thought I'd died and gone to heaven. Nothing else mattered in those hours. I was a girl on an island and life was blissful.

I remembered those days as Westley and I traveled along back roads between Bynum and Baxter in a car that came as a complete surprise. Sometime during the week, Westley had traded his Pinto in for a brand-new Caprice convertible, the color so red I thought it looked like a tube of lipstick shooting down the road. He arrived at my house at two o'clock on the afternoon of our departure for his brother's, shocking me but thrilling my mother as it bounded into the driveway.

"What in the world—" I asked. Mama and I stood at the living room window where we'd taken up vigil, waiting for the Pinto to appear.

"How utterly delightful," Mama said, a declaration that caused my mouth to gape. "Riding in a convertible. It's been years ..." And then off she went, through the dining room, the family room, and out the side door to greet her future son-in-law.

Before loading my luggage into the trunk, Westley took Mama for a spin around the neighborhood, then deposited her back on the driveway and exchanged her for me. By two thirty we were gliding past the city limits. Westley managed to wait that long before his foot pressed hard against the gas pedal. I turned to him with my hand fisted around my hair to keep it on my head and bellowed, "Can we afford this?"

Westley grinned behind his aviator sunglasses. "What?" he asked, as if he didn't know. "This?" He took his hands off the steering wheel, throwing them up in the air like a child sitting in the front seat of a roller coaster, heading down the first big dip.

"*Westley*," I screamed, horrified.

He laughed easily as his foot pressed lightly on the brake and his hands came back down. "Go easy, little girl," he said then. "I'm just excited."

"Can you just make sure you get me there in one piece," I said, as if my admonition mattered. "I'd like to meet your brother and sister-in-law without cuts and bruises. Or in a casket."

Westley laughed again, then slowed the car to a near stop, rolled the car onto the shoulder of the road until it rested between the tall blades of wiregrass and broomsedge. Before I could ask what we were doing, he gathered me to himself as he'd done the day of the engagement, kissed me for all he was worth, then pulled back. "You need a pair of sunglasses," he said as he reached for the glove compartment latch. After it sprang open, nearly hitting my knees, he reached in for a small sack with the drugstore's logo printed across the top. "Gotcha something." He handed the package to me; I opened it and peered inside to find a swanky pair of oversized, tortoiseshell Foster Grants.

"Hey," I said, sliding them on, then pulling the sun visor down in hopes of finding a mirror and smiling broadly when my wish came true. "Hey," I said again. "I like these ... a *lot*." I flipped the visor up, then turned and gave Westley the same sort of kiss he'd given me.

When we came up for air, he said, "Had I known I'd get this kind of reaction, I would have brought you a pair every time I came over."

I slapped at his arm. "I think we'd better get back on the road. I really am excited about meeting Paul and DiAnn."

Westley pulled his shades up to expose his eyes, waggled his brow, and said, "I reckon."

We slid back onto the road, a two-lane blacktop, where little traffic met us. I rested my head against the car seat, closed my eyes behind the Foster Grants, and allowed the movement of the car, the warmth of the afternoon autumn sunshine tanning my arms and face, and the lulling effect of Carole King in the 8-track to send me back to my grandmother's front porch … the joy of a good book … and the trill of insects and birds vying for God's attention.

Four and a half hours after we left my mother standing and waving in the driveway, Westley drove up a snakelike drive flanked by tall trees and thick bushes that seemed to only end at infinity. Eventually a clearing made way for a wide and lush lawn that carpeted the earth all the way to an imposing brick structure with white trim and shutters, and a dark-green door spotlighted by the front porch overhead light. "Is this your brother's house?" I asked as if Westley would have driven more than four hours and stopped at anyone else's.

Westley slid the gearshift to park, then turned with a grin. "Yeah. Nice, huh?"

"Nice? It's like a mansion. What did you say he does for a living?"

"He's in pharmaceutical sales." Westley opened his door and stuck one leg out. "He does all right by himself, but DiAnn works for her father who owns a finance company, and that helps."

"Oh," I said, completely unsure whether I should open my door or let Westley come around and do the gentlemanly thing. He usually did, but here, in front of his brother's home, I felt shy and awkward. The world we'd come from—the one we'd driven through—had been bright and sunny. We were now cloaked in near darkness, in a place I knew nothing of, about to walk into a home where I knew no one.

Westley opened my door and extended a hand. "Come on, Ali. Don't be scared."

"Do they have kids?" I asked as he all but pulled me from the Caprice.

His warm hand gathered mine as we started down a sidewalk leading from the drive to the porch. I glanced up at his face as I waited for an answer, noting the sharp features in the glow of the front porch light and the scant bit of moonlight filtering through the tall pines that swayed in a breeze. "No," he said, drawing out the answer with a smile.

"Not yet anyway."

The door opened then, and I jerked to see a young man and woman bathed in light from the foyer and the front porch. "There you are," Westley's brother said as he strolled across the wide brick porch, then skipped down the four steps to the walkway. "I was beginning to worry."

Westley released my hand and the two brothers grabbed each other in a manly hug, backslapping and laughing like two old army buddies who'd made it through the war and finally found each other after years of separation. When they released, Westley turned to me and said, "Paul, this is Ali. Ali, my brother Paul."

I reached out my hand, then drew it back, and stuck it out again. "Hi, Paul," I said.

He took my hand in his before drawing me close. "Come here, you. We're about to be family." Strong arms wrapped around my shoulders and squeezed while the scent of English Leather and the faint hint of consumed wine teased my nostrils. When he let me go, he stepped back so I could get a good look at him. Like Westley, his features were sharp, but even more handsome. Where Westley's hair held natural curl, Paul's was straight and slick-black. Kohl-dark lashes lined eyes that were blue enough to be named and given their own place in a Crayola box. When he smiled, I was met by straight pearl-white teeth. Unlike Westley's, which were not exactly crooked, but not exactly straight either. And, where Westley's chin came to a slow point, Paul's was square and held a deep cleft.

"Hi," I finally stammered, wondering how it was that, even with seeing photos of Paul and DiAnn, the matte one-dimensional illusions had done nothing to prepare me for the Greek-like reality of him. "Hi," I said again only to have Westley come up beside me, slip his arm around my waist, and laugh.

"She's tired. She's not used to all this," he said as though I were a girl of sixteen.

"Gracious, you two," DiAnn said from the porch. She neither smiled nor frowned; she simply stood. I stared up at her. Her legs were dark and shapely, shown off by a short silky skirt. My eyes climbed up from there—the flat of her stomach, the round of her hips, the tiny waist and the ample breasts made prominent by a tight-fitting V-neck sweater. "Give the girl a break and y'all come on up here. We're letting the mosquitos in, sure as I'm standing here."

I breathed out a sigh of relief, moved out of Westley's grip and climbed the steps to her. "I'm Allison ... Ali."

Bright eyes smiled while her lips stayed noncommittal. "Hello, Allison-Ali. I'm DiAnn. Come on in." She jutted her chin toward the brothers still on the walkway. "Why don't you two get the luggage so we can get these two settled and have some supper?"

Supper was barbecue chicken, asparagus, and corn on the cob, all hot off the grill. DiAnn pulled garlic bread from the oven not two seconds after we stepped into the kitchen as if she'd somehow managed to time our arrival. "What can I do to help?" I asked, terrified she'd ask me to cook something. But Mama had insisted that I do exactly that—offer. "You know little about cooking, but you can at least offer," she told me.

DiAnn noted four glasses and a pitcher of tea on the counter as she tucked a strand of her blond chin-length hair behind one ear. "Just get the ice in the glasses, if you will."

We spent most of the meal listening to Paul and Westley playing catch-up; the bond between them such that I felt a pang of jealousy. I'd never had this kind of relationship with Julia, not even as children. Any hope of connecting to her had been pretty much ruined when she married. At least as far as I could tell. But, maybe one day ...

After we'd cleaned up the kitchen, while Westley and Paul sat in the living room and continued to jabber on, DiAnn asked if I'd like to see my room. I nodded, then followed her up a back staircase to a wide hallway with doors opening left and right. "Bathroom is right here," she said pointing, "so I put you in the guest room across from it."

I followed behind her as she flipped on an overhead light revealing a small bedroom with light-pink painted walls, a twin bed located close to the nearest wall, an antique hope chest under the window and a bentwood rocker sitting diagonally in one corner. "I hope this is okay. We set this up for Heather when she visits."

I smiled. "I can see that," I said, pointing to the pink floral and quilted spread with matching dust ruffle. "Pink is Heather's favorite color."

"For such a tomboy, she can be such a girl." DiAnn nodded toward the single-door closet. "Westley and Paul must have brought your luggage up."

I blew out a pent-up breath, feeling tired and ready for bed even though it wasn't much after nine o'clock. "Do you mind," I asked, "if I take a shower and get ready for bed?"

"Not at all," she said. "I'll head back downstairs and let Westley know."

She left the room and my brow furrowed. DiAnn, who had one of the most beautiful peaches-and-cream complexions and the largest sea-green eyes I'd ever seen, seemed nice enough, but almost as if she had reservations about me. Or, perhaps, Westley and me. The two of us. Together. Then again, I told myself as I lifted my small suitcase and laid it across the arms of the rocker, I had only just met her. Perhaps, with time, I would get to know her better ...

Paul on the other hand was talkative and inclusive and had made me feel welcomed from the moment we met. I breathed in, still aware of the scent of wine and cologne.

"Hey." Westley's voice came from the doorway and I jumped, bringing my hand to my chest. "You okay?"

I nodded. "Just tired," I said.

"We were going to have a glass of wine and play some cards but ..."

I didn't want to miss out. I didn't. And I wanted to make a good impression on Paul and DiAnn. Be a *part* of the family. Their family. Because I knew how much Paul meant to Westley. But my body felt heavy and older than its years and I couldn't ... I just couldn't stay awake another minute. Hoping I had not made some faux pas, I asked, "Tomorrow night?"

"Sure thing."

"Promise? It's okay?"

Westley smiled slowly, then winked lazily, the rush of it sending me places I knew better than to go. "Promise."

I crossed my arms against a new shyness. "Um—where is your room?"

He grinned at me. "There's a bedroom and bath downstairs." Westley's brow cocked. "See? I told your dad you would be safe here."

"Yes, you did. I'm glad to note you're a man of your word," I teased.

Westley didn't move from the door but crooked his finger, silently telling me to come closer, which I did. He kissed me sweetly, his lips the only part of his body touching mine. "Sleep well, princess. Tomorrow's a big day and I want you well rested."

"I will," I whispered. "I love you."

"And I love you."

Patterson

Patterson reached for the phone on his office desk, the corner one situated at the end of a hallway in the mathematics department of Dekalb College. The room had become a favorite place of his. He kept the furnishings simple—an oversized desk, a mid-century sofa with matching chairs, bookshelves lined perfectly. The paneled walls were devoid of art, despite Mary Helen's insistence that she bring in a piece by some local artist whose work she'd fallen prey to.

The corner office meant windows and natural light, except on rainy days such as this one. Torrential, almost. Still, no one else had an office quite like his. No one.

"Hey there," a smoky voice said, and he looked up from the papers he pored over at his desk.

An easy smile crossed his face before he could stop it. "Hey, yourself," he said to the woman leaning against the doorframe, her curves accentuated by material that clung deliciously to her frame. "What brings you here so late on a Friday night?"

Rita Maledon pushed herself away from the doorway and into the room where she dropped onto the forest-green leather of one of the chairs. "What keeps *you* here?" She crossed one long leg over the other, the swish of stockings stirring him, the avoidance of his question riling him.

He pointed to the papers with the mechanical pencil dangling between two fingers. "Work. Just trying to finish up some things before the weekend."

Rita's lips—glossy and full—pursed and she pushed silky brown curls over her shoulder. "Because Mary Helen may have a million little things for you to do?" Her tiger-like eyes narrowed. "How is she, by the way?"

"Cool as always, Rita. Why?"

She stood then, high-heeled boots clipping to the opposite side of the desk, braced her palms on the wood, and leaned forward enough to bring her sweet scent to his nostrils and her intent into focus. "Look," she said. "I'm just going to say it. You and I have had a good thing since I started working here ..."

Patterson dropped the pencil and leaned back to rest his elbows on the arms of his chair. He pushed as far from the desk as he could, then crossed his legs. "Sure, as long as it suits your timetable." Outside the window, a flash of lightning brought brief revelation to the room.

She stood straight. "Are we going there again?"

"You know what I want."

Now she found her way around to his side of the desk where she perched against the edge. A roll of thunder rumbled through the room. "You want me exclusively, which I completely understand, Patterson. I do. But you're a married man and I'm a single woman. You cannot expect me to be *true* to you."

"Why can't I?"

She crossed her arms. "Be reasonable."

"I think I am. I'm telling you what I want, Rita. From you. From me. *For* us."

Rain slashed against the window now, the storm growing. Rita walked back to the chair. Sat again. Crossed her legs again, the swish stirring him further. "And Mary Helen? What do you want *for* her?"

"I told you how it is. I've never lied to you about that. She's my wife, but we don't—*jive*—in that department."

She took in a deep breath. Exhaled. "And yet ..." she said, her head tilting to the right, "you have three daughters. *Some*body's been doing *some*thing at *some* point."

He refused to answer. To rise to the bait. Finally, he pulled himself back to the desk, reached for the pencil, and said, "I need to finish this work. It's been a long day." But she didn't move. He looked up without raising his head. "Anything else?"

She smiled, slow and catlike. "All right, Patterson. We'll play it your way."

Now his head came up, his chin rose. He looked at the woman who'd been his friend, his mistress, his confidante, and—yes—his nemesis, then to the open doorway, before his eyes slid back to hers. "But how long this time? A week? A month?"

"Patterson," she breathed out. "Quit making it a math problem and just go with it. Take life by the horns and have a little fun without trying to complicate matters."

He laughed then; he couldn't help it. "Tell you what, Rita ..."

"What?"

"Why don't you get up ... prance yourself right back to that door over there ..."

One brow arched and a half smile crept toward her high cheekbone. "And then?"

"Shut the door."

She slid to the end of her seat, both feet now on the floor. "And should I lock it?"

"Absolutely."

Chapter Six

Allison

In spite of being in a strange house and not sleeping in the width of my own double bed, once I slipped between the cool of the sheets and comforter, rubbed my feet together for a moment of warmth, I fell asleep and didn't wake until the morning sun burst around the shades and draperies. I stretched my arms from beneath the cover, felt the chill in the air slap my arms, then sat up and blinked hard. I'd taken my watch off the night before and placed it on the bedside table. Now, checking it, I saw that I'd slept till nearly half past eight. "Gracious," I said. So much for getting up before Westley.

I scurried to the door, opened it, and peeked out. Indistinguishable voices came from downstairs; I hoped at least one of them belonged to my fiancé. I didn't cherish the thought of him seeing me first thing in the morning ... not yet, anyway. A quick dash into the bathroom, a shower, some makeup, a pair of jeans with a striped long-sleeved sweater, and I was ready to face the day.

And my fiancé ...

The mouth-watering aromas of bacon, eggs, and coffee reached me as I took quiet steps down the stairs, hoping not to interrupt what sounded to be an intense conversation between Westley, his brother, and DiAnn.

"I can't believe you haven't told her," DiAnn was saying. "You're going to have to sooner or later. Putting it off won't change facts, Wes."

"I will," Westley said as my breath caught in my throat and I held it there. "Just not—not right yet."

"DiAnn's right," Paul added. "This isn't the kind of thing you can hide forever."

"Nor do I want to. I just—I can't take a chance on her bailing on me. Not now." He paused. "I *love* her, Paul. I swear to—"

"And I don't doubt that. But you've *got* to come clean with the real reason behind this trip."

Air sank into my lungs as a thud indicated something had come down hard onto the table. A coffee mug, perhaps. Or a plate. "Will you just stop?" Westley interjected, anger inching its way up in his voice in a tone I'd never heard. "I'll handle it. If it's one thing I can do, it's handle things like—"

"I'd hardly call Allison a thing, big brother."

I couldn't breathe, but I forced air in by swallowing gulps of it, hoping my struggle wouldn't give away my eavesdropping.

"I'm not talking about *Allison*, Paul. And I need the two of you to *stop* talking about this. The shower shut off a good twenty minutes ago … she'll be down any second."

I blinked then took a few soundless steps back up the stairs. Okay. Okay. Westley *hadn't* been talking about me. He'd been speaking of— who knew what. But it was something. Something that would affect me. Something he didn't want me to know. Something Paul and DiAnn knew about.

But Westley would tell me. In his own time and in his own way, he would. He loved me, after all. He had just declared it in his "I mean it" voice. And he was going to be my husband. Wives and husbands didn't keep secrets and we'd be married soon enough and then all the secrets he felt he had to protect me from would disappear. Yes, yes. That was it. Westley loved me enough to protect me …

I took one more intake of breath before bounding down the stairs.

"There she is," Westley said as I rounded the corner to see the three of them sitting at the kitchen table made of thick, blond pine. Beyond them, French doors had been pushed open to reveal a screened-in porch, which looked over a lawn sloping toward a lake that sparkled under the morning sunlight.

Westley stood, walked to me as if tense words had not been exchanged between him and his family, placed his hands on my waist, then leaned down to kiss me. "You must have really been tired."

Heat rushed to my cheeks. "I'm sorry," I said, my eyes searching his, wanting desperately to know what he felt he could not tell me while, at the same time, feeling strangely embarrassed by what I'd overheard—and the fact that I'd been eavesdropping—more than by my sleepiness. But if that's what he thought ... *they* thought. These three who were obviously in on something I couldn't know about. Yet.

He kissed me again. "Think nothing of it. Coffee?"

I nodded, newly self-conscious of the physical attention, especially in front of Paul and DiAnn, both of whom I had a difficult time looking in the eye.

"Have a seat," DiAnn said as she pushed away from the table. "I put a plate in the oven on warm for you. Wes, pour her a cup of coffee. How do you like it?"

"Lots of cream and two sugars," Westley answered for me. I shot a glance over to Paul, who winked, then pointed to a chair next to him. For a moment, all seemed right with the world again.

"Come here and we'll tell you about what all we have planned for you."

I ate, forcing myself to concentrate while Paul and Westley mapped out a day of being out in their boat on the lake—DiAnn had already packed a picnic basket for a lunch we'd enjoy at a spot they'd found a few miles up toward the river. "If the weather keeps up, I may even get in a little skiing," Westley said, his exuberance reminding me of a child's.

"Do you ski?" DiAnn asked.

I took a sip of the coffee Westley had made to perfection. "No," I said after a swallow. "Never learned, to tell you the truth."

"I can't believe you've grown up in Georgia and you don't know how to ski," Paul noted.

"I'm not very coordinated," I said. "I can't skate ... I can't dance ... you should have seen me on track and field day back when I was in school." I laughed to take away the sting left behind from years of teasing.

Westley took my hand in his. After a squeeze he let me go. "But you should see her swim. She's like a fish in water. When we go to Tybee—"

"Westley," I said, keeping my eyes on my food, most definitely not wanting to discuss swimming or body surfing. "Let's talk more about our day," I said, wanting more than just to stay away from our frivolities while swimming. Wanting only to talk about anything that would keep my mind focused on the here and now rather than the giant question that hung over my head. *What was Westley—and Paul and DiAnn—keeping from me?* "What about after the boat and the lake?" I asked, which only brought a roar of laughter from him.

"All right. There's a little place downtown ..."

Westley had insisted I bring my bathing suit and by the end of the day, I was happy I'd not questioned his wisdom. Despite the lateness of the year, the sun had turned the world around us warm and had made for the most pleasant day I could imagine.

I changed into a bikini I'd purchased on sale near the end of the summer—one I hadn't worn yet, so it was a complete surprise to Westley—along with one of his long-sleeved shirts in case I got chilled. I hadn't truly come into my own womanhood yet, but even at such a young age, I recognized the combination of my swimsuit and his shirt kept nearly all his attention toward me.

Me and the pair of skis his brother loaned him.

DiAnn, who wore the most seductive gold-toned one-piece I'd ever seen, drove the boat most of the day, her eyes nearly always straight ahead, while the brothers skied behind, bouncing over the waves of the wakes, their tanned bodies lean and angled in such a way that told me the two had been doing this nearly their whole lives. True to what their parents had always told me, Westley proved to be the daredevil, performing stunts that reminded me of the ones I'd seen during a family vacation to Cypress Gardens in Florida. I clapped and cheered from my place at the back of the boat as hair from my makeshift ponytail whipped across my sun-kissed cheeks and forehead.

Paul docked the boat in the late afternoon. Westley helped me onto the pier, his hand sliding under his shirt, now wet and clinging to my body. Fiery tingles shot through me as his fingertips rested alongside the curve of my waist and he coaxed my body close to his own. "Did you have fun?" he asked, his voice low and provocative.

My arms instinctively went around him. "It was the best day I've had in a long, long time," I said, thinking what a strange place I found myself in, surrounded by three people who knew something I didn't—something I *needed* to know—and yet, out on the boat, watching Westley, for a little while, I'd drunk in the wind and sun and forgot. I'd had a good time. "What about you?"

"More than a little." He squinted down at me. "Although I've got a little bit of a headache I need to get rid of."

I glanced toward DiAnn and Paul, who worked to tie the boat off. Seeing an opportunity to help and become more a part of the family, I slid away from Westley and said, "Let me help. Just tell me what to do."

DiAnn smiled, her chin rising. "Grab that rope right there." She looked at Westley. "Show her how to knot, Wes."

Within seconds his hands worked alongside mine as we tied off the back of the boat. When we'd finished, we gathered up the skis, the life vests, and the picnic basket and made our way back up the hill toward the house.

Paul and DiAnn were treating Westley and me to dinner at their favorite Italian café located in the heart of Baxter. "Get a shower,"

DiAnn instructed me, then glanced Westley's way and back to me. "You may even want to nap a little after a day out in the sun." She turned to Paul. "I know I'm ready for one. How about you?"

"A nap?" I asked, surprised but content to comply. I wanted to be a part of whatever the evening held, and I *had* grown sleepy.

Westley pulled what was left of my ponytail from the elastic band that held it at the top of my head. "Go on upstairs," he said. "I'll do the same down here..."

I took the ponytail holder from his fingertips. "I hope a little sleep will help your headache before tonight."

"It should."

I took a long, hot shower, wrapped myself in a thick terrycloth robe DiAnn had hung on the back of the door for me, and then padded into my room wearing socks on feet that now felt cold to the bone. I closed the door behind me with a gentle click, aware that Paul and DiAnn might possibly be in their nearby bedroom, already asleep. I leaned against the door, felt a yearning to already have what they had—a marriage and a marriage bed. I wanted to be able to lay beside Westley, feel his arms around me, his breath warm against the back of my neck as we faced the same direction. I wanted to know—

The slamming of a car door and the start of an engine startled me. I crossed the room to the window, stood beside it and lifted the edge of the draperies in time to see Westley driving away from the house. My brow furrowed. Where would he be going at this hour? To get aspirin? Surely Paul and DiAnn had some here... Or maybe they were out.

I dropped the curtain, crossed the floor, and turned off the light with a flick of the switch. Minutes later, I snuggled between the bedcovers, the robe still wrapped around me, and fell asleep, not giving Westley's whereabouts another thought.

Chapter Seven

Cindie

Cindie Campbell paced from the small living room of her mother's house to the kitchen to check the stovetop clock one more time. Six-o-five and this clock was usually slow. Westley had said he'd be there by six-fifteen. No later. And she'd warned him. Warned him good. He'd better be . . . or better *not* be. Late, that is.

She'd put up with a lot from him. She'd put up with a lot from everyone. When her mother had caught wind of the fact that he was coming into town to see his brother and sister-in-law, she wasted no time in giving her middle daughter what for. "Whatever it takes," she'd said. "You get him over here and you make him listen."

The next day Cindie marched herself into DiAnn Houser's uppity finance office and let her know in no uncertain terms that Westley had best get himself over to her house at some point while he was in town.

DiAnn kept it cool, she'd give her that. Not a blink or a change of expression before she raised her brow and said, "I'll be sure to let him know."

"I mean it, DiAnn," Cindie had said. She stood over the woman's desk, her arms crossed and the toe of her scuffed boot tapping. "I've wrote him not too long ago and he didn't even acknowledge the note. I'm not putting up with much more."

DiAnn placed her forearms on top of the paperwork scattered on her desk. Paperwork full of tiny boxes filled with numbers. DiAnn was smart when it came to books but Cindie was smarter when it came to getting what she wanted. She'd place a bet on it. "Do you want to sit down?" the blonde businesswoman now asked her.

"No, I don't want to sit down."

"A cup of coffee? Coke?"

"No. I don't want—" Then again, a Coke over ice sounded pretty good. "All right. A Co-cola. But only if you serve it in a glass with some ice."

DiAnn picked up the handset of her desk phone and dialed a number. "Sherry, would you bring a Coke over ice in here for Miss Campbell, please … thank you." She hung up, raised her brow again. "Seriously. Sit, Cindie."

Cindie jerked a well-placed faux-wood and orange vinyl chair from its perfect angle to dead center in front of the desk. She crossed her legs as she sat, which only hiked her skirt higher than even she felt comfortable. She tugged at the hem without result before resting her elbows on the hard arms of the chair. "So," she said. "When was the last time you talked to him?"

The door to DiAnn's office opened and the woman who'd taken Cindie's name and "the reason for your visit" when she'd walked in off the street sauntered in with her soft drink. "Just put it there on the desk," DiAnn said, pointing to the edge.

Clever. Make her reach for it.

Which she did. Cindie took a long swallow, waited for the woman to leave, then said, "Well?"

"Paul talked to him a few days ago."

"Did he say anything about me?"

"I wouldn't know, Cindie. Paul doesn't give me a play-by-play after he talks with his brother. He only told me that—that he was coming for the weekend. Which you apparently know already."

Cindie set the glass on the desk a little harder than she'd intended. DiAnn glanced at it, then back up, her eyes never showing a care. She was a good one, DiAnn Houser was. Always been the coolest chick. The girl every boy wanted to date, and every girl wanted for a best friend. Little girls wanted to grow up to *be* her. Or like her. Cheerleader.

Tennis champ. Everything she ever wanted, she got … right down to her own horse and the latest fashions. Not like Cindie, who'd never even been close to a horse and who wore her sister's hand-me-downs, which had been someone else's hand-me-downs before that.

Cindie licked her lips. Tasted the Coke and the cherry lip balm she'd swabbed across them before she'd gotten out of her mother's beat-up excuse for a car earlier. "Like I said, you tell him I mean it. I called information and I got his mama and daddy's number. All it's going to take is a single phone call and they'll know the whole story."

"I told you I'd tell him, and I will," DiAnn said, her shoulder jerking slightly. "I'll even do you one better than that. I'll insist that he call you first thing Saturday morning. How's that?"

"Well, I hope you've got that kind of say-so over him."

"I think I can manage it."

And apparently, she had. At seven thirty that morning he'd called, sounding every bit as gorgeous and inviting as he always had. Westley Houser. Who would have ever thought that a man like him would be under her thumb? Or wrapped around her pinky?

But he was. Or at least he would be, if she kept playing her cards right. Because she sure hadn't been able to convince him—so far—to marry her. Not even with all of Lettie Mae's threats, which meant all the more to Cindie. If she was ever going to break free of her mother, she'd need a man like Westley.

And so they needed to talk, she'd told him. Alone.

And he'd agreed.

When she told her mama that he said he'd be there by six-fifteen, Lettie Mae had made sure the house was cleared out by five-forty-five. "In case he comes early," she said. Then she pointed her sharply manicured nail at Cindie's nose and said, "You don't do nothing to cause any more issues, you get what I'm telling you?"

Cindie pushed her mother's finger away. "I get you."

"And you put his feet to the flame. We ain't gonna keep this up forever. He's practically a doctor. He can do his share. More than his share. If he ain't gonna marry you right off—"

"I got it, I got it," Cindie said. "Now let me handle it."

As soon as her mother and the rest of the family skedaddled, she went to her bedroom and pulled a pair of jeans from her younger sister's closet. She had to lie on the bed to zip them and worried she wouldn't be able to breathe good once she rolled off the bed. She then pulled one of Leticia's sweaters on—a size smaller than what she normally wore. Especially since last year.

She spent five minutes at the bathroom mirror, scooping her hair up and clasping it with combs, then pulled curling tendrils toward her high cheekbones and over her forehead. A spritz of Yardley Magnolia, another application of lip balm, and she blinked at her reflection. She looked exactly the way Westley liked her. At least that's what he'd always said. Light makeup. Hair pulled up "like a Gibson girl," he once said.

She'd had to ask her older sister what that one meant. And when she found out, it made her feel pretty and special.

The doorbell rang and she jumped, knocking her hairbrush to the tile floor where it bounced slightly, then slapped against her bare foot. Shoes ... she'd decided not to wear them. Her mama would skin her alive if she knew ... but she wouldn't know ... and that was the way it was going to be.

Cindie hurried to the front door and swung it open to Westley standing there, one hand resting on the doorjamb, the other on his hip. He wore winter-white jeans with a matching denim jacket over a dark-brown turtleneck. The masculine scent of him reached her before she had a chance to catch her breath fully. "Hey," she said, smiling before she could stop herself.

Westley Houser had that kind of effect on her.

"Hey, yourself." He looked over her shoulder. "Can I come in or are we going to talk out here?"

She stepped back. "Sorry. Come on in."

He walked in with all the confidence of a man who belonged, even when he didn't. And he certainly didn't belong *there,* in the little ragtag house she and her family had been calling home since their daddy left their mama for the nurse he'd met while visiting his mama who'd taken ill for a spell. "Are we alone?" he asked.

Cindie closed the door. "Yeah. Mama thought it best."

His eyes roamed over her. "You look good. Smell good, too."

She shoved her hands into the back pockets of the jeans that didn't want to give. "Don't start nothing you can't finish."

"Oh, I can finish it," he said, then laughed. "I'm teasing with you." Then he stepped over and kissed her cheek, allowing his lips to linger just long enough that she felt her defenses slide down her spine. "Seriously. I'm sorry I haven't called. Or written." He stepped back and pointed to a chair. "Mind if I sit?"

Mind? She'd been dreaming of it all day. Waiting for it. Wanting it as bad as she wanted him. "No. Go ahead."

He slid his jacket off and tossed it on the sofa before sitting, then pulled a pack of cigarettes from the jacket's front pocket. "Want one?"

Cindie walked to him, slid a cigarette from between the rows as sexily as she knew how, waited for him to light hers, then his. She wandered over to a chair on the far side of the room and sat, feeling the waist of the jeans cut into her flesh. "There's an ashtray over there on the end table," she said, pointing.

He smiled. "I remember." He took a long drag, blew the smoke into the room that seemed dingier with the likes of him in it. She momentarily wondered what his mama and daddy's house looked like, figuring they had real fine furniture. Velvet chairs and silver-framed photos like at the Girl Scout house in Savannah she'd visited once upon a time.

"Is she here?" he asked, startling her.

"Who?"

Westley chuckled. "Michelle. Isn't that why *I'm* here?"

"No. Mama took her with them."

Disappointment clouded his face. "I'd like to see her."

"You can come by tomorrow if you want. Or maybe we can meet up—"

"I can't tomorrow. I'll be heading back home—"

"What about before you go?"

He took another long drag, then stretched across the length of the sofa and snuffed it out in the oversized tin ashtray that held her mother's cigarette butts from earlier in the day. Cindie mentally kicked herself; she should have emptied it. Made it look nicer. She bet there wasn't a dirty ashtray anywhere in his mama's house. "Can't," he said. Then he straightened. "But I'd love to see her. Maybe—"

"I need to talk to you about money."

"All right." He sat straight. Rested his elbows on his knees. "Talk."

"Raising a baby takes more than a hundred a month."

Westley nodded as if he agreed. "Have you talked to your attorney?"

"I told you I did. Told you in that letter I sent." She took a final drag, then walked the remainder of the cigarette to an ashtray resting on the fireplace mantel. One that matched the tin one on the end table. One filled with just as many butts. "He says a hundred twenty-five is fair, but I'm thinking more like one-fifty." Cindie raised her chin a fraction of an inch. "Especially from the looks of that car out there in my driveway. I 'spect you can afford it."

Westley stared at her. She tried to read his thoughts but couldn't. She'd never been able to, really. He was a man of mystery. A man of control. She wanted the same. The same over him like he had over her and everyone else he came into contact with. But she'd never have it and she knew it. She'd thought she might when she told him she was pregnant, but even then ... Westley Houser lived by his own rules. He hadn't even told his parents about Michelle and she was nearly a year old already. "All right," he said finally. "One-fifty isn't a problem. But first I want to ask you a few questions."

She didn't move. "Like what?"

"Are you working?"

"I'm taking care of your baby, Westley. That's work enough."

"What about school?"

"When am I supposed to do that?"

He rubbed the lobe of his ear between two fingers. "You'll never get ahead like this. And I want you to get ahead, Cindie. I really do."

She cocked her hip and crossed her arms. "Oh, really?"

He patted the seat beside him. "Come here."

"What for?"

His chin went up a fraction. "Come here. Sit next to me. I don't have a lot of time and I want to talk *to* you, not argue *with* you."

She walked over and sat, keeping enough distance to hold on to her wits.

Westley pulled one of her tendrils. "Always so pretty. But you can be more than that, Cindie. You can. And I want you to be. You're the mother of my child and I want the best for her and for you. Go back to school. Get a good education. A good job."

She lost it then. She threw her arms around him, pushed up against him, and kissed his neck over and over until he forcefully pulled her away. "Marry me, then," she said, her voice practically begging. "I'll make you a good wife. I promise. I'll cook and clean and you'll see Michelle *all* the time."

Westley's eyes found hers. "That's not the answer and you know it. Besides, like I told you before Michelle was born, if you want me, you'll have to do better than that."

She pulled away. Oh, he'd told her all right. Let her know right off that she wasn't good enough and this was the way it was going to be. His way or no way. But she knew—one day she'd have the biggest bargaining chip of all. His child. "I want a hundred and fifty a month," she said firmly. "Plus other things like insurance."

"She's already on my insurance and you know it." He stood, reaching for his jacket.

"You leaving?" she asked, panic growing inside her. "Already?"

"I've got dinner plans with my brother and his wife. I need to head on back."

She couldn't let him go. Not like this. She had to get things back in her favor. "Wait," she said, standing and reaching for his hand. "Wait. I got something for you." Cindie hurried into her bedroom, opened the small drawer of her bedside table and pulled out a framed photograph of their daughter, dressed in the baby-pink sun dress he'd sent early in the summer. Within a moment, she returned. "I got this for you. It's not much of a frame—I got it at Kessler's—but I thought the picture came out nice."

Westley took the proffered peace treaty and studied it. Smiled at the locks of dark-blond curls framing his daughter's cherub face. The china-doll expression made even more enticing by round green eyes—his eyes—one more almond shaped than the other. "Look at her," he said. "She's something." Then he sighed. "I really do want to see her. If I can manage it, I'll swing by tomorrow."

Cindie smiled. "Really? Will you?"

He kissed her cheek again, lingering once more. "Don't hold me to it, okay? But I'll try. If not this trip ... I'll be back real soon. And we'll do something as a family. Together."

Her smile broadened. "She'd like that. I've been trying to get her to say *daddy* and she's already pretty good with *mama*."

Westley glanced at his watch. "I gotta go. Call you later." He stopped at the door and turned to face her. "Promise."

Chapter Eight

Westley

Westley slid behind the wheel of his car, started the engine and backed out of Cindie's driveway as quickly as he could without hitting the light pole on one side and the beat-up paper box on the other. A quick check of his watch told him he would make it back to Paul and DiAnn's right on time. Hopefully, before Ali woke up or came back downstairs looking for him. He stopped at the stop sign a few yards from the driveway, lowered the top of the car, and breathed in the crisp autumn air.

Ali. His hope and his salvation wrapped up in a young woman not quite twenty. How he'd gotten so lucky to find her, or for her to find him, he'd never know. The girl was beautiful. More so than she knew. Which was a good thing. If she had so much as a clue as to how gorgeous she really was—the creaminess of her complexion, the light-honey tan her skin bore after a day in the sun, the warmth of her eyes, the upturn of her nose. And her smile. Dear Lord, did the girl have a clue how much she lit up a room when she smiled?

Ali also had more potential than any woman he'd ever met. The absolute second he saw her approaching his window at the pharmacy, he knew. She was *the one* ... the woman who would take care of the pressing issues in his life. She'd make the right kind of wife and, as quickly as he could arrange it, the right kind of mother for Michelle. She was the kind of girl his parents would approve of—the kind you brought home to Mother, as the old saying went—because the good

Lord knew both Mom and Dad would have had a conniption fit if he'd ever brought Cindie to dinner.

Yep, Allison Middleton was the kind of girl who fit in with his family—again, unlike Cindie. But, even better for Westley, she wasn't one of those women who'd ask too many questions. It didn't take a genius to know she practically worshiped the ground he walked on, which meant that, even after marriage, she would let him live his life by his own rules and standards. She was moldable to what he wanted and needed. Especially now ... him with a child and the child with a mother who'd probably never amount to a hill of beans.

Okay, okay. So in spite of the shock of her, he didn't *regret* Michelle. But he often wished he'd never met her mother. Or, if he'd met her, that he hadn't been so stinking intoxicated the night she'd wooed him away from the slightest measure of any decent level of sense.

Even with the age difference, he'd known Cindie Campbell for years—her and her family. You couldn't grow up in a town like Baxter and *not* know who the Campbells were. Years ago—gosh, how many had it been—Horace Campbell left his wife and their four kids for another woman—a nurse from another town, he'd heard his mother say. Naturally, the good women of the church had rallied to the cause, his mother included. They'd done their collective best to help Lettie Mae Campbell, despite her social standing. They'd found her an affordable house, helped her fill out paperwork for government assistance that would suffice until she could get on her feet, and even drove her to the legal appointments that concluded with her divorce. Which, of course, not a single one of them approved of but, as one woman said, "What else was there to do but divorce the man?"

Westley slowed his car as a traffic light changed from yellow to red. He checked his watch, which seemed to tick faster than what was best for him. *Keep napping, Ali. Keep napping.*

He glanced over at the photo of his daughter lying face-up in the seat beside him, the one in the thin brass frame. Well, one thing was for certain—drunk or not—he and Cindie had made a pretty child. Not that he could remember much about the night she'd been conceived.

Only that while on a weekend visit to Paul and DiAnn's to celebrate his twenty-sixth birthday, he'd gone into the café where Cindie worked, hoping for the best, greasiest burger he could find, and that at some point he and Cindie ended up on the outskirts of town, stretched out and shivering on a blanket, two empty bottles of Boone's Farm tossed into the thick, moist grass—their clothes right along with them. The following afternoon, after nursing the first and worst hangover of his life, he returned to Athens, still unsure as to how he'd gotten the girl or himself back to their respective homes, but more than a little certain of what had occurred between them and hoping she wouldn't read anything more into it than it was. A one-night stand. Done and forgotten.

Six weeks later, DiAnn called him. Cindie had spotted her in the Piggly Wiggly, she said. "She gave me a piece of news I think you may want to sit down for." Later that evening, as expected, Paul called him. "Really, brother? Cindie Campbell?"

Westley had groaned appropriately. "Never mind she's a Campbell, she's cute and I was drunk," he said by way of excuse.

"Yeah, but she's also only—what—fifteen years old? You'll be lucky if Lettie Mae doesn't—"

"She's older than that." He remembered that much. "But her mother is the least of my worries," he said. Because she was. And then, to deflate the situation, he added, "Don't *you* think she's cute?"

"Well, she's not *my* type, not that it matters. The Campbells are only after one thing, Wes, and you should know that. A way out of working. Lettie Mae has figured out a way to live without ever hitting a lick at a snake and she'll make sure her kids do, too. Other than the oldest girl, they're all headed for the same kind of life as their mother."

Oh, yes. The oldest. Velma. Sweet girl. Married a country preacher and, according to what he'd heard, made a fine wife and mother. But the rest of them ... Lord God, help.

Lettie Mae had put Cindie to work in the café at thirteen. Her younger sister right there with her. Both expected to bring half their pay to the household accounts, he now knew better than he should.

And the only boy in the family, Jacko, had made a reputation for himself when it came to petty crime before he hit his twelfth birthday.

Only after one thing ... well, Cindie had proven that. Standing there in her mother's boxed-off living room, demanding more money from him. Barely at legal age—if that—and she already had that much down to a science. No doubt in his mind she'd nickel-and-dime him the rest of Michelle's childhood. Unless ...

The light turned green and Westley pushed the accelerator a tad harder than he should, then pulled back. No need in getting a ticket. That would only make things worse. He had only a short period of time now to think things through. Somehow he'd managed, so far, to keep Michelle's existence away from his parents. For sure, he'd tell them. But first he had to marry Allison Middleton. Make everyone think he was ready to settle down. Build a life with her and, eventually, have their own children. Plus Michelle. Because instinctively he knew Michelle would be more than a child who visited every other weekend, a week at Christmas, and a week or two during summer vacation.

His fingers tightened on the steering wheel. Only a few more weeks and Ali would be his wife. He'd take her on a honeymoon she'd never forget and then, once they got home, he'd tell her the truth. Make it as matter-of-fact as possible. Michelle was a reality and—he'd say—living with a woman not fit to raise her. Somehow, they'd need to think about whatever it took to lead to full custody. Because that was what he wanted when he got right down to it. Because he'd be darned if he'd let Michelle grow up like the rest of her mother's family.

Westley made the turn toward his brother's house. Good ole Paul. He'd played life right down the line—clean and safe. No heavy drinking. No drugs. No wild women. He and DiAnn had started dating their senior year in high school. They'd remained faithful to each other all through college and, four-year diplomas in hand, they'd married and gone right to work. DiAnn's daddy had set them up right fine in the house, but Paul managed to make the payments without help from anyone else.

Westley brought the car to rest under a tall pine in the front yard, raised the top as he craned his neck to look up at the window where, he prayed, Ali still napped, then stepped out of the car. But not before slipping the framed photo of his child under the driver's seat. And not before remembering the *other* thing he had to tell his fiancée. The one thing he *could* tell her. In fact, had to tell her.

He'd not gotten six strides across toward the front door when it opened and Ali stepped out. "Are you okay?" she asked.

Westley stopped. "Yeah. Why?" He pulled the pack of cigarettes from his pocket and lit one before she could reach him, hoping there were no lingering evidences of his meeting with Cindie on his clothes. That girl and her overuse of perfume. That was another thing about Allison—she smelled like a light wash of powdery-scented body spray. Nothing more. What was it? Love's Baby Soft ... Cindie always smelled like his grandmother's garden.

Ali stopped in front of him. She had dressed for the evening— burgundy slacks that fit her like a glove with a matching multitoned sweater that hugged her in ways that nearly drove him crazy. A hint of vanilla and rose reached him and he smiled in appreciation. Yep. Cindie Campbell had nothing on Allison Middleton. Sexy without class could only be sensual and nothing more. Allison was the complete package. A woman he could have a conversation with even when she wasn't in his bed.

"Why are you smiling?" she asked.

"You," he answered. "You make me smile. And you smell good."

Her lips formed a slight frown, which was not what he'd hoped for. "I was worried about your headache."

He touched her button nose with the tip of his finger. "Yeah ..." he said, stalling. "I thought maybe a drive would make me feel better. The fresh air blowing, you know?"

Her brow rose. "Oh. I thought ... maybe ... that you'd gone to the drugstore or something. I never thought about just driving around for a while."

A low chuckle rose in him and he wrapped his arm around her

shoulders, turning her back toward the house. "You are adorable, you know that? Did you manage to sleep any?"

She nodded, then looked up at him, her eyes adoring him. "Yes, but I missed you not being here when I woke up."

He kissed the top of her head. "I wasn't gone *that* long. Must not have been much of a nap." They reached the front porch. Ascended the steps to the door, left half open. "Hey," he said, stopping. Her eyes met his. "I love you, you know that?"

Ali's arms slid around his waist as her head came to rest on his chest. "Oh, Westley. I can't wait to be your wife."

He took another draw from his cigarette. Exhaled the smoke toward the yard, then untangled her so he could toss the remainder into the shrubs. But his hand found hers. Held it. Because he loved her. He did. No doubt about that. And he'd make her as happy as a man like him—a man not always focused on what his actions could mean to anyone other them himself—knew how.

"I was thinking," Paul said during dinner that evening, "that we'd go home tonight, build a bonfire, and make s'mores."

DiAnn raised her wine glass in a toast to the idea, then asked, "Do we have the ingredients?"

"Piggly Wiggly..."

"Which is closed," Westley interjected.

"Hmmm," Paul said.

"What about a convenience store?" Allison spoke up from beside Westley.

Westley pointed to her, brows raised and smiling. "See? That's why I'm marrying this one. She's smart."

"She is that," DiAnn agreed. This time she took a sip of her wine.

They left the restaurant where they'd enjoyed a fine meal, each of them sipping on a glass of sweet dinner wine—Westley more than one—until he felt good about the rest of his life. Most especially about the conversation he planned to have with Ali later on. They stopped at a nearby 7-Eleven, purchased overpriced graham crackers, marshmallows, and Hershey's chocolate bars, then hurried back to Paul and DiAnn's.

While Allison and DiAnn set up a tray of everything they'd need, he and Paul worked to dig a pit and gather firewood. "Great idea," Westley said once the flames licked upward, the smoke curling into the dark night air. "You're all right for a little brother," he added with a laugh.

"Let's grab some chairs off the porch," Paul said, then turned toward the back of the house.

The brothers trudged the slight incline, Westley keeping his eyes on the kitchen window where Allison passed back and forth. He stopped, rested his hands on his hips, and grinned. "Look at her," he said. "Look at her, Paul."

Paul stopped beside him. "Have you told her yet?"

"About Michelle or about ... tomorrow."

"Tomorrow."

"Tonight." Westley looked at his brother. "Tonight, after we have some s'mores and, afterward, you and DiAnn go back inside. Leave us out here alone, okay? I'll tell her then."

Paul slapped him on the back. "Maybe I should tell DiAnn to bring another bottle of wine out with the s'mores ingredients."

"May-be."

"It's your funeral, big brother, but I believe I would have—"

"Never mind what you would have..." Westley said, then continued toward the chairs.

Chapter Nine

Allison

I stretched my legs in the low-sitting Adirondack chair and smiled, the flavor of chocolate and marshmallow and graham crackers and wine still lingering on my tongue. "This was fun," I said, turning so that my chin brushed against the thick, soft fabric of my coat's collar. I blinked toward my fiancé who sat no more than a foot away. "The whole night was wonderful, but ..." I grinned at him. "I'm kinda glad Paul and DiAnn left us alone for a while."

Westley pulled a cigarette from the front pocket of his jacket, lit it, then blew a thin line of smoke from between his lips where it joined the shredded cloud hovering over a dying fire. "Are you cold?" he asked.

My gaze went from him to the glowing embers. "No," I said. "I don't think I could ever be cold when I'm this close to you."

He reached over, took my hand in his. "Your hand is cold."

Cold hands, warm heart, I thought, then closed my eyes. "Westley," I breathed out. "I wish ..."

His fingers tightened around mine. "What?"

I shook my head so slowly I wondered if he perceived it. How could I answer him? I wished so much that we were married already ... that we were alone, in our own home ... that there were no premarital barriers standing in our way. I wished—oh, how I wished—that whatever I'd overheard that morning had already been made clear to me. That his trust in me was enough to tell me what Paul and DiAnn already knew. I wished ...

I took a deep breath and opened my eyes. The embers crackled and glowed, showing off the darkest outline of the few trees between us and the lake where the water rippled under a quarter moon. "I wish ..." I turned to him again, my mind as clear and as foggy as I'd ever known it to be. ". . . that we could live this day all over again. I wish we didn't have to go home tomorrow." This time, my smile was slow. Catlike.

Westley leaned toward me. "Come here," he said, his voice low and throaty.

My lips met his, our kiss so tender I believed the purity of it would kill me before we broke apart. And, when we did, I ran my tongue across my lips, tasting him ... his cigarette ... the leftover tanginess of wine and food. "Come here," he said again, this time opening his arms to me. I slid out of my chair and went to him, sitting in his lap, draping my legs over the hard, wide arm of his chair. Westley took a final draw from his cigarette, then strained to toss it toward the fire.

"Here," I said, taking it from him and bringing it to my own lips. I'd never smoked before, but tonight I felt grown up enough to try. Besides, I reasoned, there was a first time for everything and tonight seemed so perfect for acting more adult than I truly was. Then again, there were so many things I'd never done before and so many things I wanted to try. Especially tonight—

"No," Westley said, removing the cigarette from between my fingers and flicking it toward the fire where it landed dead center. "I don't want you to smoke."

I stroked his jawline with my fingertips, cognizant of a bravado I'd never known before, most likely brought about by the day, the night, and the wine. "Why not?" I asked, truly wondering. "You do."

"Nasty habit. I need to quit, and you don't need to start."

I kissed his chin lightly, then laid my head on his shoulder, again closing my eyes. "When did you start? How old were you?"

His chest lifted then fell as if it were collapsing, causing me to place my hand against the warmth of it for assuredness. The rhythmic beat of Westley's heart warmed me, and I spread my fingertips as my lips pressed against his Adam's apple. "Hmm?" I asked, truly wanting to know.

"Twelve."

My head came up. "Twelve?"

He smiled and my eyes found his—sleepy but content. "Put your head back," he told me, and I did as I was told, trying to imagine him on the cusp of adolescence, trying his first cigarette.

An odd thought crossed my mind: I would have been all of four years old. What a difference growing up makes when it comes to okaying relationships.

"I was twelve when I smoked my first cigarette," he continued. "I didn't really start until I was probably sixteen. Seventeen."

"You really were a daredevil, weren't you? Always pushing the envelope. Taking risks." I waited to see if he would answer, and when he didn't, I said, "What was the last truly crazy thing you did?"

He chuckled. "I asked you to marry me."

I slapped my hand against his chest, even as laughter rumbled within my own. "I love you so much." The words came as a whisper. A moan to my own ears. A begging and a longing.

"Ali," he said, his voice as strained as my whole body felt. "I need you to listen to me because I have something to tell you."

I nodded, wondering. Was this it? Was he finally going to confide in me? Tell me that thing he shared with Paul and DiAnn?

"Have you thought about where we'll live after we marry?"

I brought my head up again. "Not really. But I figured we'd talk about it sooner or later . . ."

Westley gently pushed my head to where it had been before. "I want you to do something for me. Okay?"

"Anything."

"I want you to think about living here."

My brow furrowed. "Here?" That certainly hadn't been in my plans. Renting a house in Bynum until we could build one of our own, perhaps. I was even willing to live with his mother and father—for certain not mine—for a season. His was the large bedroom off the kitchen—probably at one time serving as the maid's quarters. With its own access to the kitchen and its own bath, it could suffice. But move across the state? Would we live— "With Paul and DiAnn?"

He kissed my forehead. "No, sweetheart. Here. In Baxter. Actually, not exactly here. There's a town—about a stone's throw from here—Odenville. We passed through it, remember? It's larger than Baxter, but not by too much, so don't be concerned about going from such a small town to a larger one. DiAnn's grandmother lives there. She—she owns a string of pharmacies on this side of the state and she's offered me a job at the one there."

I brought my head up again; this time he didn't stop me. That was it? The thing he couldn't keep away from me forever? "Westley," I breathed out his name as though it were a prayer. "Live all the way over here? Away from Mama and Daddy?" Since the night of our engagement, I'd imagined my life as a young married woman. I'd work each weekday at the shop, stopping by my parents'—my childhood home—for a brief visit on some afternoons, then heading to *our* home, once we had one, to cook dinner. Which was, of course, something I hardly knew how to do. I could learn to do, yes. But leaving Bynum? Abandoning my preconceived notions of what happily-ever-after looked like?

His hand slid up my throat, cupping my jaw, his fingers pressing into the back of my scalp. "Ali," he said simply, his eyes never leaving mine. "I can make so much more money here. We'll have a house like the one behind us. Like Paul and DiAnn's. And we can drive over here on weekends." He cast a glance toward the lake, then back to me. "Go boating. Eat out. Sit around bonfires all the time. Whenever you want. Go back to Bynum for visits. Whenever you want."

I couldn't think. Not with him so close. Not with his fingers massaging me and his eyes and lips nearly pleading. I couldn't— "This is something you really want …"

"For you, Ali. For us. For our future and the future of our children. Odenville is a wonderful place. Paul and Heather and I used to hang out there all the time when we were kids. At DiAnn's grandmother's.

And, I know that you'll love it. In fact, I promise that you will."

I would love it. That went without saying. The one place I swore I never wanted to even visit in my whole life was the peat-filled wetlands of the Okefenokee Swamp, but that would be paradise as long as the boat ride included Westley. Still, there were so many questions. "How long have you known?"

"DiAnn called me this past week. *After* I'd asked you to come here, so I don't want you to think—She'd visited her grandmother and …" His voice trailed away in anticipation of my next question.

"Is that where you went this afternoon? To see her grandmother?"

Despite the night's drape around us, I noticed when his face darkened. "No. I told you where I went. But we are supposed to stop in Odenville tomorrow on our way back to Bynum. To see Miss Justine. And to look around a bit."

I tried to conjure it up, to recall the town we'd passed through before arriving in Baxter. Charming, yes. With more buildings than I was accustomed to. A wide main street lined with imposing houses on either side, fat columns holding up balconies secured by elaborate wrought iron railings. Would we live in a house like that? For certain my mother would be over the moon at that thought, but my father … what would he say?

I knew the answer—without question, he'd just want his little girl to be happy.

"Ali?" Westley whispered my name as his hand slid down my sleeve, sending a warm chill down the length of my legs. He tucked it then beneath the opening of my coat until his fingers found the tender flesh of my waist, moving only as far as my father would approve. Whether I wanted him to or not, Westley was sticking to the promise he'd given Daddy. And, if he could be trusted with me *now*, in this moment where every fiber of my being wanted him as surely as every fiber of his being wanted me, then I knew he could be trusted to take care of me once we married. Once we lived away from all I'd ever known my whole life. Once I'd been dropped into the period of a giant question mark.

"Yes," I said then, forcing a strength I was nearly uncertain of into my voice. "Westley, I'll go anywhere you want me to go and I promise you, I'll be happy there." My arms slid around his neck until he squeezed my body against him—an awkward imprisonment, but beyond anything I ever wanted to be released from. "As long as I'm with you," I moaned. "Oh, God, Westley. I love you so much."

We loaded up the car, said good-bye to Paul and DiAnn around eleven thirty the next morning, then pointed the car, top down, toward Odenville, Georgia—a place I reckoned I'd soon enough call home. Westley held my hand during the half-hour drive, smiled at me occasionally, but said little.

"Mind if I turn on the radio?" I asked when we were halfway there.

"Not a bit," he said.

I leaned over, fiddled with the dial until I heard a song I recognized. I smiled at Westley, my hair whipping around my face. "'Dust in the Wind,'" I said. "I love this song."

"Kansas. I saw them in concert once," he said.

"Did you?"

"Yep."

And then we drew quiet, listening to the haunting melody, both of us growing pensive by the lyrics. "Do you think that's true?" I asked him when the song had faded to a commercial for a local plumbing company.

"Do I think what's true?"

"That all we are is dust in the wind?"

"For dust thou art, and unto dust shalt thou return."

I feigned a cough. "What?"

"It's from the Book of Genesis."

I turned toward him, shifting completely. "I know that. I just—I never heard you quote a single verse of Scripture."

Westley threw back his head and laughed. "You think I don't listen when I'm in church?"

I shrugged. "I mean ... nothing personal or anything, Westley, but you don't strike me as the type."

He grew sober. "The type to what?"

"You know ... think about things like dust to dust. Mr. Daredevil and all that."

Westley raised his chin. "We're almost in town."

The car slowed and I turned to face the front. "I need to do something with my hair," I said. "Before I meet DiAnn's grandmother."

"You look fine."

"No," I said. "I don't."

We'd come to the outskirts of town, the place where crop fields gave way to low-rise buildings. A service station. A small grocery store. A couple of houses in need of repair with lawns in need of fertilizing. "I'll pull in here," Westley said, indicating the service station. "Do you need to go in?"

I took one look at the building—white brick that hadn't seen a hose or even a shower of rain in who knew how long. Single-pane windows looking into the office, cloudy with prints; the painted-white concrete black with oil. The bay doors had been shoved up and appeared to be hanging on for dear life.

"No," I said, then grabbed my purse from the floorboard. "Not even if my bladder was about to bust." I dug around until I found a brush, a tube of flavored lip gloss, and then flipped the visor to reveal the mirror.

"See?" Westley said. "You look fine."

I shook my head. "I'm hideous," I said, pulling the brush through my hair as if it had done something wrong.

"Come on now," he said to me, then craned his neck to call to one of the grease monkeys who'd stepped away from the bay where a car had been raised. "We're good," he said with a wave of his hand. "My fiancée just needed a moment."

"All right," the man said. "No problem."

I pause, watching him return to the elevated car. "I can't go meet

DiAnn's grandmother looking like a Raggedy Ann doll, Wes." His low chuckle earned my attention. "What?"

"You called me Wes. That's a first."

"Well, you call me Ali ..."

He reached over and pinched my chin. "You're a mess, you know that?"

I sighed. "I just want to impress her." I flipped the visor and looked at him. "I don't even know her name."

"Mrs. Knight. I told you that last night."

Heat rose from my belly. "I can hardly be expected to remember the details of last night," I said. For one, after my final declaration of love, Westley had kissed me so long and so hard I may have possibly lost brain cells, leaving them scattered with the ashes along the firepit. And for another, I'd never had more than a glass of wine in my life ... until last night, when I'd consumed close to three. Between the alcohol and the kisses and the headiness that comes from days like that, my whole body had gone languid. My brain to mush. I looked up. "Looks like rain."

"I'll raise the top."

I waited until it clicked into place to ask, "And she's nice?"

Westley leaned over and kissed my cheek. "You'll adore her."

Chapter Ten

I'd never seen anything like it, this palace Justine Knight called home. Justine. *Miss* Justine, as I came to call her. Which was also what the maid who answered the door called her.

A house with a maid. The full-time, dressed-in-a-uniform kind that I knew about from the movies and television, and from a handful of books but had never experienced firsthand. The kind that came once a week, yes. Those I knew. But not this.

The woman who answered the door at Justine Knight's house was something else entirely. Black cheeks overly blushed but flawless, hair styled in soft curls around her face, apron strings pulled a little too tight around an ample but not large middle, and an aura that let you know she may not be *in charge*, but she was surely second-in-command.

"I reckon y'all are the ones here to have lunch with Miss Justine," she said not two seconds after one of the stained glass double doors at the top of the wide steps jerked open. She peered up at the sky. "Come on in before it goes to raining. I 'spect it might any minute now."

Westley placed his hand on the small of my back. "I'm Westley Houser and this is Miss Allison Middleton," he said, his voice taking on a formality I'd never heard, much less expected, from him. "And, yes, Mrs. Knight is expecting us."

"Well, y'all right on time, too. And if you know Miss Justine, you know she don't like folks arriving late *or* unannounced." When she stepped back, Westley all but pushed me into a foyer I was willing to bet I could fit my entire house in. One that was, for sure, beyond anything I'd ever expected to see. A floor of black marble swirled and feathered in white. A massive table sitting dead center hosting a Chinese vase filled with fresh, long-stemmed flowers. Overhead, a chandelier dripped crystals of various size, their prisms shooting in all directions. To the right, a curving staircase, carpeted in red, swept to the second floor. And from everywhere, it seemed, light spilled over and through, shining upon an opulence I'd never known.

A quick catch of my breath and Westley's hand went to my elbow and squeezed. "Easy," he whispered.

The uniformed maid, who I guessed to be in her thirties, clasped the wrist of one hand with the other. "Miss Justine said take y'all on to the back."

"Thank you," Westley said for the both of us, which was good because, had I attempted to speak, I believe only a squeak would have come out.

We followed the sound of nylons swishing in the cavernous room. I looked up at Westley, who squeezed my elbow again. If he meant this to comfort me, it wasn't working. "Westley," I mouthed, more a plea to "let's turn around and just go home" than anything.

"There you are," a low, raspy voice said from the back where a sunroom stretched across the length of the house.

"Right on time, Miss Justine," the maid said as she stepped to one side, approval thick on her tongue. "Jus' like you like it."

I felt my mouth go slack at the sight of the woman who owned such grandeur. I had to remind myself that she was DiAnn's grandmother. And that DiAnn had come from ... *this*. Played inside the papered walls and among the imported furniture and thick wool carpets.

Justine Knight stood no more than five feet tall—five-foot-five if one counted the teased red hair and high-heeled shoes—and she held on to the petite frame of a woman who'd always been small but who had also borne children. Her creamy complexion only made astute, dark eyes beneath arched brows all the more pronounced.

But her smile—crooked and framed by deep red lipstick—warmed me immediately. "Right on time they are, Rose Beth," she said from beside a round wicker table topped with crisp linen and three place settings of fine china, silver, and crystal. She clapped as her gaze met Westley full-on. "There you are, dear boy. There you are."

Westley stepped away from me long enough to wrap the woman in a bear hug, then kissed both of her cheeks. "Look at you," he said. "You're as pretty as a picture, not that you haven't always been." After she gave him a good-natured swat, he turned to me. "Miss Justine, allow me to introduce my fiancée, Miss Allison Middleton."

Justine Knight reached for me with a stack of bracelets jangling from both wrists and most of her fingers decked in gaudy rings. Her scent, rich and heavy, enveloped me as she clasped my hands in hers, and more so as she drew me to her softness. "Land's sakes, Rose Beth, is she not darling?" She patted my cheek. "And much more child than woman, I'd venture."

"Yes'm," Rose Beth said. I looked back in time to catch a single nod. "I thought so soon as I saw her standing out there on your front stoop."

Miss Justine touched Westley's arm. "Westley, this is Rose Beth. She's been with me for a couple of years now, haven't you, Rose Beth?"

Westley smiled. Nodded. Then turned back to our hostess. "What happened to Olive?"

"Passed on," Miss Justine whispered, as if speaking the words loud enough might possibly raise her back from the dead. "Some time back now."

"Mm-mmm-mmm," Rose Beth chimed in. "Sweet Jesus, that one just dropped dead on the spot and went on to her glorious reward. May we all be so blessed."

Miss Justine shooed the maid with a wave of her hand. "Now, Rose Beth, let's get lunch served so Westley and I can have a talk." She smiled at me. "And you, too, of course, sweet child," which led me to wonder if I was supposed to go help Rose Beth or if I had been invited to be a part of the conversation between her and Westley.

Her brow went up in knowing. "Darlin', just how long have you been aware of my offer to your sweetheart here?" she asked, which quelled my wondering. "Because if I know Westley—and I do—you found out less than twenty-four hours ago."

I laced my fingers low and in front. "Yes, ma'am. He told me last night."

"Good land of the living, Westley. Son, will you ever change? Life is not to be lived by the seat of your pants. A grown man of your breeding should know that."

For a brief moment I thought Miss Justine might retract her offer, what with Westley being, in her eyes, so fly-by-night. But in the next moment she slid one arm around his waist and laughed. "God love it. If you weren't such a fine pharmacist and cute to boot, I'd throw you out right now and tell you to have your lunch at the Burger King."

I forced a smile while Westley's laughter came easily. Something in Miss Justine's voice let me know right away she had always been in on my future husband's ways. Ways I wasn't privy to. Yet. Ways his family kept mentioning and I kept telling myself were endearing. A part of his charm. One of the reasons I loved him so much.

And I did.

As lunch was served and conversation buzzed around me about the drugstore and those in neighboring towns, as talk went from profit and loss statements to salary and future expectations and the church we were slated to join, I listened. One hundred percent aware that this was *my* future being discussed and yet feeling completely not a part of it. Like I wasn't going to be Westley's partner in all this. I was no more than a textbook or a china doll that would be boxed up with the rest of our things and brought to town with him. For a moment, as my heart began to race and the lines around me started to blur, I thought to run. To jump up from the round wicker table against the glass wall overlooking a lush lawn full of gardens and statues and detailed wrought iron benches alongside a dark and brooding lake, and bolt to the car where Westley would find me, and I would beg him to take me home.

And then … "What do you think about that, Ali?"

I startled, my eyes jerking to Westley's. "About what?"

Westley laughed, then reached over and took my trembling hand in his steady one. "She's a bit overwhelmed," he said to Miss Justine.

Miss Justine's shoulders leveled. "As well she should be. Young bride-to-be. When's the wedding, did you say?"

"December," Westley said.

I supplied the rest of the answer. "Seventeenth."

"And you must simply have scads to do. Well, this will be one less thing."

I blinked several times. "What will?"

Westley squeezed the hand he continued to hold. "The house, sweetheart. Miss Justine has found us a house."

"Completely furnished," she said. "Now the furniture is not new, but it's clean and I'm sure it will be to your liking. You'll have lots of bridal showers and whatnot, so you'll have plenty of your own nice things to make it feel less like a house and more like a home."

"A house?" I said, my voice a squeak.

"Small," Miss Justine said. "But just what you'll need for now." She leaned toward me. "Sweetheart, I hope you don't mind, but I thought—"

I stole a glance at Westley, who appeared pleased beyond words. "No, I—it's just that I haven't even told my parents and I've barely wrapped my brain around the move and I—I—" And then, against my will, monstrous tears slid from my eyes.

"*Ali …*" Westley released my hand and, in one swift movement, he stood next to me, his hand resting on my shoulder. "What's wrong?"

Through a haze of tears, I saw the woman sitting across from me cock one of those perfectly arched, penciled-in brows. "Westley," she said, her tone maternal and forthright. "Leave us alone, will you?" She waved him away with the back of her ringed fingers. "Go on, now. Go tell Rose Beth we'll have coffee and dessert in the front parlor."

Westley did as he was told but not before planting a kiss on top of my head and not before the world turned nearly to night outside and, as predicted but later than expected, rain began to spatter against the glass. The next thing I knew, Miss Justine had me by the same hand Westley released. She pulled me over to a cluster of white wicker loveseats and chairs with overstuffed cushions, all nestled in the far-right corner, where I sat blubbering like the child I was.

"There now," she said, stuffing a pale pink handkerchief into my hand. "Blow your nose before you dribble all over that adorable little top of yours."

This time, it was I who did as she was told. "Mascara must be all over my face," I whimpered, thinking of how I probably looked to such a refined woman. A woman I had so wanted to impress. But, how to do that with mascara streaks down my cheeks?

"It is, but you'll survive it. Now," she said patting my knee. "Talk to me. Tell me what's going on."

And I did… I told her how much I loved Westley… and my parents … and my job … and my hometown. I told her that it all seemed to be happening so fast; faster than I could keep up with. I told her how one minute I was a single girl watching Match Game and the next I was an engaged woman whose fiancé hadn't told her about the move. He'd told his brother and sister-in-law, but he hadn't told the one person—me—who it would have the greatest effect upon. And then I ran down a completely different rabbit trail, telling her about the bridal showers my mother's friends had already scheduled and the tea the women of the church were organizing and that, so far, no one had asked me if the dates were okay. They simply expected me to be there and that was that, and so far, I'd been fine with it because all of this was really, truly exciting, but …

"But … I don't even have my dress," I sobbed. "And to top it off, I never really had an example with my older sister. I mean, she's married and all, but she didn't go through *any* of this. Not that we're even that close. I'd like to be, of course, but, well, we just never were. Not that there was much hope for that after she ran off and married the—"

A brow rose with the tilt of her head. "The?"

I managed a wobbly smile. "We call her husband 'the bum.'"

Miss Justine smiled. "And why is that?"

I squeezed the pretty pink handkerchief. Shook my head. "I-I shouldn't say ..."

She sat upright beside me. "Oh, come on now. You and I are slated to be friends, I just know it. And if you can't confide in a soon-to-be friend ..."

"It's nothing personal against him, really," I supplied quickly. "Because he's—as my sister says—a *godly* man." I shook my head. "It's because of his job ... or lack thereof."

"Oh," Miss Justine said, the word coming out in a tiny staccato. "So, he doesn't work."

"Oh, he works," I said, keeping my eyes on the handkerchief, wondering if I should take it home with me and wash it or hand it back to her in the awful mess it was now in. No one had ever taught me the etiquette for such a moment. "It's just ..." How could I explain my brother-in-law to such a woman as Justine Knight?

"Well, if he's a *godly* man, he must *do* something. If I'm not mistaken the Good Book says that *if any would not work, neither should he eat.*" She cocked a brow. "Does he eat?"

I had to swallow a smile. "Yes. Yes, of course, he eats."

"Well then. What exactly is it that he does so he can eat?"

I looked at her fully, then. At the graciousness of her. "Well, he *says* he's a writer, and I suppose he is. I mean, he's a journalism grad, but so far all he's done is turn out a few articles for some local magazines and, well, a small one in *Time*. Mostly my sister brings in the bread and butter." I spoke rapidly now, hoping Westley was not in earshot. "My parents went slap crazy when Westley and I started dating. And I mean that in a good way. I thought my mother was going to have a spasm when I told her he'd asked me—*me*—to marry him." I took a breath. "But without a dress, how am I supposed ..." Then, without warning, the tears started back up, tears I'd fought to keep at bay since I'd overheard Westley speaking with his brother and DiAnn. Tears I'd kept buried beneath the surface while wondering why my future sister-in-law seemed a little ... *cold* toward me. Or, if not cold, reserved. Tears I'd covered up while focusing on having a "good time."

Miss Justine ran her hand between my shoulder blades, told me to blow again—which I did—and then calmly noted that there were plenty of shops in Savannah that sold lovely gowns and with my cute little frame, finding the perfect dress shouldn't be a problem. "Your mother and—are your grandmothers still alive?"

I nodded as I ran the handkerchief over a now-tender nose.

"Well you should make a day of it. That's what I did with my daughter—DiAnn's mother. Sharon and myself and Sharon's future mother-in-law. Of course when DiAnn married Paul, we completely put on the dog."

"Oh," I said, "I didn't know how, exactly, you were related. I mean, I knew she was your granddaughter, but ..."

"Sharon is my oldest. Her brother Aaron is my youngest."

I let the family trivia sink in to stop thinking about my own. "So ... two children?"

Her face fell. "No," she said. "There's one in the middle. Buford Henry Knight II to hear my late husband say it. *Biff* to everyone else." She took a deep breath through her nose, then shook her head. "My son took off right after his father died. Right after he discovered that, no, he was *not* taking over the pharmacies nor was he getting a dime of his daddy's money." She pointed to her chest with a manicured nail. "That was *my* inheritance." She smiled then, albeit a forced one. "But enough about my children, dear one, especially that one. Do you feel better now?"

I nodded through a giggle. "I do."

Westley's head came around the doorjamb. "Safe to return?" he asked, stepping in as if on cue.

"Yes," I said, standing and walking to him. He put his arms around me, the safety of them wrapping me like a warm, fuzzy blanket.

"Good," he said, again placing a kiss on top of my head. "Because there is a delicious-looking red velvet cake and some piping hot coffee in the front parlor. Which is good because I just stepped outside, and I'd say the temperature has dropped about twenty degrees since we got here."

"Well then," Miss Justine said, reaching the two of us, "it's a good thing you have each other to keep yourselves warm."

Chapter Eleven

The rain let up.

After red velvet cake and coffee, Westley and Miss Justine and I stepped outside into the cooler but wet-blanket air and into our hostess's Lincoln Town Car, then drove several streets over to a neighborhood of picture-perfect cookie-cutter houses, each one flanked by fat oaks and swaying pines and each one painted a different color from the rest. "It's like a village of doll houses," I said, my nose pressed against the back-passenger's window. I turned to Westley and grinned. "I love it."

"These homes were built back in the 1940s," Miss Justine supplied as she turned the long-nosed car into the driveway of a house painted carmine red and trimmed in winter white. The front windows boasted window boxes devoid of flowers but, beneath them, a line of fat boxwoods. From the driveway, I could see that the backyard had been outlined with a white picket fence. Two steps led to the small front porch where a painted-white wooden bench perched near the door. A red-, white-, and black-striped pillow angled along with a few potted plants gave the area a "come and sit" feel. I immediately felt that I would.

"The 1940s?" Westley asked.

Miss Justine put the car in park, turned the key, then shifted so she could look at us in the rearview mirror. "Charming as they can be. Tiny, but charming. Hardwood floors—pure oak—and recently updated with lovely wallpaper and chair railing in many of the rooms." She pulled the key from the ignition. "Ready to see?"

I nodded. "I know I am," I said.

"Let's do it," Westley said.

Within a few minutes, the three of us had walked through the small, square rooms, each one more enchanting than the next. "It's like an English cottage," I said when we had returned to the living room. I crossed my arms against the chill in the house. "But without the thatched roof."

Westley tweaked my nose. "What do you know about English cottages with thatched roofs?"

I shrugged. "I saw a movie once—my sister and I—that was filmed in England. There were thatched-roof cottages everywhere in this village." I chuckled as my eyes roved around the living room—painted in burnt orange and trimmed with wide baseboards, crown molding, and chair railing, all painted in warm off-white. "And that's what this reminds me of."

"What do you think of the furniture?" Miss Justine asked.

I told her it was fine because it was. Not new, like she said, but certainly presentable. "I can purchase some pillows," I said pointing to the orange tapestry sofa that seemed to stretch for miles. Then, looking at its matching chair, I said, "And maybe one of Mama's afghans to throw over the chair."

"Sounds lovely," Miss Justine said as I stepped into the adjoining dining room.

"And I'm sure we'll have some lovely pieces from our showers to show off on the sideboard in here," I noted.

"Now, the kitchen," Miss Justine noted as she brushed past me and into the next room, "could stand some modernizing, but it has a dishwasher so thank the good Lord for that."

I peered in at the tiny square room that barely had enough counter space for a bowl, a pot and a pan, which hardly mattered given my cooking skills. And when I said so, Westley laughed behind me and quipped, "There's your excuse when it comes to my question of what's for dinner."

I turned and poked him in the ribs, and then, as he pretended injury, walked back into the living room and on into a small hallway where two bedrooms jutted off—one to the left and the other straight ahead—and a bathroom to the right.

I stepped into the front bedroom—the larger of the two—once again crossing my arms, taking in the maple-finished bedroom set, the floral bedspread with its tiny matching pillows—one round, one square—and the thick shag throw rugs cast on both sides of the bed. Late afternoon sunshine had broken through the lingering rain clouds and headed through the double window flanked by curtains matching the bedspread. The light shot straight to the bed, illuminating the place where, finally, Westley would hold me in his arms without restraint. My brow rose in anticipation, remaining there until, as if on cue, Westley's arms slid around my waist, and his lips nuzzled my neck. "Now, this is what I'm talking about."

"Westley," I whispered harshly, then broke free of him, but not before the now familiar tingle had rushed down my body and back up again. Not before the warmth had spread and settled deep into my belly.

As expected, my fiancé laughed at my embarrassment, then turned and walked into the second bedroom where twin beds had been set side by side under single windows. The walls, painted a creamy yellow, brought an added layer of warmth to the room. And, like all the other rooms, the baseboards and crown molding trimmed the room in off-white.

"Perfect for when our parents come to see us," I said to Westley, whose gaze had turned to something I didn't recognize in him. Not yet, anyway. Something that told me he saw beyond the blue bedspreads and the white throw pillows. Beyond the doily on the bedside table between the beds, the one serving as a resting place for a milk glass lamp.

Miss Justine joined us then. "Or for when you decide to expand your family," she noted, having overheard me. "Although, that would mean getting rid of the beds." She sighed then. "Oh, well. The two of us will have to shop for a crib and the other things you'll need for a nursery, that's all."

A new heat rose in me, one Westley spotted immediately. His pensive look changed to an expectant one, one that made my heart pound, both in anticipation and in dread of things happening too fast.

"Goodness, child," Miss Justine said as if the meaning behind her words only just then hit her. "No rush, of course."

Westley stopped an hour outside of Bynum, pulling up next to a phone booth, which he darted into to call my parents. To let them know we were running late and that we'd explain more when we got there. "What did they say?" I asked when he returned to the car and nearly before he shut the door good. "Who'd you talk to?" My thumbnails hacked away at each other.

He chuckled as he drove back onto the highway. "What are you so nervous about?"

"Just—Westley—they're going to be so upset when we tell them about moving. Who'd you talk to?"

"Your mother."

I leaned my head against the seat, turned my head toward the window, and peered out to the sky that had already turned the color of dark-blue ink. I allowed my eyes to roam heavenward, straining to see stars whose light might have burst through already. Finding only a few and recognizing none, I looked back at Westley. "Did she sound upset?"

"About what, Ali? They don't know anything yet."

"But—I mean—did she wonder why we were running late?"

Westley squeezed his eyes shut, then opened them again. "Do you want a play-by-play?"

I reached over, ran my fingers into the curls of his hair, not wanting him to be angry with my insecurity and knowing the effect it had on him. "Please."

"Be careful," he said then, casting a sideways glance my way. "You know what that does to me."

I leaned toward him, kissed his jaw, and said, "I'll be careful if you just tell me." My fingers left the curls that looped over his collar, then rested on his shoulder. A reminder that I was there, and I needed him. More than ever, I needed him.

"Well," he drawled. "She started off by saying hello."

"Cute."

"Then I said, 'Mrs. Middleton?'"

I could imagine my mother's fear at hearing Westley's voice. Sense her concern. "What'd she say?"

He gave a dramatic roll of his eyes before answering. "She said, Miss Worry Wart, 'Did y'all get held up?' To which I said yes and that we'd explain everything when we got there." His eyes found me again, the whites of them more pronounced against the darkness surrounding us. "She also said, 'Well, it sounds like y'all had a good time.'"

He grinned at me then and I slapped his shoulder. "Stop it," I said, aware of the blush racing madly through me.

"So," he said after several minutes of silence. Silence that held, I knew, the two of us remembering the night before. The way he'd held me. Kissed me. Drove me nearly to a place of torment without upsetting the apple cart and wishing for our wedding day to be over and our wedding night to begin. "How do you want to handle this?"

I took a deep breath as a billboard I recognized came into view. I pointed to it. "When we were little," I said, my words veering away from his question, "my sister and I used to use these billboards to mark how much farther we were from home."

Westley glanced toward the sign. "In what way?"

"There are five of them, all advertising the same motel on the other side of Bynum. The first one says ten miles and then the next one tells you that you're getting closer ... Anyway, Julie and I used to see that one back there and we'd both say, 'One ...' and then we'd watch for the next one."

"And I bet when you saw it you'd say, 'Two ...'"

I laughed. "Yes." I studied the side of the road, whirring past us in deep shades of green. I blinked at the farmland beyond the fence posts strung together with barbed wire. The shadows of trees that loomed toward the horizon. And I waited for the next sign. "I guess," I said, "we just tell them."

I looked at Westley. "They're going to be upset, Wes."

He reached for my hand and I gladly gave it, happy for the warmth and the softness of it. With one wrap of his fingers I felt that everything in the universe—no matter how awful—would be all right. There was nothing we couldn't get through as long as we held on to each other as we held on now. Even if only by our fingertips. "I know," he said, then added, "I think your father will be okay. I think he'll understand."

I returned my attention to the world beyond us. To the second sign that stood out in the now pitch-black darkness of the night. *Two ...* I heard Julie and me saying from the backseat of the car, our voices the high pitch of children who had nothing but promising futures ahead of them.

Suddenly then I missed my sister. I missed her terribly, wishing that I'd not let so much time go by since we'd talked. Really talked. Even on the Sunday after Westley had asked me to marry him, I'd said hardly two words to her when she and the bum had come over.

"I should probably start thinking of him by his name," I said out loud.

"Hmm?"

"My sister's husband. Dean. I'm just thinking that, really, I shouldn't call him *the bum* anymore."

Westley hand squeezed mine again as he nodded toward the windshield. "Three."

I followed his gaze, then smiled.

"What made you decide that?" he asked, his voice soft and kind and open-ended. As if he cared what I thought and why I thought it.

"I was just thinking about Miss Justine. She asked me why we call him the bum and, you know, around her it seemed out of line. Dean *is* a nice guy, really."

"Maybe it would help if he were a little more financially secure. Did more than hunt and peck all day."

"Maybe." I looked forward again.

"I can see why your parents don't like that so much."

"Can you?"

"Sure. Parents—especially fathers—want only the best for their little girls."

I smiled, grinning deeper on the inside at the thought of Westley as the father of our daughter or daughters. The ones we'd have one day. The ones he'd nurture and protect with every fiber of his being. I could see him so easily, there in my mind's eye. Tickling them. Nuzzling them. Reading bedtime stories as their lids grew heavy from a day of play.

I gave another glance to the world and her possibilities. "Four…" I said, then took a deep breath, releasing it slowly. "We're almost home."

Chapter Twelve

My mother cried, of course. Soft and sniffling tears that nearly drove me to stand in the middle of the family room—my mother sitting in one chair, my father sitting in another, my fiancé and I perched on the edge of the sofa—and shout, "Never mind. Do over! Do over!" I nearly had to bite my tongue to keep from pleading with Westley to forget Odenville and Miss Justine and the doll house we'd first settle in. Never mind the throw pillows and the possible afghan and the front bedroom where the sun spilled through the window and onto what would become our marriage bed.

Instead, I looked to my father for his reaction, hoping to glean my next move from him, not yet depending fully on Westley's. "Now, hon," he said to Mama. "We raised 'em so they'd grow up and make a life of their own. Seems like this one is doing just that. And it's not like they're moving to another country, now is it?"

Mama worked her hands, then laced the fingers and squeezed. "May as well be."

Westley leaned forward, resting his elbows on his knees. "Mrs. Middleton, I know this comes as a shock. And I probably should have warned you—" He looked my way before continuing his speech to Mama. "All of you. But I didn't want to cause undue worry and stress. I knew of the possibility, but until we got there and I talked with my brother and sister-in-law and then, of course, Miss Justine herself, I wasn't a hundred percent sure myself."

A flash of memory came to me as he spoke. Me standing in the stairwell. Westley and Paul and DiAnn sitting at the kitchen table, talking in hushed tones of what Westley couldn't keep from me forever. Then, just as easily, my thoughts reverted to Westley holding me near a dying fire. I could feel the pressure of the chair's wood across the back of my legs. His splayed fingers on the warm flesh of my waist as he nearly took possession of what little mind I had left. I inhaled deeply. Swallowed the heat rising in me again. How many more days … how many more days … my brain clicked furiously until Westley's words brought me back. ". . . fact is, I can provide better for Ali there. And Miss Justine has already found a nice house for us." He looked to me again and smiled, which I returned.

"It really is the cutest," I said to my parents, more than anything wanting to show solidarity between Westley and me. "And there is a spare bedroom for the two of you and …" I sent my attention to my father. "And, Daddy, if business ever takes you to Odenville, you'll have a place to stay."

Daddy nodded, his recliner rocking and creaking with the movement. "I go through there quite a bit actually."

Mama ran her fingertips through the dark curls that crowned her. "I suppose we'll need to get some things for the house," she said, her hair now tousled, and her tone resigned to the finality of a decision she wanted no part of.

"No," Westley and I said together. We laughed easily and he yielded the floor to me. "Mama, Miss Justine went out and got some furniture. It's all set up for us. Right down to the drapes and throw pillows and I'm thinking that with the stuff we get from the showers, we'll be all set. But—well, I was also wondering if maybe you could knit an afghan for the living room sofa and maybe even one for the bedroom. I can give you the color scheme and—"

"Why in the world do you already have a place to live?" Mama asked. "Complete with furniture and throw pillows and draperies?"

Westley cleared his throat as I pondered a question I should have asked myself already but hadn't. Why indeed. Why hadn't Miss Justine waited until closer to the wedding, especially seeing as she hadn't been aware of the date until earlier that day? Why had the house already been rented for a couple who couldn't move into it for nearly two months?

"Well," Westley said, clearing his throat in discomfort. "You see, I'll be moving over there right before Thanksgiving and—"

"What?" I asked, turning my whole body to look at him. "You didn't—you didn't tell me this."

"Ali," he said, his voice now low, a hint of warning in the shortened version of my name.

A tone I'd never heard before, but instantly understood. "We'll talk about this later," he said.

"We'll talk about it *now*," I said, more aware than ever that my parents sat mere feet from us. "Westley?"

His hand cupped my elbow, then squeezed as he brought me up to stand with him, the pressure nothing like the reassurance I'd felt earlier at Miss Justine's. "I haven't had a chance to talk to Allison about this," he said as an apology to my parents, one that probably seemed pretty ridiculous given that we'd just spent an entire four hours in the car together. "Will you excuse us?"

Westley escorted me—so firmly I wondered if my parents could tell—out the door until we stood next to his car where he leaned against the driver's door, directing me until I stood in front of him. "Now listen," he said, his tone remaining foreign to me. "Don't ever embarrass me like that in front of your parents again."

"Embarrass *you*? Westley, my parents now know that you just blindsided me. What kind of marriage are we going to have if you're doing that now? Before we're even married?"

"Furthermore," he continued, ignoring my questions. "Miss Justine isn't going to wait forever."

"It's not forever," I said, my voice dropping to a whisper for fear of waking the neighbors. Or worse, alerting my parents that something was more wrong than we let on as we left the inside of the house. "It's two months."

"And in two months I can make a lot more money for us, Ali. We'll be more prepared for our lives together once we're married, sweetheart." He rubbed my arms, up and down, lightly. But, for once, the thought of being Westley's wife didn't send quivers through me as it usually did. I was too stunned by his sudden revelation to feel too much of anything at all.

"But there's so much to do and I'll need you to be here with me."

"Like what?"

"Like ... I don't know." I threw my arms out, forcing his hands away from their journey, my own falling dramatically. "Wedding plans."

"Which you *don't* need me for. That's the bride's deal. Not the groom's."

"What about—I don't know ..."

"Bridal showers?" His brow rose and his eyes twinkled under the light of a streetlamp. Enough to let me know the old Westley—the one I knew and trusted—had returned. No longer angry with me. No longer on the opposing team. "Teas? Or whatever it is you girls do before you meet your groom at the altar?"

I crossed my arms. Looked down at my feet. At the clunky wedge shoes that made walking difficult but had surely improved my calf muscles. Saw his—brushed dark-beige suede—pointing toward mine, so close and yet not close enough. When I looked up again, Westley smiled at me. "Come here," he said, opening his arms, having returned to the man I loved.

"Westley," I whispered without moving, knowing that, even though we'd not finished our argument, he'd won it.

His fingers curled in a "come here," gesture. I dropped my arms, sliding them around his waist, and laid my head against his shoulder, turning my face toward his, inhaling the resilient musk cologne that lingered along his Adam's apple. "Westley," I said again, determined to make him understand. "You just can't go springing things like that on me."

His lips found my temple and rested there. "I'm sorry," he said. "I guess I thought you understood."

"How could I?"

"I know. I'm sorry."

"You didn't say."

"I know."

"And I don't like the idea of you not being here. With me. Always."

"Me either. But it's just a little while, sweetheart. Not forever. Never forever."

We remained silent for a few moments, our breath finding rhythm until it became a melody sung in unison. "Ali," he finally said.

"Wes."

He chuckled. "I only need you to trust me, okay?"

"Okay."

"I'll be back at least two days a week. Every week. Whatever you need me for, I'm there to help. And we'll talk every night. Ma Bell is free after nine o'clock."

"Okay." I squeezed my arms tighter around him.

"Are you cold?"

"Yes. But there's not a fire nearby or a chair for you to hold me in."

He kissed my temple again. "Goodness, woman. You're really something, you know that?"

I grew warm under the fullness of the compliment. "I may be, but I still don't want to plan a wedding without you."

"You won't have to. Whatever you need me for, I'm here."

"We have to pick a china pattern. And silver. And crystal and linens."

"Whatever you want, Mrs. Houser."

I snuggled closer as a giggle rose from inside of me. "I want to *be* Mrs. Houser."

Westley shifted, forcing me to look at him. Truly look at him. To see the softness in his eyes. The care that rested there. The tenderness that laid against his lips like roses on the vine. "I love you," he mouthed more than said.

My senses nearly caught fire and my knees threatened to buckle. "I love you, too. And we need to go back inside and talk to my parents some more. Let them know we're okay."

"Are we? Okay?"

I nodded. "We're more than okay, Westley. We are."

Within a week, Westley had moved to Odenville, leaving me to stay busy with work and showers and teas and all the things that, as he'd said, went with planning a wedding. Flowers. Candelabras. Bridesmaids dresses. Every night at 9:01 on the nose, our home phone rang, me practically sitting on top of it. Mama wanting nothing more than to hover as Westley and I talked and Daddy doing whatever it took to keep her occupied. My grandmother continued to come over, recipes in hand, bent to make me into the next Julia Child and failing miserably. And, when Westley returned two days a week, true to his word, we chose china and silver, crystal and linens and stole every moment we had to be together. We went over wedding party lists and guests lists and, once Westley had returned to Odenville, I addressed envelopes and licked stamps until my tongue stuck to the roof of my mouth and my mother brought in a relieving damp cloth.

The days passed to weeks and the weeks spun toward our wedding day. And, as it turned out, Miss Justine had been correct about my dress. My mother, grandmother, Julie, and I made a "day of it," driving to Savannah to a little shop where I found a simple but elegant dress with an empire waist and a high-neck collar formed of delicate lace and sheer puffy sleeves with wide cuffs. The long skirt fell in folds of satin overlaid by chiffon and the bodice had just the right number of pearls stitched into it. Grand declared it "beyond perfect for my little figure" and, while the seamstress did a little tuck here and a pinning there, Julie walked around the store, returning only when she'd found the "perfect headpiece and veil."

"Don't you think?" she asked, holding it out to me.

I looked into her eyes then, dark and lovely and hopeful. In spite of being—at least as far as I knew—fabulously happy with the man she'd chosen, she'd never had this moment. Instead, she'd run off with Dean during what was supposed to be a Friday night date but ended up a wedding across the South Carolina line followed by a honeymoon in a cheap Charleston hotel. So I wasn't surprised at the waltz her eyes danced. She'd never had *this*. Never played "dress up" for real. My moment would be all she ever experienced of this until, perhaps, she had a daughter of her own who would one day ask her to accompany her to Savannah for "a day of it."

I took the veil as if it were the most prized possession in the world and smiled at her. "It's beyond beautiful," I said. "Thank you."

Chapter Thirteen

Westley

A two-week vacation so soon after joining a company for most employers was unheard of, but that was exactly what Westley had included in his employee package when he came to work for Knight Pharmacy Odenville. That and a decent increase in pay from what he made in Bynum. And every Wednesday afternoon off, which enabled him to drive over to Baxter for a visit with Michelle. At least for the time being.

Treasured as those afternoons were, they also meant dealing with Michelle's mother, who did everything but open the front door in her birthday suit in an effort to lure him back to her bed. Whether Lettie Mae or Leticia or Jacko were at home didn't seem to matter. She wanted what she wanted and what she wanted was him.

More specifically, what she wanted was his cash flow and whatever easy life she thought being married to him would afford her. And, now that he'd had more time with her and more time to think about how he'd gotten himself in this situation, he'd come to realize that the moment he walked through that greasy spoon of a café where she worked back in February of the year before, she'd seen him as her ticket out.

Well, her flirtatiousness may have worked back then, but it no longer held any power over him. Now, the only thing that mattered was Allison. Allison and Michelle. Marrying one and getting custody of the other. A long-term plan. A *life* plan that minutes of pleasure were not going to steal from him.

With each visit he toyed with the notion of telling Cindie the truth—that come Christmas he'd be a married man. Especially when she talked about how they could celebrate the holiday, finally, as a family. That he could come over that morning—or the night before if he wanted to spend the night—and be there when Michelle spied what Santa left for her under the tree.

As wonderful as that sounded—seeing his daughter's eyes light up over the presents he'd already purchased and given to Cindie for safekeeping—it couldn't compare to waking up Christmas morning with his new wife. His arms wrapped around her and hers around him, if he had his way about it. Most likely at his mom and dad's home. They'd get up, exchange gifts, eat his mother's delectable French toast smothered in butter and homemade maple syrup, then get ready for church. Then, after church they'd drive to Bynum where they'd spend the rest of the day with his new in-laws.

Miss Justine had already declared the day after Christmas to be a holiday, so they'd finally return to Odenville and their new home sometime Monday. And nothing, or no one—not even his adorable Michelle—would alter those plans.

Now, staring at himself in the bathroom mirror at his parents' home the day before his wedding, he arched a brow as he slid a chrome razor over his jaw. "For a man who likes to live by the seat of your pants, young man," he said to himself as he shook the cloud of lather from the double-edge razor in the sink half-filled with murky water, "you sure have planned this one out."

With one caveat. He had to tell his parents about Michelle. Had to do it today, in fact. Cindie had pitched a little teenage hissy fit when he told her he'd be spending Christmas with his family, not hers. Or theirs, in fact. She'd gone on and on about him not loving Michelle as much as he loved himself.

"That's not true," he'd told her, fury rising in him at the very suggestion. Of course he loved his daughter more than himself. In fact, he'd hardly known that he *could* love someone as much until recently. But in the few weeks of afternoons that he'd had with her—the chubby-armed hugs and the bright green eyes that looked at him with heart-palpitating trust and adoration—he'd come to realize what true love meant. And that gaining custody of her at *any* cost was at the forefront of necessity.

"It *is* true," Cindie pouted, making the most of her immaturity while reaching for the child they shared, a child snuggled in her father's arms, sleeping like the angel she was. "*We* are your family now. Me and Michelle. You should be with us."

Westley slid over on the sofa. "She's fine with me," he said, his voice firm. "I mean it."

Cindie had taken the hint and backed away, her face pinking at his admonishment. Two rooms back, Lettie Mae banged around in the kitchen, while Jacko sat cross-legged in front of the television not eight feet away, his attention captured by an episode of *Good Times*. Across town, Leticia put in a shift at the café—the same restaurant where one burger and an order of fries had changed his life. The thought of it brought his lips to the crown of his daughter's head. He inhaled the sweet scent of baby shampoo and talcum powder and the scent that comes simply from being a toddler, then snuggled her heart closer to his own. "I bet you haven't even told your parents yet," Cindie's tirade continued, her voice rising in hopes of getting Lettie Mae's attention. Of having her mother come in and help fight this battle for her. God knew he and the older Campbell had gone around and around enough in the last few weeks over money and responsibility, the irony of the arguments never skipping past him.

"I'm telling them over the holidays," he told Cindie then. "Kind of an early Christmas present."

And at that, Cindie's face brightened. "Really?"

"Really." Not because he necessarily wanted to, but because he needed to. He had to tell his parents before he told Allison. Had to somehow have them on his side in case things went south with his new wife. Not that they would. They couldn't.

Cindie slid closer. Placed her hand on his arm, her fingertips playing with him. One more attempt … "And then Michelle and I can go with you to their home for weekends. She can get to know them, and they can get to know her." Her eyes brightened at the thought.

Westley had only smiled. Kissed Michelle one more time before handing her over to her mother. "Here you go, little one," he cooed. "Here's your mama."

With that, the suggestion defused.

But that was then. This was now …

He finished shaving, then dressed. He strolled through the house in search of his mother, not locating her, then into his father's study where he found him standing at his desk, flipping through pages of a book. "Hey, Dad," he said.

Benjamin Houser turned to look at his son, his reading glasses perched on the tip of his nose. He removed them before smiling. Before laying them on top of the book that had held his attention. Whatever thoughts had occupied his mind before this minute, Westley knew, were about to take a backstage to what he had to tell his father now.

"By this time tomorrow," his dad said, "you'll be a nearly married man."

Westley chuckled. "And by this time two days from now …"

His father crossed his arms. "What's up? You look like you have something on your mind."

Westley glanced over his shoulder. "Where's Mom?"

"Beauty shop. Tonight's the rehearsal and tomorrow's the wedding and if her hair isn't absolutely perfect, you and Miss Allison are going to have to cancel the whole shebang."

Westley nodded, a smile breaking across his face and easing the tension that twisted between his shoulder blades. "I'm not so sure Ali will be okay with that. Um—" He glanced over his shoulder again. "Hey, Dad. Can we go into the family room? I'd like to talk to you about something."

"Sounds ominous."

Westley rested his hands on his hips. "Ah, no. No. Not ominous exactly."

"Don't tell me I've got to have *the talk* with you," his father teased. "I distinctly remember going over all that when you and Paul were kids."

"No, sir."

"Well, then what is it, son?"

Westley took a step back. "Can we—ah—can we just go sit down?"

"We can. But let's go into the kitchen. Mom made a fresh pot of coffee before she left, and I have a feeling this conversation will call for it."

It would call for it, all right. In fact, if they had something stronger in the house—not that his teetotaling parents would—he'd suggest adding that to the cups. Especially since he'd quit smoking. Cold turkey, of course. Instead, they prepared their coffee with milk and sugar, then sat across from each other at the Formica table that stood center stage in the room. "Dad," Westley began. "I've got an issue—and I need you to just hear me out before you say anything—I made a mistake—not a mistake. No." He shook his head. "An error in judgment."

Concern registered on his father's face. "Are you wanting to call off the wedding? Because—"

"No." Westley gripped the coffee cup, then relaxed his fingers and brought it up to his lips for a slow sip. "Gosh, no. I love Allison. I do. I can't wait to make her my wife." He gave his father a knowing smile "And not for the obvious reasons."

"She's been a good girl, then," his father confirmed.

"Yeah. She has. But your son ..." How would he say this? How could he possibly tell his father what he should have told him months before. A year before, if truth be told.

"Has sowed some wild oats? Son, I think that's natural." He raised his coffee cup toward his lips. "Most young men these days have—"

"I have a daughter, Dad."

The cup came down, its contents sloshing over the rim, pooling onto the saucer. "What did you say?" his father asked, ignoring the mess.

Westley rose from the table and walked to where a roll of paper towels hung over the counter. He tore off two, then handed them to his father who only wadded them into his fist. "Say that again."

"I have a daughter, Dad," Westley said, returning to his seat. "Her name is Michelle. She's a year old and, Dad, the cutest thing." He attempted a smile, one that went unanswered.

"Who is the mother?"

Westley took in a deep breath, letting it go slowly enough to buy him the time he needed to say the name. "Dad—it's—it's Cindie Campbell."

His father's ears turned bright red, the color spilling down his neck and throat, until the shading crawled back up his face. "Lettie Mae's girl?"

"Yes, sir."

"Which one? The oldest one? I'd heard she married a—"

"Middle girl."

His father paused, his natural color returning to him as his brow furrowed and dates and timeframes calculated through his brain. "How *old* is she?"

"She's almost eighteen."

More calculations. "She was what, then? Seventeen?"

"Sixteen … but, almost seventeen."

His father's hand came down on the table, rattling the dishes, sending more coffee into the saucers.

"Dad."

"You're lucky you're not in jail."

"Well, I'm not, Dad," Westley said, his voice on edge. "It was one night, and we were drunk and now I've got a little girl. Bottom line." He took a breath, which caught in his chest. "Michelle Elise. And she's—she's beyond amazing." He stood, walked to his room where he retrieved the cheaply framed photo he'd hidden between the mattresses, then returned to the kitchen where his father busied himself cleaning up the mess, his jaw as tense as Westley had ever seen it. "Here," Westley said. "This is your granddaughter."

With that, his father's face softened, and he reached for the photo.

"Dad," Westley said, keeping his voice soft. Calm. "I know I've done some things over the years that have aged you and Mom ten years or more with each event. And I know I was reckless having sex with a girl I didn't really know and, yes, I should have used protection, but that's water under the bridge, quite frankly. What's important now is—"

"Have you told Allison? Because if you haven't—" His father's admonition was interrupted as the kitchen's storm door opened and both men turned to see a thoroughly coiffed Olive Houser standing at the threshold, her eyes wide.

"What is it?" she asked, her face a canvas of concern. "What's wrong?"

Chapter Fourteen

Allison

Finally, everyone and most especially Mama had left the bride's room—a secluded chamber within the church decorated in antiques and chintz—leaving me alone with Elaine. I turned from the floor-length gilded mirror where my reflection revealed a bride about to lose her breakfast, had she bothered to eat one. Despite my mother's plea to "at least swallow down a piece of toast, Allison."

"Elaine," I said to a young woman I feared may show the bride up in her beauty. One good look at her and Westley may grab her by the hand and take off running. I shook away the notion. "Let me ask you something. Last night, did you notice anything? Anything at all? Like something going on between Westley and his parents?"

Elaine bent over a Queen Anne coffee table where my bouquet—a cascade of miniature red and white roses with green ivy spun between the petals—lay protected within a large box filled with white tissue paper. She picked it up, then straightened it and handed it to me with a serious shrug. "I don't really know them, so I can't say. But you insisted all last night that something was going on and you know them better than I do. So ... okay."

I took the bouquet and turned back to the mirror for a glimpse at the results of weeks of planning and choosing and picking over. "Something's up," I breathed out. "Do you think they think that maybe Wes shouldn't marry me?"

Elaine came to stand behind me, looking resplendent in the red, white-dotted swiss maid of honor gown I'd chosen for her. "Stop that. This is just nerves talking. They're lucky to have you in their family. In spite of the fact I think you're getting married too soon, it's obvious Westley loves you. One look at his face and I knew."

Before I could ask her to pinky swear it to me as we'd done so many times over the years about so many childish things, the door behind us opened and we both turned. Julie stepped in and I smiled at the sight of her. The white, red-dotted swiss gown I'd chosen for her (and Heather) gave a shimmering glow to her always-bronzed complexion. "Are you about ready?" she asked, then stepped over and ran her long fingers through my hair, fluffing it enough that it lay over my shoulders like a shawl. "You're gorgeous," she whispered.

Tears stung my pupils. We'd never been much on deep conversations, but for once the situation warranted being open and vulnerable. "Julie, did you notice anything with Wes and his parents last night? Did they seem to you like they wished Westley would marry someone else?"

She kissed the air around my cheek, careful not to mess up her lipstick or the tiny bit of makeup I'd carefully applied earlier in the day. "Don't be silly."

"That what I say," Elaine chimed in.

"They're lucky to have you in their family."

"That's what I *said*," Elaine concurred. She had stepped in front of me, close to the mirror. Leaned in to check her reflection as my shoulders sagged, their words of assurance not quite hitting the mark of good intentions.

"If you think something like that, Allison," Julie began, "then you should have asked him about it last night."

"Well, I *did*. Right after the rehearsal dinner ..."

"And what did he say?" Elaine asked. She turned, then stood on tiptoe to bring the veil over my face. "That's perfect." She stepped to the coffee table for her own bouquet.

I shook my head and peered through the veil at the mirror, not fully seeing the picture it reflected. A beautiful bride was supposed to look back at me. Instead an anxious inner voice clouded the view. "He said everything was fine and that I was being a nervous bride," I answered her.

Julie smiled at me, one side of her mouth rising higher than the other. "And are you?"

I coughed a tiny giggle, which caused the veil to poof. "I'm scared out of my mind."

Julie's brow rose. "About tonight?"

Heat rose in me. "A little ... but ..." No. Not really. Whatever was in store for me as a young bride, I knew enough about my groom to sense that he'd take his time ... allow me to take mine.

She grinned. "Don't be. I can't say the first time is the best time, but I promise you it will get better." She threw up her hands then and air-quoted, "Did Mom have *the talk* with you?"

I rolled my eyes. "Are you kidding me? You're talking about *our* mother, right? Whatever I learned, I learned from Elaine."

"I beg your pardon," Elaine laughed, knowing full well she'd managed to study up and share more on the subject than Masters and Johnson ever dreamed of.

"Yeah, she didn't tell me anything either. Then again, I ran off and got married so I guess she decided that—by the time we got back from our honeymoon, such as it was—I had it all figured out."

"Did you?" Elaine asked, her grin showing a side to her I knew all too well.

Julie shook her head. "No, but I'm working hard to. Maybe that's what we do," she said, her expression oddly contemplative. "Maybe we spend our whole lives just trying to figure it out." She stood straight, all notions gone. "All right, little sister. The mothers have been seated. The grandmothers and grandfathers are getting older by the second and they're probably restless for cake. Your future sister-in-law is out in the vestibule waiting and our father is pulling at his collar as if it's a noose. It looks like we've done all the damage here we can do." She threw her arms wide. "What's say we go get you married?"

"And when you return from your honeymoon," Elaine threw in,

"you can tell us if you figured it out or not."

I shook my head with a sigh. "Elaine," I said. "You simply will not do."

"Whatever *you* do," Julie said as she opened the door to lead the way, "*don't* bring this other stuff up again with Westley tonight. It's not the time. Just ... wait."

"Okay."

Then she added, "Now ... *go*."

The afternoon went by in a blur of tears and stomach knots. Of vows and directions and camera bulb flashes. Of punch and cake and grinning so much my jaws ached. Of holding on to Daddy's arm as he guided me toward Westley and then my new husband's arm whenever I needed support to get through the next moment. Later, when Mama helped me into a wrap-around, long-sleeved dress, she fretted long enough to make her final point to me. At least for the day. "Westley is a good man," she told me as we stood almost exactly where Elaine and Julie and I had stood mere hours before.

"I know, Mama."

She grabbed a shoe box from the floor. Opened it. "Here, put these on."

I did, slipping them over feet kept in line by nude-colored pantyhose while holding onto the side of a wingback chair for support.

"And he comes from a good family."

"I know."

"He's going places."

I straightened, then pressed my hands over the front of my skirt. "I need my bouquet."

"Not like your sister's husband."

"Dean."

She frowned at me. "I know his name."

"Then you should say it from time to time."

"Don't get smart. Just because you're a married woman now ..."

"Mama ..."

"Whatever he wants, Allison Grace."

My breath caught. "Is this *the talk*? Here? Now? Because if it is—"

Mama stood straight. Raised a thick and perfectly arched brow. "Impertinence. I won't have it."

I attempted to laugh. "I'm teasing you—"

Her index finger found my nose. "I won't get a chance to say this again, so listen up. I'm telling you that Westley Houser is the kind of man who needs to run his own household. Whatever he wants, Allison, you just follow his lead. Don't mess this up. Don't shame me and your daddy. We've done good by you and—"

I reached for her then, drawing her close, feeling the frailness of a woman who spent too much time cooking and not enough time eating. "Mama," I whispered. "I love you so much and I love him so much and I promise you—I *promise you*—I won't do anything to embarrass you or Daddy."

She held on to me with a passion I'd never known from her—at least not that I could remember. She'd been a good mother. A worrisome mother. A mother who made sure we minded our p's and q's, Julie and me. And she'd always been there for Daddy, now that I thought about it, whenever he strolled into the house. And once he stepped through the door ...

"Make him the king of his castle," she whispered. "That's what my mother told me, and I've never regretted it." She broke the embrace, her eyes now washed in tears, finding mine. "No more flying by the seat of your pants, Allison. This is your purpose in life now. *He* is your purpose."

I'd never heard anything remotely like this from Mama's mouth. Had no idea how deeply she felt about the relationship between a man and his wife. Between a mother and her children and the way they all hung in the balance, one with the other. Even in my naiveté, the notion that her instruction somehow related to her own mother and the loss of her father came to me by instinct. Mother to daughter.

Daughter to mother. "*Mama ...*"

She swallowed hard, pushing a repression down that I had no understanding of. Not yet. "As far as tonight goes ..."

I waved a hand between us; the conversation had gone as deep as I dared it to go. "Julie has already talked to me."

Mama's chin rose. "Good. That's one less thing I have to worry about then." She turned for the door. "Are you ready?"

I blinked at her. "I don't know, Mama. Am I?"

Her lips formed a wobbly smile. "I'd say you may as well be."

"Then I am," I said. But I wasn't. Oh, no ... I wasn't.

We left the church around five o'clock that afternoon, the car graffitied and wrapped in toilet paper, the customary tin cans clamoring behind us until Westley pulled over just beyond the outskirts of town and snapped them off. I stayed inside, my knees pressed together and my hands clutching the handle of a suede handbag. Within a minute Westley slid back into the car, his smile broad. His manner easy. He looked at me as he put the car in drive and said, "Happy?"

Finding it difficult to speak, I nodded.

"Nervous?"

I shook my head, slowly at first, then with more certainty.

"Then why does the cat have your tongue?"

I turned my face to the windshield, ever mindful of my sister's admonishment *not* to bring up my concerns. "I dunno," I all but whispered. But I smiled to lessen the tension.

Westley reached over and took my hand in his, the warmth of it spreading through me, providing more heat than from what came through the air vents. The sky had darkened, changing to shades of deep purple struck through by magenta clouds. The sun winked as it dipped below the treetops, many of them bare, some still holding on to their autumn colors. A few refusing to release their summer green. "Look at me," he said.

I brought my eyes to his.

"I love you. I want you to know that."

"I do," I said. "And I love you. So much." So much it hurt. The very life of me had ached for him. And now, he was mine and I, his.

Westley's hand gripped mine, then released and he rolled the car back onto the highway, heading toward Savannah ... and a beachfront house owned by an old classmate of his from their days at UGA. Or, his classmate's parents, really. Not that it mattered. We were going somewhere quiet. Someplace completely ours for a week. A secluded little stretch of paradise, we'd been told. We couldn't lay out or swim, of course, what with it being December. But there was a fireplace and plenty of wood and Westley had promised evenings snuggled under a blanket. A roaring fire crackling in the fireplace. The whitecaps of the ocean rolling toward us from under a black sky dotted with stars that twinkled "nearly as much as your eyes," he'd said. "Right now ... while I'm telling you about it."

"Will we drink hot cocoa?"

"With tiny marshmallows."

"I like the thick ones."

He had kissed the tip of my nose. "Whatever you want."

"I *don't* want Swiss Miss. I want real hot cocoa."

Westley smiled, a new knowing showing in his face. "Do you know how to make it?"

My shoulders sank. "No." I brought my chin up in defiance. "But Mama can teach me. We still have a couple of weeks ..."

And so she had. Now all I had to do was buy the ingredients. First thing Monday morning. After a long walk on the beach with my new husband. Holding hands. Talking. Laughing. Allowing the ocean breeze to pull gooseflesh from under our skin until we could bear it no longer. Until we were forced to run back to the beach house where we'd dash into the bathroom and maybe even take a shower. Together. We could do that. We were married now.

Yes, that was how it would be. And then we'd return to his parents' home on Saturday—Christmas Eve—enjoy an afternoon and evening with them. Hopefully, whatever tension existed since the night before our wedding would have floated away on the cloud of joy. Then, on Sunday—Christmas Day—we'd head over to Mama and Daddy's where we'd return to the church where we'd just married. We'd eat Christmas dinner with Grand and my aunts and Julie and Dean. Then, on Monday morning, we'd load up the gifts that had come in since Westley's last visit. And, finally ... we'd head home.

And everything would be fine. It would.

It would.

Chapter Fifteen

A week later, I stretched between the linens and under the blanket and down-filled comforter in the bedroom Westley had left behind at his parents' home the day we married. I blinked in protest at the morning's light intruding from around and between old venetian blinds. A glance at the ticking alarm clock propped on top of a copy of Cosmo I'd purchased in Savannah left me wondering if I read the time correctly.

I pushed myself up from the warmth of the bed, the cover dropping to hips entrapped by a twisted nightgown. I straightened it. Blushed under the memory of Westley's hands beneath it the night before. Of my strained protests. "We're at *your parents*," I hissed between uncooperative giggles. "We can't do this *here*."

His breath warmed my ear as he whispered back. "I know *where* we are. And I know *who* you are and whatcha wanna bet my parents already figure this is what's happening tonight in this very room?" Westley's kisses smothered whatever protest was left in me, just as they had during our glorious days at the beach.

The door opened and my husband strolled in, already dressed in flare-legged jeans and a ribbed turtleneck shirt, his cheeks wind kissed. "What's wrong?" I asked.

He closed the door, then crawled onto the bed with me. "Nothing, why?"

My hand cupped his cheek, the cold of it iced my fingertips. "Why is your face so red?"

Westley chuckled as he pushed me back, my head plopping onto the feather pillow that had gone flat during the night. He lay over me. Wrapped his arms around me. "Warm me up," he said. "Dad and I were out back taking care of something for Mom."

I placed my palms flat against his cheeks as if it would help, inwardly sighing at the sight of the filigree, white gold wedding ring wrapped around my finger. "I can't believe it's really after ten," I said. "Why'd you let me sleep so long?"

He rubbed his nose over mine several times before answering. "Mom insisted you needed the sleep and to leave you alone."

His mom. Whatever tension I'd felt before the wedding seemed to have dissipated, leaving me to chalk it up to something personal. Private. Not yet my problem. Or perhaps, I had reasoned, she was as distraught over our moving as my parents had been. Or, at the very least, my mother.

I grinned. "Then why are you in here?"

He nuzzled my neck, kissed the hollow of my throat. "I couldn't bear another minute away from you." A playful growl came from the depth of him and he pretended to gnaw at me until I forced myself out from under him.

"Go away, you," I said. "I need to get up and get ready." I dropped my feet to the floor, shifted my gown again, then stood. "And I don't care what your mother said. She must think I'm absolutely spoiled rotten."

Westley propped up on his elbow and crossed his ankles as a smile spread catlike across his face. "Not *absolutely*."

I shook my head at him. "Wes . . ."

"Ali."

I held my breath for a moment, then released it. "I'm going to shower now."

"You do that. And brush your teeth," he added, a full grin breaking through. "You have morning breath."

I threw my hand over my mouth. "You're horrible," I mumbled, feigning horror as I giggled around my fingers.

Westley bounded from the bed to stand beside it. "Not as horrible as your breath ..." He threw the bed linens back, then jerked them toward the head of the bed—his attempt at making the bed—before glancing my way. "I'm kidding you. Stop looking like a little girl whose best friend left her for the new girl at school."

My brow rose. "Really? I mean, I know my breath is ... but it's not *horrible*, is it?"

He straightened before leaning against the wall and crossing his arms. "The only thing horrible right now is that we aren't already in our own home, because if we were ..." He started toward me.

"What would you do?" I taunted, although my arm stretched out in protest, my hand forming a solid "stop."

"You know what I'd do." He waved his hand toward the bathroom, teasing. "Go. Take a shower. Brush your teeth and your hair and dab a little bit of makeup on and, for heaven's sake, try to make it to the kitchen by lunch."

I shook my head slowly, mesmerized by him. His easy manner. His way with me. Sometimes I felt like his wife. Other times like his child. How could that be ...

"I hate you," I said, the words even. Skilled, as if I'd practiced them.

"I love you, too. Now ... go."

My mother had never insisted I help her when it came to cooking meals. Instead, she insisted my role started *after* the meal with the cleanup. Something I had down to a science. So after a hearty lunch of homemade vegetable soup and grilled homemade pimento cheese sandwiches, I took over kitchen duties by washing and drying the dishes and wiping down the countertops while Westley and his father continued working in the back, and Mrs. Houser—who insisted I call her "Mom"—laid down for "a quick nap."

I took my time, occasionally glancing out the window to the

graying and brown grass of a winter's lawn. A lonely, wire clothesline stretched under naked pecan branches and between two unpainted T-shaped posts. Toward the back of the property Dr. Houser's—Dad's—shop stood with the double doors open, as though unaware that a chill remained in the air. I smiled, knowing that just past them, my husband and his father worked on a project together. What, they hadn't said. Or wouldn't say. But instinct told me that it had to do with me … and Christmas.

After placing the final dish in the cabinet, I wiped my hands on the red dishtowel before hanging it over the oven's handle, then stood in the middle of the kitchen with my hands on my hips, wondering what to do next. The house was eerily quiet, and a sense of nostalgia ran over me, tickling me. I stepped past the opened swinging door between the kitchen and the den where a fat Christmas tree in the corner had replaced an overstuffed chair for the holidays. I looked at it for a moment, noting the perfectly wrapped gifts for the rest of Westley's family who were expected before dinner—Heather, Paul, and DiAnn, namely. The large multicolored bulbs sent rays of Christmas lights to gleam off handed-down ornaments and the deep green of the live and richly scented branches.

No fake trees for this family.

I dropped onto the sofa and stared at the lifeless screen of the console television, remembering the day two months earlier when I'd been in this same spot, watching *Match Game*. I closed my eyes, thinking back to Westley walking in from the outside. Him taking off his shirt—something I'd grown accustomed to in the past week—and kissing me until I'd nearly lost my mind. Something *else* I'd grown accustomed to. Still, my cheeks flamed at the memory of his father walking in and I opened my eyes again, picturing Westley smiling at me. Teasing me. Joshing with his father and then walking down the hallway, his shirt clutched loosely in his hand … an envelope jutting from his pocket.

I stood. Funny I should remember that right at that moment. Funny and yet, somehow, telling. But I shook it off, figuring that the silence of the house and the memory had collided to confuse a young bride.

I started back toward the kitchen, thinking I'd head back into Westley's bedroom—*our* bedroom—then stopped and, instead, went to the front of the house where I'd snooped two months before. Back to the living room, the serene opulence of it drawing me like a moth to the flame.

As always, the room's lighting was subdued. The hushed hues of dusty rose and olive green greeting me. Welcoming me. I walked over the thick rugs to the piano, again taken by the old photographs, most particularly the one of a young woman with sleepy eyes and a wispy head of hair piled atop her head.

"My grandmother," a voice from behind me said. I turned to see my mother-in-law standing in the wide arch of the doorway. "Her name was Hillie. Hillie Lenore Jones Martin."

I had picked up the silver-framed photo, holding it gently between my fingers, but I returned it to the piano with a clunk. "I'm sorry, Mrs.—Mom. I wasn't trying to be nosy."

"Don't be silly." She walked over, picked up the photograph, and then handed it back to me. "Our house is now your house, no? She was a real beauty, wasn't she."

I nodded. "How long ago was this taken?"

"Nineteen twelve. An interesting time in women's history, did you know that?"

I shook my head. "I never did that great in history class, I'm afraid."

Mom's chin rose an inch. "Then you should learn, Allison. Our history is what shapes us. Even the history of those women who came before us—or, I should say, *especially* those who came before us."

I looked at the photo again. Studied it. My goodness, but the woman was a beauty. "Maybe it's the black-and-white photo—I don't know—but there seems to be such a softness about her. A gentleness."

"Hardly. She was a tough one." Mom laughed before motioning to the sofa behind us. "Come here and sit down and I'll tell you all about Hillie Martin."

I placed the photo back on the silk scarf that protected the piano from its sharp edges, then joined my mother-in-law on the antique sofa with its carvings of swans' necks within the wood frame. Mom had turned pensive, it seemed, and I could tell she loved her grandmother Hillie very much. "Is she still alive?" I asked.

Mom patted my knee. "Oh, no, no, no. Hillie died back in ... 1970."

"You called your grandmother Hillie?" I grinned. "I call my mother's mother Grand."

Mom returned the smile. "Hillie was always just ..." She shook her head slowly, her smile fading to the place where memories become sweet and tender. "Hillie."

I turned toward this woman I wanted so desperately to feel a closeness to. One who, other than right before the wedding, seemed to want the same from me. "Tell me more about her."

She sighed. "It's interesting, I think ... that you should be drawn to *her* photo."

"Why's that?"

"Because Hillie... well, Allison, when Hillie married my grandfather back in 1912, she had no idea, really, what she was getting herself into."

Nineteen twelve. The year of the photo. Confusion clouded my thinking and the room seemed to grow dimmer. "Do you think *I* have no idea—"

Mom waved a hand in the air as though she was erasing a blackboard. "No, no." Then she chuckled. "Well, no more than any of us know what we're getting into when we're first married." Her brow shot toward the curls sweeping over her hairline. "I know I sure didn't."

I glanced across the room toward the photograph. "And Hillie?"

"Hillie ... well, let's start at the beginning. My grandmother was born in 1889. Hard to imagine, isn't it?"

"Wow. That's ... nearly a hundred years ago."

"When she was sixteen," Mom continued without acknowledging my math skills, "she went off to school and got her teaching certificate. Now, you have to understand that a lot of women in Hillie's social standing back in those days didn't do things like that. But Hillie was determined, I suppose, to make her own way—her own mark—in the world."

"Her social standing?"

"Her father—my great-grandfather—was a businessman in Savannah. Not wealthy, but certainly not hurting. When I was a little girl, we used to visit their house and ..." She smiled again. "I used to pretend I was a princess and the house was my castle." Her hand fell lightly to her breast before she continued. "Well, one day Hillie up and decides she's going to be a teacher and there was no stopping her. After a while, Hillie took a teaching position and then, one by one, her younger sisters started having beaus and getting married. And, the way she told it to me was this: she got to thinking she'd never get married because of her lazy eye."

"Her—?"

"Look closely at the photo. You'll see it. One eye is what they call *lazy*. So, about that time Hillie's best friend—I never got her name, I don't think—tells her that she read in the want ads about a widower farmer with five young children living on the outskirts of Baxter who needed a wife for himself and a mother for his children. And Hillie—who knows what possessed her—wrote to the man and the next thing you know he comes by train to Savannah to marry her." Mom pointed toward the piano, then stood, walked over, and turned on the antique lamp to shine a light on the subject of her story. "This lamp was hers, you know."

"No, I didn't ..." How could I?

"It was an oil lamp, but Benjamin wired it for me after Hillie died."

I clasped my hands in my lap. "He's very handy."

"He is," she said, picking up Hillie's photo, caressing it. "Hillie and my grandfather—his name was Isaac—married in the middle of my great-grandfather's protests and my great-grandmother's anguish. They'd not so much as kissed before they went straight to the justice of the peace and got married, then boarded the train and headed for Baxter."

"They'd never kissed?"

"They'd not even held hands, Hillie told me."

I couldn't begin to imagine. "Goodness." Waiting to sleep together I could relate to. But holding hands? Kissing?

"Of course, eventually they did more than hold hands or ... because a year later—after getting the house set back to rights and working on the children's educational needs—Hillie had her firstborn child, Bonnie."

"Bonnie is *your* mother."

"You met her at the wedding."

Yes, I had. An older, shorter version of Mrs. Houser, for sure. "She was nice."

"Mother always told me that Hillie never let on that the oldest five were not her own. In fact, Mother said that until she was old enough to calculate things, she'd had no idea."

Understanding settled over me. "Because Hillie loved them as her own."

Mom returned the photo, but her eyes didn't quite meet mine as she said, "After Grandpa died, Hillie went to live with the youngest of the original five children. She had three of her own, but for some reason, her heart was tied closest to the first wife's baby. And she lived with him and his family until she died." Tearful eyes met mine. "She taught me a lot about ... love. That it extends far beyond what you think it should. It can go straight from your heart to those who occupy an unexpected place there."

"I—"

"Listen to me, Allison," she said in such a way that I knew—I *knew*—our conversation had somehow left Hillie's story and come to mine. "Every woman's child is precious. Every *child*."

"Mom," Westley said then from the same position his mother had occupied earlier. Both she and I turned suddenly, as though we'd been caught doing something we shouldn't. I smiled at him instinctively, but his attention was focused solely on the woman who'd brought him into the world, *not* on the woman he'd married. "What are you doing?" he asked, his tone confused. Accusatory.

But Mrs. Houser was not intimidated. She stepped away from the piano and to her son, whose chin she cupped in maternal tenderness. "I was telling her about *Hillie*," she answered matter-of-factly.

And, with that, she left the room ... Westley right behind her.

Chapter Sixteen

Westley

They had promised each other no Christmas gifts—and they'd stuck to that—but, nevertheless, on Monday morning Westley's car pulled a small U-Haul trailer full of gifts—both Christmas and wedding—toward their new home in Odenville. Including a hand-carved cedar hope chest, a gift from his parents. Unbeknownst to his new bride, her mother had sent over her wedding dress—already dry-cleaned and boxed—which Westley's mother lovingly placed within its depths along with two family heirlooms from the Houser family—an antique soup tureen that had belonged to his father's grandmother and, nestled for Allison to find later, the photo of Hillie.

Westley's brow furrowed at the heated, yet whispered, argument he'd had with his mother after she'd shared Hillie's story with Allison.

"I know what you're doing, Mom," he'd said to her.

"Son," she'd said, her voice as firm as it had been after the after-prom shenanigans he and his best pals had executed. "I love you more than I have words. But you *have* to tell her. In fact, she should already know."

"She will. I promise. Soon." And he would. Right after the first of the year. Right after he sought out his attorney—an old friend from childhood—to discuss all the options.

Now, nearing their new home, Allison swiveled to look behind them and he smiled inwardly, remembering how she'd made certain he'd wrapped her special gift in old army blankets her father kept in the attic before supervising its placement into the farthest corner of the trailer.

"It's still there," he teased.

"Just making sure," she said before turning to face front again. Before readjusting the blue suede faux-fur-lined maxi coat her parents had given her the day before. A final time, he figured, that they'd make such a purchase. Winter coats were for husbands to purchase, not parents.

They arrived back in Odenville around three thirty, Westley driving straight to their house, anxious to have her in it. To feel her presence there. To see how she'd supervise, this time, the *unloading* of the trailer ... the placement of the gifts. Determining "this goes in the kitchen ... the dining room ... the living room ... the bedroom." The last room being the one he'd had on his mind most of the day, if not all.

He'd honored her wishes the night before and stayed on his side of the bed. But tonight—if he survived until tonight—they'd finally be home. In their own bedroom. In their own bed. And, once again, she'd be his.

He grinned at her as he reached behind the steering wheel to put the car in park, then said, "Welcome home, Mrs. Houser."

She clasped her hands as if in prayer. "Gosh, I love hearing that name," she said before waggling her brow at him and saying, "Is this the part where you carry me over the threshold?"

He opened his door. "If I can, after all that turkey and dressing you ate ..."

She waited for him to come to the passenger's door. To open it and help her out. Because she was, first and foremost, a lady. Which was, after all, one of the reasons he'd married her. Had to have her. "Ho-ho-ho," she said, her voice indicating that she'd understood the joke.

"Come on," he said. "I'll walk you to the door and then ..." He stretched playfully. "I'll see if my back holds out for this tradition you think so important."

Naturally, it did. She was light as a feather, as the old saying went.

And she kissed him as soon as they'd stepped inside. Before he could send her feet to the floor. "I love you," she said for the first time inside their new home.

"I love you," he repeated, as he always did. Always would. Because he did. He was sure of it.

Allison looked around then. Inhaled. "It smells lemony fresh in here," she said, her brow furrowed. "I figured with it being locked up for a few days ..."

Westley kissed her turned-up nose. "Miss Justine sent Rose Beth over this morning. Told me before I left for the wedding that she would so you wouldn't be faced with what a house looks like after a man has been in it alone for a few weeks." He blinked furiously in jest.

The still-moist lips of his wife turned downward. She wasn't pleased. "Oh."

"Something wrong?" he asked, his arms still circling her waist, still pulling her to him.

She shrugged. "No ... I just ... I figured I'd ..."

"What?"

Allison shrugged again. "Never mind. I'll be sure to thank Miss Justine when we see her again." She looked over her shoulder. "Well, then ... let's get that U-Haul unloaded."

Two hours later Allison had managed to have every piece of luggage unpacked and every gift put in its place, including the hope chest, which she positioned perfectly centered and at the foot of their bed, followed by one of her mother's knitted afghans placed lovingly on top. "What do you think?" She stood away from it, hands on hips, hair tucked behind her ears then pulled over one shoulder.

"I think it looks like we're home."

She couldn't have given him a brighter smile; his own heart leapt at the sight of it. "Home," she breathed out. "Yes." Then, as if reality struck, she added, "Are you hungry?"

Westley patted the toned abs of his stomach. "I could eat. You?"

"A little."

She walked past him and straight into the rest of the house without another word. On into the kitchen where he found her standing in the middle of it, looking at the stove as if it were a phenomenon of nature. "What is it?" he asked.

"I'm not really sure what to cook."

Westley chuckled. "What *can* you cook?"

Allison looked at him, her eyes wide. "Well, Grand has been working with me, but ..." She sighed. "I *can* boil an egg ..."

"And do what with it?"

She pressed her lips together. "I can make a tuna salad. A pretty good one actually. Grand taught me. And Mama taught me how to make tuna hash."

Westley grimaced. "How about we go out to dinner tonight and tomorrow you can stock the kitchen and then tomorrow night you can cook."

"But how will I—Julie and Dean aren't bringing my car until this weekend, remember?"

Yes, he remembered. His wife had been too afraid to drive all the way across the state alone, so her sister and brother-in-law had risen to the task. Which also meant they'd have another couple in their home within days of them being in it—something Westley wasn't sure he was quite ready for yet. "Yes, but—"

"How can I get groceries without a car?"

Westley leaned against the frame of the back door. "Well ..." he said, pondering their issue. "I suppose you'll have to drive me to work. Pick me up afterward."

She stepped over to him and looked up. "Oh, Westley. I'm so sorry about the car. Really, I am. I'm just not ready for such an undertaking as driving all the way across the state—"

He smiled down at her. How could he do anything else? "Don't worry about it, sweetheart. We can make do with one car for a few days." He kissed her forehead, breathing in, already intoxicated by the floral scent of her shampoo. "Why, if I remember the story correctly, Hillie and Isaac only had the one horse and buggy."

Allison slipped into his arms without reservation. "Oh, Westley.

I must have done something so wonderful when I was a child. So fantastic. But I cannot remember it to save my life."

He leaned back as best he could to tip her chin and her face toward him. "Why do you say that?"

"Because I don't deserve you. I don't."

"I'm the one who doesn't deserve *you*." And he didn't. He knew he didn't. She didn't. Not yet, anyway. So, he hoped—no, he prayed—she would still love him … would forgive him after she learned the truth about Cindie. About Michelle.

"Westley?"

"Hmmm?"

She smiled, all pre-bridal coyness gone from her. "I'm not hungry anymore …"

Cindie

Too much time had gone by since she'd last seen Westley. Since he'd seen his daughter. Yes, he'd said he was going to his parents' for Christmas, but to her way of thinking, there hadn't been much reason for him to have left over a week before.

Her mother felt the same way. And she'd drilled it into Cindie's head nonstop since the day after Westley left, the day after he'd stopped by with a few more holiday-wrapped boxes filled with what turned out to be Fisher Price toys suitable for a one-year-old. He'd also managed to hide two gifts for her under the tree. Gifts she'd found on Christmas Day, hidden, supposedly, when she'd gone to get Michelle from her crib. Waking her from her afternoon nap just so she could see her daddy and then him not even calling since.

She looked at herself in the dresser mirror that had clouded with time, leaning in for a better look at the gifted dangling opal earrings, wishing he'd been around to put them on her for the first time. Hoping for so much more than a token of his feelings, but happy to get whatever portion of him he gave nonetheless.

"You going on over there again today?" her mother asked from the open bedroom door, startling her.

Cindie turned to look at the woman who had, once upon a time, been a pretty woman. Thin and shapely. But who now looked like a woman who'd had life beat out of her and all its joys with it. "Yeah. Will you watch Michelle?"

"Course. Don't I always?"

Yes, she did. And she might as well. She didn't do much of nothing else all day. "Mama. Don't start."

Her mother crossed her arms over breasts that hung thick and large against her midsection. "I'm telling you, girl, something is up with that one. Him coming around like he did for a while there and then suddenly—poof—he's gone? And right at Christmas? Don't make no sense to me."

Cindie looked a final time in the mirror for an approval of the form-fitting ecru sweater, denim skirt, and the boots her father had mailed to her for Christmas. At least he still remembered his kids during the holidays. On birthdays. Not much any other time, but at least then, always leaving her to wonder if he'd had to sneak the presents out when his new wife wasn't looking. "How do I look?" she asked.

"Too pretty for your own good."

Cindie pulled at a tendril of hair, her mother's answer sending a rush of fear through her. She looked so much like photos of Lettie Mae in her youth. Would she still look like her when her age had doubled? Would she act like her, holding on to the same bitterness? Or was it envy. Anger. "Well, as long as I look good enough for Westley Houser, that's all that matters." She turned again. "All right. I'm going to Odenville to see if he's come back to work by now. The sign on the door yesterday said they'd be open today, so I reckon—"

"Bring me back a box of Salem Lights while you're over there, hear?"

Cindie walked past her mother, the heels of her boots clomping on the hardwood floor that needed a good mopping. "All right."

"Two if they're on sale."

Cindie reached for the strap of her purse she'd left in the living room and brought it over her shoulder. "Yes'm."

"And don't stay gone too long," she said as Cindie reached the front door, her mother's car keys now jangling from her fingertips. "I got a life, too, you know."

Cindie rolled her eyes but not so she'd be seen. The last thing she needed was Lettie Mae's palm print across her face when she saw Westley. Then again …

She turned back into the room, caught her mother's eyes with her own. "What life, Lettie Mae?" she said, daring the woman who'd given her life to end it.

And, right on cue, a hand came across her cheek, stinging it soundly, snapping her head sideways, bringing tears to Cindie's eyes without trying. "Don't you sass me, little girl. I don't deserve it."

Cindie blinked slowly as a smile spread across her soul. "No, Mama. You don't. Sorry."

She found Westley behind the raised pharmacy counter, head down, lips moving slightly. Like he was counting or something. She stopped dead in front of him. Waited until he sensed her presence. Looked up.

"Hey, there," he said.

She thought she saw a blush rush across his cheeks, like he was embarrassed for her to be there. Not that he should be. She'd dressed up nice. Done her hair like he liked it. Worn the earrings. Then again, maybe the sight of her did to him what the sight of him did to her. "Hey."

"What are you doing here?" he asked, but he came around the counter to where she stood, hands shoved loosely into his pants pockets, letting her know that her being there was okay. He wasn't mad or nothing. "Is Michelle—hey … what happened to your face?" His right hand came up quickly; his fingertips brushed across her still-reddened cheek, sending shivers down her body.

"It's nothing," she lied. Because it was surely something, mostly half-planned and purposeful. "Lettie Mae just didn't like something I had to say about her life."

His brow furrowed. "She doesn't hit Michelle, does she?"

"Never. I'd never—"

"Good, because—"

"I waited until nearly lunch to come up here, Westley. Hoping maybe you and me could go somewhere and get a little something to eat. Because I—uh—well, you didn't call or nothing on Christmas Day like I'd hoped you would and I—I wanted to show you the pictures I took of Michelle with that Instamatic camera you got me. I already got 'em developed."

Westley returned his right hand to the pocket, then looked over the counter toward the large-faced clock hanging on the wall. "Yeah … um … yeah. Okay. I'm about done here for the morning, but I—why don't you—why don't you go on down to Mama Jean's Restaurant and grab a table for us there." He smiled in that gentle way that made her know everything between them was good. Better than good. Might even have a future to it. "I'll be right behind you."

She smiled as the warmth continued to spread through her. Yes, yes. A future with the father of her child. "I can do that."

He started to walk away, then stopped. "Um—see if you can grab one near the back, okay?"

"Sure," she answered with a sigh that caught her off guard. Yes, yes. This just may go better than she'd hoped.

Chapter Seventeen

Westley

After slipping out of his lab coat and hanging it on the brass hook near his desk, Westley picked up the phone and dialed a number he still had to look up—his own.

Allison answered on the third ring, her voice sounding confused. "Hello?"

"Hey, sweetheart. You okay?"

She breathed a sigh of relief. "Oh, Westley. I couldn't imagine who'd be calling. I don't know anyone here."

He tucked his chin and grinned. "You know me."

"I definitely know you," she said, once again understanding his banter. Something she seemed to have gotten better at since their wedding.

"Did you go to the grocery store?"

"I did. Took me longer than I thought it would. I'm not used to shopping on my own."

"Did I give you enough cash?" He glanced up at the clock knowing he had to hurry. "We'll go to the bank soon and get you added to the account. Get the checks printed with both our names."

"You gave me plenty. Came back with extra, actually."

The very soul of him smiled. Beautiful *and* thrifty, his wife. "And you had no trouble finding your way there and back?"

"I did fine." She giggled. "Okay. I got a little lost, but I figured it out."

"I'm sure you did," he said around a grin. "Well, I've got to get back to work. I just wanted to check on you."

"I love you so much."

"You too ... say, what are you doing with yourself the rest of the day?"

"Well, I just got back from the grocery store so I'm going to put things away. After that, I don't know. What time do I need to pick you up?"

"Six."

"I can't wait. I miss you so much."

"Miss you more. Gotta go, hon."

"Love you," she said again.

"More."

Westley stopped at the post-Christmas sales display and grabbed a small stuffed Santa, then snatched the tag off and handed it to Miss Ramona, the fifty-something who'd worked the register since "Moses was a boy," as Miss Justine put it. "Miss Ramona, hold on to that for me if you will. I'll pay for it after lunch."

One dark, penciled-in brow shot up over cat-framed glasses. "Mind telling me who was that young woman who came in a while ago?"

Westley gave the spinster his best smile, one that always worked when it came to the fairer sex. "Just someone I knew from Baxter. Went to school with her sister." He waved the Santa back and forth in the air. "Be right back," he said, then scooted two blocks over to Mama Jean's. Along the way he pulled his wallet from his back pocket, then tucked his wedding ring behind his license before sliding the wallet where it belonged. He glanced at his left hand, worried that the barely-a-week impression of nuptial vows would give him away before he had a chance to share his secrets. His torment.

With Cindie, that he was married.

With Allison, that he was a father.

He found Cindie exactly where he'd asked her to be, near the back, two cups of coffee on the table, steam curling and hovering like the Spirit over the deep. And, as luck would have it, he didn't recognize a soul in the restaurant. Give him another month, and they'd all know him and he them. But for now...

"For Michelle," he said as he handed Santa across the table and dropped onto the seat left vacant for him.

Cindie smiled. Rubbed it against the cheek that didn't seem nearly as red as it had earlier under the florescent lighting of the pharmacy. "She'll love it," she said, then dropped it onto her purse.

"Your cheek looks better."

"Don't worry none about Lettie Mae. I rile her up every now and then and she just has to let off steam, I reckon."

"As long as—"

"She don't hurt Michelle, Westley. I promise you that."

He nodded. Looking at her. Taking her in. She tried; he knew she tried. Still, she couldn't come even remotely close to Allison's beauty. Her purity. Her intelligence. Everything about the woman sitting across from him reminded him of how stupid a bottle of wine—okay, two bottles of wine—could make him. How desperate, perhaps. What's more, how quickly he needed to act to get his daughter away from the day-to-day influence of Lettie Mae Campbell, if not from her own mother. "Earrings look nice," he said, mainly because he needed to say something. The air around them was changing to something he may not be able to control—her wanting more than he would ever give her again and him wanting to blurt out the truth then and there and be done with it. He peered over his shoulder. "Where's the waitress? I've only got an hour."

"Oh, I already ordered," she said, and he looked back at her. "Burgers and fries... like that night."

He blinked. "What night?"

She pinked. "The night we—you know..."

And he understood. "Ah. Yeah."

Cindie leaned forward, her arms tucked under the table, her hands in her lap. Probably clutching each other if he were to bet. "So, are you coming over tomorrow? I mean, now that you're back in town and all? I figured... Wednesday is our day."

He would, had he a car. And that might take some explaining. "We'll see."

Her face fell. "Well—why wouldn't you? Michelle misses you."

The thought of his daughter looking for him turned his stomach to beach sand—the kind closest to the shoreline—and brought about a surprising expectancy. "I miss her, too."

"And me?"

Westley his opened mouth to say something trite like "yes, of course," but the waitress appeared at the exact moment, the aroma of grease and burger and crinkle fries brought to a perfect golden brown causing his mouth to water, reminding him that he was actually pretty hungry. He and Allison had skipped dinner the night before and he'd only had a bowl of cereal with a sliced banana for breakfast. No coffee; Allison hadn't learned how to perk it yet and he didn't have time to show her or make it himself. He inwardly thanked God for Miss Ramona and the pot she made each morning, fresh and hot and waiting in the employee's lounge at the pharmacy. "Wow," he said, then glanced up at the waitress. "My compliments to the chef and I haven't even taken a bite yet."

The young woman with a slicked-back ponytail and too many teeth for the size of her mouth smiled, her chewing gum peeking out from where it rested on a molar. "Y'all need anything else?"

Westley searched the table, spied the Hunt's Ketchup, which Mama Jean's continued to serve in the commemorative Spirit of '76 bottle, and said, "Mustard?"

"Be right back."

Westley watched her spin on a heel and leave, aware that Cindie stared at him, conscious that she waited for a reply to her question. Knowing it was time to be honest—at least partially. "Look, Cindie …" he began, then stopped as the waitress returned with the mustard bottle, then left again. "I know what you're hoping for …" He watched her expression change. Hope giving way to honesty and then again to heartbreak. What was it the preacher said at his wedding? *Hope deferred maketh the heart sick: but when the desire cometh, it is a tree of life.*

"Keep hope alive," he'd coaxed the bride and groom who stood side by side, their hands clasped in union. "Fulfill *desire*," he'd added with a wink toward the groom. He could do that with Allison, but not with Cindie. Never again with Cindie. But he didn't have to crush her. That certainly wasn't his intent. "Look," he said again. "I know what you're hoping for and it's not—"

"Why not?"

"Because, sweetheart, I don't feel that way about you." He brought his hands up, then placed them on the table. "I'm sorry. I'm probably the biggest cad in the world—"

"What's a cad?"

"A—a cad is a—a *scoundrel*." Right there. Right there was another reason ... Not knowing a simple word like *cad*. "Cindie, I want you to fulfill your potential. I told you that." He popped a fry in his mouth; if he was going to eat at all, he'd have to work it in between the beginning and ending of her undoing. And, perhaps, his own.

"I can, Westley. As your *wife* I can."

"No," he said around a swallow.

"Why not?" Her eyes widened. Her lips pursed. Understanding dawned. "Is there someone—someone else?"

Here it was. His chance. Or, at least, half a chance. "Yes."

Cindie pushed at her plate, which hit the mug of coffee she'd yet to drink from, sending the contents over the edge to form a small waterfall, its tiny pool lying around the base like a mud pond. Somewhat like, he had to admit, his father's reaction to finding out about Michelle. And now, this ...

Westley grabbed a napkin from the dispenser and handed it to her, but she slapped his hand away. "Is it serious?"

"It is," he answered, now mopping up the spill himself.

She stood so quickly he had to grab at his plate to keep from wearing the contents. "Don't bother coming tomorrow," she said. Loudly. Too loudly.

"Sit down," he told her, the tips of his ears growing warm. Cindie causing a scene was the last thing he needed.

"No. I won't. And I don't have to let you see her. I *don't*," she all but screamed before throwing the Santa at his chest, then stomping toward the café's front door like the near-child she was.

"Cin—" he called after her, half turning in his seat to see that—seemingly—every diner now focused on the argument in the back. He raised his hand in apology, then turned back to the unconsumed meals that grew cold.

"Is everything okay?"

He looked up. The waitress had returned. "Yeah," he conceded, then pointed to his plate. "Can I have both of these in a couple of to-gos?"

He'd eat back in the break room . . . and take Cindie's meal to Miss Ramona as a token.

Of what, he wasn't quite sure.

Cindie

By the time she reached her mother's car, the tears that threatened to spill over did exactly that. She jammed the key into the lock, twisted it with such force she surprised herself that it didn't break off, then scrambled into the car as quickly as she could. Within seconds she gasped, her hands gripping the cold, cracking vinyl of the steering wheel. They flexed. Once. Twice until she held onto it as though holding onto a life raft in the middle of a tumultuous ocean. She brought her forehead down hard on the wheel. Moments later, she raised up, then slammed her hands down on the dashboard as a primal growl rose from inside her. Against Westley. Against this girl, whoever she was. Against herself. Against Lettie Mae and her father and everything that life had sucked out of her.

"I hate him!" she shrieked, then looked around to see if she had brought any attention to herself.

She hadn't . . . for such a busy little town, nothing stirred right then. But she noticed a phone booth nearby and, as if she were an actor in some movie playing at the Mahoney Theater in downtown Baxter, she knew her next move.

First, wipe her nose and dry her face, which she did with an old McDonald's napkin she found on the floorboard. She opened the car door, then stepped out. One foot on the pavement. Then another. She hoisted herself up and out. Slammed the door behind her with little effort, mainly because that was all that was left inside. She then made her way to the phone booth that smelled like old beer and perspiration. Stuck her finger into the 0 of the rotary dial and waited.

"Operator."

"Operator," Cindie said, keeping her voice as steady as she knew how. "Do you have a listing for a Westley—W-E-S-T-L-E-Y—Westley Houser in—um—Odenville?"

"Hold please," a soft voice replied, then: "I have a new listing—"

"That would be it."

"On Rosemary Street."

She wasn't sure, but ... "That's it."

The operator gave the number. "Oh," Cindie said. "Wait ..." She dug into her purse until she found a pen and an old receipt for baby powder, then scribbled the number down and repeated it back. "Thank you."

Within a minute she was back in the car, unsure what to do next. Another minute and she was back out on the sidewalk, waiting for someone to walk by. And when they did, she asked, "Do you know how to get to Rosemary Street?" A minute after that, her car was pointed in the right direction, her eyes scanning the houses—little cookie cutters standing between pretty trees and edged lawns—until she found exactly what she was looking for: Westley's hot new car.

Cindie slowed Lettie Mae's to a crawl, her heart racing, her breath coming in rapid beats. Was that her? The young woman sitting on the front porch, legs crossed, dark hair falling over her face, nose pointed toward a book opened on her lap—was that her? And what was she doing *there*? Cooking? Cleaning? Waiting for Westley? Had to be because she seemed to have possession of his car.

She kept going until she was at a safe distance, then pulled into a random driveway, backed up and drove past the house again. Yes.

That was definitely Westley's car and, this time, the woman looked up. She was—okay—she was pretty in a *Seventeen* Magazine cover sort of way. Fresh-faced. Almost ... nearly ... perfect. But Cindie had one thing that chick didn't—Westley's baby girl.

A few minutes later Cindie turned the car back in the direction of the house for one more look. To assure herself. Or maybe to convince herself. And, again, the young woman spied her, their eyes practically shooting messages across the distance between them. Cindie continued on, this time driving farther down the street, turning into a different driveway. This time gripping the steering wheel so hard she worried it would come apart in her hands.

She swore at Westley again, this time between her teeth. A hiss like the snake he was. He was the father of her child ... but he had some woman living with him. Not her. Not plain Cindie Campbell. Plain and stupid Cindie Campbell.

No. She had to face it, the woman on the porch was ... *everything* she was not.

A brow rose as two facts collided—yes, that girl was everything but one thing. She wasn't Michelle's mother. And she never would be. If Cindie needed to use her child to her advantage, so be it.

Chapter Eighteen

Allison

As soon as I spotted Westley coming out of the pharmacy, I moved to the passenger's side of the car, anxious for my husband to get in and kiss me. He all but trotted toward me, then opened the door and, before sliding in, stuck his hand in and waved a small stuffed Santa toward me.

"What's this?" I asked, taking it. "A Christmas present?"

Westley drew the seat belt over him, buckled it, then leaned over for the much-anticipated kiss. "Just a little something that says I love you."

"Oh, Wes," I sighed. "Can we go home? I mean, we don't have anywhere else to be, do we?"

"Yes, ma'am, we can and no ma'am we do not."

As I hugged the Santa to my breast, he backed the car out of the parking space and into the slow-moving traffic. "So," he said, "tell me about your afternoon. What did you do with yourself?"

I glanced out the window, placed my hand upon it, felt the chill from the night air pushing against it. "Well … I sat outside on the porch for a while. Did some reading." I gave a little shrug, not sure how to tell him about the car that had passed back and forth in front of the house. "Something … well, something kind of odd happened."

"Odd?"

I looked at him—the point of his nose, the angle of his chin, the curl in his hair that took on a slight frizz in the moist winter air—and shook my head. "Truth is, I wasn't reading for pleasure. I was looking through that Betty Crocker *Cooking for Two* cookbook that Grand gave me for Christmas and—"

Westley shot a crooked smile my way. "God bless Grand."

"Funny."

He turned down a not-yet-familiar road where the streetlamps had all come on, casting soft funnels of light along a sidewalk. "So, something strange happened?" He laughed. "Did you spot a recipe you can't wait to try out on me?"

I ignored the tease. "Not strange. Odd."

"Okay."

"While I was outside, there was this car that drove past really slow. I looked up and—I know it's probably crazy on my part—but I thought the girl behind the wheel was—you're going to think I'm silly, but, I thought she was staring at me." Westley looked at me sharply, but only for a moment. "And then she pulled into a driveway and turned around and did the same thing and—not too long after—she did the same thing again."

For a moment I thought Westley stopped breathing, or that perhaps he'd not heard me. Then he asked, "What kind of car?"

I shook my head. "I don't know cars, Wes. But it was long and brown and kind of old. Beat up."

"And the girl?" he asked, keeping his focus straight ahead.

"From what I could see, she had blondish hair. It was pulled up. A nice face ..." I touched his arm. "I wasn't scared or anything. She looked too young to be dangerous. I just don't understand why she kept driving by and staring at me."

The car turned into our driveway. "I see you left the front porch light on."

"Mama always did ... made me feel all grown up turning it on before I left to come get you."

Westley all but shoved the gearshift into Park before saying, "Let's get inside." The dimness of light from the porch found his face; he'd aged. In the past five minutes. I could see it. Something I had said. Or done. Something had added time to his face and taken it away from his soul.

I squeezed the Santa. "What?"

He looked at me. "Let's—I need to talk to you about something and—all right, it may as well be now."

I spent the rest of the evening and most of the night sobbing into my pillow, my arm wrapped around the little Santa, sleep occasionally coaxing me to itself with puffy eyes and swollen lips. Anguish gripped me as I'd never experienced. As though someone—or something—had died.

But no one—and nothing—had.

The man I loved—and *still* loved—had a child. A daughter. With the woman in the long brown car. The girl with the pretty face and blond hair swept up, soft tendrils curling to her shoulders.

Westley had shown me the cheaply framed photograph—Michelle, he'd called her—as he told me everything. Or everything he chose to tell. Which was fine; if there was more, I couldn't take it. What he'd said as he reached across the table to hold my hand was enough. "That girl—and that's really all she is, sweetheart—is Cindie Campbell." His eyes never left mine, as though begging me to believe him. Telling me I should when I couldn't. Or maybe that I could when I couldn't. I was too young, too inexperienced in the rules of love and deception to be sure. "And she and I have a child together. A daughter ..."

Life intersected with his words and pulled me into a vortex. Drew me with such speed and power I felt like Alice falling through the rabbit hole. Westley's face grew fuzzy. Time slowed and sped up all at once. His words garbled like Charlie Brown's teacher when she spoke from the head of the classroom—*wah-wah-wah-wah.* Or a record playing at the wrong speed. I stood, pushing his hand away, and retreated to the bathroom where I threw up the three bites of tuna casserole I'd managed to eat before he'd lowered the boom, then went into our bedroom and slid between the cool sheets to bury my face.

Westley had the good sense to leave me alone, sleeping in the spare bedroom. The *guest* bedroom—the one where my sister and her husband would sleep come the weekend. *Dear God, where will Westley sleep then?*

The only words spoken between us came early in the morning when he'd walked into the bedroom to get his clothes. "Sweetheart," he whispered from beside the bed, his fingertips brushing my hair from my face.

"Go away," I told him.

And he had. Which was, truly, the worst part. Because it was and wasn't what I wanted. What I needed. No, I *needed* him to tell me that the whole thing had been a joke. A horribly bad joke. Or a dream. A nightmare. Something every new bride dreams on the second night in her new home. Instead, he pulled clothes off hangers, went into the bathroom, showered, and several minutes later, left the house, taking the car and leaving me alone.

I stayed in bed until nature forced me out. I took a shower. Brushed my hair, pulling it into a ponytail, and then my teeth because, God knew, I didn't want morning breath. Westley didn't. He'd made that clear, hadn't he? And I stupidly wondered if this Cindie Campbell person had morning breath after . . .

I slid into a pair of jeans and a sweatshirt, then made both beds, before shuffling into the dining room, surprised to find the table cleared. And, in the kitchen, everything had been left spick-and-span. The percolator stood in the center of the stove with a note taped to it: JUST PLUG ME IN. I'LL PERK THE BEST CUP OF COFFEE YOU EVER HAD.

I tried to smile. In fact, I may have, especially after I took the first cinnamon-laced sip from where I sat in the living room. From where I stared out the wide window onto the street outside, thinking about that long brown car and hearing the words Mama said to me after the wedding.

"I won't get a chance to say this again, so listen up. I'm telling you that

Westley Houser is the kind of man who needs to run his own household. Whatever he wants, Allison, you just follow his lead. Don't mess this up. Don't shame me and your daddy. We've done good by you and—"

"Mama," I had whispered. *"I love you so much and I love him so much and I promise you—I promise you—I won't do anything to embarrass you or Daddy."*

I sighed into my coffee, my vow choking out any thoughts I had of calling Mama ... of asking her what I should do ... of asking her if I could come home. If I could pretend none of this—meeting Westley, dating him, marrying him, becoming his wife in every sense of the word—had ever happened. But what kind of shame would I bring on her and Daddy—or Grand—if I left Westley after less than two weeks of marriage? They'd never be able to hold their heads up again, especially not in a town like Bynum.

Movement from the driveway jerked me from my melancholy long enough that I was able to walk over to the window and peer out. To see Miss Justine bounding out of her car as though she were no more than a twenty-one-year-old. The much-needed smile broke across my face at the sight of her—such a petite woman dressed in the middle of the morning as if she were heading for a late-night downtown dinner. Black boots . . . a full-length mink coat ... hair teased high. A rope of pearls wrapped around her black-gloved wrist.

I opened the door, setting my coffee on the console TV simultaneously, to find her already on the porch, arms opened wide.

"Come here, darlin'," she said before I had a chance to greet her.

And I did. Even though I towered over her, I folded into the maternal warmth of her, remaining there until she said, "Let's go inside before rumors start."

I offered a cup of coffee, which she took, then complimented me on the flavor. "Rose Beth couldn't have made a better cup," she declared after we'd returned to the sofa and she'd removed her gloves and coat to show off a sporty suede skirt and coordinating sweater. Thick gold chains hung around her neck, low enough to lie askew over her breasts and her makeup was, as before, a tad too much for my taste, but seemed to represent who Miss Justine was at the very core of herself.

"Westley made the coffee," I admitted. "A peace token, I guess." I looked up at her. "How did you know, Miss Justine?"

She took a sip of coffee before answering. "Westley called me the minute he got to work. Confused as I've ever heard him. Told me in that little-boy-with-his-hand-in-the-cookie-jar voice that he'd messed up everything. He thinks you'll never forgive him." She cocked a penciled-in brow. "Will you?"

"Should I?"

"Of course, you should. He didn't have the child while the two of you were married, did he?"

"No, but—"

"And he hasn't slept with the girl since the two of you met, has he?"

"I don't think so—"

"He hasn't," she clipped. "I know, because I asked him. And he swore he hadn't." She pointed at me. "When you've been married a whole lot longer, you'll learn to ask the right questions right up front. You'll also learn how to put Westley in his place and keep him there. Which, by the way, is in knowing yours."

I placed my cup on the low, oval coffee table. "But, Miss Justine, how can I believe that? That he hasn't *been with* her since ... the baby ... was conceived?"

She laughed. Actually laughed. "Oh, child. If there is one thing I know about Westley Houser it's this—if you ask him a direct question, he will *not* lie. He may hold some things back—and believe *me*, that boy's untold shenanigans could fill a book, but he won't lie." She cupped my chin, her long nails lightly scraping the tender flesh of my throat. "He's not a *bad* boy, he just made a bad *decision*."

"Marrying me?" I asked, wondering what a woman like Miss Justine really thought. Shouldn't he have married the mother of his child? Shouldn't he have done better than keeping Michelle a secret, all the while dating me? Proposing to me? Meeting me at the altar? How could she possibly justify such behavior? How could *I*?

She released me, her pearls clunking against each other. "Heavens no. That was the best decision of his life, if you want my opinion. No ... going out with that Cindie Campbell is what I mean. Honey, listen. That family—you don't know—they're a mess. White trash, some people would call them." She waved a hand laden with gemstone rings. "Not me, mind you. I'd never call anyone that. But even over here in Odenville we've heard tell of Lettie Mae Campbell and her lot. And I'll tell you another thing: if I know women like her—and I do— she thought her daughter giving birth to Westley's child was her meal ticket." Her shoulders squared. "I'm surprised she didn't have him in a court of law, but for whatever reason ... maybe she thinks she'll get more out of him this way."

I looked toward the spare bedroom. "My sister and her husband are coming on Friday night," I said, mainly because I didn't know how to respond to the information. I'd been sheltered most of my life, but I knew white trash. I understood ... I thought. And this new piece of information made me more confused than sure. How could Westley— *Westley*—date a girl like Cindie Campbell? I couldn't picture it. Couldn't bear it. Not another word of it. "They're driving my car in."

Miss Justine blinked. "Well, I don't know what that has to do with anything, but if I had to guess, I'd say Mister Westley spent last night in one bedroom and you in another."

Shame washed through me. Maybe my actions had been no way for a bride to behave. I didn't know. I hadn't been at it long enough. "Yes, ma'am."

Again, her laughter filled the house like a dog's bark. "Good for you, princess. Good for you." She scooted closer, gathering my hands in hers. "Want my advice?"

"Yes, please." Because I surely couldn't ask my mother for any right then. Or my grandmother. *Maybe* my sister when she arrived.

"Keep him in the guest bedroom another night. Make him sweat just the teeniest weeniest bit. But, tonight, make a meal he won't forget and then listen to what he has to say about that little girl. And about his plans."

"His plans?" My heart hammered. Westley had plans? Plans he could have and should have told me about before now, certainly.

"He's got some," she said, drawing me back from the angst that wanted to simmer below the surface. "He told me all about them and I support him 100 percent." Her hands squeezed mine. "If need be, with my money. And if you knew the Campbells you would too."

I sighed. Westley. Had. Plans. Plans Miss Justine knew about and I didn't. Not that I'd given him a chance the night before to tell me anything. And not like he hadn't had months to do so previously. "I only know how to make tuna casserole." I nodded toward the back of the house. "Decently, I mean. In spite of my grandmother's attempts to teach me." I pointed toward the kitchen. "The one I made last night is in the fridge."

"Good land of the living," Miss Justine said as she stood and reached for her coat and gloves. "Then let's get going. Go change into something presentable, child. Can't have you out and about in jeans and a sweatshirt. Then, you and I will run to the Piggly Wiggly, get what we need for a nice, big salad to go with that tuna casserole, and first thing tomorrow you'll come over and Rose Beth will start your cooking lessons."

I stood. Took a deep breath and forced a smile I didn't quite feel yet.

Raise your radish, Allison…

All right, Grand. All right. If you could keep going with all your tragedy, then so can I… "Miss Justine?"

She shoved her arms into her coat. "Yes, lamb?"

"How'd you get so wise?"

Again, she laughed. "Honey, when you get to be as ancient as me, you'll be wise, too. It's the gift the good Lord gave us—a reward for putting up with our men for as long as can be."

The table was set when Westley came home, the house dimly lit and inviting. I didn't dress up—I wore the same slacks and top I'd worn to the grocery store—and I didn't put on makeup or spritz on body spray. But I stood in the dining room behind my chair, hands gripping it, waiting as he walked in, a sense of relief etching away at the look of concern. "Hi," he said.

"I'm still upset," I told him right away, just as Miss Justine instructed. "But we have to eat and I—I want to hear what your plans … are."

He hung his coat over the back of his chair, then leaned against the wall, eyes squeezed shut. "You talked to Miss Justine?" he asked, his face declaring that he was, indeed, a man with both everything to lose and everything to gain by our conversation.

"She talked to me." I pulled out my chair and sat. "Sit, Wes."

He smiled as he complied. "Ali …"

"Salad?" I asked, tossing it again before scooping it into a bowl for him. "And I bought several kinds of dressing."

"How did you—"

"You owe Miss Justine twenty-three dollars and eighteen cents, by the way."

He smiled again. "I see we're having tuna casserole again."

"Leftovers."

"That's fine."

He'd best believe it was. Right then, I figured, he was lucky he wasn't eating radish stew. "Will you say grace?"

He did, and after our nearly harmonized "amen," I said, "So, tell me." My insides quivering at the new Allison whom Miss Justine—and Grand—had introduced me to as I reached for the Thousand Island and he reached for the Bleu Cheese.

"What do you want to know?"

"I want to know everything, Westley. I want to know about your relationship with Cindie—"

"There is no relationship." He capped the bottle of dressing and placed it near his plate.

"There must have been at one time," I said, forcing away the vision of my husband, naked and writhing all over another woman. Her beneath him ... over him ... blond hair spilling over ...

He had the decency to blush. "Look, Ali, I don't want to get into ... *that*. Because you knew that ... *our* first time wasn't *my* first time."

"Yes, but I never thought I'd have to come face to face with anyone you'd been with and—here I am—" I said, throwing my arms out, nearly knocking over my bottle of salad dressing in the process, "almost two weeks a bride and I already have."

"I'm so—"

"Please don't, Wes. Please don't apologize. If you apologize, I'll know this whole thing—dating, falling in love, marriage—all of it was a plot on your part. And, if that's true, I don't think I can handle that right now. Maybe later, but not now. So, just ... *talk* to me."

"All right. If it matters, I was drunk. She was drunk. And I was stupid. And I didn't know you at the time or that anyone like you could ever be in my life." He leaned toward me. "I love you. I swear I do. Us—you and me—was never a plot. And I never, ever loved her, Ali. Not even close to it. I'm not even sure I *like* her."

"Then how could you ..."

"Come on," he said, frustration rising in his voice. "You're not stupid, Ali. You're bright as a bulb. I *love* you. That's why I was always willing to wait. Why I never ... pushed you."

The thought of the night at Paul and DiAnn's swept past me, knowing how close we could have come but ... Westley had drawn a clear line for both of us, out of respect for me. Out of respect for Daddy. I hadn't drawn the line. Westley had. Without his fortitude, I may have thrown myself on the wet grass and the crackling fire in front of Paul and DiAnn and God and anyone else who may have walked by. "I know."

"Because I do love you. She was before I met you and she was just ... there."

"And then she was pregnant."

He stabbed at his salad but didn't eat from it. "Yes."

"How long have your parents known?" I asked, quickly running through the questions my brain had calculated all afternoon.

"I told them before the wedding."

That explained it. That explained everything. "And Paul and DiAnn?"

"They've always known."

Oh. *Oh* … "It wasn't about the job," I whispered, feeling oddly as betrayed by my brother- and sister-in-law as my husband.

"What?"

"Nothing." I shoved a bit of salad into my mouth and chewed on it, giving myself more time to think as he did the same. "Okay," I said after swallowing. "I know she's not from the best family."

"No."

"But is she a good mother?"

"I cannot say she is a *bad* mother. But she's—she's not living up to her potential, even for her. For one, she needs to get away from Lettie Mae. If she does, she *can* be a better mother. That's why—that's why I saw an attorney today."

I set my fork down before I dropped it. "An attorney?"

"I plan to sue Cindie for custody of Michelle. And I can only pray you'll be there with me."

I blinked several times, understanding not yet complete. "*With* you?"

"Yes. With me. We have an appointment with an attorney next Wednesday afternoon."

A new question rose up within me, one that demanded an answer—straightforward and without reservation. "Westley," I began slowly. "Did you marry me for this? Because you need a woman in the house in order to get custody of your daughter?"

His eyes found mine without blinking, not even once. "No," he said. "I told you, I married you because I love you."

I wanted to believe him. To *not* believe would mean walking out on a marriage that had barely begun. Returning home. Facing questions. Ridicule. Shame.

I wanted to believe. And, perhaps, believing—for once—was the easiest route to take. "All right," I said. "I guess we just have to begin again from here."

Chapter Nineteen

Cindie

Westley had come over the day before as he always did on Wednesday afternoons to see Michelle, but she'd made sure their daughter wasn't there. Cindie had some things to say, and she intended to say them without the baby there to draw his attention away. Because, no matter what he thought, *she* was in control. She was. Somehow, she would get him back—she would—and she would make him listen to reason. Whatever and whoever this sweet chick was sitting on his front porch like she owned the place ... well, she would be toast. And, once again, Westley would be hers. All according to the plan.

But the plans of one are not always the plans of another, she learned and learned quickly when he stepped up on the porch and knocked on the door. The second she opened the door and told him that Michelle was at Velma's house, he turned and headed back to his car, sending her plans into the frigid January air. "Hey!" she called after him, panic rising in her chest, squeezing out all good sense and logic. "Don't you dare walk away from me." Because all she needed was the right amount of time ... and the warm beer sitting out on the stained Formica countertop in the kitchen.

He made it close enough to the car—that *fancy* car he was so proud of—with her on his heels, until he spun around. "What?"

"You don't have a right to be mean to me." She took a step back. Forced the tears that threatened back to where they belonged. Back to righteous indignation. Back to the want of him. The *need*.

"I'm not being mean, Cindie, but I am not about to get into a war of words with you." His tone came from a man as sure of himself as her daddy had been the night he and Lettie Mae got into their own war—Lettie Mae declaring rights as his wife and her daddy stating his love for another woman, pure and simple. "Your little tantrum at Mama Jean's was enough for me to know right off where this is going," Westley said, reminding her to stay focused. "If Michelle is not here, then there's no reason for me to be."

Cindie crossed her arms over her chest, her heart beating wildly beneath the flesh. And, suddenly now, not from the sight of him. "Who is she?"

He cocked his head, the afternoon sunlight calling out to the red undertones in his hair, drawing them to wink at life. "Who is who? The woman you saw sitting on my front porch?"

Heat rose in her, enough to ward off the chill in the air that begged her to go back inside for a coat before she could say all that was on her mind. Yet, from somewhere deep down, a shiver had begun. A shift in her life. She could feel it, even around the embarrassment. "How'd you—"

"Ali told me. She found it odd that you kept driving in front of the house, staring at her."

"*Ali?*"

"Allison." He held up his left hand, a filigreed band of white gold wrapped around his naturally tanned third finger. "My wife."

She stepped back, her head spinning, her thoughts muddled, her fists tight. He was married. Westley was married. To the pretty girl on the front porch. She was his *wife*. They shared a house. A bed. A *life*. How stupid could she be to have ever thought—"You will *never*," she spat through clenched teeth, "*ever* see your child again." She ran halfway to the house, gasping. Turned again and screamed for all it was worth. "*Ev-ver!*"

Westley came toward her, storming, and she ran as fast as her feet allowed—because every inch of her had become dead weight—until she reached the front door. She jerked it open, darted inside, and spun to shut the door. Lock it. Away from him. Away from everything.

But he'd reached her. Shoved against the door, sending her backward. She stumbled to the floor, hitting her backside hard against floorboards that hadn't seen a mop in a month. At least, not a clean one. "I'll call the police," she threatened, fear now sliding over her as she scooted back. Had she gone too far?

Westley stood with his legs braced apart, his jaw firm. He reached down, grabbed her by the wrists and righted her. "You do that," he said before pointing toward the phone. "Go on, Cindie. Do it."

Cindie jerked the handset from the receiver, not because she would really call, but because she couldn't give him the upper hand. Her own daddy had done that to the mother of his children and look how that little scenario had turned out. "I will—"

He stood his ground. "All you've got to do is dial zero. Put your finger in the hole and pull to the right."

"I hate you," she screamed, slamming the phone back into its place, sending the lamp behind it teetering until it settled again to shine a ghostly light on her mother's ashtray filled with old butts and flicked-off ashes.

Westley breathed out, slow and easy, the scent of musk and spearmint reaching her. Taunting her. "Well, I don't hate *you*, Cindie. But you're not going to threaten me with Michelle."

"I swear to God," she said, ire tying her jaws into knots. "You ain't *never* seeing her again, you hear me? Lettie Mae already said so. She means it, too. She knows how to deal with the likes of you, Westley Houser."

"I'm sure she does." With that, he turned, stopping at the door to look at her again. "I'll see you in court, Cindie. You and Lettie Mae can count on that."

He left her then, not shutting the door behind him, making her walk across the room to keep the cold from infiltrating the barely warm room. Cindie watched him as he backed the car out of her driveway, not looking toward her, even for a last glance.

Other than her mother's tirade and her daughter's frightened shrieks at all the fuss Lettie Mae kicked up, she'd not heard anything since. But it hadn't been twenty-four hours yet. The next morning, Lettie Mae met her in the kitchen with a cup of coffee in one hand and a cigarette dangling from puckered lips, her tattered robe hanging loosely about her pudgy frame. "Tell you what you're going to do, little girl," she said after perching the cigarette on a nearby tin ashtray. "You're gonna get yourself put together and you're gonna go see that DiAnn Houser first thing. Ain't no two ways about it; that woman knows what's what, you can count on it."

"So what if she does?" Cindie asked, the weight of her anguish almost too heavy to get the question out of her mouth. "What good will any of it do?" She poured coffee into a chipped cup, then added two large scoops of sugar and a wide pouring of milk.

Lettie Mae slid a chair out from under the table, the scraping of metal against old linoleum sending a flinch through Cindie's muscles.

Dear God, how she hated her life. Hated it with every fiber of her being.

"You make that woman tell you the truth. You know how to do it. As long as you got that baby, you got the upper hand."

As long as she had the baby... No. Michelle wasn't the upper hand with a man like Westley. But something else was. All she had to do was figure out what.

Cindie took a long swallow of the coffee that warmed her clear through with a taste so perfect, she could almost believe that life *could* get better. "I got a shift this morning, Mama."

"Then right after that. Don't waste a second. See if she knows if he means it."

"Means what?"

"About the lawyer. We can't afford no lawyer, Cindie, so you'd best find out what's what, like I said. We'll plan what we need to do onc't we know for sure." She nodded toward the counter. "Bring me my cigarette, will ya? And pour me a bowl of cereal before you go get ready. Two scoops-a sugar like you know I like it."

As soon as her shift was over, Cindie went to the restroom her boss set aside for his employees—not the better one for customers, but the one with the rust-stained sink and the toilet with a broken seat that pinched every time she sat on it, and the cheap paper towels they were ordered to use only one of per visit. There she washed off the smell of grease and coffee before changing into the best dress she owned, a new pair of nude pantyhose she popped out of an egg-shaped container, and the boots from her daddy. She swatted her lashes with another coat of Great Lash before applying a touch of lip gloss, and—for her final act—slid the posts of Westley's earrings into the tiny holes in her earlobes.

Ten minutes later she was at DiAnn's office and, this time, the receptionist recognized her. "Here to see Mrs. Houser?"

"Yeah. Tell her Cindie Campbell—"

"Yes, I know. She said if you ever returned, she'd see you."

Cindie just bet she did. She waited while the woman punched numbers into a large office-style phone that would connect her to DiAnn's office. She wondered fleetingly if DiAnn would offer her another Coke poured over chipped ice, and hoped so because, with everything at stake, her throat was as bone dry as she was bone weary. Dear God, she was still a teenager. Why then, did she feel seventy?

"Mrs. Houser said for you to come on back," the receptionist said in her clipped tone. "Do you remember the way?"

"Yes."

DiAnn Houser was standing behind her desk, dressed like the professional she was, when Cindie entered the sanctity of her office. "Close the door behind you," she said, then smoothed the back of her wool skirt as she sat. She leaned back easily, crossing her legs and resting her elbows on the soft leather of the armrests with complete command. "Have a seat."

Cindie kept her jaw firm as she tried to sit in the same relaxed manner, knowing the act wasn't coming off the way she'd hoped.

Would she ever have the grace and poise this woman possessed in her smallest finger? "I reckon you know why I'm here."

"Westley called me this morning."

Cindie leaned forward. "Look, DiAnn. I ain't—I'm *not* trying to act like we're some great friends or something, because we're not. Even back in school you hardly paid attention to me—"

"I hardly *knew* you, Cindie. What's the age difference here? Several years?"

"Probably. But we're not in school anymore. We're not kids."

"No, we aren't."

"So you need to tell me right up front so I'll know. Because like it or not, I'm the mother of your niece, and you owe me for that."

DiAnn's chin dipped. "I don't owe you anything, Cindie, but I'm happy to try to help you if I can."

"Is Westley really married?"

"He is."

"Since when?"

"He and Allison married right before Christmas." She pulled a drawer open and reached in, then held up an envelope marked by a logo of a leaping rabbit. "I have pictures here if you want to see them."

She didn't. But she did. She stood, snatched the envelope from DiAnn, then walked over to the window to allow for better lighting. One by one she sifted through the matte photographs with the rounded edges, gazing at the young woman in the white bridal gown—*white*—and the man Cindie loved standing beside her, dressed so uptown: black tuxedo, red sashy-thing around his waist, topped off with a red bow tie. Picture after picture ... Westley looking into his new wife's eyes. Adoring her. Kissing her. Dancing with her. Cutting a slice of cake with her. Laughing as they shared it . . . his eyes teasing her as he pulled a blue-and-white garter from midway up her thigh, while she . . . *blushed.*

The photos seemed to grow heavy; they depicted everything Cindie had always wanted—always dreamed of—Cinderella and her Prince Charming ...

And nothing she would ever get. Not at this rate. Certainly not on this path. No fairy godmother for her. No pumpkin turning into a coach or mice becoming horsemen. Even Cinderella was a cut above Cindie Campbell and there wasn't a doggone thing she could do about it. Nothing... *nothing*... would change her. Could change her. She was exactly what she was and she could never be more.

Cindie tossed the photos and their envelope back on DiAnn's desk, then returned to her chair and attempted to breathe past the heaviness that had settled in her chest. "Did he tell you he's going to see a lawyer?" she asked, using what little bit of oxygen remained in her lungs.

"He did." DiAnn gathered up the photos and slid them neatly back into the envelope.

"Do you think he means it?"

"He already has an appointment."

Cindie nodded, reached into her purse, and dug around until she located her pack of cigarettes. She pulled one out, then continued digging for her Bic. "You mind?" she asked, looking up.

Again, cool as a cuke, DiAnn reached into another drawer and brought out an ashtray, fancier than anything Cindie had ever seen.

"What if I give him good visitation?" she asked after blowing a long line of smoke from between her lips.

"You'll have to talk to Westley, Cindie. This isn't between you, me, and him. It's between you and him."

Cindie drew deep on the cigarette, allowed it to remain in her lungs. Burning. Punishing her for every wrong deed, including that night with Westley. "What's she like?"

"Allison?"

"Yeah."

"She's lovely. And pretty, as you know. Smart. Funny. Enjoys life to the fullest." DiAnn paused. "She's the perfect girl for him."

Yes. Lovely and pretty she already knew. Smart, though. *Unlike* her. She'd not even made it through high school. "She go to college for a long time like he did?"

"I don't believe so."

A thought tickled her then. Nudged her from the inside. Poked at her until she stood. "Tell Westley to call me when he can," she said, crushing her cigarette in the elaborate ashtray, keeping her eyes locked on DiAnn like Lettie Mae would expect her to.

"Is that it?" DiAnn rose without a single blink. Darn her. *Darn* her.

Cindie walked to the door, her legs filled with dishwater. She opened it, took a deep breath, and hoped for the courage she'd need to face her mother. The courage she'd need—God help her—to say three more words before she bolted. "Yeah," she finally managed. "For now."

Chapter Twenty

Allison

My sister's visit brought more than my car.

On Saturday morning, after Westley took Dean up to the pharmacy to purchase a disposable razor—Dean had left his Gillette at home—Julie and I curled up like kittens on the sofa, our hands nestling a cup of Westley's delicious cinnamon coffee heavy with cream and sugar the way we both liked it. "Dean didn't really forget his razor," she said, her voice set in a confidential tone I could scarcely remember her using with me. Perhaps now that I was married ...

I tilted my head at her, at the beauty of her. The glow about her. She wore not a bit of makeup so early in the day, and yet her loveliness—the dark of her hair against the cream of her skin—was undeniable. My whole life I'd been envious of her natural good looks, but right then I only felt a sister's love. Perhaps marrying Westley had changed things for me. For us. "Then why did he—"

"Because he knew I wanted to talk to you for a while and I knew I'd never get you away from Westley long enough that we could—you know—chat."

I clutched the mug tighter in my hand. Had she sensed that something was wrong between Westley and me? Or—could it be—had something gone wrong between her and Dean? They didn't act as if they had too many cares in the world, considering. Then again, Westley and I were putting on a pretty good show ourselves. "Are you—are you okay? You seem okay ..."

Julie laughed, her near-perfect lips forming a delightful smile. "We're more than okay. We're ... pregnant."

"Pregnant?" The word came out half whisper, half gasp. The thought struck me in the gut: my sister was going to have a baby. My husband's one-night stand had a baby. Babies seemed to be coming at me from everywhere and yet none were to be found. For a modicum of a moment I wanted nothing more than to jump up and run from the room, but Julie's face ... oh, her face! And her confiding in me. How long had it been since we'd shared anything of this magnitude?

Julie's hand reached for my knee, bent toward her. "What's the matter? Aren't you happy for me?"

I blinked several times. Swallowed hard. My sister's joy had fallen to concern. "Of course I'm happy. *Julie,*" I exclaimed eagerly, then leaned over to hug her, careful to keep the contents of our coffee mugs from spilling over.

She laughed again as relief replaced the worry. "I couldn't *wait* to tell you. Now that you're a married woman, too, and all."

"Do Mama and Daddy know?" I asked, wanting *not* to go down that trail.

"We told them Thursday night."

"And?"

"Well, first we had to tell them that we're moving to Savannah because—"

"Savannah?" My hand flew to my chest and rested there. "Gracious, Julie ... Whatever for?"

"Dean was offered a job with the Savannah Morning News. We felt like ..." She threw one hand up in the air. "Like it was such a blessing from God, really. We found out about the baby a month ago—"

"Before—"

"Your wedding, yes. I wasn't about to rain on that. I couldn't."

"Oh, Julie ..."

"And I was so bummed because, I mean, how in the world were we going to survive on my salary alone? And you know, Dean ... always talking about me *not* working."

No, I hadn't known that. How would I?

"But I trusted that Dean would do the right thing and he did. He applied at the paper and got the job. Not exactly what he wants to do with his career, but it's what's necessary for now and, well, I won't have to work anymore—Dean says that's God's way. So ... we're moving."

"And having a baby."

The smile broke wide again. "And having a baby," she parroted as she pressed a hand to her still-flat stomach. "In six months." And then she looked at me. Really looked at me in that way only sisters can do. "Allison, what's wrong?" she asked, her voice soft. "Are you and Westley okay? Because, if you don't mind my saying so—and I know I have little right—but, Dean and I both noticed last night that there's a tension in this house. I mean, you're playing the role just fine, but, it's still there."

I nodded yes, but the tears welled up in my eyes, betraying me, calling me a liar. "It's just that ..." I dabbed at the corner of my eye with my index finger, careful not to smear Revlon mascara all over my cheekbones.

"Is it—is it the sex?"

I shook my head no as a flame rose in me. Goodness, it surely wasn't that. Even two nights before, as hurt and bewildered as I was over Cindie Campbell and her child, and in spite of Miss Justine's advice, I couldn't hold back the passion and want I felt for Westley. "No. We're—we're fine." I caught another tear, this time with my pinky, determined not to tell my sister the truth, still unsure of her loyalty to me. What if she told Mama? Or worse, Grand?

"Hold on," Julie said, already rising from the sofa and turning toward the bedrooms. "I want to show you something." She returned a moment later extending a book toward me, one I'd heard about on television but hadn't seen in person. The white cover was slick, the single red rose arched over the elaborate lettering of the title: *The Total Woman*.

"You're reading this?"

She nodded as she sat, this time keeping her feet on the floor. "And you should, too."

"Does Mama know?"

"Does she *know*? Mama's the one who insisted I read it. She said that if I were a better wife, Dean might get a job." Julie's laughter came like tiny wind chimes on a breeze. "I swear, Allison, she thinks her advice on my reading this book is what led to Dean getting a job and me getting pregnant. She has no clue it was the other way around."

I thumbed through the pages. "Does she really talk about showing up at the door dressed only in Saran Wrap? The author ..." I looked at the cover. "Marabel Morgan, I mean. Not Mama."

"Oh, gosh." Julie feigned disgust. "I haven't even thought about Mama and the whole meet-him-at-the-door-in-Saran-Wrap notion."

Our eyes met and we both pretended to have the willies, which—if nothing else—gave me a moment of reprieve from my angst.

"Honestly, Julie," I said with a sigh. "Sometimes I feel like you and I are a part of a generation caught in between."

She cocked her head in curiosity while the merriment from a moment before lingered in her eyes. "Meaning?"

"Meaning there are times I don't know whether I'm supposed to act like Donna Stone and Samantha Stevens or Ann Marie and Mary Richards."

Julie laughed again. "Seriously, I *do* know what you mean. Do we tie a kitchen apron around our waists or burn our bras."

But then, as the gaiety subsided, Julie spoke softly and said, "You don't have to tell me what's going on, Allison. All young brides have to get through something or another. I know I did. But, read this for kicks, okay?" She pointed to the book. "And if you can take anything away from it ... great."

I stood. "I'll go put it in my—*our*—room," I said, not wanting Westley to walk in and see me holding it. Not wanting him to think he'd have even a hope that I would *ever* greet him at the door wearing nothing but a smile and clear plastic.

Days after my sister and her husband and Westley and I had celebrated the arrival of 1978 in festive style—Westley and I drove in silence toward an attorney's office—the same one who had drafted the legal document ordering his child support payments. Money I hadn't realized had been coming out of his—now our—bank account.

Westley wanted custody of Michelle. I kept saying the words over and over in my mind, hoping they would stick. Because he'd not asked how I felt about it. Not questioned whether I thought I was ready for such a thing as being a mother to a one-year-old. Not taken into consideration that I was barely nineteen. Or that a month ago I was happily planning my wedding and working for the Fosters who fluttered around me like second parents, hoping I wasn't jumping into a fire. Which, in the end, I suppose I had. No ... I thought we'd wait a while. Give us time to allow us to grow up a little as a couple. Two years, at least, I figured. Wasn't that about the norm?

And Michelle wasn't even my child. It wasn't like I'd gotten pregnant on my wedding night—I'd heard such stories. Instead, this was another woman's baby. Yes, Westley's too, but mostly the mother's. What would Marabel Morgan say about *this*? Or my own mother? Although I wouldn't have to wonder long when it came to Mama. She had made it clear before I left for my honeymoon that I was to let Westley call the shots. Whatever he wanted. And from what I could tell from Mrs. Morgan's book, she would tell me the same. *His child has now become your child,* she'd say. *She is a part of your husband therefore she is a part of you.*

Westley parked the car and I followed, stepping past him after he opened the front door of the office—a converted small house right off Main Street. We stepped into a room that, with the exception of a woman sitting behind a desk at the far corner, looked as if it could be someone's grandmother's parlor. The walls were wallpapered in muted-yellow grasscloth, the framed artwork large and expensive-looking, and the accenting pieces old and rich. Westley's hand touched the small of my back as he guided me forward to the woman with the Mary Tyler Moore hairdo. "Can I help you?"

"We're the Housers," Westley said. "Here to see Mr. Donaldson."

"Have a seat. I'll let him know you're here."

We sat close on a footed love seat's thin cushion that lay like waves lapping a shoreline. Westley's hand found mine, our fingers intertwining. He squeezed, a silent signal to look at him, and I did. "Thank you," he mouthed.

I nodded, my eyes blinking, fear threatening to overtake me.

"I love you," he whispered.

Again, I nodded. I loved him, too. I did. But I wasn't sure I was ready for what he had asked of me. Not this soon. Not so young.

"This is going to be fine. I promise." He reiterated words spoken countless times since the week before, leaving me unsure as to whom he hoped they'd convince.

And, again, I nodded.

"Mr. and Mrs. Houser," the receptionist said, startling me, having not quite gotten used to hearing our names spoken in such a way. "I can take you back now."

Westley stood, bringing me with him. "I know the way," he told her, raising his hand to stop her from getting up.

We walked down a short, narrow hallway until we reached a room on the left, its door half open, the brass nameplate reflecting the blurred colors of our image as we approached. Trevor Donaldson, it read.

I relaxed as soon as we entered. Trevor Donaldson—Trev, he introduced himself—was barely older than Westley, reminding me more of a big brother than a stuffy lawyer. He wore suit pants without the coat, and he'd rolled the cuffs of his dress shirt up to his elbows, displaying naturally tanned arms and a nice gold watch. He chuckled as he shook my hand. "You expected some old fogey, didn't you," he said.

Heat penetrating my face betrayed any thoughts of lying. "Yes," I admitted.

"Ah," he said, sitting behind his desk and motioning for the two of us to take our seats across from him. "Westley and I go way back, don't we, Wes?" He looked at me again. "Wes didn't tell you?"

"No. He didn't." But, then again, there were so many things my husband had chosen not to tell me. "He just said we were seeing his attorney today."

Westley turned toward me, a look of conspiracy washing over him that came with a desire to steer the conversation in another direction. "Don't believe anything this boy tells you."

Trev leaned back, the leather of his chair squeaking in protest at the motion. "Allison, I could tell you some things about this one." He pointed to his friend. "Me and him and Marty Cone—the things we used to get into."

"The things he's *still* getting into," I said before I'd had time to think about the impact of my words. I looked at Westley, waiting for his reaction, but he only looked at Trev and grinned.

"She's got a point there, Trev."

"That she do." He leaned forward then, resting his arms on the edge of a massive desk topped with books and files and scattered papers. "Talk to me, son. What's happened?"

"I want custody," Westley said. "Plain and simple. Cindie's more like a child herself and she's got Lettie Mae Campbell's influence all over her."

Trev winced. "Wes, listen up. No court in this state is going to take a child away from its mother unless you can prove she's mentally unstable—and I mean like Central State Hospital nuts. Or that she's messing with drugs ... or bringing men into her bedroom in such a way that the child witnesses what the law calls carnal acts." His brows formed an attractive upside-down V at the bridge of his nose as he continued. "Cindie Campbell may not be the best choice of mothers but the first thing a judge is going to ask you about is the night Michelle was conceived, which brings *your* character into the equation. Not hers."

Westley shook his head, defeat flickering in his eyes as hope managed to settle in my stomach. Maybe I wouldn't have to make such a sacrifice so early on. Maybe there was another way. "There's got to be something—" my husband's voice pleaded.

"Not with a one-year-old, Wes. And not a little girl to boot."

Westley sighed, the very essence of him deflating, filling the room now with heaviness and—I could see it then—heartbreak. He loved his daughter. He may not love her mother—or, as he said, even like her—but Michelle was *his* child, too. Flesh of his flesh. Bone of his bone. His blood running through her veins. "Isn't there *anything* you can do?" I asked.

Westley looked at me then, startled by my question. Yes. Whatever he wanted ... just like Mama and Miss Marabel and maybe even Hillie would tell me if the three of them were here. Because if his heart was broken, mine was broken ... didn't he know that? Hadn't he begun to realize how much I loved him? How, without him, I was ...

The song that played on the radio during our trip back from Paul and DiAnn's skipped through the airwaves of a memory. The one we'd talked about. Philosophized about. *Dust in the Wind.* Without him, that was every bit of who I was. And without Michelle, the same could be said about him.

He reached for my hand and I gladly gave it.

Trev opened a manila file and scanned the pages of notes within. "You don't have set visitation, do you?"

"No. And she wouldn't let me see her last week."

Trev glanced up. "Well, now ... there's something I *can* help with. Let me draft up a motion for the court asking for a modification on your child support order." He smiled at me. "You're married now. There's a woman in the house—and, might I just add, one that makes a nice statement—so that's good. What would you like me to ask for?" He reached for a pen and an absently tossed legal pad buried under a stack of loose papers. "Every other weekend?"

"Every weekend."

"Not gonna happen."

"All right then. Every other. Yes."

"The norm is Friday at six until Sunday at six. Work for you?"

Westley scooted forward, stretching my arm to the point of

discomfort. "Yes."

Trev scribbled a few words onto the paper before continuing. "How about one night a week. Wednesday?"

Anticipation returned to his face and I slipped my hand from his. "Yeah ... yeah."

"All right. Let's talk holidays ... school vacations as she grows older ... we may as well get all this in so you don't have to keep coming back every couple of years." He winked at me. "Not that I mind the business ..."

Over the next half hour Trev went over everything we could expect. The questions we'd be asked in court. The fight we'd be sure to get from Cindie—mostly Lettie Mae—after the papers were served. The difficulties we might encounter along the way if and when she refused to comply with the judge's orders.

"How long are we talking before she's served?" Westley asked. He propped his elbows on the armrests, laced his fingers together.

"Couple of weeks." Trev pointed his pen toward Westley. "Meanwhile, do everything you can to get her not to fight this. Promise you'll dance at her wedding if you need to, but if we can keep this thing from going to some kind of long, drawn out day in court ..."

"Got it," Westley said, confident, while I wondered what the *everything* might entail.

We stood to go. Trev walked with us all the way out to the parking lot. He shook my hand again, then slapped Westley on the shoulder. "Son," he said, thickening his drawl and winking at me again, "You done good. Got lucky and married up."

"Yes, I did," Westley said, gazing at me with all the love I could have ever imagined or hoped for.

I smiled a thank you, but deep inside, I knew better. *I* was the one who had married up, not Wes. No one of Westley's caliber—his intelligence, his good looks—had ever given me a second glance before that day in the pharmacy. So, if becoming a part-time mommy to a one-year-old meant keeping Westley, then so be it.

I was the lucky one.

Chapter Twenty-one

Cindie

The "something" she was looking for came over a BLT served with a side order of coleslaw.

"Just passing through?" Cindie asked the man with dark eyes and thick brows that, on anyone else, would have appeared wormlike. The man sitting in the farthest booth from the café door, shoulders back, legs crossed like he was somebody, reading a book like it was the most interesting thing he'd ever picked off a library shelf. A smart man, no doubt. A man like Westley.

He looked up as if he were surprised that she'd brought him his order or that he'd forgotten completely where he was at. "Sorry?"

She smiled, giving it her all. Whatever "it" was. "I don't recognize you as a local." She allowed her smile to grow. "And believe me, if you were a local, I'd know you."

The man smiled back as he slid the thick eggshell-white platter closer to his edge of the table. "Ah … yes. Small-town woes."

"You could say that."

"I did say that."

Cindie laughed then. Lightly. Not too much. This man was uptown. High class. She could spot it on him as easily as she had the night Westley walked in. The night he took her for a drive and changed her life. Of course, she had known Westley already. Had known him since she'd been a little girl. But still … that same air of sophistication Westley wore like aftershave settled around the stranger in the booth who now looked up at her as though—the book aside—she now held the title of "Most Interesting."

"Yes, sir. You did," she admitted, because she knew that men like him needed to hear they were right about the things they said. Lettie Mae hadn't taught her a whole lot, but that much she'd made sure her three daughters knew.

His eyes traveled from her face to her chest—something she was accustomed to—but didn't linger—something she was *not* accustomed to. "Cindie, is it?"

She pressed her hand against her nametag. "Yes."

"How old are you, Cindie?" He picked up the slice of dill pickle stretched out next to the sandwich. Took a bite.

"Why?"

"Graduated from high school yet?"

What was this? Twenty questions? Was he planning to ask her out on a date? Trying to figure out if she were legal enough to— "No. I had to—I dropped out." And not because she wanted to—although she couldn't tell *him* that. No, she dropped out because a fickle man named Westley Houser used her for his own need ... then left her alone and pregnant ... didn't marry her . . . married someone else ... and hadn't even bothered to *try* to come see his daughter yesterday like she'd thought he would.

The man took another bite of the pickle, small enough to swallow right away. "Did you get your GED?"

Cindie frowned now. Seriously, what *was* this? "No, sir, I did not," she said as if she were proud of it. As if she dared him to say anything against not having a high school diploma.

The man chuckled then. "I'm sorry." He pulled a napkin from the holder, wiped both hands, and extended the right. "I'm Dr. Miller," he said. "Harry Miller."

"Oh," she said, then looked over her shoulder because any minute now her boss would come around the corner. Would catch her talking to the customer longer than he preferred. Keep it moving, he always said. But Cindie knew that a little personal time spent gabbing nonsense equaled a better tip. And tips was what she lived on. "What kind of doctor?"

"Am I holding you up?" he asked. "You've got other customers. I'm sorry." He picked up one side of the sandwich that had been cut on the diagonal. "I don't want to get you into trouble. You go on. I'll eat."

Cindie nodded, then turned as the ever-annoying *ding* rang from the back. "Order up! Cindie!" She hurried to the counter, grabbed two plates of spaghetti with meat sauce, waltzed them over to Table Five, then rushed to where large pitchers of iced tea and water were stationed. She grabbed the handle of the sweet tea, taking it immediately to the booth with the doctor who had finished off the first half of his sandwich and now worked on the coleslaw. "More tea?"

The doctor looked at his glass, which had hardly been touched. "Sure."

"So … since we've pretty much established that you are not from here, where *are* you from?" Cindie asked as she topped off his drink.

"Atlanta," he said after a swallow of tea and a lift of his glass. "This is good."

"A little heavy on the sugar, if you ask me."

His eyes shone. "Like my mother used to make it."

"Oh," she said, noting that he hadn't said his wife. Noting that he also didn't wear a ring. Not that this necessarily meant anything. "So … what kind of doctor?"

He glanced at the book now closed and abandoned on the table. "I'm a professor at Dekalb College," he said. "*That* kind of doctor."

"Oh," she said again, mostly because she had no idea what he was talking about.

"I'm the head of the business department there." He reached into his shirt pocket and drew out a business card, then chuckled again. "Just happened to have one of these." He handed it to her, and she took it, rubbing her thumb over the raised lettering of his name. His title. His office phone number. "Tell me something, Cindie—and forgive me if I'm being too forward—but you've dropped out of school, you're working in a diner probably not making a lot of money, and you don't have your GED." The brow shot up. "I can't help myself here—when I see a young person, I look for the potential." He picked up the other half of the sandwich. "And you, Cindie, should be in school somewhere and not serving strangers in town BLTs."

"Well, somebody's gotta do it," she mumbled, but smiled anyway. "So, let me know if you need anything else." She left, coming back only one other time—refill on the tea again—but not to talk. Mainly because she wasn't sure she liked his insinuations—even though he was—if she were honest—completely right. She *should* be in school and not working for the nickels and dimes and sometimes quarters and half dollars left tossed on the tables for her to claim like some prize. And as if to prove himself to her, the business doctor left a tip larger than she usually totaled in a whole shift.

Days crawled by—days of carrying plates heaped with food to customers who barely understood the concept of tipping, much less actually leaving her anything to live on. Days of her mother's nonstop complaints and demands. And that's when the plan came like a much-needed breeze on a muggy summer's day full of gnats that swarmed and stuck to skin.

She left early for work that Monday morning—the start of a new week as she saw it—stepped into the phone booth just outside the café and inserted the necessary coins before dialing the number on the card.

"Dr. Miller's office," a female voice answered on the second ring. "Rita Maledon speaking."

"Um …" Cindie said, then grimaced at her stammering. She pictured the woman on the other side of the line. Pretty and slender and probably rolling her eyes. "Yes, ma'am. I'm calling for Dr. Miller."

"Dr. Miller is not in right now."

Cindie's shoulders sank. "Oh."

"May I take a message?"

"A message?" She had to think. And she had to think fast. She couldn't give her home number. Lettie Mae would want details and she didn't have them to give. And, if she did, she certainly wanted her mother as far away from them as possible. "Yes. Could you tell him that Cindie from the café in Baxter called? He-um-he left me his number. Tell him I'd like to talk to him about something. Um ... do you know when he'll be in?"

"Should be any minute now," the woman answered and Cindie now pictured a woman with styled hair wearing a pink cashmere sweater and a strand of pearls. As smartly dressed as she was smartly educated. "Did you say *Baxter*?"

"Yes. Yes, ma'am. And I'm Cindie ... from the café." She left her work number, hopeful that Dr. Miller would call back sooner rather than later. Which he did. Not fifteen minutes after she tied an apron around her waist, her workmate Midge answered the wall phone while Cindie poured coffee into the five mugs of the Monday Morning Men's Coffee Club, her heart thumping at the possibility that her future could be on the other end of the call.

"Cindie," Midge hollered out while holding the phone's handset up in the air. "For you."

Cindie rushed over. "Thanks, Midge." She brought the phone to her ear, nearly breathless, her heart hammering, so much so that she wondered if it could be heard over the din of customers and Lynn Anderson's *Rose Garden* playing from the overhead sound system her boss was so dang proud of. "This is Cindie," she said, a little too loud. She swallowed, repeated herself, this time keeping her voice low and businesslike ... the way Dr. Miller's secretary had spoken.

"Cindie? Cindie from the café in Baxter?"

Cindie turned her back to the noise around her, a smile sneaking up on her at the lilt in Dr. Miller's voice. "It is. Um—" She had so little time; she had to make each second count. "Dr. Miller, I wanted to talk to you. And it's a little busy right now, being a Monday morning and all. But I wanted to talk to you about what it would take, say, if I wanted to go to college up there where you teach."

"You'll need your GED, Cindie," he said, his tone now controlled and almost parental.

"Okay."

"Once you get that, if you need help getting in, all you have to do is call me back and I'll see what I can do from here."

"Is it—does it cost a lot of money?"

"It can. But there are grants and scholarships. Loans. Of course, you can always work part time while you go to school full time. Do you know what you want to study?"

She didn't. She only knew that Westley required a smart woman and she was nothing but a dumb girl. But she could *learn* to be smart. Surely she could. She'd learned her ABCs once upon a time. And she'd learned to add. To subtract. And she'd always been good with fractions. "Well ... what do *you* teach, Dr. Miller?"

"Business."

Oh. Yes. How could she forget? Because she was stupid, that's how. Stupid, stupid, stupid. But, business. *Business.* "I'm good with fractions," she blurted out, then gritted her teeth.

Dr. Miller laughed, but not *at* her. She could tell. She amused him, and being able to amuse him fell in her favor.

"Well, here is the part that's kinda tricky, Dr. Miller. You see, I have a little girl. She's a baby, really. A little over a year. Will that mean I can't go to college up there?"

"I already figured that was the case ... And, no. It's not impossible. A baby will make things more difficult; I'm not going to lie. But you won't be the first woman to pull it off."

Woman ... he thought of her as a woman. And he thought she could do this ... and she *could*. She had to ...

"Listen," Dr. Miller continued as the cook hollered out her name and rang the godforsaken bell. "When you get your GED, call me back. I'll see what I can do."

"I gotta go," she said.

"I know. I heard. I hope I'll hear from you again, Cindie. I have a feeling you're a very bright girl."

No. She was stupid. But she was *going* to be bright. And, when she got that way, she was going to outsmart them all.

❧

Although Cindie's body felt beat to a pulp, when she got home her mind whirred with possibilities. Of course, Michelle decided that *that* evening was a good one to be fussy. "Teething," Lettie Mae announced like Cindie didn't know the difference between cutting a tooth and diaper rash. "Rub some whiskey on her gums. That always helped with you young'uns."

Cindie retrieved her mother's favorite toddy elixir from a kitchen cabinet, shook it, caught a drop or two on her index finger, and rubbed Michelle's swollen gum. Her daughter sucked on her finger, her eyes holding to Cindie's, her lashes soaked with tears. They glistened in the moonlight streaming through the window over the sink, and Cindie swiped them with her thumb. "Sweet baby," she cooed. "Mommy is so, so sorry those nasty teeth have to hurt you. But pain is all a part of growing up … and one day, those little teeth of yours are going to be so pretty. You'll have the prettiest smile in all of Georgia. In the whole wide world."

Within a minute, Michelle had calmed, laid her head against her mother's breast, and fallen asleep. Cindie breathed a sigh of relief, then poured herself a finger's worth of the same elixir into a glass she found turned upside down in the drain. She downed it in one swallow, then shuffled into the living room where she stretched on the sofa, her daughter still asleep on top of her.

She spent the rest of the night caught between the fog of sleep and Michelle's restlessness, between her tears and drops of whiskey. She woke the next morning with a stiff neck and a headache and gratitude that she didn't have to go into work that day but also with a new reality. Many a woman may have gone to college with a baby, but she didn't see any way clear to do it.

Not that she had changed her mind on going. There were just other things to consider. And so she came up with another plan … a plan as clear in her mind as anything had ever been. She could see it. Taste it. Practically touch it. Her heart fluttered at the mere thought of it.

"Mama," she said after a hot shower, after getting herself dolled up for the first step in her independence from stupidity and toward her path of becoming Mrs. Westley Houser. "Can you watch Michelle for me? She's settled down now and I need to run an errand."

Her mother narrowed her eyes at her. "What kind of a' errand?"

Cindie sighed, counting the seconds she'd be free of all this. "I need more Kotex, for crying out loud. Must you know *everything*?"

"Don't you sass me. And don't go down there to that drugstore in Odenville neither. You don't need to come into contact with that boy. Make *him* come to you. You listen to me on that."

"Keys?"

"You hear me?"

"I *hear* you ... Keys?"

"In my purse."

She drove straight to the drugstore in Odenville where she found Westley in the Nose and Eye aisle holding a small box containing a bottle of Afrin, his eyes scanning the back of it. "Hey," she said.

He looked over at her, a smile on his lips until he recognized the bearer of the greeting. He frowned but smiled again as if he'd not known her until that moment. "Hey, yourself." He placed the box of nose spray back on the shelf with the other remedies for stuffy noses.

"You got a cold?"

"What? No ..." He pointed to the box. "This stuff is addicting. Don't ever use it."

Cindie frowned. Once she got to Atlanta, Westley would be one less person to tell her what to do. "I don't get many colds."

"Good." He turned toward her. "Are you here to tell me I can see my daughter tomorrow afternoon?"

"I need to apologize ..."

He raised a brow. "You ought to."

There it was again. Control from someone she should have the upper hand over. She could—should—resume their argument on such a line. But, if she wanted to win the war and not just the battle, she'd have to bite her tongue. For once. "No. Really." She looked around, spotted the old biddy who usually stood guard at the cash register now staring down the aisle at them. She made a face at Westley, one she hoped would ease things between them. "We have company."

Westley smiled as he raised a hand. "I've got it," he called. To Cindie he motioned toward the pharmacy and said, "Let's go back here."

Cindie followed him until they found an alcove of privacy. "Is everything okay with Michelle?"

"Oh, yeah. She's teething. Kept me up most of the night."

"I can give you something for that."

"Whiskey worked just fine."

He gave her a look that made her feel stupid all over again, which only affirmed her decision. "You gave a baby whiskey?"

"No ... I just rubbed some on her gums. That's what Mama used to do for all of us and it works." His face turned a light shade of red and she raised her hands. "Look, Wes. I didn't come to fight none. I came to ask you a favor. A big one and it's hard enough as it is. But I think you might ... not mind it ... so much."

Westley crossed his arms. Raised a brow. "A favor?"

"I need your help. See, I want to go to college. Up in Atlanta. There's one up there and I'm pretty sure I can get in, but first I got to get my GED and then I'll need help with what to do next and with things like housing and paying for schoolbooks. And see, I can work while I'm in school but—well, you've done all that and—here's the tricky part—Westley, Mama cannot know nothing until I'm already there and the deed is done."

Westley leaned toward her, eyes large and steely. "Cindie, you are *not* taking my child to Atlanta."

"What?"

"I mean it. My attorney—"

"No." She slipped her fingers over his forearms and stepped toward him. Close enough to wrap herself around him if she could. Not that she would. Not now. Because that wasn't in the plan. Not for at least another few years. "No," she said again. "I just need your help with the steps I need to take because I have no idea what to do after I get my

GED and ... Westley ... stop looking at me like that."

"You're not taking her."

"No..."

"Then—"

"I thought maybe you'd want custody of Michelle while I'm gone. You and—" Cindie swallowed back the heartache of what she was about to do. What she *had* to do. "—your wife. Allison, is it?"

His face softened and he took several shallow breaths. "Are you serious?"

"But just while I'm in school."

He blinked several times. "Are you truly, truly serious? Cindie, don't mess with me."

"*Just* while I'm in school," Cindie reiterated. She took a deep breath. Squeezed his arms to give herself strength. Strength she'd need if she was ever going to see this through. "Will you do it? Will you help me?"

Chapter Twenty-two

August 1978
Allison

Iwoke with a ton of bricks lying across my body. Not literally, but it certainly felt that way. Or, perhaps at some point during the night, I had walked into the street, a Mack truck had run over me, the driver had gotten out, thrown me over his shoulder, rushed me back into the house where my poor, unsuspecting husband lay flat on his back softly snoring, dropped me unceremoniously onto my side of the bed, and then left by the same door he had entered.

One of those two things had happened. I was sure of it. Otherwise, why would I feel so awful? Simple fatigue? Could most certainly be. Going from new bride to the full-time "mother" of a one-year-old practically overnight had taken every bit of strength I'd ever hoped to have. My days and nights were filled with her. She hadn't slept well at first, which meant restless nights for me. Nights soothing her while hoping Westley wouldn't wake up, seeing as he had to work the next day. Gradually, she became accustomed to being in her new bedroom, which brought some relief. But during the day, Michelle was a full-time job and, on his days off, Westley was bent on "doing stuff." Sometimes we went to Paul and DiAnn's and sometimes we drove up to Calloway Gardens. Other times we headed for Panama City, which wasn't far for two adults, but for two adults with a baby, the drive was an eternity.

Of course, no matter what we did, we went at it in Westley's way:

full throttle. Periodically, Miss Justine insisted that we leave Michelle with her and Rose Beth for the weekend so Westley and I could have some "alone time." As much as the thought thrilled me—and nearly sent Westley over the top with anticipation—once we were back home from dropping her off, all I wanted to do was catch up on laundry and housework... and sleep. Marabel Morgan would be sorely ashamed if, somehow, she could know.

Most of our days—mine and Michelle's—were spent at Miss Justine's. There, standing next to Rose Beth in the kitchen, I learned to cook food that Westley declared to be better than his mother's. And when I wasn't standing next to Rose Beth or tending to Michelle who had grown quite used to the layout of the massive house, I could be found sitting next to Miss Justine learning how to manage both household and business affairs, namely hers. How to balance a checkbook. And how to pay bills *before* they were due, unlike Westley who paid them a day or two *after*. Miss Justine insisted I save back at least ten percent of Westley's earnings and put another ten percent in the offering plate on Sunday mornings. "You cannot—I repeat—you cannot outgive God," she told me more than once. "I'm living proof of that."

"That's right," Rose Beth would second, were she around to hear it. "That's right." Which always left me wondering exactly where it was Rose Beth lived and to what degree God had given back to her compared to Miss Justine.

I also became quite masterful at something Miss Justine was superior at: investments. She taught me to read the stock market reports in a way no man ever could. "With a woman's eye," she said. "If we women don't learn to take care of ourselves, by ourselves, who will teach us?"

Words which always brought a hearty, "Mmm-hmm. That's what I say. Ever time," from Rose Beth. Again, this left me wondering...

But that morning in August, I sat on the edge of the bed, my hands balled into fists and pressed against the mattress, my head hanging low between my shoulders. I took deep breaths as I tried to decide whether to lie back down and hope for another half hour of sleep or to go ahead and get up. Push through.

Westley came in from the bathroom then, his hair spiky from his shower and a towel wrapped around his waist, tucked in at the hipbone. "Decided to wake up?" He started for the chest of drawers, then changed his mind and came to sit next to me. He nuzzled behind my ear, letting me know that he and I were clearly riding on different wavelengths that morning.

"Westley," I said, shrugging away from him. "I don't feel so good."

Knowing I'd yet to dissuade or refuse him, he leaned back, lifted my chin with his fingertips, and peered into my eyes. "You don't look so good either."

I hung my head again. "Thanks. And I'm serious. I feel like I'm going to throw up."

"I think you're just tired," he said, standing. The mattress rocked and I held on as if I were in a wave-pitched boat. "But if it continues during the day, let me know and I'll bring you something from the drugstore." He placed a cool hand on my forehead. "No fever."

"No."

"You've been overdoing it ..."

"Overdoing it?" I looked over at him. He'd dropped the towel to the floor and now stepped into his underwear followed by a somewhat wrinkled undershirt. "The house is a mess, the laundry's piling up again, and I feel like I hardly accomplish a single thing all day. *Every* day."

He returned to the bed with a pair of slacks he'd taken from the closet. I stared at its door, which he'd left open. "Well, I think I know how you can get caught up ..." He shoved first one leg into the pants, then the other.

"How?"

He shifted to face me. "I got a call from Cindie yesterday."

A shiver ran through me. Gooseflesh covered my body, something I'd hardly expected. Had she changed her mind? Was school not working out as she'd thought it would? Things rarely did. I could certainly attest to that. Not to too much else, but at least to *that.* "Why didn't you tell me last night?"

"I needed to process it."

"And?"

"She's coming home for a week between terms. And she wants Michelle while she's here."

As much as the idea of an entire week without the munchkin should have thrilled me, it didn't. For one, I'd grown so attached to her ... and her to me. We *fit* together. When I held her . . . the way she cradled against me. When I rocked her, the way she laid her head against my heart to hear its steady beat. When I carried her on my hip, the way her chubby hands held on, one of them usually against my breast. Something maternal had taken over me. Holding and caring for Michelle came as naturally as I ever expected holding and caring for one of my own would feel. But something else concerned me, something more important than my own feelings. "Do you think that's wise?"

"What do you mean? She's her mother, Ali. I promised her when we signed the papers that I'd never keep her from her own child."

The words stung. Yes ... Cindie was Michelle's mother. I knew that. I did. And I never wanted to take her place. Because I couldn't ... surely, I could not. "I know, Wes, but ... Michelle is just now getting used to being here. She just this week started sleeping through the night ... we'll have to start all over again."

Westley kissed my forehead and stood, once again rocking the mattress in ungodly ways. "She's a baby. She'll get over it." He looked down at me. Sick as I felt—not only physically, but now emotionally as well—I found nothing but love and compassion in his eyes. Understanding. "Look," he said. "The last thing in this world I want is Michelle over at Lettie Mae Campbell's for a week—"

"Then—"

"But I made a promise, Ali. Much as I hate it ... a promise is a promise. And she *is* her mother. Put yourself in her shoes."

I tried, but I couldn't. I could only put myself in Michelle's and my own ... and the heartache I expected to feel at having her gone for so long. Or the fear that Cindie wouldn't bring Michelle back. That she would find it impossible. "When?" I asked as a slow wave of nausea rose within me.

"She's driving home on Friday ... so she said she'd come get her Saturday morning."

"Here?" The wave grew larger. I had yet to meet Cindie and I knew, without a doubt, that I didn't want her coming to my house with it looking such a mess.

Westley's eyes narrowed as he studied me. "You look like you're going to throw up ..."

I bolted from the bed. "I am," I said around a gag. I stumbled into the small bathroom, my knees barely reaching the cold tile before I vomited into the toilet.

The wave had crashed.

Michelle woke shortly after Westley left. By then the nausea had passed and I'd managed a shower and getting dressed. I ate a slice of toast with butter and even started a load of clothes. In the sudden rush, Westley had failed to tell me—assure me—if he planned to meet Cindie somewhere other than our home. So, just in case ...

The baby and I arrived at Miss Justine's a little after ten. Rose Beth—now referred to lovingly as Ro-Bay by Michelle and, subsequently, Westley and me—opened the door with admonishment on her lips. "'Bout time," she said as the door swung wide. "Miss Justine," she hollered over her shoulder, "they're here and one of 'em looks like death warmed over."

I stepped over the threshold and into a foyer that continued to impress, but no longer intimidat me. "I take it you mean me," I said wryly.

"Well, I don't mean that sweet chile ..." She stretched her arms for Michelle, who struggled to be free of me, the irony striking harder than expected. "Come on to Ro-Bay," she said as Miss Justine's house shoes slapped against the floor in rhythm to her walk from the back of the house. "What's kept you so …" She stopped and stared at me with her fists planted on her hips. "Good land of the living, what's happened?"

"I woke up sick and then Westley …" I didn't continue. At twenty-one months, Michelle had begun repeating my words, sometimes to my delight. Often to my chagrin. "I feel fine now though."

"Mm-hmm," Ro-Bay said with a knowing look toward Miss Justine as she closed the front door and Michelle reached for one of her large-hoop gold-filled earrings. "You thinking what I'm thinking, Miss Justine?"

"What are you thinking?" I asked them both.

"Auntie Flo come to see you in a while?" she asked.

"Auntie who?"

Miss Justine chuckled as she reached me. "Come on, darling. Let's go have a talk. Rose Beth, bring us a little hot tea, will you? We'll leave you in charge of Little Bit for a while."

"Ain't I always …"

Miss Justine and I walked arm in arm toward the back of the house, Michelle's giggles becoming more distant. "Cindie's coming into town this Friday," I said both confidentially and quickly.

We stopped and Miss Justine looked up at me. "Oh, dear. I reckon I'd hoped … but of course not. She's the baby's mother." Her face grew firm. "How did Westley take it?"

"Like you," I answered with a grimace. "She's …" I couldn't say the word. I wanted to, but right then, I couldn't.

We continued toward the sunroom. "Westley is in a tough place." She tapped the center of her chest. "In his *heart,* he'd like nothing better than for you and him to be all the family that child needs. But he made a deal with Cindie and he's trying to keep it. Can't fault a man for being a man of his word."

"No, and I don't, but is this the way it will always be?"

We reached the sunroom then, its comfort and light welcoming me as it did most weekday mornings. "Until Cindie gets tired of the game and simply goes her own way ... makes another life for herself ... or ..."

"Or she comes back and takes Michelle for good."

"Is that what made you sick? The thought of losing that baby?"

"No, but it didn't help any. I woke up sick." We sat on one of the wicker sofas and I sighed. "I felt so bad when I woke up that I thought a truck had run over me during the night and left me for half dead ... but I-I really do feel better now."

Miss Justine raised her chin as Ro-Bay ambled in carrying a tea set kissed with tiny rosebuds and green leaves and all on a silver tray. Michelle waddled behind her, her Tommee Tippee cup clasped between both hands, the morning's sun casting an angelic halo over silky blond curls. "We come up with a date yet?" Ro-Bay asked as she placed the tray on the coffee table.

"A date for what?" I asked.

"The last time Auntie Flo came to visit." I scrunched my brow as Ro-Bay poured the tea and Michelle leaned her weight against my knee. "Honey, didn't your mama ever teach you nothing 'bout Auntie Flo?" She handed first one cup of tea to Miss Justine and then one to me.

"*Aunt* Flo," Miss Justine whispered, her tone filled with dignity. "Your period."

"My—"

"When was the last one?"

I paused a moment. Thinking. Calculating. "I've been so busy with Little Bit ..." I rubbed her back and she grinned at me, her clear green eyes smiling.

Ro-Bay scooped Michelle into her arms. "Y'all let me know what you work out. Me and Missy here are gon' color a pretty picture." She kissed Michelle's neck and the child giggled. "Aren't we, sweet thing?"

"Yes!" Michelle sang out.

I smiled at the child who had stolen my heart, a smile that fell when I turned back to Miss Justine. "Well?" she asked.

"Six weeks? No ... eight. Yes, eight."

"And you and Westley ... what kind of birth control are you using?" Flames ignited in my cheeks.

"Never mind. That is 100 percent none of my business." She nodded toward my cup. "Drink up. I'm going to make a phone call ... see if we can't get you in to see Dr. Sharpe this afternoon." She was halfway to the telephone bench that sat angled in the corner of the room.

I took a sip of tea, then set the cup and saucer back on the tray. "You don't think ..."

"Only one way to find out." She picked up the handset and dialed a number she apparently knew by heart. "We need to see—as we used to say back in the day—if the rabbit dies or not."

I reached again for my tea, my hand shaking. *A baby ...* a baby of my own. Not that I didn't love Michelle enough to call my own ... but a baby ... formed from the love Westley and I shared. Purely and wholly ours.

Another thought hit me ... a baby ... *and* a toddler. Not that it hadn't been done before. Hillie ... Hillie had five of her husband's children when she gave birth a year into the marriage. Which meant that Hillie and I were nearly on the same schedule.

"We're set," Miss Justine said. "Two o'clock this afternoon." She plopped down on the sofa. "Now, tell me. Have you ever had your feet in a doctor's stirrups before?"

Chapter Twenty-three

Cindie

She stood in front of her mother, hands on her hips, fingers splayed wide. Shoulders back. Breasts jutted forward. Chin up. "What do you think, Mama?" she asked the woman who filled the occasional chair in the corner of the room. A cigarette dangled between her lips and her eyes narrowed before she took a long drag, then exhaled slowly.

"What do I think about what?"

"How do I look? I'm picking up Michelle from Westley this morning."

"And since when do you care what I think about anything?"

Cindie's shoulders dropped. "Come on, Mama. Don't start this again. For the love of all that is holy, do not start this nonsense again."

Lettie Mae pulled another drag into her lungs. Held it for a few seconds before exhaling. The distance between them filled with smoke, adding to the overall dinginess of the place. If she looked hard enough, long enough, Cindie would swear she saw it clinging to the walls, adding a coat of gray to what used to be pure white. "Well, aren't you just all high and mighty? Talking to *me* about what's holy." From somewhere near the middle of the house, a door opened, then closed, followed by another door shutting. "Your brother's up, I reckon," Lettie Mae added. "Leticia sleeps to near noon on days she ain't working."

"Mama ..." Cindie took a deep breath. "Are we going to go at each other all week? Because if we are, I am not bringing Michelle here. I can tell you that much."

Lettie Mae hoisted herself up, sliding to the end of a cushion that had seen better days years prior, the center of it concave. Unsupportive. Even the flowers in the pattern looked wilted and forlorn. "And just where do you think you'll go, Priss?"

"I'll go to Velma's." Cindie waltzed over to the end table next to Lettie Mae's chair, grabbed up the pack of Salems, then pulled one out and lit it with her mother's Bic. She blew a thin line of smoke before sashaying to the sofa. "She told me I could," she said, then plopped on it.

"She ain't said no such a thing."

Cindie nodded. "Yes, she did."

"When?"

"Thursday night, when I talked to her on the phone. Told her I was coming home and that I was concerned about how you were going to behave—"

"*Me* behave?"

"And that's when she said for me and Michelle to just go out to her and Vernon's house."

"I reckon now that you got your own car you think you can just up and do whatever."

Cindie tapped her cigarette against the edge of a nearby ashtray. The gray-white ashes crumbled over the edge. Part of her deal with Westley was that in addition to getting her set up in Atlanta, he would provide a decent car. Something that wouldn't break down every five miles. He'd done better than that. "It's a fine car," she said, now taunting her mother.

"Ain't a new one."

The Fairlane was a few years old, that much was true, but it had barely been used and Westley had insisted that a mechanic give it the okay before he purchased it. Cindie hated the color—some putrid yellow—but the radio and the air conditioner worked so she kept that much of her opinion to herself. "It's better than anything you ever drove."

Jacko shuffled in on bare feet. He hadn't bothered to pull on a shirt or button the rumpled pair of jeans that hung low on his narrow hips. A line of dark hair ran from the opening to his navel. Another formed a V between his breast bones while the hair on his head stuck out in all directions. Chocolate eyes bore the telltale signs of a night of drinking. "Could y'all keep it down, please?" he mumbled. "You could wake the dang dead with all this carrying on."

Cindie stood and walked over to the young man who had grown at least two, maybe three inches since she'd seen him last. She slipped her hand under his chin as she strained to make eye contact. "You sure tied one on last night, didn't you, baby brother?"

He jerked away from her. "I need coffee," he said before ambling to the back of the house.

"Bring me a cup," Lettie Mae hollered. She ground out the nub of her cigarette. "And you," she said to Cindie, "leave him alone. He works hard over to the plant. If on a Friday night he wants to go out with his friends, then there ain't nothing wrong with it."

Cindie crushed her half-smoked cigarette before stalking after her brother. She found him in the kitchen, two mugs in front of him, pouring coffee from the percolator into the empty one. "Hey," she said, keeping her voice soft. "Wanna go with me to Velma's this weekend?" Because, for sure, she wasn't going to be able to tolerate a whole week at Lettie Mae's. She hadn't learned a whole lot in Atlanta yet, but she'd at least learned that much.

He eyed her. "For what?"

"I thought maybe you and Leticia and me and the baby could spend some time with our big sister." She looked around the room, frowning at the previous night's dishes still piled in both sinks. The trash overflowing from the can. The Formica table that needed a scrubbing in the worst way. "Don't you want to get out of this rat trap for a couple of days?" Obviously, since she'd left, the house had gone to the dogs.

Jacko chuckled as he took a sip of black coffee. "You mean get away from Lettie Mae."

"Come on," she coaxed. "We'll have a sibling weekend. We'll cook out and enjoy Mother Nature and on Sunday we can go listen to Vernon preach. I bet Velma will make a big Sunday dinner afterward ... fried chicken ... fried okra ... you know how much you love her fried okra ..."

Jacko's face lit up as much as humanly possible considering the hangover Cindie felt sure he must be nursing. "Makes Vernon's hellfire and damnation stuff worth listening to."

Cindie reached for the second mug of coffee and began fixing it to her mother's liking. "So, you'll do it?"

"I think Leticia's working this afternoon."

"Yeah, well ... I've got my own car now. I'll just drive back to town and pick her up from the café."

He took another sip as their mother called from the front of the house. "Is someone bringing me my coffee?"

Cindie rolled her eyes and Jacko chuckled again. "I'm coming," she hollered back. Then, to Jacko, "I'm meeting Westley at the drugstore in about a half hour and then I'll be back here about a half hour after that ... if I'm lucky. That gives you a whole hour to throw some things in a sack so we can get out of here as quick as possible."

Her brother nodded. "All right ... Let's go on out to Velma's."

Cindie started for the door, then turned. "And get a shower. You're too cute to go around looking and smelling like the something the dog drug into the yard."

She worried that Michelle wouldn't recognize her. After all, she'd been gone for months. And while she thought of her baby every day of the world, she was smart enough to know the same wouldn't be—couldn't be—true for Michelle.

She talked to Westley often enough. Knew the day-in-day-out of their daughter's life. Knew she was adjusting. That she wasn't sleeping through the night, but that she had stopped crying for her mama in the daytime. He never said much about his little wifey ... how she and Michelle might be getting along, but he didn't sound strained over the relationship either. Whether that gave Cindie any comfort or grief, she couldn't say. What he had done was assure her that she—*Cindie*— would always be Michelle's mother. The one who had brought her into the world. The one she would always call *Mommy.*

"You got that right," Cindie now said under her breath as she pulled her car into the wide and vacant space in front of the drugstore. She slid the gearshift to Park, then looked through the windshield stained with bug guts from her trip, to the flapping green- and white-striped awning over the store's front door. Nostalgia washed over her, and she smiled at the arched lettering of the store's name, painted across the width of one of the wide pane windows. The advertisements welcoming folks to come inside for an ice-cold Coca-Cola at the fountain ... or to pick up a box of Goody's headache powder in case the kids get too loud during summer vacation. Another showed the face of a beautiful woman, her eyes downcast, lids deeply shadowed in baby blue by Maybelline's powder-twist invention. The poster startled her; the model looking so much like the young woman she'd seen on Westley's front porch. The one who now raised her child. Held her. Fed her. Tucked her in at night. "Stop it," she admonished herself and not for the first time either. She had a plan. One she had to stick with. Because if she didn't, all would be lost. Not just for a couple of years. For a lifetime.

Cindie popped open the door and got out, made quick steps on weak legs to the store's front doors. She jerked the right open wide and stepped through to see the old woman behind the cash register looking over the rim of her cat glasses and down her nose. Cindie stopped short. Had she spied her outside? Thought that she could persuade her to turn around and go back to Lettie Mae's without Michelle?

"May I help you?" she asked.

Cindie shook her head. "Pharmacy," she answered, then made her way to the back. Her stomach turned into knots and she wondered when—if ever—she'd feel like she was as good as someone else. Or better than. Knowing she'd settle for half as good.

Anxiety kicked at her. She was about to see Michelle again. What if her daughter cried? What if she ran from her? What if—

"There's Mommy." Westley's voice cut through the cacophony of her thoughts a split second before she saw him standing at the end of the row, holding their daughter—a glorious sight of blond curls and large green eyes and rolls of baby fat that had thinned out considerably. The wide hem of her pink-and-white gingham dress lay draped over her father's protective arm, the one that held her close—his face nestled against hers.

Hers against his.

Cindie stopped. "Baby girl," she cooed.

Michelle squirmed for release and Westley gave it. Cindie squatted as her little one waddled toward her—half running, half walking ... all smiles and giggles. The overhead light reflected joy in her eyes, a clear indication that Cindie had not bargained and lost. Cindie caught her as soon as she neared. Stood. Tightened her hold. Breathed in the baby shampoo and powdery goodness of her. The light scent of her father's aftershave. She dipped her lips between her child's shoulder and neck and kissed it over and over, repeating the same words again and again. "Baby girl ... baby girl ... Mommy missed you so much."

"See," Westley now said as he drew close. "I told you she would remember you."

"Westley," Cindie breathed out. "I missed her so much." *And you,* she wanted to say, but stopped herself.

"She missed you, too."

Cindie kissed her daughter again before adding, "Not too much, I hope. I couldn't bear it if I thought she was miserable."

"She's not. I promise you, she's not." He shoved his hands into the pockets of his lab coat. "How's it going up there?"

"It's going. Job's working out ... school is good." She tossed her laughter into the air. "I forgot how hard it can be, but it's good."

He rubbed their daughter's back who turned to him before clinging again to her mother. "And your housing situation? Still good?"

"I have two roommates now...Karen works long hours downtown, goes out most evenings with her officemates. And then there's Kyle."

Westley's brow shot upward. "Karen and Kyle?"

Cindie smiled as she nodded. "Kyle is Karen's twin brother...He's hardly ever home, either, which is fine by us as long as he pays his third of the rent. He's a year ahead at DeKalb. Same program." She grinned, loving the way talking about school—about higher education—made her feel. "Oh and one of the girls I work with has been helping me with Algebra I, which is great, but I'm already dreading next term's calculus with Professor Thacker. I met him the other day and both Professor Miller and Kyle say he can be a real bear in class."

Westley pulled his hands from the pockets. Crossed his arms. "I thought you said the apartment was a two bedroom ..."

"It is," she said, shifting Michelle to the other hip, delighting in her daughter's hands on her face and even more that Westley didn't want to talk about academics. Clearly, he was more focused on the fact she lived with a guy, even a guy like Kyle. Nice and all, but no Westley Houser. "We turned the dining room into a bedroom. It's not perfect, but Kyle doesn't seem to mind." She took a step back. "By the way, we're going out to my sister's today ... to Velma's. We'll spend the weekend there."

"Let me get her little suitcase," he said before heading toward the pharmacy.

Cindie followed behind. "I made pretty good grades this term, I think. Probably no As but some Bs. Maybe one C."

Westley nodded his approval as he reached behind the counter and brought out a small suitcase, one she'd never seen before. Pink with white hearts swept upward from the base to the top, as though they were leaves caught by the wind. "That's cute ..."

"Miss Justine ..."

"How *is* your boss lady?"

He nodded. "She's good. Michelle spends a lot of time with her, don't you, sweetheart?"

Michelle squirmed toward her father's question. "And Ro-Bay..."

"Ro-Bay?"

"Rose Beth. The housekeeper."

"Oh. What about—" Cindie faltered, not wanting to say his wife's name out loud. Not now. What if Michelle heard and asked for her? Wanted her father's wife more than her own mother? She squeezed her baby closer.

"She's there, too. Don't worry."

"I wasn't." She looked toward the front of the store. "Do you want to walk us out?"

"Sure thing," Westley answered. He picked up the suitcase with one hand while the other came to rest against the small of Cindie's back, sending an electrical current through her. "I gotta get you past ole eagle eyes, don't I?"

Cindie wrapped Michelle even more tightly in her arms. "That woman gives me the willies."

Westley chuckled. "Whatcha wanna bet that if we'd have sent her over to Vietnam, the war would have not only been won, it would have been over before it got started good."

"No doubt..."

Chapter Twenty-four

Westley

He missed her. Couldn't stop thinking about her. Wondered what she was doing.

Not that it wasn't like that every day, but today was different. Today his daughter wasn't with his wife. *Or* his "boss-lady," as Cindie had so crudely called her. Or "Ro-Bay." Today she was with her biological mother who—okay, he'd admit it—looked different somehow when she'd walked in earlier. Not altogether different ... just ... changed. And it wasn't like she'd grown up much in the last few months or become smart enough to carry on an intelligent conversation past the general chitchat. But there was something about her clothes. A nice summer's dress—white, trimmed in red with matching sandals—and the way she wore her hair. That Farrah Fawcett look, it was called. And, on her, it looked becoming.

A few weeks earlier, Ali had mentioned doing the same to hers, and he'd balked, letting her know he preferred the sleek style of Jaclyn Smith to something that looked like it belonged on a Playboy bunny. "Jaclyn's got class," he'd said, pulling on Ali's tresses before gathering her to himself. Feeling her body against his own. Driving him crazy in a way he believed only she could. And, because he knew himself well enough, prayed only she would.

He glanced at his watch. Somehow, he'd made it to the middle of the afternoon. Two more hours and he could go home to Allison and, maybe, a cleaner house than they'd been living in lately. She tried. God knew she tried. But, having a toddler to run after all day—even at Miss Justine's—didn't allow for a lot of domestic tidiness. For one thing, if Westley had to guess, her mother hadn't taught her a lot on the art of home economics. Not that Mrs. Middleton didn't keep a tidy home. She did. A man could eat off the woman's floors. But he recognized in his mother-in-law the tendency to do everything for her family ... except prepare her daughters for life outside of their familial home.

Westley counted twenty-eight capsules of erythromycin, careful now not to allow his thoughts to get in the way of his job. Whatever waited for him at home would be whatever waited for him at home. What with all the new expenses—Cindie's initial demands, Michelle's needs, and a new wife—his life had catapulted to a place where the notion of losing his job—not to mention his career—over a silly mistake was unthinkable. Still, his mind wandered, if only for a moment. He and Ali should use this week for more than the day to day. They needed to get away. He was off Sunday and Monday; they could ride over to Paul and DiAnn's. Enjoy the lake. A little time on the boat. Maybe even stay over.

It had been a while.

He labeled the prescription bottle, slid it into a small white bag with Knight's Pharmacy logo plastered across the front, then dropped it into the basket marked with a large "M" before picking up the phone and dialing a number scrawled on a nearby pad of paper. He waited through three rings before Naomi Morgan answered the phone. "Mrs. Morgan?"

"Yes," the thirty-something woman answered, her voice groggy with the infection her doctor had prescribed the antibiotic for.

"This is Westley Houser over at Knight's Pharmacy, Mrs. Morgan. Just wanting to let you know that we've got that prescription ready for you."

"Oh," she said, and he briefly pictured her, lying in bed, hair sticking up on all sides, dark circles under eyes that typically sparkled with life. "I-um ..."

"Mrs. Morgan, do you have someone who can come by to pick it up or do you need it delivered?" She coughed. Hard, the phlegm breaking from her lungs. Westley held the phone from his ear and grimaced. "Tell you what," Westley said then. "I'll have our delivery boy run that on over to you. You don't sound like you need to be outside."

She coughed again before agreeing and calling him "sweet for doing this."

"Not a problem, Mrs. Morgan," he told her. Because, *sweet* as he could be, this wasn't about his kindness. Home delivery was something Miss Justine prided herself in, reminding those who worked for her that if their customers were sick enough to need a prescription, they surely didn't need to be out and about, getting worse while spreading their germs. "We'll have it over there to you in about a half hour and we'll bill you first of the month."

"Thank you, again," she said, then hung up.

Westley smiled. *Morgan.* The last name made him think of the author of that book Ali was reading. The one she didn't know he knew about. The one she'd slid between the sofa cushions and he'd found one evening while she bathed Michelle. He'd flipped through it. Saw that the first part of it instructed women on being organized. Apparently, his lovely bride had skipped most of that part and headed straight to parts two and three, which were about adoring your husband and having playful sex with him. Westley shook his head as he flipped the pages and chuckled—Allison Houser could have *written* that part of the book.

He glanced at the clock again; he was even more ready to go home.

He pulled into the driveway a little after five thirty. Spied his wife's face peering around the front window draperies. Wondered if she was going to meet him at the door wearing something crazy like the Morgan woman wrote about in her book. Decided he really didn't care if she did or she didn't. Besides, he had a surprise for her.

She opened the door before he reached the front porch. She

wasn't wearing pink baby doll pajamas and go-go boots, but she looked stunning in a moss-green, one-piece jumpsuit that hugged all the places it should and flowed around the rest. Instead of the typical ponytail she'd found easier with a near-two-year-old, she wore her hair down. It lay upon her bare, tanned shoulders in thick waves. "Wow," he said, stopping.

Ali turned, slowly, allowing him to admire her in the way a husband should. And he did. God knew he did more than he could have ever imagined he would. "Wow," he said again. "If I'd known this was waiting for me, I would have clocked out sooner."

She giggled. "Come in before the mosquitos do."

Westley crossed the threshold and stopped again, breathing in the scent of lemony furniture polish and a collection of vanilla-scented candles in various heights that flickered on the dining room table. He scratched his head, teasing. "Am I in the right house?"

His wife slid her arms around his shoulder and kissed him soundly. Passionately. "Don't get too excited," she said, and he wondered exactly what she meant. About the house or over her?

Westley grabbed her waist and squeezed. "Too late," he muttered.

Ali leaned back. "And don't get any funny ideas," she said. "Dinner is ready."

He pulled her back to him. Nuzzled at her ear. "What are we having?"

"Your favorite—glazed pineapple chops with scalloped potatoes and green beans."

He looked at her. Raised a brow. "Ro-Bay has been here, hasn't she?"

She pouted, playfully. "All right, you found me out. She cleaned while I cooked."

Westley kissed the tip of her nose. "Does that mean I get to cuddle with Ro-Bay, too?"

She snuggled up close. "I better be the only woman you *ever* cuddle up to, Westley Houser."

This time he kissed her, kissed her with as much passion as she had him. "I promise," he told her. "You're the only one for me."

And he meant it.

Allison

"I love you," I whispered.

Westley lay on the sofa with me up against him. Our dinner had been eaten—the dishes left on the table, the kitchen back to its old messy state—and the candles glowed from the next room. Only moments before, while Westley adjusted the sofa's pillows and stretched along the full length of the old couch, I dropped *The Carpenters: A Song for You*—my old go-to album—onto the turntable of our stereo, then turned the volume high enough that the music filled the room, but low enough that we could talk. Now, as Karen Carpenter's throaty and soothing voice cooed into a microphone, I did the same along the lobe of my husband's ear. "I love you so much," I said.

He brushed my hair from my shoulder, the teasing of his fingertips sending chills down my arms. Up my legs. "You know you're the only girl for me, right?" he asked.

I nodded, wondering what made him say such a thing. He'd seen Cindie that morning. Handed their child over to her. Had she come on to him? Had he been intrigued by her? I'd only seen her in those veiled moments as she drove up and down our street all those months ago, so she seemed a mere shadow to me. A shadow that hovered over our house and sometimes crept into our rooms.

"We have a good life here, don't we, Ali?"

I nodded again, trying to squash the molecules of trepidation that requested a ride on the coattails of my gooseflesh.

"You, me, and Michelle?"

Yes. Him, me, and Michelle. But not Cindie. Oh, thank God, not Cindie. The last person in the world I wanted in the mix of the news I'd waited nearly two days to share with my husband was *her*. It was enough that I had to deal with the shadow ... enough that I looked at Michelle and wondered what part of her mother rested in her face ... curled her hair ... determined her mannerisms. I nodded, closing my eyes for a moment to gain control. Knowing I could not let Cindie Campbell be a part of this evening, not even in the slightest of ways. "What if ..." I began, then laid my cheek against his shoulder and inhaled the honied muskiness of what was left of his cologne. "What if it could be even better than that?"

Westley pressed his lips against my forehead. "Tell me how that's even possible," he murmured.

I lifted my face to his, fearful from the sound of his voice that he was about to slip off to sleep. That he would miss my announcement. "Westley," I whispered. "I'm pregnant."

Half-closed eyes grew full and dilated with surprise. He rose slightly, though not enough to disturb the pattern of our bodies. "What?"

I grinned. Nodded.

His hand slid up my hip and to the flat of my stomach where it rested. He shifted more fully, bringing me flat to my back, him hovering over me. Protectively. Seductively. "Are you sure?"

I nodded again. "Miss Justine took me to the doctor."

His fingers stretched. Gripped. "So that's why—"

"Mmmhmm."

He kissed me. Lightly, then without reservation. "I love you," he groaned, then sat up as if a revelation had come to him, bursting through the room on a flash of lightning. He blinked several times. Ran his fingers through his soft curls.

I raised up on my elbows, stunned by the suddenness of his movement, needing him to return and yet wanting to know the source of his actions. "What is it?"

My husband chuckled and his brow rose. "We're gonna need a bigger house," he said, reminding me of Brody in *Jaws* when he said, "You're gonna need a bigger boat."

I laughed, more with relief than anything else. "I think we'll be fine here for a while. I've already thought of how we can turn Michelle's room into half nursery, half toddler's room."

But he shook his head. "No. Michelle will need her own space.

She'll want to play with her toys and the baby will be sleeping and—*a baby.*" He looked at me, his expression wide with wonder, lips parted in the sweetest of smiles. "I simply cannot believe—a baby..."

I wondered then, ridiculously, how Cindie had told him of her pregnancy. How he'd reacted. Obviously not with joy. Or expectation or wonder. "March," I said then.

"March?"

"The baby is due in March. So, it's still early. We have plenty of time to think about nurseries and new houses and all that." I sat up, adjusted the material of the jumpsuit that had become twisted around me. "But whatever you want to decide, Westley. Stay here or find a bigger place ... whatever you say is fine by me."

He slid closer. Kissed me again. "How did I ever find someone as wonderful as you?"

I grinned at him, tilting my head to make myself look more cartoon than wife. "You didn't," I reminded him. "I found you ... behind the pharmacy counter." I pointed to my throat. "I was getting sick, remember?"

My husband tweaked my nose. "Luckiest day of my life."

I sobered. "Mine, too. I'd take a hundred sore throats—the sorest— if it meant finding you."

We stared at each other for long moments, barely blinking, lips parted. From the next room the candles flickered, sending shadows dancing across the walls and into the living room. One song came to an end, fading into a musical measure of notes. The crackling of the album replaced it ... and then another song began.

I rested my head on Westley's shoulder, awkwardly. Not that I cared. I didn't. I only knew one thing—the words of the song were true. "I won't," I whispered.

Westley moved us into a more comfortable position, then kissed my temple, his lips warm and moist. "You won't what?"

"Last a day without you ..."

Chapter Twenty-five

Westley and I rose early the next morning, assuring enough time for me to get over my morning sickness and for us to gather a few things together, throw them in the car, and head over to Paul and DiAnn's. With the top down, August's sun beat down on our bodies, already tanned by the summer. With Westley anxious to hit the lake as soon as we arrived, we were in our swimsuits—me with a cover-up and Wes with a V-neck tee.

"What do you think they'll say when we tell them that I'm pregnant?" I asked, already excited.

Westley grinned as he stared straight ahead. "They'll be happy for us," he said.

I crossed my legs, looked out the window at the now-familiar roadside. We'd made this trip so many times since we'd married, usually with Michelle. She adored the water . . . the boat . . . delighted in watching her father ski. Paul and DiAnn doted on her, showered her with gifts every time we came. So much so that I'd asked Westley to talk to them about it, to tell them that she would become spoiled and learn to expect something every visit. "It's fine," he said, dismissing my concern. "Don't worry so much. They love doing it and they can afford it."

I looked again at my husband—so amazingly handsome. Like an ad in a fashion magazine. "Do they know that Michelle is at her—is at Cindie's?"

He glanced at me then, catching my hesitation and knowing its source. "It's okay, sweetheart. You can say it ... Cindie *is* her mother."

"I know. I just—it had all felt so real and then, especially now ..." I pressed my hand against my stomach. "I don't know how to feel."

"Meaning?"

I paused long enough to—for once—think before I answered. What had I meant? Did I *want* to be Michelle's mother? Did I wish in some crazy way that it had been me who gave birth to her? Me, who she called her best spin on Ali—*Adi.* I had fallen in love with her; that much I knew. I knew and I now understood why Westley had been so determined to gain custody of her—not just because of whatever Cindie lacked, but because of all that Michelle gave from her tiny little self.

"Ali?"

I shook my head. "I'm hormonal. Ignore me."

But he reached for my hand just the same. Gave it a warm squeeze. "I think they'll be thrilled."

"I think they'll go broke if they keep up the gift giving once the baby comes." I turned a little toward him, the seat belt pulling against me. "Wes, why do you think they haven't had children yet? They've certainly been married long enough."

Westley shrugged. "I don't know. Paul's never mentioned anything ... I don't even know if they're trying." He chuckled. "I mean other than ... you know, the usual *try.*"

I slapped at him. "Now there's a picture in my head I don't need."

Within minutes Westley parked the car in front of the large house—so much larger when I compared it to ours. Not that I cared. I loved every square foot of our home, especially since Michelle had come into it. I grabbed my beach bag and slung it over my shoulder.

Unlike our first trip when Paul and DiAnn practically waited at the door in anticipation of our arrival, the front porch stood quiet and empty. Now, with our frequent visitation—sometimes just for dinner, other times for the weekend—we were no longer guests at all. As Paul quipped, "You're family, by golly, so act like it and just walk on in."

DiAnn hadn't seemed too charmed by that idea, so I insisted we knock upon arrival. Once we got inside, I did everything I knew to make DiAnn see me as her sister-in-law. I happily helped in the kitchen. On weekend excursions, I stripped the beds and put on fresh linens before we left to go back home. I even washed the sheets, threw them in the dryer, and folded them, placing them back in the tiny upstairs hall closet as my final act of "family" duty. Still, DiAnn remained somewhat distant to me. Accepting, but distant.

After knocking two or three times and getting no answer, we decided to walk around to the back of the house. Sure enough, Paul and DiAnn—both clad in their suits—were at the dock—Paul on his knees, appearing to tinker with the boat's engine. "Hey there," Westley called out, waving as if we'd just returned home from an extended trip at sea.

"Ahoy," Paul called back as if he'd read my thoughts. "Got some issues down here."

"Oh, no," Westley muttered, leaving me to wonder if his disappointment was for what this may mean for his brother ... or for him and his weekend plans.

We hurried toward the dock, my flipflops slapping against my heels. The grass—which needed a cut—licked at my ankles, while gnats, already up and pesky, fluttered around my face. I blew them away with the trained act of every southern child. Bottom lip out and *whew*. "What's going on?" Westley asked as soon as we stepped onto the dock and over the skis that had been laid there half forgotten.

"Engine sounds funny..."

DiAnn shook her head as she pulled large sunglasses to the top of her head, pushing her blond hair back to reveal the elegant lines of her face. My shoulders sank. How could one woman be so put together without makeup? Not to mention so early in the morning? Even the humidity refused to torment her. She walked toward us as I ran my hand over my ponytail, hoping to slick some of the frizz out. "Wes," she said in a commanding tone I hadn't grown accustomed to, "your job is to convince him there is absolutely nothing wrong." She nodded toward me. "Come on, Allison. Let's go up to the house and get the picnic ready."

I turned obediently and headed back up the slope of their backyard, this time with DiAnn by my side, asking her usual field of questions. How have I been ... how was her grandmother ... did she still insist on a proper tea at four o'clock ... and that sort of thing. I'd often wondered if it bothered DiAnn that I spent so much time with Miss Justine, but she never mentioned it outright, so I figured not. After all, DiAnn, like her grandmother, wasn't one to beat around the bush. Whatever she thought, she said. "So, how does it feel not to have Michelle in tow?" she asked when we reached the back door.

"Odd," I admitted. "I have kinda gotten used to the little squirt." We slipped inside where cold, manufactured air met us and I breathed out a sigh. "Already hot out there."

"Too hot." Most of the ingredients for making sandwiches had been placed on the bar between the breakfast nook and the kitchen. "Get the mayo for me, will you?" she asked as I dropped my beach bag onto a chair.

"Sure thing."

DiAnn worked the twisty-tie free from a loaf of bread as I fished the mayo from a refrigerator that stood full to overflowing. Unlike ours. I only purchased what I knew we needed for the week, using nearly all of it before heading back to the store seven days later. Not because I worked economically as the housewife of our home but because I couldn't think any further ahead than a one-week period. "Have you met her yet?" DiAnn asked as I brought the mayo to her.

"Who?"

"Cindie." Her expression told me I should have anticipated the answer.

I shifted a little, then grabbed the packet of sandwich meat and pried it open. "No."

"A piece of work, that one is."

"That's what Westley says. But he ... he also says she is Michelle's mother and ..."

DiAnn slapped mayonnaise onto a slice of bread. "And how are you feeling about that?"

I shrugged, suddenly concerned as to where our conversation was headed. We'd never had anything close to this kind of moment. Not really. "I don't know. He's right. She is." I started placing the meat on the prepared bread, then brought my attention back to her. "Do you want me to get the cheese?"

DiAnn gave me a half smile. "Sure." Then, after I opened the refrigerator door again, she added, "Well, I'd watch out for that one."

I peered over my shoulder, aware now that the room had grown darker, as if the sun had decided to find a cloud to hide behind. "Cindie?"

"Yes."

I returned to the bar, a large package of sliced cheese in hand, my stomach suddenly revolting against any thoughts of Cindie. Or, perhaps morning sickness had returned on their wings. "Why?"

DiAnn shook her head; the overhead light reflected in the dark lenses of her sunglasses. "Cindie isn't the brightest bulb in the box, but she's cunning. Trust me. She grew up under the leading of Lettie Mae Campbell."

"I've heard some things ..."

My sister-in-law reached for the mustard and unscrewed the top. "Whatever you've heard, multiply it by about a hundred." She opened a drawer near her hip, grabbed a knife from the silverware tray, then dipped it into the jar. "The only decent one—in my estimation—is the oldest sister, Velma. But if you ask me, she would have done better to have left town instead of just moving out in the country."

I found that a strange thing for her to say considering she and Paul lived *out in the country*. "Westley told me about her. She's married to a preacher, right?" I tore the protective covering over the cheese, then pulled six of the wrapped slices from the stack.

"How she turned out so well, I'll never—" She stopped as the back door opened and our husbands walked through. I looked at her. Studied her. Wanting to see some telltale sign of being caught talking about Cindie. About her mother and her sister. Wondering if she'd feel the need to explain herself to Westley as though she'd breached a confidence I'd yet been made privy to.

But there was none of that. Not from DiAnn Houser, at least. "Well?" she asked. "Are we going or is the boat out of commission?"

"I think we'll be fine," Paul answered, "if the weather behaves."

Westley ambled in, sliding his arm around me, his hand gripping my waist. "You feel all right?" he said, low and in my ear.

I stared up at my husband in wonder that he had sensed my sudden queasiness and hoping he couldn't guess why as Paul explained the complexities of the engine and how he and Westley had master-mechaniced it back to rights.

"What's wrong?" Paul asked, abandoning his tale. "Have you been sick, Ali?"

I shook my head. "Just a little ..."

"Pregnant," Westley blurted, not waiting for the perfect time to announce our news.

A flurry of activity broke out around us—DiAnn reaching for me with a firm but quick hug. Paul patting Westley on the back, quipping, "You don't wait long, do you?"

"It was a—not planned," I stammered, heat rising in me, hoping they were not picturing Westley and me in bed, making this tiny person who grew inside me.

"You look like you could use some fresh air," DiAnn now said. But she stole a look out the storm door and said, "Dark clouds are gathering," as though the weather had some nerve.

"Nah," Westley answered. "It wouldn't dare rain. Not today. Not on us." He walked around the bar and began to insert the sandwiches into small bags. "I say let's get this party started. I'm ready to feel the water beneath my feet."

By the time we made it back to the boat, which the tempestuous water rocked and bumped against the frame of the dock, my knees had gone to butter. My stomach to jelly. "Westley," I said, turning toward him and away from the motion. "I think maybe I should go back inside. Lay down a while."

"Don't be silly, sweetheart. You'll be fine once you get out there."

I looked over my shoulder to where DiAnn and Paul yanked knots from the ropes that tethered the boat to the dock's security ... on out to the lapping water against the shorelines of the narrow canal that, if we followed the snaky path, would lead us to the Flint River. On the other side of Paul and DiAnn's property, trees stretched upward from a tangle of shrub, their leaves dancing, the pine needles shimmering in the dim sunlight of a morning that wanted to retreat as badly as I did. "Westley ..."

"Come on," he said, turning me toward the boat and Paul's extended hand. "You'll sit up front with Paul and help him navigate and watch DiAnn and me do our tricks. What with all the fresh air you'll breathe in, you'll feel fine in no time."

"I'm not so sure," I protested, my voice sounding more like a whimper than a roar.

His eyes found mine, pleading. "Would I ever lie to you?"

"No," I answered, wondering if his lie by omission fell into the same category.

I stepped toward the boat. Toward Paul, who took my hand and guided me until the fiberglass flooring rocked beneath me without provocation. I breathed in and out, found the cushy seat that swiveled from front to back, and lowered myself onto it. I closed my eyes as the boat continued to sway and attempted to absorb the sounds around me. The rhythm of DiAnn and Westley gently tossing skis into the back of the boat, then slipping into their life vests. Paul donning his.

"Sweetheart." Westley's voice came from overhead. I looked up. He held another vest—mine—wide for me to slide into. I held out my arms and he placed it on me as though I were a child. As though I were Michelle and it was time to go to school or church ...

... something Westley had become strangely adamant about in the time since we'd gained custody of his daughter. *Our* daughter.

"Here you go," he said. He knelt before me and clasped the sides of the vest together, locking them to keep me safe. "Can't have you going overboard and drowning," he added with a wink, which made me smile. "That's my girl." He kissed me. "You're looking better already."

"I feel ... strange ..." I said to him. "Hot."

"It's just the rocking of the boat with a touch of morning sickness and a soaring temp of about ninety. Once we get it out, it'll get better." He kissed me again, then stood and joined DiAnn at the back of the boat.

Paul turned the key and the engine came to life. He backed the boat out, glanced upward and said, "The sun's making a dent in the clouds." Then, to his brother, "I think you're right, Wes. I think it's going to break."

Westley grinned as he turned on the portable radio, twisting the knob until he found the station of his choice. Until Peter Frampton's guitar permeated the air around us. Within fifteen minutes we were in the river, DiAnn and Westley performing their tricks. My husband's lack of fear became more and more evident each time we came here while I shuddered to think of all the things that could happen, even as I kept Michelle wrapped in my arms, listening as she cried out, "Me, too, Daddy! Me, too!" and wondering at what point her father would purchase little baby skis for her and have her out there, slicing into a wake.

I shifted in my seat, tucking one foot under.

"You okay?" Paul called out over the whipping wind that pulled his hair straight back and mine forward so that it hit my face like needles from a pine bough.

I nodded. "My back hurts a little. I just needed to shift."

He smiled. Brought the speed back up. I turned my attention back to Westley who lay nearly flat against the water now, teasing nature with his flamboyance. I laughed then, the sound of it catching in my chest as intensity pulled low and unwelcomed.

Something was wrong ... horribly wrong.

I shifted again and, feeling a familiar but unwanted wetness, twisted to look at the white vinyl seat beneath me.

It was smeared with blood.

Chapter Twenty-six

September 1979
Patterson

Dr. Patterson Thacker stretched on the sofa in his home office, arching his spine and feeling it pop. He blinked at the room made of heavy draperies, rich colors, dark wood wainscoting that gave way to bookshelves, a multipaned picture window, and double doors leading to the remainder of the house. The furniture was masculine and smelled of pipe tobacco and the lemony wax the housekeeper applied weekly. Axminster rugs that had cost him a near fortune lay somewhat flat and somewhat wrinkled and mostly curled on the corners, showing scant lines of the hardwood beneath. The bookshelves held a library of rare books as well as those he'd studied from in college and those he simply liked because they were considered classics and the writing was good. Books he'd read time and again. Would read time and again. This was his place of comfort. His reprieve. Where he stopped being who or what everyone else wanted and became only himself.

His home rested along the outskirts of Druid Hills—an Atlanta suburb recently added to the National Registry of Historic Places—in a house made solely of red brick. A gothic sort of home where his wife entertained lavishly, inviting only those who hailed from the city's A-list, and he retreated to his study as often as possible. Nightly, in fact.

Patterson chuckled as he crossed his legs at the ankles on the leather-tufted sofa that both warmed and chilled him, thinking that this was one thing he and his old man had in common. That and a penchant for living life like a dead man. Going through the motions for the sake of what was expected. Obtaining an impressive degree, marrying the right girl, siring the right number of children—not too many, not too few.

He adjusted the large earphones that kept him bound to the enormous stereo system Mary Helen had given him for his birthday a week ago. Since then, he'd hardly come out except to go to work ... eat dinner ... and then sleep on one side of a large king-sized bed while Mary Helen lay like a stone on the other.

Ah, music ... The one constant in his life had been music. He couldn't play a single instrument. Didn't know middle C from F sharp. But he took pleasure in the power and majesty of it. The boasting of it. He could determine all the instruments in nearly every work. Knew the French horn from the piccolo. The acoustic guitar from the 12-string, the bass from the lead. He could also tell anyone who may be interested about nearly every form of music, from Chopin to Dylan, from Sinatra to The Eagles, from Billie Holliday to Fleetwood Mac, which—amped up—pulsed through his body at present.

He closed his eyes, tapped one socked foot to the beat of Mick Fleetwood's straightforward drumming, breathed in and out, enraptured completely by the contralto voice of Stevie Nicks. By the sultriness. That low rasp and the way it warbled as it climbed the scales. He imagined her, for a moment—one longer than he intended—lying possessed in his arms ... begging him to love her as she'd never been loved before. Certainly better than Buckingham ever could. Or Henley. Or Fleetwood, according to the latest music gossip.

A tap on his shoulder startled him and he jerked upright to see his wife standing over him, her arms now crossed and a frown on an otherwise flawless face. He blushed as though she'd read his thoughts—and perhaps she had. They'd been together long enough that she should be able to. But, if that were so, she'd have divorced him by now. Divorced him and taken him to the cleaners, as the saying went.

How could so much sweetness have turned so sour in fourteen

years? He'd often wondered if perhaps they shouldn't have married on such a hot day—that the gods had aligned against them, starting with that. Or that they should have waited a little longer. Or perhaps that he shouldn't have dallied around with Dani beforehand or Rita since. But he'd thought—no, believed—back then, that it would all turn out okay. That they'd have everything and more. A beautiful home, which they did. Although, compared to his childhood home, the rooms were smaller but the closets larger. A perfect number of family members—three wonderful daughters who excelled at everything they did, even five-year-old Helen-Leigh. A social life to rival his parents'.

And they did. They said all the right things, moved in all the right circles, dressed in all the right clothes, and sent their girls to all the right schools—from preschool on.

But what they didn't have was passion. Not an inkling of it. What Mary Helen had declared as chastity before wedlock had turned to duty in marriage. For all their years together, he'd never once made her cry out. Never once felt the earth move in the throes of their lovemaking. It was all ... just ... duty.

"You scared me," he said, pulling the headphones off.

"Well, if you wouldn't act like you're still in college ..."

"Did you need something?" he asked, ignoring the jab while keeping his voice in the same tone as when his secretary buzzed him or poked her head around his office door.

"You have a phone call."

He furrowed his brow and looked at his watch. "This late?"

"Harry Miller's secretary. She says it's important ..."

He turned his head in case heat rose to his face again, making a bigger to-do out of putting the headphones away than necessary. "I'll take it in here," he said.

Mary Helen left on the same chilled wind she'd most likely entered. He stepped around to the back of his desk. Picked up the handset and waited until he heard his wife on the extension. "I've got it," he said, then waited for her to hang up, which she did. Loudly. "Rita?"

"Sorry to call you at home, but you said it was urgent."

Patterson sank into his chair and it squeaked, then sighed. "I didn't say urgent, Rita. I said *as soon as you can.*"

"Sounded urgent to me."

He pulled a small notebook from one of his desk drawers, flipped it open to a clean sheet, then grabbed one of the half dozen pens scattered on the cluttered desktop. "Did you find out anything?"

"You know," she said, her voice taunting, "only an ex-lover who still cares for you would go to all this trouble ..."

"The *ex* part was your decision. Not mine." And not just once either, he reminded himself. Between his wife's frigidity and his mistress's on-again-off-again mindset, he'd wondered at what point he'd simply lose his faculties and commit himself to a residential hospital. Preferably on a deserted island.

Or, perhaps, he could have the next best thing.

"I know," Rita finally said, and he brought the pen upright. "You're right."

"As you've said before. So? You have information for me?"

"I do. Her name is Cindie. Cindie Campbell."

"I know that, Rita. She's my student."

"Well ... *Dr. Thacker* ... I found out from her files that she came here, you may be interested to know, on Dr. Miller's recommendation."

A gust of breath pushed itself from Patterson's lungs. "Harry?"

"Don't go overboard. You and I both know Harry Miller is as faithful to his wife as a church mouse is to his cheese. When I oh-so-casually questioned Harry about her, he said he'd met her on a return trip from Tallahassee and found her—and I quote—interesting. You know Harry and his lost causes."

"Hmmm."

"There's more, of course, if you're ready."

He poised his pen over the paper; the dim light from the desk lamp caused a long shadow to slice across the page. "Yes."

"She's from some little town in southwest Georgia I've never heard of and you probably haven't either. Has a nearly three-year-old child who was born out of wedlock—"

"Stop. She's only—what—eighteen? Nineteen?"

"She'll be twenty in about two months. January twelfth, if you were thinking to buy her anything."

"Is the child with her? Here?" Because that would change things. Most things, in fact, if not all things.

"No. The child—a little girl—lives with her father back home, according to Dr. Miller, while the object of your interest resides in a small apartment off campus with two others—a brother and a sister. And she's working over at Rhinestones. Which means—"

"I know what it means." Rhinestones was known for its scantily clad waitresses who flirted with the predominantly male patrons while serving tables, which meant Cindie was exposed to too many other men for Patterson's liking.

"Patterson, please tell me you're not thinking of doing anything stupid," Rita said, sounding more like a sister than a woman who, once upon a time, kept him warm in bed.

Again, heat rose to his face. Rita breathing down his neck was the last thing he needed. "No, no. She's having trouble in my class," he said matter-of-factly. "I only want to see what I can do to help her. I thought a little background would help—would help me know where she's coming from. It's obvious she's a fish out of water."

"But such a darned pretty fish ..."

Yes. Yes, she was. And she reminded him so much of Stevie, who he could *never* have beneath him. And a little of Dani, whom he'd most likely never see again. But her ... Cindie Campbell ... "What else do you have?"

"She's a high school dropout. Got her GED before applying to DeKalb. Comes from the poorer side of town, as Billy Joe Royal used to sing it—"

"Poor."

"What?"

"Johnny Rivers—not Royal—sang *The Poor Side of Town*. Not poorer." He'd also written it, but that was beside the point.

"Well, pardon me for living." She paused long enough for him to apologize, which he didn't. For pity's sake—Music of the '60s 101. "Anyway. She got her GED, came up here on some scholarships and Dr. Miller's recommendation and there you have it," she fired off.

"Thank you," he said after scribbling a few undecipherable notes onto the paper. "I owe you one."

"You're darned right you do."

He closed his eyes, squeezing them as he gripped the phone's handset tighter than need be. "I'll see you tomorrow ..."

"Patterson," she said then, her voice whispery soft.

"What?"

"Tell Mary Helen I'm sorry for interrupting her evening."

"Shut up, Rita."

She laughed, then disconnected the call.

Patterson drew a circle around the initials of Cindie's name—CC— and smiled. Everything in his life had been heading for the dumpster until two weeks ago when *Little Stevie Nicks* walked into his classroom. He'd seen from the first day that she was out of her element. That calculus didn't—and wouldn't—come easily to her. And while he'd tried to get her out of his mind—while he'd tried to stop the plot from forming—he found that he could not. Somewhere down the line he had to have at least one thing—one person—he could control, rather than feeling as if the whole world controlled him.

He had hoped it would be her. Now that he knew about the child born out of wedlock, he was pretty sure he could bank on it. Unless, of course, she'd had some kind of spiritual conversion, which the job at Rhinestones negated.

Everything balanced; he'd make certain she both understood and passed calculus and she'd give him the one thing Mary Helen and Stevie could not.

Tomorrow, a new life would begin. Piece of cake.

Chapter Twenty-seven

Allison

The second chapter in Mrs. Morgan's marriage book talked about redeeming time. Not yesterday's time. Tomorrow's. Which, in some sense, becomes today's. According to her theory, to *redeem time*, to make it work with you rather than against you, the *total woman* will sit down at night and compile a list of all the things she needs to do *tomorrow*. Then she numbers them according to importance. Priority. She then tackles them, Mrs. Morgan says, one at a time, never skipping to #2 until #1 has been completed. And certainly never worrying about #5 until numbers one through four are done.

According to Mrs. Morgan, Mrs. Kennedy kept such a list that was maintained hourly during her time as First Lady in the White House.

So who was I to go against the tide of Mrs. Kennedy?

To be honest, at first, I had no intention of keeping such a list. It seemed almost *too* adult, even for someone like me who, in the short course of a year, had grown up way more than I ever thought possible. But then Julie talked about her list as though it were the Ten Commandments, never to be deviated from. And, I noticed, Miss Justine kept a list—although the notion that Miss Justine had ever read *The Total Woman*, much less put its mandates to practice, seemed too far-fetched. So I finally broke down, purchased a composition book, and began my own daily lists of tasks—some of vital importance (like making dinner, dressing Michelle, dressing *myself,* and going to work) and some not quite so important (sweep the back porch, organize my sock drawer, write a letter to Grand). If I got to those things, more power to me, but if I didn't, they'd save for another day.

My only concession—my only personal stamp—was that I didn't compose the list at night in some cosmic expectation concerning the next day. Instead, I got up before the sun—who would have ever guessed I was a morning person—made coffee, and then sat at the dining room table with a steaming cup, my composition book, and a Bic pen.

Remarkably, Mrs. Morgan was as right about the making of a list as she was about most of the things in the book. At least as far as Julie and I were concerned.

Julie, whose second child was due in about three months. Julie, whose life—in spite of being married to a man we'd originally deemed "the bum"—had turned out more perfect than any of us could have imagined. Dean's job had not only provided steady income, in one year he'd won an award for a piece he'd written, published in a column he'd created. *Lowcountry Profiles of Chatham* had become—to my father's shock and my mother's delight—the *must-read* of the Sunday paper. Right after their first child—a boy, my nephew—had been born, Dean and Julie purchased a ranch-style home in a subdivision so new, the front-lawn sod hadn't fully rooted to the earth. Three bedrooms, all of which would soon be filled.

I, on the other hand, had managed to miscarry not once but twice. And while Westley had become the darling of downtown and Michelle was the princess of everywhere she went, I had morphed into the shadow who stood behind them both. Even Cindie—according to the reports she gave Westley who then thought it was his duty to share with me—glowed in every hall of DeKalb College, her academic scores impressive. Except, as Westley had informed me a few nights earlier, for calculus, which she worried would be her undoing.

"When did you talk to Cindie?" I asked, my hands busy wiping a dish already dry enough to go into the cabinet where it belonged. I looked over my shoulder, wanting to read his expression, but finding nothing noteworthy.

He leaned against the kitchen doorframe, a cup of instant decaf coffee in hand, and blew at it, his eyes locked on me. "This afternoon." He took a sip of the drink, then swallowed as if it may have still been too hot to consume.

"She called?" I placed the bowl in the cabinet; my angst over Cindie's calls was no need to rub the pattern off.

"Like clockwork. Every Monday, Wednesday, and Friday."

"And Saturday," I reminded him.

"You know that's to talk to Michelle."

I wrangled another dish—this one a plate—from the avocado-green-coated dish drainer. "Which always leaves her upset," I reminded him.

"Hey," he said, his word soft but commanding. "Stop."

I turned and leaned against the sink. "You're not the one who has to deal with it, Wes."

"I do, too, deal with it."

"No ... that's when you usually run whatever errand you feel has to be taken care of right then, leaving me to be the one who holds her and rocks her and reminds her that Mommy loves her and Daddy loves her and—"

"And *Mama* loves her, too."

I placed the plate on the countertop and reached for another. Yes. *Mama*. The name she'd started calling me a little over two months ago. The name that brought both sunshine and heartache, especially after the second miscarriage. "Yeah," I said, now studying the design of the plate with more intensity than it deserved.

"Hey," Westley said again.

When I didn't look up—when I couldn't for the layer of tears clouding the pattern and threatening to give my feelings away—he set his cup of coffee on the nearby stove and moved to me. Pulled the plate from my hand, placed it back in the drainer, and slid his arms around my hips, drawing them to his. "It's going to happen," he said, having read my thoughts in a way only he could.

The dam broke. "I know," I whispered through the sobs I

deliberately kept silent. Michelle sat alone in the living room watching television and playing with her toys; I didn't want her to hear my cries. To leave her perfect little world for my torn one. "But when?"

Westley drew back, smiling. "How about nine months from tonight?"

I slapped his arm, now smiling myself. "You know what the doctor said. We have to wait a little while longer."

His brow rose. "But can we practice?"

I stepped away from him. "Stop," I half-teased before throwing the dishtowel over the remainder of the dishes that, I figured, could keep till morning. I reached for my ever-present composition book with the pen shoved into the metal coil that held it together. "I've got to get Michelle's bathwater ready."

Westley's fingers found my upper arm and squeezed. "I'll do it," he said. "I can do it."

I looked at him, studying him. He'd had a haircut recently, which had whacked away at many of the curls I so loved to weave my fingers through. His face bore the tan that never seemed to fade. His eyes the same soft and gentle nature that had drawn me to him in the first place. I smiled. Briefly. "No," I said. "It's my job. I'll do it."

I woke early the next morning, shuffled into the kitchen aware of an early-autumn chill that had seeped into the house. After starting the coffee, I went into the dining room, flipped on the light, and then sat at the table where my notebook waited. A yawn found its way through me. I gave in to it, blinking back the moisture it brought to my eyes as I flipped pages until I came to a new sheet. I scribbled the date across the top, followed by placing a #1 in the left-hand margin.

Put coffee on ...

I then placed a checkmark next to the words, which brought an instant sense of satisfaction and a smile.

By the time I'd completed the list, which included *Start planning*

Michelle's b-day party, the coffee had gurgled its last perk and I was enjoying my first cup while placing numbers based on the order of importance next to each assignment. As I wrote #3 next to *Start a load of whites*, Westley walked around the corner from the living room. "Morning," he mumbled.

I lifted my face for a kiss, which he gave. "Coffee's ready."

He strolled into the kitchen, prepared his drink, then returned to lean over my shoulder. To read over what would constitute my day. "Michelle's party ... You already thinking about that?"

I glanced up, noting the stubble of his beard. "Why wait? Especially with DiAnn ..." Both my sister *and* my sister-in-law were expecting now—DiAnn's baby due on Michelle's birthday, which had made for a lot of family joking—*We can just celebrate them together*—but a hindrance when it came to planning our little girl's third birthday party.

Westley pulled a chair from under the dining room table and lowered himself into it. "Has Miss Justine said anything to you about DiAnn's baby shower?"

I shook my head, then jotted a note at the bottom of my list. "I'll talk to her about that today." I shrugged one shoulder. "I mean, she *mentioned* it, but ..." But, she hadn't said too much, knowing how fragile I had been over the past few weeks since the last miscarriage. She'd been one of the select who'd even known I was expecting again. She and Westley and Julie and me. Only the four of us.

Well, possibly Dean. If my sister had told her husband, she hadn't mentioned it.

Westley stood. "I'm jumping in the shower."

"Okay," I said, looking up. Forcing a smile.

He kissed the top of my head. "It *will* happen, Ali."

I nodded, keeping my eyes downcast, the words on my list blurring as all logic left my brain. Which it always did when I thought about the two babies I'd not been able to "grow" to full term.

I'd lost the first baby on Paul and DiAnn's boat—a boat I refused to ever get on again. Illogical, I knew, but I didn't care. Not that it stopped Westley from going out with his brother and sister-in-law and Michelle every chance he got, leaving me sitting at the dock to read whatever book I currently immersed myself in. Or inside the house "starting dinner."

The second baby had been lost at home while napping with Michelle, my arms tucked around her, my body curled like an "S" around hers. After a trip to the hospital where a D and C was performed, the doctor warned Westley and me strongly that we shouldn't "do anything" for several months that could lead to another pregnancy. "Give her body a chance to rest," he said. "To heal."

"How long are we talking about ... *exactly?*" I had asked, not wanting to waste a single second.

"Six months would be my recommendation. Especially in cases like yours, Mrs. Houser, where the second pregnancy resulted in a second miscarriage."

Six months. I'd marked February 15, 1980 on the calendar with a big heart drawn with one of Michelle's red crayons, then began counting down by months, weeks, and then days. Six months. Approximately twenty-seven weeks. One hundred and eighty-three days.

And only a month and a half had managed to snail by. Only six weeks. Only forty-two days.

"Wait till you see what the cat drug up to the house," Ro-Bay said from Miss Justine's front porch. She stood there, a broom in one hand, the other fisted and planted between the folds of flesh at the hip. I had a notion she'd been sweeping in wait for Michelle and me to arrive.

"Wait, wait," I said as I pulled Michelle from her car seat. The moment we climbed the steps, Michelle left me to rush to Ro-Bay and I added, "What's happened?"

"That boy of Miss Justine's," Ro-Bay muttered. "Come home last night like he was the king of some castle. Got Miss Justine all upset this morning, I'll tell you that much."

I glanced upward to the span of the second floor, half expecting the face of the man I'd only seen in a few photographs to stare down at me from a windowpane. "Biff?"

"Well, it ain't Jimmy Carter passing through on his way from Washington to Plains." Ro-Bay propped the broom against the closed front door to gather Michelle in her arms. "Hey, sweet baby," she cooed before turning back to me. "That boy ain't nothing but trouble. *Nothing* but smooth-talkin' trouble. Miss Justine's been wringing her hands all morning. You best get on inside." She nuzzled Michelle. "I got this one."

I found Miss Justine in her usual place—the sunroom. Sure as Ro-Bay had said, she was out of sorts. Not her usual "well-honey-come-on-in" self. I walked over to where she sat, looking out the wide windows at the vast backyard and the lake glistening under the midmorning sun. "Ro-Bay said Biff is here?"

She turned and looked at me, her red-rimmed eyes unblinking. Then she stood and extended her hand, silver bangles jangling at the wrist. "Come with me, darlin'. Let's walk down to the lake."

I took her hand. She pulled me toward the back door, letting go to open it and step outside. Her arm linked through mine as she guided me down the gentle slope of the yard. The ground was soft beneath my canvas flats, the grass thick as carpet. Our footsteps kicked up the scent of water and grass and summer flowers as we trod toward one of the benches along the water's edge, neither of us saying a word over the hum of insects until we sat, hip to hip.

"He's my son," she said, her tone strong. "And, of course, I love him."

I looked at her, squinting against the harsh light overhead, saying nothing. It wasn't my turn. Or my place.

"But he's been—how do I explain to someone so young—*like this* since he was a child." She laughed then. A short chuckle to soften her words. "Sharon," she said, patting my knee. "Sharon was born blond-haired and blue-eyed and happy as the day. And then, sometime later, here came Biff." She looked at me, tears forming where typically only fortitude resided. "Dark hair. Brooding eyes that shift from blue to green. Even as a baby. His daddy was as proud as a peacock in a Sunday

227

afternoon parade. Said we had to name the baby after him—which
we did—but demanded he not be called *Junior.* Oh, no. According
to Buford, we were going places and we had to make sure that our
children's names reflected that."

"Then ... how did the name *Biff* come to be?"

"Started in kindergarten." She waved a hand to swat away a gnat
who'd buzzed by to eavesdrop. "Grabbed hold and never let go." Her
laughter—painful and poignant—rose and, just as quickly, dissipated.
"You should have heard folks talking." She glanced at me again, then
back to the water. "Sharon with her blond hair and her laughter—like
her father's—and Aaron with his red hair and spunk—I guess you
know where he got that from—and then there was Biff, in the middle
with his dark hair and those exquisite eyes."

"Were there *milkman* jokes?" I asked, hoping to ease the severity
of her memory as I shooed away the gnats that sought refuge in the
glistening moisture along the top of my arms.

Miss Justine frowned. "Constantly." She sighed. "I think it all made
him very angry with me. There was always a—disconnect between us.
As if he believed I held something back from him." She turned toward
me without blinking. "Like the name of his real father."

This was no laughing matter; I could see that now. Decades of
hurt rose in the syntax of her voice and lay within the fine lines of her
powdered face. "But surely he knew better. I mean, a woman such as
you, Miss Justine."

She stood then, dismissing my words as she started back toward
the house, me scuttling behind and then beside her, sad to be going
back inside so soon. "He says he's here for a week. Says he took
some time off from his job—I may have mentioned, he's the hospital
administrator over in Dothan."

She hadn't. "Alabama?"

"Is there another one?"

I shrugged, genuinely unsure.

"Actually, there is. Or, so my son tells me. Six, he says, not that the
others matter if he's not in them." Miss Justine stopped as her sarcasm

lay like weights around us. She took my hands in hers, warm and soft. Fleshy in a bone-thin sort of way. "Now you listen to me, Allison. I have to leave to go to my junior league meeting. We have the charity art exhibit coming up and I'm the chairwoman, so I *have* to be there." She squeezed my hands. "Biff hasn't gotten up yet—as far as I know— but when he does, you make a wide arch around him, you hear me?"

I shook my head. "No ma'am. I mean, yes ma'am, but why should I make—"

"He'll take one look at you and swarm like a bee to a marigold..."

This time, it was I who laughed. "*Miss Justine*. First of all, isn't he a little old for me? Or, should I say, aren't I a little *young* for him? And secondly ... no man—I promise you—could ever turn my head in *any* way." I took a step toward her. "You know how I feel about Westley."

Her hands squeezed mine again. "Just mind me, you hear?"

And with that, she let go and trod back into the house, leaving the glass-paned door open for me to follow after.

Chapter Twenty-eight

Biff found me in Miss Justine's library, which doubled as the office where she and I—mostly I—did our work. At one time, it had been her husband's, then masculine in color, design, and scents. But when he died—she once told me—she brought in a new floral sofa and a baroque vase she'd "spent entirely too much money" for, which she filled with flowers. Within weeks, she had replaced heavy draperies with chintz and window sheers and added a cluster of cranberry-scented candles that stood like soldiers on a gold-dusted charger in the center of an elegant coffee table. Candles she insisted stayed lit while we worked, poring over the financial reports and books from the small empire her husband had created from a single hometown apothecary.

Miss Justine had been correct about her son—his eyes *were* brooding. Nearly mesmerizing, which—in all the years I would know him and no matter how close our faces came, one to the other—I could never pinpoint in color. His hair, so black it shone nearly blue, had been cut to wear stylishly long, but neat. He was tall and well-built. Bronzed and polished and much more appealing than any camera could ever capture. His nose, which was more Italian than English, only served to make him more handsome in a not-quite-perfect sort of way. But his shoulders were squared like those of a man who life had treated with smiles and favor. Respect, even if from a distance, but most definitely, up close. He stood in such a way to express the suave ease of being in his own presence. Years later, when I sat still long enough to look back on the story of my life, I could say with clarity that this was the first moment I ever remembered gasping at the sight and scent—fresh and moneyed—of someone. Even Westley—adorable and sexy as he was—hadn't had that kind of effect on me. Not so all of a sudden. Until that very second, I'd not been aware that a human could hold that kind of power—to literally take one's breath away. No wonder Miss Justine had warned me.

He stood in the doorway, dressed in a pair of blue-and-white tennis shorts and a crisp white tee, matching socks and shoes, looking for all the world like a Sears and Roebuck catalog model, not that I could ever, as time went on, imagine Biff stooping to such a degree. His lips, exquisitely bowed and shaded, bore a slight curl and over those magnificent eyes ran an arched brow. "I hope I didn't scare you."

His voice bore something between the genteel lilt of a refined Southern man and an aristocratic Brit. I had to bite my tongue to find my voice. "No. Why?"

"You gasped."

"I just wasn't expecting—" I looked down at the papers and ledgers scattered on the desk before me, then back up.

"You must be the wonderful Allison I've heard so much about," he said, now brandishing a smile that would well please those four out of five dentists that went about approving toothpaste and mouthwash and such.

I stood. Closed the ledger as inconspicuously as I knew how, then walked around the desk and toward the door. "I don't know about wonderful, but the Allison part is right."

Biff took the necessary steps to meet me, his hand extended for a shake, which I obliged. His cologne—rich and spicy—met the wafting scent of the candles, forming a most intoxicating aroma.

Like Miss Justine's, his hands were warm. Soft. Not the hands of a man who'd spent any time working in his mother's garden.

Or tending to his own.

"Buford Henry Knight II," he said. "Or so my parents named me.

My friends call me Biff." The smile broadened, which surprised me. I hadn't thought it possible. "I hope you'll be my friend."

When I didn't answer, he roared with laughter at my expense, then sauntered into the library and plopped into one of the two old leather wingback chairs left over from his father's days of occupying the room. "My mother . . ." He opened a small drawer of the table propped between the chairs, pulled out a box of Virginia Slims along with a silver-plated lighter. ". . . has told you to be wary of me." He held up the cigarettes. "She also hides her ciggy-butts in here. Thinks I don't know." He extended the pack toward me, his brow raised again in the offering.

"No. No, thank you," I answered the unasked question. "I don't smoke."

"Neither does my mother," he said, then pulled a cigarette from the box as I found my way to the sofa. The candles flickered and, for once, I wished I could blow them out before leaving for the day. The light, the scent, the ambiance was too much, especially in the company of this man. "Yet, somehow, these little beauties ..." He lit the cigarette, then placed the box and lighter back into the drawer and slid it shut. "... always manage to find their way into this drawer. There are twenty ... then nineteen ... eighteen ... all the way down to one. If you were to ask her, which no one would ever dare, she'd tell you she has *no idea* how it happens. Or who they belong to." He studied me then. Studied me through the veil of smoke that floated between us and added to my comfortable discomfort. "So, you married young Westley."

"You know my husband?" I asked, fingering my wedding band. An involuntary action he picked up on with a lazy blink and an even slower smile.

"He and Paul and DiAnn used to come here to go skiing out on the lake when they were kids." He took a long draw of his cigarette, then stood in search of an ashtray, which he found hidden behind a few books on one of the shelves. After thumping ashes into it, he returned to his seat. "Of course, I know Paul much better now."

"Oh, that's right. He would be your nephew-in-law."

"Something like that," he said, crossing one long leg over the other in a way that told me he owned the moment we both occupied.

"Well, they still love to ski," I said, "only now at Paul and DiAnn's."

"I hear their spread is nice."

I sat back a little. "It is. Pretty impressive, actually."

"Well, it doesn't hurt that her father and my mother gave them a leg up after they married. Or that they both landed sweet jobs."

"I guess not," I said, because—really—what else was there to say. His confession was none of my business.

"So, tell me, Allison, how it is that you started working for my mother?"

I chuckled. "I'm not entirely sure. She wanted me to come over—right after Westley and I married—so she could show me how to balance a checkbook and Ro-Bay could teach me to cook." I smiled at the thought of the awful tuna dishes I'd served Westley in the beginning. If there was a way to prepare and serve the canned meat, I'd found it. "Then, one thing led to another and she—she hired me."

"Does that make you happy?" He drew on the cigarette again.

"It's not bad as jobs go ... I certainly couldn't ask for a better employer."

He nodded in agreement. "And what about the other? Is it everything young girls dream it will be?"

"What?"

"Marriage."

"No," I said, then blinked furiously at my own admission. "I mean," I recovered while he chuckled. "Well ... no. And I'm not complaining, it's just that ..." I couldn't continue. Wouldn't. Not with a stranger. I wouldn't tell him that I thought there would have been—should have been—more time for just the two of us. Or, how we'd fallen into a pattern—sweet and familiar, but nevertheless, a pattern. I wouldn't tell him of the ghosts that hovered in our home—Cindie, and unborn babies, and babies not yet conceived. Instead, I said, "I'm *not* complaining. I love my husband, and I really like working for your mother, and sometimes we go to Paul and DiAnn's and that's a lot of fun."

Biff leaned forward, snubbed out the half-smoked cigarette, and said, "Well, that was a mouthful." He leaned back again. "Does she scare you?"

"Miss Justine?"

"Goodness, no. My mother has obviously taken you in like a stray kitten in a rainstorm." He tilted forward again. "DiAnn. Does she scare you?"

I couldn't help but choke out a laugh. "A little. But, how did you—"

He laughed with me. "She scares *me* and I'm her uncle. Should be the other way around. I should terrify the living daylights out of her."

"I remember when Westley and I were dating," I confided as though I had made a new best friend. "He told me that she was smart, but she never makes anyone feel that they are beneath her." I shrugged. "I think he can say that because he's got a college degree and is about the smartest person I know. And she—she's just so—so sure of herself."

"And you're not."

"Not really."

"Why do you think that is?"

I frowned. "I don't know…"

Silence now hung between us, pushing the cigarette smoke aside, the tick-tick-tick of an antique cuckoo clock from one of the bookshelves its only interruption. I glanced toward it, this timepiece I imagined had belonged to Miss Justine's husband. Biff's father.

Biff stood, returned the ashtray to its hiding place, then turned and rested his shoulders against the case. "But you, of all people, shouldn't let her do that." His words came in a half-whisper-half-command.

"Why? Why not?"

"Because you're a beautiful young woman who my mother says is quite intelligent—despite the fact you didn't go to college." He took in a breath. "And not to mention your level of compassion."

I narrowed my eyes, teasing. "How do you know I'm compassionate? I might be as heartless as Cruella De Vil."

He smiled. Crossed his arms and legs at the same time. "That little urchin in there with Rose Beth for starters. My sister told me…

about her mother. About you taking her in not two minutes after you became Westley's bride."

I stood now, not liking the idea that he had brought Michelle into our conversation. Westley, yes. DiAnn, fine. Even his mother ... but not my little girl. "She *is* my husband's child."

Biff angled himself toward the door, then took a half step, dismissing my attempt at bravado. "I'm meeting an old high school friend for a game of tennis in a few. Care to join us, Cruella?" He winked, most probably at my choice of fictional antagonists.

"No. I—" I looked at the desk. "I still have work to do," I said as though I *would* consider a game of tennis with two strangers. Men, at that.

"Ah, yes. Well, then. Would you do me a favor and tell Mother I'm taking her out for dinner tonight and to please be ready by seven."

"Of course."

He started for the door, then stopped and smiled at me a final time. "And, if you will, there's some air freshener in the powder room down the hall. Maybe ... spray the room for me. Those candles over there won't fully erase my sins."

I offered a half-smile. "Your mother keeps a can of Glade in one of the desk drawers."

He laughed again, the voice booming. Commanding. "That funny thing. She's so full of secrets and surprises." He winked again. "Isn't she?"

Patterson

The whole thing had gone easier than he ever expected it could. Especially considering that he'd never done anything quite like this before. Dani didn't count. And Rita surely didn't. His affair—or affairs—with them both had been consensual. He'd not had to plot or plan. But, desperate times. Desperate measures ... and all that.

Patterson Thacker needed both something in his life, oxymoronically, to take control of and, at the same time, be someone who would love him. Or, at the very least, to warm him. To make him feel alive again. Worth having around for more than a paycheck or a lifestyle or a pair of high-top leather and suede Adidas sneakers, which was the focus of his oldest daughter's latest tantrum.

And it had all come so easily.

Then again, Cindie Campbell wasn't the brightest bulb in the box. Cute, yes. Absolutely adorable, quite frankly.

Beautiful, really.

But just not bright enough to recognize a wolf dressed in sheep's clothing.

He'd orchestrated everything. First, contacting one of his old high school friends—one whom he'd gone off to college with ... joined a fraternity with ... graduated with honors alongside—one who'd kept his finger on the political pulse of Atlanta while living, mainly, just outside of DC. Leesburg, Virginia, he thought it was. Not that it mattered. What was important to Patterson was that his old buddy furnished a home in one city and kept a small apartment in another. An apartment he'd visited once or twice a few years back.

And Patterson had been honest with his old friend. He'd give himself that much. He'd asked Ronald if they could possibly talk the next time he came into Georgia and, as luck would have it, his friend said that he was coming in that weekend. That they could meet for drinks at an Irish pub known as Connolly's, located down the street from his Atlanta place.

How did five o'clock sound?

Patterson said it sounded perfect and he'd see him there.

He was spot-on time. They shook hands, then embraced in that type of hug male friends do when they haven't seen each other in a while. A clasp on the shoulder. A pat on the back. A chuckle for old time's sake. Afterward, Patterson followed Ronald to a table near the back where a candle offered scant light in the dusky, smoke-filled room. Patterson couldn't help but notice that Ronald was a favorite among the staff—they called him by name as he passed, one young lady dashing over to take his order. "Jameson Irish Whiskey" he said, then looked at Patterson, brow raised.

"I'll have the same," Patterson said.

They exchanged small talk as they waited for their order—but once the drinks had been placed on the table and the customary *sláinte* had been given, Patterson dove right in. "I'm going to be honest with you," he said. "You remember Mary Helen, of course."

Ronald nodded. Yes, of course he did. He'd been one of the many guests at their wedding.

"My home life is ... well, it's not as good as I hoped it would be. As I believe it could be." He waved a hand as though he could dismiss the words, but continued with, "The girls are fine. More than fine actually. But they are their mother's daughters. I'm just ..." He took a sip of his drink, swallowed slowly, then returned the glass to the table. "Sometimes I feel like an afterthought."

Ronald studied him; Patterson could feel the gears of his brain clicking way down to the marrow of his bones.

"You probably—probably don't know what I mean. What I'm saying."

Ronald's fingers twirled the glass and its napkin beneath it in a slow circle. "I know exactly what you're saying." He smiled, but the upturn of his lips dropped nearly before they'd fully risen. "Look, Patterson ... we're men. We have needs."

Patterson leaned in, rested his forearms on the table where the candle cast dancing shadows. "Exactly. Maybe—maybe women have needs, too, but they're a different kind of need. Maybe what they need is—you know—the nice house and the family-sized car and the children to look after. Some need to work. And I'm not talking about those who need money to survive. There are women out there who actually *want* to work."

"I hear what you're saying. And I know quite a few in Washington. But I don't think you brought me here to talk about women's lib and all that."

"There's someone."

"I gathered that." He sipped from his glass. "Anyone I know?"

"No. She's a student."

Ronald brought his glass down, though not quite to the table. "Good Lord, man."

"She's—she looks like—don't laugh, but she looks like Stevie Nicks."

He laughed anyway. "Well, that would certainly explain it. Remember that girl you kept on the side in college? The one you always said looked like Grace Slick?"

"Dani ... and she *did* look like Grace Slick."

"Maybe." Ronald smiled at the memory. "Go on. I interrupted you."

The memory of Dani wrapped around Patterson and wouldn't let go until he shook it free with the thought of Cindie. "It's more than the way Cindie—that's her name—looks, quite honestly. It's ... she seems to have something to offer. She—I don't know—when she's in my classroom I feel like she's wanting something. Or ... someone." He shrugged for good measure. "Wanting someone the way I want someone."

Ronald studied him again. "So, why come to me with this?"

"Straight up?"

"Have we ever been any other way?"

"I don't want stolen moments in a hotel or a motel and I remembered that you've got—"

"The apartment." He tilted his head in understanding. "Of course."

Patterson extended a hand, palm up. "If the answer is no, I'll understand. I will. I'll rent my own apartment. I can certainly afford it, but—"

"No, no. I'm only here once or twice a month and then only for a couple of days and typically on weekends." He drained the rest of his drink. "You know where the place is, right?"

Patterson sat back. "Yeah. I remember."

"I'll give your name to the doorman. He knows—ah—how to be discreet. Especially when he's tipped on the way out."

"Got it."

"I'll leave a key for you with him. Just return it to him ... afterward." He smiled. "It's nice, you know?"

"What is?"

"Having someone who loves you. In … *that* way."

Nice. Yes. Patterson hoped he'd soon find out. Step one had been accomplished with success. Now, all he needed to do to convince Cindie that passing calculus and a little of her time—a little of her warmth—went hand in hand.

Sure enough, that had gone well, too. At first, she seemed perplexed at his offer, which he'd laid flat out on the line. No pretenses. No "let me tutor you" lies. Just raw honesty. "You're beautiful," he'd said. "And I want to spend some time with you. A *lot* of time with you. I think you understand what I'm saying."

Initially, she said she'd need to think about it. Asked if she could let him know the next time she came to his class. Afterward.

An inner quiver began in him then. What if she took his offer over his head? Reported him? Well, it would be her word against his … and he had tenure and she was a girl who'd managed to get herself pregnant before she'd even graduated from high school. Who would they likely believe? "Of course," he said.

Two days later she returned to class. Smiled at him each time his eyes happened her way. A subtle answer without words. Without acknowledgement of an offer accepted.

Yes, indeed. Piece of cake.

Chapter Thirty

May 1982

She lay on her stomach, her hair fanned to one side, her face turned toward the other. Toward him. She'd scooted down in her sleep so that her head now lay on the mattress near his chest. Patterson turned slightly, enough that his fingers could rake through her blond mane. Enough to wake her without disturbing her slumber. Or startle her.

Long lashes batted against upper cheekbones until her eyes were wide and staring at him. She stretched, catlike, as a slow smile broke across her face. "Hey," she said, the old drawl not nearly as noticeable as it had been when he'd first met her.

Patterson reached over and kissed the top of her forehead, inhaling the scent of floral shampoo. "Hey, yourself."

Cindie raised up to prop on her elbows. "How long have I been asleep?"

"A couple of hours."

She laid a hand on his bare chest, allowed her fingers to play with the small tuft of hair at the top of the breastbone. "I can't believe it. I must have been tireder than I thought."

"More tired," he corrected. Her language skills had improved greatly over their two years together. Still, sometimes—

But then she grinned at him again and he knew he'd been had. "I know ... I just like to see if *you* know."

He pulled her to him then, laughing as his arms wrapped around her, pressing the warmth of her to the warmth of him. "I'm going to

240

miss you," he said with a kiss to the tip of her upturned nose. "Do you have to go?"

Cindie laid her cheek against the hollow of his chest. "My brother's wife just had a baby, Professor. Of course, I have to go."

"A baby," he said. "They're too young to have a baby."

"I think you forget..."

"That's different. They had a baby on purpose."

Her fingers drummed against his upper arm. "Things are different in the country. They marry young, have their babies young, and grow old together." She looked up, kissed him as though she intended to start something, but then scurried off the bed, dragging the sheet with her, wrapping it around herself as she stepped toward the bathroom.

"Promise you won't be gone any longer than you said."

She turned back, rested her shoulder against the doorframe where the light from a side window shot in and spilled over her like the goddess he wished her to one day be. "Sunday night. I promise. I'll see you—when? Monday afternoon?"

He sat up with a shake of his head. Pulled the spread, which had become bunched at the foot of the bed, up to his waist. "No can do. Patricia has a piano recital. We're going out to dinner afterward." Her face darkened and he added, "Hey. Don't do that. You know how I feel."

"I know."

They needed a change of subject. "Will you get to spend much time with Michelle?"

"I pick her up tomorrow morning," she said, her whole face bright again. Flushed, which gave him cause for worry.

"Will you see him, too?"

"Only for as long as I have to." She returned to the bed, walking the length of it on her knees until she was directly in front of him. "Hey," she said, now mimicking him. "Don't do that. You know how I feel."

He reached for her, tickling. She laughed, the melody of it filling the room with its song until he had her flat on her back, him over her. "Do we have time for another moondance?" he asked, referencing the lyrics from a Van Morrison tune he'd introduced her to, the one she called "their song."

She shook her head and whispered. "I have to go. But I'll miss you every second of every minute of every day until we *moondance* again." She smiled, offering radiance to her words of "no."

"You have made me so, so happy. Do you know that?"

Cindie nodded beneath him, her eyes searching his, her hands pressed on the sides of his face. "Say it," she said, her voice a whisper.

"No," he teased. "And you can't make me."

She squeezed until his lips puckered. "Say it."

"Can't with my lips like this," he managed.

She softened her hold on him. "Say it."

"I love you," he answered. Not necessarily because it was true—not entirely—but because it made her happy. And she made him happy. A little something in his life that made his soul smile. Something that filled the gaps left by Mary Helen.

She kissed him again—his jaw, his brow, his eyes, and finally his mouth—until, once more, she darted out from under him. "I've really gotta go," she said. "Traffic is a bear and if I don't leave soon ..." She made it to the bathroom this time.

"Tuesday afternoon," he called after her, already counting the days and every maddening minute that filled them. Only the antics of his daughters kept him from going stark raving mad.

"With bells on," she sent back.

Patterson fell back against the pillow. If only Mary Helen's voice sang to him the way Cindie's did ... well, then. There would be no need for a mistress, would there? His brow tensed under the pressure of the conflict that often sparred within him. His relationship with Cindie was wrong—on a number of levels. He knew that. But he was in too deep now, completely uncertain if he could live without her or not.

Not that they should have to. They could keep this up indefinitely. She'd graduate soon. Get a good job. Find her own place. He'd no longer be beholden to Ronald for the use of his place.

And then what, Professor?

The question came and went so quickly, he'd almost not heard its echo. But it was there. His life as a husband and father were set like the European silver epergne Mary Helen insisted on purchasing recently for their formal dining room table. His life with Cindie, however, balanced precariously near the edge of a cliff. Quick to fall. Quicker, still, to shatter.

Cindie

She thought she'd walk into an empty house—the little gingerbread she and her roommates had started renting over a year ago—grab her suitcase and be on the road within fifteen minutes. By now the early-evening Atlanta traffic had backed up along I-75, which meant stop-and-go for the next hour or so. Just the traffic between downtown and home had been bad enough. No doubt about it, her time spent with Patterson—not to mention the long nap afterward—had cost her. She'd arrive at Velma's long after lights out. Probably endure the scathing stares of Vernon who always made her feel like he knew what she'd been up to these past two years.

Instead, when she jerked the front door open—it jammed from time to time—she found Kyle stretched out on the sofa, watching the console television Karen purchased in a congratulatory gesture to herself after she'd secured a job with Delta Airlines. "Oh," Cindie exclaimed over the subdued tones of the news. The aroma of a half-eaten pizza wafted from the coffee table to where she now closed the door.

Kyle sat up, then scooted back on the sofa. "Sorry," he said. "I thought you'd already left for home."

Cindie wanted to remind him that *this* was home. That what she'd left behind—apart from her brother and sisters and, of course, Michelle—was no longer of any consequence to her. She had plans—new plans—and they included this little suburb of a great big city. "No," she said. "I had to—to run by Connolly's to pick up my paycheck." The half-truth came so easily. Before meeting Patterson at the apartment, she *had* gone to Connolly's where her doting professor had secured a job for her shortly after they'd begun seeing each other. Close enough to the apartment, he said. Perfect for making more time together.

Not to mention that Connolly's required more clothing than her previous job. A notion that sent a smile to her heart. Patterson Thacker cared enough about her to keep her virtue intact. "I'm just here long enough to get my suitcase ..."

Kyle chuckled. "You'll never get out of Atlanta now," he said, pointing to where the traffic report showed its usual Friday night fate. "May as well have a bite of pizza and wait it out."

Cindie checked her diamond-face watch—a gift from Patterson—and frowned, knowing Kyle was right. She dropped her purse into a nearby chair before joining him on the armless sofa. "Shoot. I guess you've got a point." She tore a piece of the nearly cold pizza from the pie before folding it in half and taking a bite.

"Want a Coke?" Kyle asked, now standing to his full six-feet-if-he-were-an-inch height.

She nodded at him before swallowing and taking another bite. An afternoon with Patterson had left her hungrier than she'd realized. Or was it *more hungry?*

Kyle went to the kitchen, then returned with two bottles of Coke and a couple of napkins. "What are you doing tonight?" she asked as he sat, handed her a drink, then a napkin.

He pointed to the television. "This."

"No date?"

Cindie couldn't say she knew Kyle all that well, so whether he had a steady or not was anyone's guess. They'd been roommates for a couple of years, yes, but what she knew *about* him she could write in a small paragraph. Sure, he had dated some girl during their time at Dekalb—Lisa? Lila? Lydia?—but they'd parted ways as soon as they'd graduated. She'd gone back to wherever she came from and he'd gone to work in a bank in Tucker. Since then, Cindie couldn't say. But he was a good-looking enough guy with dark-blond hair and caring eyes who made pretty good money, which made him a good catch. He also liked to go places. So far this year he'd been to Aspen followed by a quick trip to Orlando to check out Disney World. The year before he'd ventured into Canada to see their version of Niagara Falls, which he'd told her was prettier than the American side. She, in turn, suggested a trip such as that to Patterson, who'd only said he'd "see what he could do."

"I'm having a Kyle weekend," he said with a smile, his one and only dimple slicing into his left cheek. "Karen is flying the friendly skies to Chicago I think she said, and you're *supposed* to be in—"

"I'm going," she quipped around another bite of pizza.

"I know." He rested his elbows on his knees, clasped his hands together. "I'm kidding. Anyway. My plan is to lie on this sofa all weekend. Watch some TV. Read a book ... maybe. Take a couple of hundred naps. Work has been a pressure cooker lately and I need the quiet."

Cindie shook her head. "You're not going out at all?" She couldn't imagine. Number one, this didn't sound like Kyle, and, secondly, if she and Patterson *were* free to go out, she'd take advantage of every minute of their time together to explore Atlanta with him. Or Niagara Falls. Or anywhere, really.

He glanced at the front door. "Only to get the paper and—maybe—the mail."

She laughed, then brushed the crumbs from her fingers into the pizza box and took a long swallow of her drink, keenly aware that he watched her as she placed the bottle to her lips. "Why is there nothing like pizza and Coke?"

"Because it's the food of God," he said. "I swear, if I get to the Pearly Gates and I don't smell pizza coming from some nice little Italian eatery around the corner, I'm turning around."

"Sure you will." She took another sip, then pointed to him. "And if my brother-in-law ever heard such blasphemy, he'd condemn you to ..." she turned her finger now in the direction of the floor. "You know... the other place."

Kyle reached for his own drink and took a swallow. "Your brother-in-law, huh?"

Cindie nodded as she eased back on the sofa. Arranged herself by tucking one foot under the back of her knee and angling toward her roommate. "He's a preacher. The hellfire-and-brimstone kind. I stay with him and my sister Velma—his wife—whenever I go home."

Kyle jutted his chin toward her. "Not your parents?"

"My father and mother divorced years ago. I lived with Mama until I moved up here. For a while … for a while I stayed with her whenever I went home, but she's sort of … well, she's a miserable person. About a year and a half ago, right after one of the worst fights ever recorded in the history of mothers and daughters, I decided that from then on, I'd stay with Velma when I went home." She took another sip of her drink before returning it to the table. "Which means enduring weekends with Vernon and his preaching."

"*Velma* and *Vernon*?"

"I know," she laughed. "What is it about living in the South? We think we have to name our kids so their names go together—like Karen and Kyle—" she said with a wink, "and if not that, we make sure we marry someone whose name is close enough to our own."

"Like Velma and Vernon."

"And Jacko and Jasmine," she offered, even though she knew he wouldn't know who they were.

"Jacko?"

"His name's Jack—that's my brother—but we've always called him Jacko. He's the one whose wife—*Jasmine*—just had a baby."

Kyle leaned back until his body formed a funny S and his neck rested against the curve of the sofa's cushion. "So, what about you?"

Heat rose in her, then quietly dissipated. "Me?"

"Any fellas out there named Cameron?"

"Cameron?"

"Or …" He chuckled easily. "Give me a sec. I'm trying to think of C names."

"Clifford," she said, falling into the game.

"*Clifford?* I cannot imagine you with a Clifford."

"Wait, wait!" she said, now leaning toward him and swatting at his leg. "Calvin."

"Oh, I know ... marry Calvin Klein and we'll get all our jeans for free."

Cindie slipped into her sexiest voice. *"Nothing comes between me and my Calvins."*

Kyle sobered then. Blinked in a way that said he just now saw her. Really, truly saw her. "Brooke Shields has nothing on you."

Their eyes locked long enough—too long perhaps—until Cindie forced herself to laugh again, Kyle right along with her. "She has more money than me, that's for sure."

"More money than both of us." He righted himself. "So, Jacko ... is he the brother whose wife just had the baby."

"Isn't that what I said?"

He nodded, his eyes still focused on hers. "Yes, you did." Then his brow shot up and the dimple cut through the left cheek again. "Boy or girl?"

"Girl," she answered, grateful for the question. This was the most she'd ever talked to Kyle—strangely enough, seeing as they'd been roommates as long as they had—and she didn't want their banter to be misunderstood. As available and adorable as he was, nothing and nobody was coming between her and Patterson. "Six pounds, one ounce. Velma says she's like a little baby doll."

"Is your brother older then?"

"No. Younger. Patt—" She caught herself, swallowing the name. She'd never once told a soul about her relationship with Patterson. Not even Leticia and certainly not Velma. She'd promised him that she would keep their relationship solely between them. Because it was sacred, almost. A togetherness to be treasured. "A girl I work with—*Pat*—says they're just babies themselves. And I suppose they are. But ..." She looked down then. Down to the newish, shaggy tan carpet that carried a few coffee stains already—mostly hers—to the base of the console where the local news had changed to national.

Pope John Paul II left Rome today, traveling to Africa ... Dan Rather reported.

"But Jasmine loves my brother—in spite of his wild ways at times. And they both seem excited about the baby."

"Babies are nice."

"They are," she said, now missing her own. Some days were easier than others, but the closer the time came to her seeing Michelle, the more she missed her.

"You seeing your little girl while you're home?"

Cindie nodded. "Of course."

"Think you'll ever have another one?"

Cindie blinked at the intimacy of the question, unsure how to answer. She hoped so. At least, she supposed she did. Although her plans had changed drastically since she'd left Michelle with Westley and his wife, she still wanted to get married one day. Have more children. A houseful would be nice; a chance to prove that she was a better mother than Allison. For sure a better mother than Lettie Mae ever dreamed of being. But ... if she continued to see Patterson—and she couldn't imagine that she wouldn't—that would prove sticky. How long they could keep seeing each other the way they had, she wasn't sure. Would she be satisfied with things as they were now? Or would she want more?

Would he?

She believed he loved her. And, goodness, how she loved him. But she also felt certain he would never leave Mary Helen. Never leave his daughters. At least, not until they were older. Maybe.

Then again, the age difference between Patterson and herself stood up and begged to be noticed. Nearly a quarter of a century. Not that she minded. She didn't. But Patterson, having already raised his daughters, might not want more children. Gracious, if she could bide her time, and if he left Mary Helen and they got married, and if they had kids, he'd have children and grandchildren nearly the same age. But that had been done before, hadn't it? Men could have children at *any* age. Not that Patterson was just any man. He was a man who wanted certain things to be certain ways. So ...

"Sure," she answered when she realized she'd left Kyle waiting long enough. "I guess I'll need to start dating someone seriously first though, huh?"

Kyle stood, reaching for the mostly empty pizza box as he did. "Won't we all ..." He looked over at her. "Want the last slice?"

She stood with him. "No." She pressed her hand against her stomach now paunchy from her dinner. "I really need to see if I can get out of here before too much longer."

He straightened. Raised the box and gave her a nod. "Hey. This was nice. Kind of a shame we haven't spent more time together before. Karen will have to go off to Chicago and you'll have to run late more often."

Cindie crossed her arms. "Yeah. It was nice." She started around the coffee table and toward her bedroom. "I'll—uh—I'll just get my suitcase and then you can start your *official* Kyle weekend in earnest."

Kyle was halfway to the kitchen when she crossed her bedroom's threshold. "Let the official non-party begin," he called out. "Woo-hoo!"

Chapter Thirty-one

Allison

"Look, Mama. Somebody spilled ink on the moon."

I lay on my back next to Michelle in the cool backyard grass, my fingers clasped around hers. "That's right, baby girl. And what kind of moon do we have tonight?"

"Full."

"Very good."

"And there's Oh-RYE-on," she said, pronouncing the constellation Orion in her own special way.

I turned my head toward her; she did the same toward me and I rolled over, gathering her, kissing her soft cheek and smelling the baby shampoo that lingered in her freshly washed hair. "I'm going to miss you this weekend," I whispered.

"I'm going to miss you more," she whispered back.

"But you'll have a good time with your mommy," I said, my throat closing in around the maternal moniker.

"I like my Aunt Velma," she said, then rolled on her back with a furrowed brow. "Mama, is it okay if I lay on the grass in my new shorts and shirt?"

I laughed easily. Oh, my goodness, this child. "Yes, sweet baby. It's okay. It's not like we're wiggling around or anything."

Michelle said nothing back for a minute, then: "Do you see that start over there?"

"Star," I corrected gently. "No T. Just star. S-t-a-r. Can you spell that?"

"S-t-a-r."

"Very good. You're the smartest little girl I know. Did you know that?"

"Uh-huh. But do you see it?"

I laughed again. "Yes, I see it. I actually think it's Venus and Venus isn't a star, but a planet."

"What's a planet?"

"*What's a planet?*"

Westley's voice brought me onto my elbows and Michelle scrambling to reach her father. "Daddy," she squealed as she ran to him.

"You made it home," I said. "I was beginning to think you'd decided to spend the night at the drugstore. What time is it anyway?"

My husband grimaced. "Felt like I needed to—after eight thirty—too much work, not enough time." He kissed Michelle's face, then neck, which brought a melody of giggles. "You packed?" he asked, as though she were heading out on vacation. "Mommy ought to be here soon."

Michelle nodded and I pulled myself to my feet, brushed the grass from the back of my damp shorts, then crossed to my family. "Does Mama get one of those kisses, too?" I asked Westley.

"You'll get more than that later on," he said, bringing his lips to mine as Michelle wrapped her arms around us both.

"I love you guys zoo muuch," she said in her way of over-emphasizing "so much."

Westley turned. "Is that the phone?"

I paused, listening. "Yeah. I'll get it." I took off in a sprint, bounded up the back-porch steps and through the door to the kitchen. "Hello," I panted into the wall phone's bright yellow handpiece, the one that coordinated with the floral wallpaper I'd hung earlier in the spring.

"Let me speak to Westley."

All joy rushed out of me. *Cindie.* I could imagine what she wanted, but I couldn't imagine who'd taught her that *Let me speak to Westley* bordered on good manners at any level.

But at least my mama had raised me right. "Of course," I practically cooed. "Hold on." I turned as Westley—Michelle still cradled in his arms—entered the room behind me. "Cindie," I mouthed.

Westley's face became like stone. "Hey," he said into the phone while transferring Michelle to me. I held her against me as he continued with, "All right . . . all right . . . yeah, okay . . . I'll see you then."

I set Michelle's feet on the floor and suggested she go watch a little television. "Y'all gone talk?" she asked, straining her head backward to look up at us.

I raised my brow as Westley smiled. "You are a very smart little girl, *Michelle Ma Belle*. Do what your mama said now."

She left us in a wake of giggles, her footsteps growing faint as she neared the front of the house.

"What is her excuse this time?" I crossed my arms, knowing Michelle would not see Cindie that night.

"Atlanta traffic."

I sighed. "Doesn't she care—"

"Don't start, Ali. It's not a big deal. She stopped at a phone booth south of Macon and called, meaning she's not going to make it until way after Michelle's bedtime, which . . ." He glanced at his watch. " . . . is about twenty minutes from now."

I pursed my lips. "So, what are you going to do?"

"I'll meet up with her in the morning." He raised his hand to stop me from saying what he knew I wanted to say—that a mother—a *good* mother—would know that Atlanta's traffic on a Friday afternoon was bumper to bumper. That a mother—a good mother—would leave early enough to beat it. But Cindie had some perfect excuse, no doubt. She always did, especially over the past couple of years.

"All right," I said. "Are you going to break this news to Michelle, or will you leave that for me?"

Westley shook his head, his hands coming to his hips. "Stop it, Ali. It's not *that* big of a deal. Don't martyr yourself. It's unattractive."

But it was a big deal for me. I hated seeing Michelle disappointed and I told him so.

"Life is full of disappointments. She'll learn that eventually. May as well start now." He opened the refrigerator door, leaving me with the harsh reality of his words. Yes, life was slap full of disappointments. "I'm starving," he said, then closed the door without removing a single item and turned to me, his face now full of the tenderness and love Michelle and I both counted on. "I'm sorry, sweetness," he said, his eyes on mine. "I'm frustrated, too."

I stepped into his arms, felt the power of them. The surety. He would make everything all right, I knew. He'd make a fun game out of it with our daughter and she would be okay, too. Truth be told, she was more excited about seeing Aunt Velma than she was about seeing Cindie anyway.

I leaned back to look into his eyes. "Are you?"

He kissed me gently, then nibbled on my lower lip. "I had *big* plans for you and me after I took her to meet her mother."

"Oh, did you now?"

"Mmm. The neighbors were *probably* going to have to call the cops."

I groaned as my legs turned to jelly. "I can *probably* be persuaded to wait until tomorrow night."

He narrowed his eyes. "Tomorrow night we're supposed to have dinner with Trev and Marilyn."

Ah, yes ... our monthly dinner with our friend and attorney and his new bride—a couple I'd come to enjoy getting together with. "All night?" I teased, pushing myself closer to him.

"Woman ..."

"From what time to what time?"

"We're supposed to meet them at seven."

"Can we be done by seven thirty? In bed by seven-thirty-five?"

Westley laughed as he stepped away from me. "Tell you what let's do—right now, you fix me a sandwich and some chips, and I'll go break the news to Michelle."

"Good," I said. "Because I believe I hear the theme song to *Dallas* playing and I think she may be a tad too young for *that* drama."

Westley closed the gap between us and whispered, "Tomorrow night..."

I kissed him. "With bells on."

He wiggled his brow. "Yeah, we can try that."

He left the room on the melody of my laughter.

"So, what's next for her?"

Trev and Marilyn Donaldson sat across from us in a booth at an off-road seafood restaurant that had opened only a few weeks previous to rave reviews. From the aromas permeating around us, I could see why. *Everything*—and they did mean *everything*—was beer-battered and deep-fried.

Phil Collins' "In the Air Tonight" pulsed from the sound system and Westley had just finished telling Trev about his meeting with Cindie earlier that morning and of how she had not arrived on time the night before. Trev followed up by asking the question I'd been wondering but dared not ask.

Westley took a long sip of sweet tea before returning the sweating glass to the vinyl red-and-white-checked tablecloth while I glanced over at Marilyn with a slight roll of my eyes. She smiled inconspicuously, then looked at Westley with wide, smoky eyes. "Yes, do tell," she said.

After a slight shifting, Westley leaned his elbows on the table and clasped his hands. "Well, now," he began, "there's the rub. See, in the beginning she couldn't get enough of telling me about this class and that event. I got every minute detail on her social calendar and then . . ." He shook his head. "I dunno. She just stopped talking about it."

"Maybe she really is serious about school," Trev noted. Then, when no one said anything, he added, "It could happen."

"Does she say anything about her grades?" Marilyn asked, ignoring her husband's wit.

Westley's fingers shot up, then fell back into the grasp. "That's another thing. To my knowledge, Cindie has never been an ace student. But she's actually doing well. I mean . . . like the dean's list well. She told me recently that she'll graduate after summer term."

Heat rose within me, but from where, I was unsure. Anger? No. Embarrassment? Perhaps. Was it not enough that Cindie had given birth to Westley's child—a child I called my own, but nonetheless came from her own womb? Was it not enough that I couldn't seem to get pregnant and *stay* pregnant, no matter what the doctors tried or how hard I prayed? Did Cindie now have to find herself on the dean's list and near to obtaining a degree as well? Something I'd never wanted, really. Especially after meeting Westley. All I'd ever really wanted was *him*. Yet here I sat with three educated adults—Westley a pharmacist, Trev an attorney, and Marilyn, the principal at Michelle's elementary school. And me? Well, I'd graduated from high school, hadn't I? And I worked for Miss Justine, didn't I? And I raised Michelle . . . Michelle, the little girl who had somehow taken the place of—by now—the three babies I'd not been able to carry to term.

Yes, well, that and thirty-five cents could get me a cup of coffee at—

"Ali?"

I jumped at Westley's voice, my eyes coming to his. "What?" He looked up and I followed his gaze. The waitress had returned with our plates of food; she stood waiting for me to lean back so she could place them on the table. "Oh," I said as another warm wave bathed me. I offered a smile as she completed her tasks. As she asked if we needed more tea. As Westley said, "Yes, please" and she said she'd be back in a moment.

My husband took my hand in his. "You okay?" he asked, and I nodded.

Now was not the time. Later . . . later I would ask: *After graduation, what then?* Would she return to live here? Would she want Michelle back? Would Westley allow that disruption to our daughter's life? Or would he think that now, with her degree, Cindie would be fine as a mother as he'd once promised her?

The pain started low, near my uterus. Cramping that, at first, I attributed to too much fried food the night before. I rolled onto my back, careful not to disturb Westley who snored lightly, then turned my head to the digital clock glowing amber and red on the nightstand on his side of the bed.

Four thirty-eight.

I breathed out slowly. In through my nose, out again between slightly parted lips. Another cramp, a twisting almost, and I knew. This wasn't nausea. My period was back after only two weeks.

I frowned as I raised up, wincing. Had I purchased pads and tampons since the last time? Never mind the tampons; they tended to hurt for some reason now.

But, had I? Getting them was on my list. Written neatly in my notebook.

I swung my legs over the side of the bed and felt it then, that first gushing of blood. Not wanting it all over the sheets, I stood, pressing my hand against my lower abdomen while the sensation of my bottom about to fall onto the floor let me know that taking soft steps to the bathroom wasn't an option. I nearly stampeded. Westley moaned as I reached our bedroom door. *Don't wake up ... not yet.*

Blood spilled down my legs as I stepped into the bathroom, plopped onto the octagon-shaped tiles. My hands shook as they jerked my soiled nightgown over my hips in frustration, then lowered the toilet seat Westley left up at some point during the night. Men.

Blood poured into the toilet as if I urinated and what felt like a rock pressed against my bottom, distending me. I bent over, nearly blinded by the stabbing pain. Breathing in, then out, I pulled a wad of toilet paper from the roll. Held it against me. But it soaked almost instantly and pooled into my hand.

"Westley," I called out, grateful Michelle was at her aunt's and not a wall away. I drew in a quivering breath and waited. Hearing nothing, I called out again. "Westley!"

Within a moment he stood as a silhouette in the dark hallway. He took one look at the damage, another at my face, then dashed in and dropped to the floor in front of me. His hands, warm but trembling, pushed my hair from my face. "I'm here." Then, looking down, he said, "I've got to get help."

"I need a towel ... or something," I said, panic rising in my voice.

He grabbed a hand towel from the linen closet—off-white with gold daisies—and handed it to me. "Not that—" I started, then shut up and folded it until it formed a large pad.

Westley called for an ambulance from our bedroom, speaking words and phrases that grew faint as the room dimmed. I stood, my breath shallow, grabbed hold of the sink for support. But my legs, streaked with drying blood, had turned to jelly. *Westley ...*

He stood over me then, holding me up, chastising me for standing, for trying to reach the safety of him. But as he scooped me into his arms, he whispered, "I've got you, Ali. I've got you."

I closed my eyes and allowed the pain to sweep over me until I simply slipped away.

There would be no babies.

I woke, blinking into the bright hospital room I'd been in for three days and willed my tears to stay put. At least for as long as my mother and father sat in the hardback chairs against the baby-blue-painted wall.

Baby blue ...

The irony.

For days I had slept, especially once the narcotics had been administered—the ones that came after the surgery. The surgery that ended any chance, ever, of me getting pregnant. Ever again.

I glanced toward the sleeper-chair where Westley sat looking up at the television, then followed his gaze to where *Match Game '82* flickered images into the room. "*Match Game*," I whispered. More irony.

Westley slid to the end of the seat. "Awake again, huh? You okay?"

I nodded at him. "Yeah."

"Pain?"

"A little."

"Thirsty?"

"Yeah, but not enough to ... how ironic that *Match Game* is on right now."

His smile was tender. "How's that?"

I gave him a weak smile in return. "The day you proposed to me ..." I reached for the bed's remote to raise the head a tad. "I watched *Match Game* while you pulled weeds."

Westley stood, then took the remote from me. "Not too high."

"I wasn't—"

"I think they are all about three sheets to the wind," Mama noted.

"Probably so," Daddy agreed, which brought a grin to Westley's lips.

"No doubt," he said.

"This is the last month," my mother said as she placed the sweater she knitted into the sewing basket at her feet.

I looked at her as Westley adjusted the sheet around me. "What?"

"I read it in the *TV Guide*. This is the last month they're gonna air the first-run series."

"Oh." More irony ...

"Your mama loves the *TV Guide*," Daddy said then. "Reads it cover to cover."

"You do the crossword," she said back to him.

"Yes, I do."

I glanced back at the television. "Who's that?"

Mama stood so she could see the screen. "Who?"

"The man next to Brett Somers."

"Skip Stephenson."

"I don't know him." Then again, lately, if it wasn't The Muppets...

"He's on *Real People*," Mama said, returning to her chair and her knitting.

"Oh." I looked at Westley. "When will you get Michelle?"

"After we get you home." He leaned over and kissed my forehead. "She's fine, Ali. Velma's got her and you know how much she loves being with Velma."

Yes, I knew. I swallowed. "Did Cindie leave?"

"On Sunday. I told you this."

He had, but I wanted to make sure. And more than anything I wanted to know if he'd told her the truth. About the surgery. About how I was only half a woman now. About how she would have it all, really.

The education we practically paid for.

And the little girl with her curls and Westley's smile.

Chapter Thirty-two

Daddy left the following day to go back home, but Mama was staying until I got back on my feet, which the doctor said would be within a few weeks. Mama being with me for so long brought both comfort and despair.

The next day—a Thursday—Westley returned to work after dropping Mama off at the hospital. She entered my room with a vanilla milkshake from the new McDonald's that had opened up on the outskirts of downtown, her basket of knitting, and a stack of get well cards bundled together in multicolored envelopes. "Which do you want first?" she teased. "The cards or the shake?"

"Both," I said, sliding up a little in bed and offering her a smile. The prospects of the milkshake having a cherry on top brightened my somber mood.

"Have they had you up and walking yet?" She placed the shake and the mail on the rolling bedside table, then slid it over my lap. "Here you go."

I reached first for the drink, peering inside to fish out the cherry. "Yes, and it hurt like the dickens. Sometimes I think they took a hacksaw to me on that operating table."

"Well, get through it. They're not letting you leave here until you walk enough and—you know—go to the bathroom." She dropped into the sleeper-chair; it sighed softly under her light weight.

"I know," I said around the straw. Drawing on the shake pulled at my stitches, so I started spooning it with the straw.

"Look at the top card."

"Let me just finish this first ..." I said. "It's too good to let it turn to soup and breakfast was awful."

"Soon we'll have you home and I'll make you a good breakfast like I used to."

Words—and memories—that brought another smile.

Later, with the entire milkshake in my happy tummy, I slid the first card off the stack, read the return address, then looked at my mother. "Elaine?"

"She's gone and done it from what her mama told me. Said she would and she did."

I opened the card, my fingers quivering. "She couldn't have ..."

The last time I'd spoken to my old best friend, she'd mentioned taking her hot-off-the-press diploma and heading west to the reservations to serve as a medical missionary. I'd laughed at her, reminding her that she had planned to bake on the beach for a while first. "No, no," she'd said to me. "The beach for a few days, but ..."

"Come on, Elaine. You? A missionary?"

"Yes, me. I'm serious now," she'd said. "Serious as a heart attack."

"You are not ..." I just couldn't imagine Elaine doing anything so far above herself. A great girl and all, but ...

"If I'm lying, I'm dying," she quipped.

I opened the card, which included a child's drawing of flowers growing wild under a golden sun. The words "Get Well Soon" had been scrawled in crayon along the top left corner. I turned it toward Mama who had already gone to work on her knitting. "Look," I said.

"Did she include a letter?"

"She wrote in the card."

"Read it to me ... if you want to."

I did and I didn't. Elaine, of all people, working with the American Indians. Working, specifically, with American Indian children. *Children.* Little Miss "Let's Live Life by the Seat of Our Pants" had actually started living for someone else. For something greater than herself. I almost couldn't believe it, even with the color-crayoned proof lying in front of me, still half folded.

"She says: Hey, Sweet One!" I looked over at Mama. "She's never called me *that* before."

"Sounds just like her mama." Mama's needles clinked against each other in the familiar tapping of my childhood. "That's what happens to daughters when they grow older. They start to sound like their mamas. I know I did."

Oh, dear Lord...

"Bound to happen to you, too," Mama continued as though she'd read my thoughts, her eyes on her handiwork.

Maybe so. But who would it happen to after me?

"She—um—says: Greetings from the Nizhoni Reservation in glorious northern Arizona. *Nizhoni* is the Navajo word for 'The Beauty Way.' Sounds like I'm working at some kind of spa, huh?" I looked at Mama again.

"It does, I reckon," she said.

I took a deep breath. "Okay... some kind of spa, huh? But it's not. I wish I had enough room to tell you all about it, but I don't so I'll write you a long letter soon. I'll even tell you how I was persuaded to move here (oh my gosh, you should see Sedona!) to work with these amazing people." I paused. Swallowed around the words I saw coming. "I love you bunches and wish I were there to help you mend. Sending prayers." I closed the card. "Elaine."

Mama didn't miss a beat. "I declare I need to talk to Rose. I sure hope Elaine's not going to take up with some strange religion while she's out there."

I lay back against the cool of the pillow and closed my eyes, trying to picture Elaine holding Native American children. Comforting them when they were sick. Laughing with them when they were not. Reading to them... the way I read to Michelle.

Michelle. Could I possibly miss a child more? "Mama," I said, my eyes still closed.

"Hmm?"

"Do you know if Westley talked to Michelle?"

"He called over there last night," she answered, her needles still working. "I heard him saying prayers with her. Or his side of the prayers, anyway."

I smiled. "She's so precious when she prays."

"Are you going to read the rest of your cards?"

I shook my head. "Not right now," I said. "I think I'll nap a little while I can."

"You may need to try to get up and walk a little ..."

"I'll nap, Mama," I said, a tiny breath escaping my lungs. "Then I'll get up and walk a little."

I woke when the candy striper brought my lunch tray in. Mama took that as her cue to go downstairs to the cafeteria where she'd eat the sandwich and a snack-sized bag of chips she'd brought from the house with her. But she'd order a cup of coffee to make herself look less conspicuous, she told me. Less ... thrifty.

After nibbling at the rubbery Salisbury steak, fairly decent potatoes with gravy, and canned peas, I devoured the chocolate ice cream that came in the little tub like those we'd had in school. The ones served with a stick-spoon. Done, I pushed the tray to the edge of the bedtable and reached for the second card, this one from Julie who had recently moved to Nashville after Dean was offered a new job. The job he'd always wanted, Julie had told me in a previous letter. This one at an impressive publishing house—the kind that puts out Bibles and such—working as an editor. Financially they'd hit pay dirt. In fact, everything for them seemed almost too good to be true. Two children. Another on the way.

I opened the card, hoping Julie would not have included a new photo of my niece and nephew. As much as I loved them ... as much as I loved seeing their cherub faces grinning up at the camera ... I didn't think I could bear their latest moments of life captured on film.

Patterson

He didn't like what he was hearing.

Not three days ago when he and Cindie had finally been able to meet up for a stolen hour, she had been all over him. Doted on him. Smothered him with kisses and hugs and everything that followed. Afterward, she'd sat in his lap, her head against his shoulder, and told him about her weekend with Michelle. About how she'd been late getting out of town due to the traffic—due to the late start, thanks to him she added with a giggle—but that she and her daughter had more than made up for lost time. She'd told him about her brother's baby and mentioned, casually, how she wished—just once—she could take him to her family's house way out in the sticks. He'd get a kick out of it, she'd said. Especially on Sundays.

"And I'd love it if you could meet Michelle," she'd added.

"One day," he said with a pat to her hip, cuddling her as if she, too, were a child. Knowing that the chances of his ever being in the same room with Cindie and her daughter were slim to nonexistent.

She'd not once mentioned the father of the child, not even in passing. She rarely did anymore. But she had spoken of someone new to him, although not altogether unfamiliar. He knew Kyle Lewis, of course. He'd had the young man in a few of his classes. He was also aware that Kyle and his sister shared a place with Cindie. But Cindie had never spoken much about the young man. In fact, she'd made a point that the three of them rarely encountered each other.

"Ships passing in the night," she'd said, borrowing from the old metaphor.

And then, today, as they lay burrowed under the bedcovers to ward off a late spring chill that had descended upon Atlanta, she nuzzled her nose into the curve of his neck and said, "Didn't you tell me once that you like Fleetwood Mac?"

He had nearly fallen asleep, but at the name of the band, his eyes opened. "Yes," he said. "I do."

"Kyle just got their new album. Have you heard it?"

He prickled. Of course he'd heard it. He'd purchased it the moment it had become available. "*Mirage.* Yes."

"Kyle bought it last night and played it in his room. I couldn't help but hear it from mine." She flipped to her side and ran a hand up his stomach to his chest, then slipped her fingers through her tresses. "Do you think I look like Stevie Nicks?"

His eyes caught hers and narrowed. "There's a resemblance."

Her lips pursed. "Do you think she's beautiful?"

Patterson smiled. "Yes, I think she's beautiful," he said, which brought a sigh from her. "Why do you ask?"

"Kyle said I look like her."

"Did he now? And when was this?"

Cindie's eyes widened. "Last night," she said. "I just told you. When we were in Kyle's room listening to the album."

"In his room?"

"I told you."

Patterson pushed back enough to let her know of his displeasure. "No. You said that he played the album in his room and that you heard it from yours."

"Yeah ... and then I went into his room and asked him if it was Fleetwood Mac." She ran her fingers through her hair again, bringing it to rest along her shoulder until it cascaded over her breast. Blood rushed to his head, pooling there. "I've always liked their music and I remembered you saying that you—"

He captured her then, bringing her close to him, pushing her back against the mattress.

"Patterson, you're hurting me—"

His fingers clamped hold of her chin. "Listen to me, Cindie. I don't want you in another man's bedroom, you hear?" The tears that sprang into her eyes did little to soften his mood. The very idea of her ... in a bedroom ... with another man. A younger man. A single, younger man. "Do you?"

"*Patterson ...*"

"I'm asking you a question," he said, squeezing tighter.

"Yes," she whispered, her eyes filled with something he'd never seen before. Something he'd not meant to place there, so, as the blood began to dissipate, he wrapped her in his arms. Buried his face in the hair she had tempted him with a moment before.

"Cindie, Cindie," he moaned. "I'm sorry, sweetheart." Words he half meant brought a torrent of tears from her. He shushed her, rocking her, kissing her until he thought she understood. "I just cannot bear the thought of you with another man."

She slid away from him then, sitting straight up, drawing the sheet to her chin. "That's not fair, Professor."

He sat up, too. "What does that mean?"

"I mean, it's not *fair*. You are in another woman's *bed,* every single night. But I'm not supposed to even listen to an album with my roommate?"

"You knew about Mary Helen when we first—"

"Yes, but ... don't you see? I was just listening to an album with Kyle. That's *all*. But you and Mary Helen—I mean, you *do it* sometimes, don't you?"

Rarely. In fact, he couldn't remember the last time. "Leave my wife out of this."

She flung herself out of bed and reached for clothes that lay crumpled on the floor. "I gotta go."

Cindie leaving now—like this—frightened him. Tortured him, nearly. He couldn't stand the thought of it, but at the same time he couldn't have her stay with an upper hand. Nor could he deal with her living with Kyle Lewis another minute. Not after this. One foot in the man's bedroom was one step closer to his bed.

"We should think about getting our own place," he said as she shoved her legs into her jeans and tugged at the zipper.

She stopped for a moment, then reached for her bra ... her sweater. "What are you saying?"

"I'll set you up in an apartment. A place just for us."

Cindie didn't speak until after she'd pulled her long hair from the back of the sweater. "You just don't want me living with Kyle."

He leapt from the bed—too quickly. She took frightened steps backward, her eyes darting toward the door as if she were looking for a means of escape. "Cindie," he said, keeping his voice calm, wanting to regain control now more than he had even a moment before. He reached for his own clothes, draped across a chair. "Just think about it."

She found her way to the door. "I gotta go," she said again, then shot out before he could stop her.

Tomorrow. Tomorrow he'd send her a dozen roses. Long-stemmed. Pink. He rarely did things like that, and he knew she'd melt at the gesture. Then he'd wait a few days—a week maybe—before bringing up the idea of her own apartment again. Yes, that should solve everything.

Piece of cake.

Chapter Thirty-three

The first week of December 1987
Allison

"Michelle wants to wear her hair like the girl in *Full House*," I informed Westley after the final touches of putting our daughter to bed.

He raised his eyes from the boating magazine he had engrossed himself in. "What does that mean?"

I dropped into my favorite chair—one Westley had decided would be *just mine* after we moved into our new home three years earlier—a comfy armchair, complete with a thick bottom cushion and tufted back. "Like Candace Cameron's. The oldest daughter on the show."

Westley shook his head, his eyes filled with confusion. "I still don't know what that means."

I reached for the library book that rested on an occasional table and raised my brow. "That's because you don't watch *Full House* with Michelle and me. She is absolutely in love with DJ Tanner." I grinned. "The Candace Cameron character."

Westley's attention returned to the magazine. "As long as she doesn't want to look like Madonna, I'm good with it."

I chuckled. "Well, it means a haircut. Are you okay with that?"

His gaze returned to my side of the room. "How short?"

"Below her shoulders, so about five or six inches."

Westley frowned. "Is she dead set on it?"

I gave him a nod. "I'd say so. And, to tell you the truth, I could use some reprieve when it comes to what it takes to get her hair brushed every morning." Michelle's thick, waist-length hair had become a source of tears no detangler could rectify.

He glanced back at the magazine's slick page. "If that's what she wants."

Of course. Westley had denied Michelle few things she wanted. Our new home stood as proof. We now lived in the same tree-dotted, lakefront neighborhood as her best friend, Sylvie, a precocious child with errant brunette curls and the largest brown eyes I'd seen on such a petite child.

Michelle and Sylvie did everything together—school, ballet, piano, Girl Scouts, church, hours of play. Anything two little girls could possibly do together, they did it. Their friendship was as deep and solid as the one I'd once had with Elaine, who had recently married a doctor who shared her love for Native Americans and their plight. Together, they ran a medical mission in northern Arizona, returning home only during the Christmas season, if then. With the holidays right around the corner, I hoped to see her during her stay. To date, we had come to rely mostly on letters and the occasional phone call.

Westley held up a photo spread of a boat and asked, "What do you think?"

I squinted across the semidark room. "About what?"

"This. I think we should get it."

"A boat?"

"Yeah."

"How much?"

"Affordable."

"Do you *need* a boat?" I asked, though in all honesty I had expected Westley to purchase something to tie to our dock two minutes after we signed the papers for the house.

"Of course," he said. "And Michelle will, too. Something for her friends to come over for."

"The pool out back isn't enough?"

Westley's appreciative stare went back to the magazine. "You can't ski in a pool, Ali."

But you can lose a baby on a boat, I thought irrationally, even after all the years since my first miscarriage. "Wes," I said, now wanting to change the subject. "Michelle also wants to know if we can pick out our Christmas tree this weekend. And," I added, "she asked me to remind you that Sylvie's family has theirs up and that it's decorated trunk to star."

"I'll get off early on Saturday," he said, looking up at me again. "We'll head out to Samson's Tree Farm as soon as I get home."

"Miss Justine wants to come with us. Wants to pick out her tree and then have Mr. Samson haul it to her house in his truck."

Westley chuckled. "All right. Let her know we'll pick her up around three."

I opened my book to where I'd last dog-eared it and found my place on the page as a smile crept into my heart. Westley and I were doing okay, I reminded myself. We had a spacious home—as lovely as Paul and DiAnn's, although filled with half as many children—that rested on a lake as inviting as theirs. We both had jobs we enjoyed, good friends to complete us, and we stayed active in the social workings of our community and church. Our daughter was growing into a well-rounded young lady—socially, academically, and spiritually—only sometimes having her life interrupted by Cindie or Cindie's family. Something Michelle always took in stride.

Cindie—I thanked God every day—had remained in Atlanta after graduating five years before. My constant unraveling at the notion that she would return and demand her daughter had been for nothing. My fretting that she would want Michelle to spend every week of summer vacation in her new apartment—one she moved into shortly before her graduation—had also been for naught. Instead, Michelle spent two weeks of her summer with Cindie, a week of Christmas vacation, and every other spring break and every other Thanksgiving.

I had finally met her. Had seen what pieces she'd lent to Michelle. Finally understood what had drawn Westley to her. She practically oozed sexuality I believed I'd never have. Even at Michelle's kindergarten graduation, where I'd dressed in a simple wrap-around dress, Cindie had donned a long bohemian number that made her look part flower child and part love child. And although Westley seemed to give her no more than a passing glance after their initial hello, I found myself drawn to her. A moth to the flame. A fly to the spider's web. My focus more on her and her reaction to Michelle receiving her diploma than to the five-year-old who pranced across the stage with a smile that showed off a missing front tooth.

Westley had noticed—of course he had noticed. Later, while Michelle spent the night with Cindie at Velma's, he chastised me, reminding me that I'd missed the whole point of the day because I had been so focused on Cindie.

"I couldn't help it," I declared, slamming the bangle I'd worn all day into my jewelry box. "My gosh, Westley. She's ... she's *gorgeous*. I mean, seriously, seriously gorgeous."

He flung his shirt onto the bed. "So what? So *what*, Ali? She's pretty. Did I ever tell you she wasn't?"

Tears stung the back of my eyes, threatening to unleash years of wondering. "I don't want to talk about this anymore," I said, then headed for the bathroom where I drowned my tears in a cascade of water from the shower.

From what I knew—from what little Westley told me—Cindie had graduated from college and immediately gone to work for a county parks and recreation department, working as an assistant to the director. Her old roommate—the male one—had helped her secure the job, he and the director being long-time friends. "Still amazes me," Westley told me one night, "that she and that Kyle fellow never ... you know ... got together."

"How do you know they didn't?"

He rolled his eyes and laughed lightly. "No. Cindie's got someone, but it's not her old roommate."

"*How* do you know?"

"I just know. I know her ... or women like her." He pointed upward. "And she's being quiet enough about it, I'd wager he's married. With kids."

"Maybe she's being quiet because she doesn't have a man in her life right now," I countered, though I hoped that wasn't true. The idea of Cindie returning with a diploma and her sights set on Westley kept me up as many nights as the thought of her returning for Michelle.

"Not possible. Women like Cindie need men in their lives. Someone to use." He blew out a breath. "Or use up."

I blinked now at the words in the book in front of me, forcing the memory away. The last thing I needed to worry about tonight was Cindie Campbell. She lived her life in Atlanta; we lived ours in Odenville.

Patterson

His life had become complicated.

For starters, Mary Helen had begun to demand more of his time, declaring that the children would be grown and gone soon, and they needed to spend as much time with them as possible. That much was true. Patricia had grown into an exquisite beauty, like her mother, but with a zeal for life, like him. She had also been granted an impressive scholarship at Boston's New England Conservatory of Music and had been living there since midsummer. When she called home—typically on Thursday evenings, because she had nothing else to do then, she said—she spoke of classes and new friends, outings, and—too often—of her new job working as a teaching assistant for Dr. Bauder, who, she said, insisted she call him by his *Christian name*—her words—which was Lance.

"Don't neglect your studies, Patricia," her mother had warned from their bedroom phone while he listened in on the office extension while wanting to shout, "And don't sleep with this—this—*Lance!*"

He also wanted to grill his daughter on everything she spoke of, especially when it came to her friends. How many of them were male? Occasionally, when she brought up a young man's name, Mary Helen fluttered about as mothers of young adult daughters do, wondering if Patricia was getting involved too soon. He, on the other hand, continued to conjure up a vision of her chastity being stolen by some slick professor. Or worse, given away.

But when it came to her musical outings—the theater, concerts, jazz clubs—he wanted to drown in her excitement. For nearly her whole life, and despite him not being able to play an instrument, it had been the one thing he could connect with her on that Mary Helen could not. His wife could *play* a piano, but as with most things in life, she didn't have the passion for it.

No passion for much of anything until recently when she became friends with Nola and Eldon Edwards. Predominately Nola, a woman who seemed completely at ease in her role as a wife and mother. And, Patterson couldn't help but note, a woman at ease in her own skin. The two women had met during one of Mary Pat's lessons at Bryce Park Equestrian Center, which the Edwardses happened to own. Bryce Park and a slew of others. Mary Helen and Nola became fast friends as did their middle daughter, Mary Pat, who recently turned seventeen, and the Edwards' oldest son who neared twenty at an alarming rate of speed. Which, of course, was another cause for concern, although Mary Helen didn't seem to think so.

But, she wouldn't.

Before Patterson could wrap his mind around his two oldest girls having lives with romantic interests, Mary Helen was scheduling nearly every free minute with Nola and Eldon. Dinners. Horse shows. Even jaunts to the North Georgia mountains where the Edwards had a "weekend home."

Making things more complicated was the fact that Mary Helen had warmed up since meeting them. Making herself available in ways she'd never done before. He couldn't quite put his finger on *why,* unless Nola's innate sensuality had somehow rubbed off on his wife. But, while he relished the newness of their relationship, it certainly made things more difficult where his mistress was concerned.

Cindie had become just as demanding, but in a different way. Her new job had changed her. She'd grown into a savvy young woman with a head for business and had grown the program beyond her boss's expectations. From the way she put it, Murray Kendricks couldn't say enough good things about her. Indeed, to hear her tell it, Kendricks was ready to sign over the moon to her, were he to own it.

The one thing he had not been able to accomplish where Cindie was concerned was completely getting rid of the old roommate. Cindie made certain Patterson knew she still saw Kyle often enough, despite the fight they'd had years before.

Good Lord but that had cost him. The long-stem roses had been the easiest part of regaining her affections—and her trust. Cindie had used his slight upset to her full advantage.

First, there had been the down payment on an apartment with plush white carpeting, gold-tone walls, oak furnishings, and all the amenities she could think up. Then, there had been the jewelry. She wanted a pair of diamond earrings large enough to "mean something." He'd bought them for her and threw in a matching tennis bracelet for good measure.

She'd rewarded him kindly that night. But tonight, Cindie was agitated, which wasn't going along with his evening plans.

She'd received a letter from Michelle, who had turned eleven the month before. Her "once a week" letter that came typically on Wednesdays helped soften the time between the Sunday evening phone calls mother and daughter enjoyed. And, usually, Cindie read the child's letter to him with giggles and sighs and exclamations of adoration. But tonight . . . tonight Cindie's bare feet peeked out from beneath the too-long red satin pajamas he'd recently treated her to as she paced back and forth on the thick white carpet and shook the letter at the ceiling.

"I don't understand why you are so upset," he told her. He'd kicked off his shoes and draped himself on the sofa in hopes that she would join him, but so far, she had not. "Come here. Let me hold you."

Cindie folded the letter and shoved it back into its envelope, then slammed the whole thing onto the end table, before plopping down beside him. "Don't you understand?" she whined as he wrapped his arms around her, aware of what lay beneath the cool material shimmering in the glow from the fire that gave the room its only light.

"All she seems to talk about these days is what she is doing with ... *her*."

"Allison?"

"Don't say her name to me."

"What would you like me to call her then?"

Cindie pondered the question before answering, "Witch."

"Is she?"

"Yes." She turned toward him. "She's stealing my daughter," she said, then muttered, "They've beaten me at my own game."

"You can go get her any time you want, Cindie."

"No. I can't. Westley has things sewn up so tight, managing to keep me at arm's length all these years, and *she's* put a dadburn bow around the whole thing."

"Who has?"

"*Allison*," she shouted, then swatted him. "You did that on purpose."

He laughed as he slid a hand up the back of her pajama top, hopeful until she stood and walked across the room to peer out the window. To the parking lot where icy rain slicked the asphalt and turned the world into a Monet painting. "Girl Scouts. Piano. Dance. School. Her friends." She turned and pointed toward the envelope. "That letter? All about the stupid tree in their stupid house and that *she* had bought a little fake one just for her room and *they* had decorated it with all pink and white ornaments."

Patterson glanced at his watch, mindful of the time they were wasting. "Well, if it makes you feel any better, dinner was good tonight," he said.

Cindie looked toward the kitchen where dirty dishes littered the countertops and filled the sink. One thing she never did—the dishes in front of him. Because she didn't want to waste a single second of their time together, she'd once told him. "Glad you liked it," she mumbled, then sighed as if she meant to expel all the air from inside her. "I've still got to get a tree before Michelle comes for Christmas break. I should have done it by now, but we've been so busy at work and—"

"Why don't you wait until the two of you can do that together," he suggested. "We're waiting until Patricia gets in ..." He allowed the words to fade; best not to bring up the domestic life he had with Mary Helen and the girls. Especially since it had improved so greatly.

"Why don't *you* stick a knife in my heart and *twist it,*" she said. "First ... a letter from my own kid telling me about ... *her* and all *she* does ... and now you want to paint me a pretty picture of Christmas warmth and love over at the Thackers'?"

Patterson rose from the sofa and shoved his feet into his loafers. "I'm going to leave while the going is good," he said. "You're in a mood I cannot fix." He walked over and kissed her forehead. "I've been around enough women in my life to know when I'm beat."

"No, wait," she said, surprising him by throwing her arms around him. Kissing him. "Don't go home tonight," she whispered.

His arms slid around her. "I have to go home tonight, sweetheart."

"Then let's plan a getaway. We haven't done that in a while. When is your next conference?"

He nibbled at the lobe of her ear; the obtrusive earring nearly cut his top lip. "March."

"I can't wait that long," she breathed out. "Patterson, seriously, how much longer can we go on like—"

He stopped her words by pressing his mouth on hers, deepening his kiss until her body went slack against his and he was forced to hold her up. "What's say we make good use of the time we have left this evening," he suggested when they broke apart. "May I have this *moondance?*"

She nodded. Took him by the hand and guided him to the floor in front of a fire that had become a low flame emitting only the occasional crackle. Something she had never done before. Or, maybe in a long time. "Merry Christmas, baby," she sighed with a smile.

Months later, when he looked back on that night—on that moment, that sigh, that smile, that letting her call the shots—he clearly saw his own undoing. And complicated didn't begin to explain it.

Chapter Thirty-four

January 1988
Allison

The winter of my discontent began after our celebration on New Year's Eve, on a Saturday to be exact. Michelle had returned from Cindie's a few days before, her arms laden with gifts, her mouth running ninety to nothing about how fun it had been in Atlanta because, wonder of wonders, Christmas Eve brought snow and "we went outside and made snow angels." My daughter was also bent on showing me every gift left for her under a tree she described as "skinny but loaded with lights"—a Caboodles filled with appropriate cosmetics and toiletries for an eleven-year-old, clothes that looked more Cindie's style than Michelle's, a 14k half-a-heart charm necklace (Cindie had the other half), and a glossy poster of Stevie Nicks.

"Stevie Nicks?" I asked from the second twin bed in her room. "Not your hero DJ Tanner?"

"I know, but don't you think she looks like Mommy?" Michelle asked, startling me. For months she had only referred to Cindie by her given name, despite my protests but with Westley's approval.

"Giving her life and giving her *a* life are not the same thing," he'd said, thereby ending our argument. I supposed it only made sense now that, after spending a week with Cindie, she would refer to her, again, as Mommy.

"She *does* look like ..." I swallowed. "Mommy. But ... why did Santa leave you a poster of ..." I looked back at the color-washed reproduction. "Stevie Nicks?"

"Mama," Michelle said with a chuckle from her bed. "Santa? This was one-hundred percent Cindie." She shook her head. "She thinks you won't let me have a picture of her in my bedroom, so she bought me this."

I glanced over at the framed five-by-seven of Cindie and Michelle taken at Six Flags Over Georgia the previous summer. "But you *do* have—"

"I told her that," Michelle said with a shrug. "She doesn't believe me." She looked back at the now rolled-up poster of Stevie. "Do you care?"

Yes. "No. Why should I care?"

"She thinks you're jealous of her." Michelle kicked off her shoes before crossing her legs.

I mimicked the movement. "Of Stevie Nicks?" I asked, trying to lighten the conversation.

Michelle chuckled. "No, silly. Of *her.* Cindie."

So, we were back to calling her Cindie. "Why would I be jealous of her, Michelle?"

She shrugged again. "She says because she's my real mommy."

I smiled the fakest smile of my life. "Sweetheart, I would be completely stupid if I didn't know that."

Michelle threw herself back on her bed, her feet popping out and pointing toward me. I reached over and tugged on a big toe. She sat up, propped herself on her elbows. "I love you to bits," she said. Words I'd heard Sylvie and her say to each other time and again in a torrent of giggles. Now, amazingly, also for me.

"I love *you* to bits," I told her.

At about five o'clock on the afternoon of New Year's Eve, we piled into Westley's car and headed for a downtown park where fireworks would explode in colorful displays of welcome to the new year beginning around midnight. Leading to that, a carnival, a few local garage bands, and some housewives-turned-craft-makers selling their goods entertained a crowd growing by the hour. Sylvie had ridden to the event with us rather than her family, but the girls vacillated between Westley and me and her parents whenever our paths crossed. For hours we meandered the park and rode the rides. I purchased a large homemade basket perfect for holding my books at the foot of my chair while Westley's great purchases included cotton candy, candied apples, and footlong hotdogs. And, as the night's chill grew, hot coffee for the two of us and cocoa topped with mounds of whipped cream for the girls.

Near midnight, Westley returned to the car while Michelle, Sylvie, and I found the perfect spot to enjoy the fireworks. He returned moments later with a picnic basket filled with champagne for the grownups and ginger ale for the girls along with a variety of snacks I'd prepared earlier. For more than an hour we laid back on an old quilt brought from the recesses of a chifforobe at Miss Justine's. "Perfect," she'd said to me, "for such things as picnics and fireworks." The four of us oohed and aahed at the displays of pyrotechnic brilliance shot into the blackness arching overhead. At one point, I looked at the girls who lay between Westley and me. Despite the noise and excitement, both were asleep, their hair tousled, their mouths agape. What little bit of their faces showed from the hoods of their jackets appeared wind-kissed.

I sat up, sent a *psst* Westley's way. He looked at me. I nodded toward the girls and he sat up, too. Looked. Smiled broadly, then leaned across them to share a kiss with me. One that began simply enough, then deepened. "Happy New Year, sweetheart," he said.

Who needed a coat? Warmth melted through my veins. My arteries. Every muscle in my being went to flame and marshmallows—something that had not happened in a while. I wasn't blaming anyone—least of all Westley and certainly not myself. Between our jobs, Michelle's schedule, and keeping up with a halfway decent social life, we had fallen into a "too tired to care" pattern. Or, perhaps we cared, but had become too tired to worry about it. But tonight, having shared a fun evening and a bottle of champagne ...

"Westley," I breathed, his name forming a cloud around us.

His brow raised. "How quickly can you pack all this up?"

"How quickly can you drive us home?" I countered.

He stood.

I stood. "Go warm up the car."

But by the time we arrived home and put the girls to bed, Westley complained of being "just too tired."

That had been Thursday night. Or, Friday morning, according to how one calls it.

Friday evening the weather went from cold to frigid. Rain that had fallen intermittently during the day turned to ice and grabbed hold of thick branches and limbs and snapped them like twigs. The electricity went out before nine. While Westley lit a fire, I pulled sleeping bags from our camping supply closet, then gathered the necessary items for making s'mores. After roasting and eating, we fell asleep to the sound of nature giving way to nature.

The next morning the sun rose from her slumber to create even more of a mess. By midafternoon, Westley declared war on the chaos defacing our lawn, and insisted we all head outside to tackle "this unsightliness" as a family. For nearly an hour I gathered limbs and twigs, fanning pine needles and prickly cones that littered the front while Westley did the same in the back. Michelle carted the wheelbarrow back and forth between the two, all the while singing some song she'd learned at church, loud and off-key. I grinned at her enthusiasm, humming a little myself as the warmth of her childlike abandon filled me with contentment. This was life, I told myself. This was *living*. I had everything I never knew I wanted—a loving husband, a beautiful little girl, a job I enjoyed, a lovely home. We had friends we enjoyed and money enough in the bank that we could breathe and enjoy the time God blessed us with.

I gathered what I hoped would be the last of the cones, then pulled off my gardening gloves in time to see Michelle darting around the corner of the house. Her arms and legs flailed about and her eyes held concern too mature for someone so young. "Mom!" she said, using a new term of endearment. "Daddy says come quick."

"What's going on?"

She stopped a few feet in front of me, hands dropped beside her powder-blue puffy jacket, her panting breath forming a cloud in the cold air. "He just says he needs you. He also says I'm to stay put."

There is a moment we can all look back on. A split second. A timestamp that divides everything from the beginning to that which will, eventually, play out to be the end. A moment when we don't know something that is immediately followed by the knowing. Or ... *a* knowing.

I ran the same path Michelle had arrived on until I reached the expanse of our backyard. Westley sat on the edge of one of the Adirondack chairs that encircled a firepit in the far-right corner of the property. He'd been wearing a baseball cap earlier, but it now lay at his feet. His head was down, his shoulders dipped forward. Even from a distance I could see the pallor of his skin.

I reached him, breathless. "What is it?" I asked.

He looked up then, his eyes watered in fear and his face devoid of color, his skin glistening with sweat. He held his left arm against his chest with his right hand.

"What is it?" I asked again.

"Ali," he breathed out. "Something's wrong."

I dropped to my knees in front of him, the still-wet grass immediately dampened my sweatpants. "What? Westley? What?" I gripped the arm of the chair and began to cry. "Oh, God," I said, which was more prayer than exclamation.

"Listen to me," he said softly. "I don't want to scare Michelle. So dry your tears, you hear me?" I nodded. "I need you to go inside and call an ambulance."

"Why?"

"Sweetheart ... do *not* scare Michelle."

"Are you—"

"*Allison*. Just. Do. This."

I stood and, when I did, he released his arm to grab my hand. "Tell them—tell them *no* siren. Hear me?"

I ran inside and dialed 9-1-1, giving them Westley's instructions, explaining that we had a young child who didn't need to be unduly frightened and telling them that we would be in the backyard. I ended the call, then dialed Sylvie's mother. "I need to send Michelle to your house," I said, my voice quivering. "I think Westley's having a heart attack or a stroke or something."

"Oh, Allison," Nikki said. "Of course. Do you want me to come get her?"

"No," I said. "That may scare her. I'll send her to you on her bike."

I hung up the phone, ran to the kitchen, and peered out the back window. Westley hadn't moved and I couldn't tell if he was breathing. "Okay," I said to no one, then turned and dashed to where Michelle lay on her back between the trunks of the pines, arms and legs spread wide, face peering out from around her coat's hood. She stared at the clear blue sky as though it were the most natural thing in the world to do in the middle of a cold, desperate January day. And, I suppose, for a child, it was.

"Michelle," I said, steadying my voice.

She sat up, her expression focused. "Hey, Mom? Is it okay if I call you that? Sylvie calls her mother 'Mom' and I think I'd like to call you that, too."

My smile wobbled but I managed to nod. "I—I like it," I said.

"Is Daddy okay?"

"He's fine ..." I didn't want my next words to become a lie, so I added, "Just not feeling real good. I think he tried to do too much." I took a breath that then left my body in a cloud. "Speaking of Sylvie's mom, she and I were just on the phone ... she's asked if you'd like to ride your bike down and play."

No questions asked, Michelle bound up, skipped to the opened-door garage, pulled her bicycle from where it rested against the wall near the stepladder and Westley's power saw, and hopped on. "You don't have to ask me twice," she hollered as she pedaled down the driveway.

"Have fun," I yelled back, then returned to the backyard to find Westley sitting with his eyes closed. "*Westley.*"

"Take my pulse," he said when I reached him. "I'm trying, but I can't seem to ..."

I dropped to my knees again, fear slicing me in half. What if something horrible happened to my husband because I didn't know anything about anything when it came to medicine? I should have gone to school like Elaine, I reminded myself. I should have become a nurse. Then I'd know what to do. "Westley."

He extended his right hand, palm side up. "It's not hard. Put the tip of your index and middle fingers on my wrist below my thumb." His instructions came in pants. "Don't use your thumb."

"Not my thumb."

"Your thumb has a pulse of its own, so ..."

"Okay." I laid my fingertips along the edge of his wrist, felt it throb where cold met clammy flesh. "I feel it. But how do I—"

"Your watch has a second hand, doesn't it?"

I looked at my watch as if I didn't know the answer. "Yes."

"Wait until the second hand gets to a quarter hour and then count the beats for fifteen seconds."

"Okay."

I held my own breath as I counted the thumping under my fingertips, nearly losing count twice within the fifteen seconds. "Thirty-two," I said.

Westley took in a slow breath through his nostrils then released it from between his lips.

"What does that mean?" I asked him.

He turned his face toward mine, then glanced over my shoulder. "There they are," he said, and I stood as two men in dark-blue uniforms rushed toward us. They carried black duffel-looking bags that appeared to weigh more than the two of them combined.

"His pulse is thirty-two," I said, wanting to be a part of the solution, a force behind the healing.

"One twenty-eight," Westley said, correcting me. "Shortness of breath, angina." He took another breath. "I'm diaphoretic, as you can see..."

Diaphoretic. Diaphoretic. A word I didn't know. Elaine would know. But I didn't and it sounded ... *not good.* I took a step back and then another and another to watch through a tunnel of fear and apprehension as the paramedics worked effortlessly on my husband. Gasped as one of the men ran back to the front of the house only to return pushing a gurney. I crossed my arms against a chill that penetrated my bones, then looked down and took in my attire. A long-sleeved turtleneck under a sweatshirt with matching sweatpants, the latter wet from the knees down. Should I go to the hospital dressed like this?

"Ma'am." The remaining paramedic walked toward me. "You'll want to follow us to Brady General," he said. "We're going to transport your husband—"

I looked at Westley who peered over his shoulder at me. "It's going to be okay, Ali," he said. "It's going to be okay. Just drive to Brady and go straight to the ER."

I walked to him, a knot forming in my throat, tears stinging my eyes. "Wes," I said, leaning over to kiss lips that quivered beneath mine. "Don't you dare die on me."

He chuckled. Actually chuckled, which brought a sigh of relief from me. "I'll see what I can do," he said.

Encouraged by his humor, I added, "I'm too young to be a widow."

"And you'll have to go out and buy a new black dress ..."

"And pearls. Miss Justine would demand pearls." With that, the paramedics continued onward.

I started to turn away, to return inside for my purse, but he stopped me with, "Ali."

"Yes?"

"Call Paul."

Chapter Thirty-five

Michelle spent the following week with Sylvie's family, the two girls joyfully pretending they were sisters while I spent the time sitting next to Westley's hospital bed. Or pacing in chilled hallways while the doctors performed first this test and then that one. Praying. Begging God. Making every deal I knew to make as long as the Almighty held up his end and kept my husband alive.

Julie called every day, offering wisdom and hope and letting me know that the folks Dean worked with were praying alongside me. Although certain none of them were making deals, I thanked her and them. Yet, I knew they were sincere in their petition. Still, I doubted they loved or cared about Westley—or even Dean—enough to strike a deal with God.

Heather also called daily. She had, in the years of my marriage to her brother, met and married her own Prince Charming, Nathaniel, who programmed bank computers but who talked nonstop about leaving the rat race behind to plow his own farm. Heather also worked within banking—which was how she and Nathaniel met—during her days and tended to the most rambunctious three-year-old I'd ever encountered during her "off hours." With each phone call she apologized profusely that she couldn't "let go and come help me," but I assured her I had all the help I needed.

Paul and DiAnn took leaves of absence from their jobs, leaving their kids with Westley's mother and father who drove across the state to help. Even though I slept at the hospital, my brother- and sister-in-law returned to our home each evening. But they kept daily vigil with me, listening to what the doctors said, what they advised. Then, on the day two men pushed my husband through double doors where he would undergo a double bypass, they stood on either side of me and held my hands until time to head for the waiting room. There they reminded me that Westley was young and strong and that he would come through this. DiAnn fetched coffee for the three of us, coffee we barely touched. It grew cold and formed a gray layer along the top until we tossed the remains into a lined trashcan. We made small talk, glancing occasionally at the television where a soap opera played out in all its drama.

As if we needed more drama.

Paul looked at his watch incessantly, an act that should have worked my last nerve, but instead prompted a "what time is it now?" from me. And each time he'd say, "Ten minutes since the last time I looked," and DiAnn would sigh.

"I'm going to get more coffee," she said, not thirty minutes after we'd thrown away the first cups, then disappeared down the hall.

"She's stressed. She's worried about Wes, missing the kids ..." Paul explained. We sat side by side in the yellow-gold faux leather and wood chairs, the kind you only find in medical offices or cheap beachfront motels.

"I worry about your mom and dad if—"

"Don't, Allison. Don't even go there."

"And Michelle," I choked out, knowing the only person in the hospital I could be completely honest with was Paul. I didn't dare mention my fears to Westley. Didn't dare add to his concerns of life and death. And I was still too afraid of DiAnn.

Paul leaned over to rest his elbows on his knees then turned his head toward me. "What did you tell her?"

"Only that Daddy had gotten tired the day we worked in the yard and that he was in the hospital, but he'd be home soon and not to worry," I spilled. "To enjoy her time with Sylvie."

A long exhale escaped from Paul as his attention went to his shoes. "Listen, uh—I should tell you that Cindie called last night."

"Oh, God. What did you tell her?"

Paul straightened. "Nothing. I didn't actually speak to her. She left a message on your answering machine."

"For Wes?"

"No. Michelle."

Tears stung my eyes until a lone traitor slipped down my cheek. "Paul," I whispered. "If anything happens to Wes ... Michelle ..." I couldn't say the words. Couldn't fully share my greatest fear. Losing Westley would be one thing—devastating—but losing Michelle on top of that would mean the end of my existence. She had become more than just Westley's child, the toddler I took in so soon after we married. She was now my daughter as well. My little girl. Nearly every minute of every day revolved around her. How would I—

DiAnn returned then with three fresh cups of coffee in a carrier, steam curling above the Styrofoam. She handed mine to me, then Paul's to him before sitting and producing three donuts from a small white sack.

"I told her Cindie called," Paul said, reaching for his donut.

"Don't let her worry you." DiAnn extended a donut toward me, but I shook my head. "Eat it," she all but ordered. "You'll be happy for the sugar rush later."

I took the pastry and bit into it, relishing its delectable warmth. "You heated them?" I asked, marveling at her consistent attention to detail.

"They were under a warming lamp," she said around her own bite, then swallowed. "Back to Cindie—seriously, do not give her another thought. You have to stay focused on Westley."

"They sort of go together," I reminded her.

"The three of you go together. Besides, Wes will be fine."

"I just don't want Cindie to find out about ... all this."

DiAnn took a long swallow of her coffee. "Not bad for a hospital cafeteria," she said, then added, "Paul and I will handle everything where Cindie is concerned. Do *not* give it another thought."

I nodded at the woman whom I'd been so unsure of the first time I met her. Of course, she'd put a wall up back then; she hadn't wanted to see me hurt. Even now, with her strong personality, I felt intimidated, all the while knowing she only had my best interest in mind. "All right," I said, but I couldn't *help* but give it a thought. More than one. A million and one. What would I do without Westley and Michelle? What would I do with the little bit of happiness I called mine?

Westley returned home in fine spirits eight days after he'd entered the hospital. Release orders stated that he was to make a cardiologist appointment in one week, not to return to work for at least six, and to forego any strenuous activities for at least three months. The first order was easy to adhere to; the next two were problematic.

Westley found it nearly impossible to stay home and relax. Never mind *nearly* impossible. Within days he managed to talk me into taking him to the drugstore where he promised to walk in only long enough to make sure his fill-in didn't need anything or that he had all of his questions answered. "Five minutes," he pleaded after I had given him several exasperated "nos." But when I put my foot down with a firm "absolutely not," he simply retorted, "Fine. I'll drive myself."

Knowing he meant business, I relented and drove him to the store where he stayed for more than an hour. And when he returned to the car and to my horrified if not furious expression, he looked at me as if I should not have expected anything less.

Within two weeks, he returned to work part time, and no amount of arguing on my part or Miss Justine's mattered. He did what he wanted to do, in true Westley style, defying fate and logic. His prescribed half-mile walk began at a mile. The later prescribed two miles became four. By the time six weeks passed, he was out riding bikes with Michelle, had returned to work full time, and was planning a ski trip to Boone, North Carolina "before the snow melts."

The only thing he hadn't done by his typical standards was reach for me at night, a circumstance he blamed on his medication.

"Are you sure?" I asked him one night. I knelt beside him in our bed, him on his stomach with me massaging his back. "You promise it's the meds and not me?"

He craned his neck to look at me. "How could it possibly be you?" he asked with a smile. "You're beautiful, you're sexy, and I love you like mad. Always have. Always will."

I returned the smile as I continued to knead his warm flesh, wishing I could feel his muscles move and stretch above me rather than beneath, the warmth of his breath sighing onto my skin. But he returned his face to the crook of his arm, leaving me unsure as to whether he'd placated me or told me the truth. I leaned over and kissed the line where neck and shoulders meet, slid my tongue upward toward his earlobe. "What about now?" I teased, hopeful.

"Ali," he mumbled. "Stop." He rolled onto his back, drew me into his arms and kissed my temple. "You'll have to trust me on this one, okay? I know the side effects and I've talked with the doctor about it. As soon as I can wean off, Mother Nature will take over and I'll be back in the saddle."

"Back in the saddle?"

"You know what I mean."

"It's just," I whispered around the knot that threatened to choke out the words, "that I love you and I miss ... that."

"Me, too," he said. "Now let's get some sleep."

Cindie

Everything had to be perfect.

Everything. From the meal to the music. From the words to the timing in which she spoke them.

Patterson had been on a Kenny G kick lately, so she went out and purchased the latest. Had it playing loud enough that he'd hear it when he slid his key into the front door lock.

A bottle of his preferred wine was open and breathing on the bar. She'd timed his favorite meal from her kitchen—smothered pork chops with asparagus and seasoned baby red potatoes—to the minute. And, of course, she had taken great pains in choosing what she'd wear. Had gone shopping for the right outfit, settling on a white knit too-short skirt with matching sweater accentuated by a wide red knit belt. More sash than belt, really.

She nearly broke her budget with the purchase of gold mesh earrings that dripped seductively from her earlobes toward her shoulders, then decided to go all the way and purchased the complementary necklace. Then, keeping with what made Patterson happy, she met him at the door barefoot, despite the chill in the air. The fire in the fireplace would take care of that.

And, hopefully, her news.

He smiled as soon as he saw her, and she hurried over to him. Locked her arms around his neck and kissed him. When he pulled back, his eyes narrowed, but his grin grew broader. "Do I smell smothered pork chops?" he asked.

Cindie pretended to pout. "Really?" She stepped back. Turned slowly. Seductively. "Is that all you're interested in?"

"Well," he said, giving her a quick peck on the cheek, "No, but I am hungry, and you know how much I love your smothered pork chops." He took a step toward the dining room, stopping short at the view of linen and crystal and gleaming china. "You brought out the good stuff," he said. "Did I forget something? I know it's not your birthday."

She wrapped her arm around his and guided him toward the table set for two. "No, silly. Have we been together so long that I can't treat you to a special dinner? Light the candles, will you?" She released him, picked up the plates, and started toward the kitchen. "I'll serve the food."

"Kenny G," he called out as she spooned a generous helping of potatoes onto his plate.

"You like?" she answered back.

"Yes, I do. When'd you get it?"

Cindie returned to the dining room carrying two plates of steaming hot food, one with noticeably larger portions. "Today," she answered as he took the plates from her. She looked down; he'd kicked off his shoes, his black socks a stark contrast to the carpet. When Patterson took their plates, she turned back toward the kitchen. "I'll get the wine."

She returned less than a minute later to hand him the dark-green bottle. "Do the honors?"

"You're beginning to make me nervous," he said with a chuckle that failed him.

"Sit," she said, then slid onto her chair. "Why's that?"

Patterson sat across from her. "Muted lights. Kenny G." He leaned back. "Is that a new outfit?"

"It is," she answered, picking up her fork. "Eat before it gets cold."

"And new jewelry?" he asked, reaching for his knife and fork.

"You like? The light, the music, the outfit, the jewelry?"

"Very much so." He took a bite of pork chop. "Dear Lord in heaven, this is ... so ... good." He swallowed then. "Cindie."

"Yes?"

He pointed the fork at her. "Tell me the truth right now. And no funny business. What is this about? Is your checking account in the red again? Do you need money?"

"I'm doing fine, Patterson." And she was. More than fine. That was the one and only good deal in her allowing Michelle to continue to live with Westley. No "child expenses" and no "child support." Her money was hers to make and hers to spend. "When was the last time I asked you for money?"

"It's been a while."

"See? A little education and a good job go a long way."

"Indeed, they do." He took another bite, swallowed. "But you and I both know this isn't our typical evening at home."

That much was true. Then again, they had no *typical* evenings at home. Nor did they have typical evenings anywhere else. Every "night out" was in secret. Every trip a rendezvous.

Patterson started for his wine, then stopped. "Seriously," he said.

"Is there something you need to tell me? You weren't fired today or anything?"

"Of course not. You know how much they depend on me at work."

His face brightened. "A promotion then?"

She gripped her fork, then set it down. "That would be nice, but ... no."

"Cindie ..."

"Drink your wine," she said, because clearly this wasn't going as she'd hoped. Her plan had been dinner. Wine. A half glass for her, at least three for him. Her plan had been snuggling on the sofa. Making out. Making love. Then ... then when he was half drunk and completely spent and relaxed in her arms she'd ask if he loved her. He would assure her that he did. The way he always assured her. And then, she'd tell him her secret. Beyond that, she had no clue.

But, as always, Patterson was running the show. Whatever Patterson wanted ... whenever he wanted ... wherever he wanted ...

Cindie took a sip of her own and said, "It's the good stuff in case you didn't notice."

"I noticed."

She forced a smile. "Then drink up," she said, reaching for the bottle to add a small portion to the half-filled goblet.

"Not until you come clean," he answered, but his fork speared one of the potatoes.

She had to gain control. She had to ... "Patterson," she said, her voice strong. "Seriously. Take a sip of your wine. It's delicious and I spent a great deal on it."

Then, for reasons she'd never fully understand, he did. "Now," he said. "What's this about? Because I can tell when something's up. If you are having a problem—with your job, with your bank account, whatever—tell me now so we can get it out of the way, and I can enjoy this evening with you. We don't get nearly enough time, so—"

All right then. She'd have to skip ahead. No snuggling. No making love. "Do you love me?"

He rested his knife and fork on the edge of the plate, and she did the same. "How long have we been together now? You know I do."

"Good, then we *don't* have a problem."

"Then it stands to reason that if I didn't love you, we would."

"Yes." She picked up the utensils again, holding them the way he'd taught her. The way she made sure Michelle held them when they ate together—the one thing Westley had apparently failed to teach her properly. "You're right. It stands to reason."

"And why is that?" Patterson pressed.

"Because," she stated, bringing her eyes to his. "I'm pregnant."

Chapter Thirty-six

Nothing had gone as planned.

Patterson hadn't swept her into his arms. He hadn't caressed her. Told her that he loved her and that, "Somehow, sweetheart, we'll work through this. I'll leave Mary Helen tomorrow, I'll file for divorce, and you and I will marry, and our baby will grow up in a loving home, happy with his sisters who will come every weekend and Michelle who will come when she can." Instead, he became demanding. Ordering her about. Blaming her. She'd done this on purpose, he ranted. She'd not taken her pill at just the right time. She was a woman, he said. "You know the way these things work."

She'd assured him otherwise, but he didn't believe her—the worst sting of all.

"So then? What do you expect of me?" he asked, his hands splayed on his hips as he paced in front of her on the living room floor. "What do you want me to do about this? Because if you think I'm leaving my wife ... my girls ... my career ... you're sadly mistaken, Cindie."

She sat on the sofa, feet tucked under her. They were freezing now; no amount of heat from the fireplace could warm them. In fact, her bones hurt, the whole of her was so chilled. She'd known he wouldn't necessarily be thrilled, but she'd not expected this.

And, of course, she cried. Tears, unrelenting and uninvited, slipped down her cheeks in a cascade, which only riled Patterson more. He pointed at her, face red, eyes blazing. "Crying isn't going to help."

Even worse than being called a liar was the fact that she had somehow, inexplicably, found herself here again. In such a position. Telling a man she loved—or thought she loved—that she now carried his child, only to have him become angry. Unsympathetic to her needs. Her emotions. Her desires.

Always what *they* wanted. Always.

Well, she didn't need him. She could have a baby on her own— she'd proven that—but this time she'd figure out a way to raise the child. Over her dead body would Patterson and Mary Helen bring her child up. It was bad enough that Westley's wife had sunk her teeth into Michelle. Molding her into what *she* wanted her to be—like *her*. But not this time ... no. And she sure as sunshine on a July afternoon wasn't going to let her family know she'd gotten pregnant by another man—a married man—anytime soon. Velma would call hellfire down on her. Leticia, who flitted from one bad relationship to the next, would try to figure a way to make her older sister's situation work to *her* benefit, and Jacko—who drank too much but still managed to marry a sweet girl and raise his kids halfway decent—Jacko and Jasmine would probably offer to make her child one of theirs. Then there was Lettie Mae who would, as she'd done the first time, call her a slut. Tell her she was only getting what she deserved, and then, in the next breath, try to find a way to extort money from Patterson much as she'd tried from Westley.

Patterson. A man she could kill right now as good as look at, but at the same time had to protect. The irony struck her, seeped into the soul of her. Somehow ... *somehow* ... she had to stop being a victim. Had to be on top and remain there. If only once in her life, she had to.

She stood. Faced him, her lips taut as a rope holding a rabid dog. "Get out," she said.

"Don't tell me—"

She pointed to the door. "Get. Out."

His face softened and his eyes became tender again. "Cindie," he whispered, reaching for her. She took a step back. If this was going where she thought it was going, he'd best know right up front that she wasn't the stupid teenager she'd been when she'd faced Westley with this news. Oh, no ... No man was going to sweet-talk her again. Talk her into something she didn't want to do so he could get what he wanted ... again. "Sweetheart ... I'm sorry. I wasn't expecting ... *this*. I know you didn't do this on purpose." He raised his hands as if he were addressing a jury about to sequester and reach a verdict. "What we have to do now is figure out what we will do from here."

"I know what I'm going to do, Patterson."

His shoulders sank, the idea of losing it all—wife, daughters, career, and a mistress—weighing them down. "Look. I know a good doctor. He can take care of this, discreetly, and we'll get back to what we had—what we *have*."

She blinked. "I'm not aborting this baby, Patterson." She laughed then. A light chuckle that came from the saddest place inside her. "You and Westley," she said, breathing out their names as though they were poison. "I sure know how to pick 'em." At least Westley hadn't asked her to abort the child.

"Them. Pick *them*."

"Shut up, Patterson. I know how to speak. And I'm not as stupid as you seem to believe."

"I never—"

"Then shut up. You ..." She took a step toward him. "You were never, *ever*, going to marry me, were you? You were never going to leave Mary Helen. It wouldn't have mattered how old your girls got to be." She laughed again. "I can hear it now... *I can't leave, Cindie, because the girls are too young ... in school ... getting married ... having their own babies.* Well, Patterson, I hope you enjoyed what you had since the day I walked into your classroom with a 'yes' practically tattooed across my chest because you'll never have it again. You'll never touch me. Kiss me. Love me." She shook her head. "You sure saw me coming, didn't you? And for some reason you thought you could use me ... for how long? For another few years?"

"Stop it."

"No." She took another step. "You stop it. Get your shoes. Get whatever you think you have here that is yours ... and get. Out." She turned away from him, but his hand came around her arm, gripping.

"You will not walk out on me," he told her. "And you will not threaten me, do you hear? I'll ruin you from one end of this globe to the next."

A moment of fear ran through her, a moment of remembering the time he'd hurt her. But what else could he do, really? How much worse could life get? She raised her chin and brought her eyes directly to his. "*You* will ruin *me?*" Cindie jerked her arm from his hold. "I suggest, Professor, that you go home tonight, snuggle up to your cold little wife, and pray to God that *I* don't ruin *you.*"

His slap came fast, leaving a trail of heat. But she didn't collapse, nor did she clutch her cheek in distress. Instead, she turned, somehow made her way toward the bedroom door, and then tossed over her shoulder, "Leave your keys on the table. You won't be needing them again."

She entered the dark of her bedroom and closed the door behind her, locking it with fingers that quivered so much they were nearly useless. Then, with her forehead pressed against the jamb, she waited. Listening ... first to the slow shuffle of feet, the sitting on the sofa— was he putting on his shoes?—to the sigh of fabric as he stood, the drop of a single key to the table ... She listened ... until the front door opened and clicked shut.

It was over. How long had it been now? How long had they been together? How long had she been such a stupid little fool? How much time had she wasted? Or nearly wasted, since one thing she had learned had been that nothing in life is ever wasted. The good, the bad. Nothing. If you learn from it, it becomes useful and worthwhile.

Who'd said that to her? Westley? Sounded like something he'd say, but . . . no. Surely not Lettie Mae and certainly not her father. Vernon? No. Vernon was all about doing the right things all the time and not having to learn from the bad.

Then who?

Cindie flipped on the light switch—the one connected to the

bedside lamp. A soft glow filled the corner of the room, dimming as it neared her, giving her just enough light to step over to her dresser and, without a glance in the mirror, remove first the earrings, then the necklace, followed by her clothes, which she left discarded on the floor. Like a puddle.

She pressed her hand low on her stomach. Squeezed eyes devoid of tears shut and tried to imagine a life raising a child on her own. She hadn't been able to do it before. To do it with any measure of success. How could she possibly do it now? And how long before she told anyone? How long before she—

Kyle. Kyle had been the one to tell her about the good and the bad in life. Her old roommate and oftentimes friend. The man Patterson despised for no good reason except that she loved him like a brother.

And he loved her, too. Sometimes she thought more than as a sister, although he'd never played that card.

She turned. Spied the phone on her bedside table as a slow smile crept from the corners of her mouth. She slid beneath the covers dressed only in her bra and panties. Shivering, she picked up the phone and dialed a number she knew by heart.

"Hello," a sleepy voice answered.

"Did I wake you?" she asked.

"Nah," he answered. "Who's this?"

Cindie giggled. "Silly…"

"Hey…" he said as recognition came. "What are you up to?"

She took a breath. She could do this. She could. She had to. "I've had kind of a bad day … and I was … well, I was remembering what you said that time about bad stuff. You know? That even the bad stuff can be good if we learn from it."

"Truth." The rustling of body against cotton met her as he shifted in bed. She tried to imagine him, thick hair tousled, muscles stretching, eyes blinking. "Did something bad teach you something good today?"

Oh, yes… "I'd say so."

"Want to talk about it?"

"Not really."

He groaned. "All right. Want to talk about anything in particular?"

Cindie paused. Waiting long enough to gather her courage and become coy at the same time. "Kyle, can I ask you a question?"

"Anytime."

"Why haven't you ever—you know—asked me out or, I mean, even tried anything with me? Do you not find me attractive?"

His sigh was long. Poignant. "Gosh, no. I mean, yes. Yes, I find you attractive. You're downright gorgeous, Cindie. Did someone tell you otherwise?"

"In a way. I guess—I guess what you could say is that someone told me I'm not good enough."

"You listen to me, you hear? You're beyond good enough. If I ever thought for a second that our friendship could be something more …" He chuckled lightly. "I would have been all over you like white on rice."

She smiled in spite of her circumstances. "Kyle," she said, breathing out his name. "What if I told you that I wish—that I often wished— you'd want more than just friendship? What would you say?"

He didn't answer at first, making her wait while he gathered his wits, she figured. "What are you doing right now?" he asked.

"Just lying under a mound of covers, shivering."

"Don't move," he said. "I'll be right there."

She smiled. "The door will be unlocked."

When the line went dead without a "good-bye," she threw back the sheet and blanket and the thick comforter, ran to the closet for her robe, then across the room and opened the door. With a dash she entered the dining room, blew out the candles, cleared the table, and then tidied the kitchen as best she could in the little time she had. She found Patterson's discarded key and threw it into a junk drawer. Finally, she poured two fresh glasses of wine and took them into her room, where she removed the robe and slid back into bed. She took a moment to calculate. To her best guesstimation, she was right at four weeks. All she had to do now was let nature take its course tonight with Kyle. And then tomorrow … tomorrow would come and, hopefully, he'd want more of her. And, with any amount of luck, she'd want more of him. Then, in a few weeks she'd tell him of a baby—their baby. Kyle being Kyle, he'd marry her right away. Never hesitating. Never imagining that Professor Thacker was the biological father. He'd marry her and together they'd raise *their* child. No one but no one would be the wiser. Except Patterson, and he no longer counted. Finally, with one simple plan, she had the upper hand.

Cindie smiled. Stretched. Reached for her glass of wine and took a sip.

And then she waited.

April 1988
Allison

Cindie had decided that, instead of Michelle coming up to Atlanta for Easter, she would come down and that they would spend the holiday with her family—primarily Velma and Vernon. Which was fine. Better than fine because, at least, Michelle didn't have to go all the way to Atlanta for a week during spring break. Instead, Cindie told Westley, he could bring Michelle to her sister's on Saturday morning and she'd have their daughter home Monday before heading back to the city later that afternoon. Double hurray, because now I could make plans with Michelle for the school holiday.

But Cindie had also said something in her call to Westley that left me unnerved in the interim between his taking Michelle to Velma's and his return to the house. "She said she needs to talk to me about something once we get there."

I felt blood rush from my head. "What do you think she means by that?"

"I don't know, Ali. I guess we'll have to wait and find out."

And so I waited. I waited and I paced until I nearly wore a groove in the polished bricks of the kitchen floor. Waited for my husband to come home and give me whatever news Cindie had to give. Waited and wondered what she wanted and, even more so, what had gone wrong in our marriage since January. December, really, which was the last time I could remember us consummating our marriage. His lack of attention toward me was only the start of it. Medication or no medication. We seemed farther apart than any two people had a right to be and call themselves husband and wife.

If only I could find that copy of Marabel Morgan's book. Maybe, then ... But I'd long ago misplaced it. Long ago stopped adhering to the principles, except for making sure I looked every bit the part of Westley's wife. I kept my wardrobe updated to the latest fashion trends acceptable for married women—straight skirts worn just above the knee or flattering slacks, all of which I wore with silk blouses or turtlenecks made from soft cotton. I'd had my stylist cut my hair in layers, which gave it a bouncy look, and I wore my makeup in the smoky, sultry way that graced the face of every fashion magazine cover girl tempting shoppers at checkout counters. I also continued to make a list first thing every day. That I stuck to, although I didn't always know why. Seemed to me that, lately, every day only mirrored the day before. Every week the week before. Yesterday and today and tomorrow had blurred into a haze I couldn't see my way out of.

Furthermore, Mrs. Morgan, I couldn't begin to remember the last time I'd been playful in the bedroom. Westley kept me at arm's length, unable to physically love me but clearly able to purchase and ride a new motorcycle and certainly capable of skiing—both on snow and water, despite the frigid temperature. Why, he'd just wear a wetsuit and stay toasty and dry, he said.

But it was more than the trip to Boone or the days on the lake or his driving the Harley much too fast for my liking. And it was more than the lack of passion or even conversation in our bedroom. It was every room. Sure, he was kind. Polite. And he doted on Michelle as he'd always done. But there was a difference in the air around us. Something I couldn't put my finger on—I felt sure it wasn't another woman—but something I felt all the same. Something separating us. Worse still, it was something I couldn't identify enough to discuss with Miss Justine or Julie or even my mother. I'd almost said something to Marilyn once, but before I could find the words, she began telling me of a trip she and Trev were taking. By the time the itinerary had been covered I was too emotionally drained to say, "Oh, by the way, I think Westley and I are heading for a divorce."

Okay. Maybe not a divorce. But there were certainly moments when I feared the only thing holding us together was Michelle ... and now ... now I wondered if Cindie wasn't about to tell him she wanted Michelle back. Full time. She had graduated from college. She had a good job according to what she told Westley. And, according to Michelle, a "cool apartment in a really cool complex where some other really cool kids lived."

No. Cindie wasn't the same girl she'd been when I first married Westley, that much was for sure. She had made a difference in her life and now, through her job, she made a difference in the lives of others while I recorded numbers for Miss Justine and made the perfect home for Westley and a life for Michelle.

The door to the garage opened and I turned, startled to see Westley enter, a strange mix of amusement and bewilderment drawn across his face. Somehow, in my angst, I'd not heard the car as it rolled up the driveway.

"What?" I asked, stopping long enough to wring my hands.

He tossed his keys on the countertop. "Do I smell coffee?" he asked.

I glanced at the Mr. Coffee that stood empty and gleaming in the corner near the sinks. "No," I answered, stupefied. "Do you *want* coffee?"

"Please," he said, then plopped into the nearest chair at the kitchen table with a deep sigh.

I set about to make a pot, my heart hammering. "Oh, gosh, Westley. Just tell me. Is she going to fight us for custody of Michelle? Because a fight is what she'll get if she thinks she can just—"

"She got married."

I spun around, the carafe in my hand, poised beneath a spray of water from the tap. "What?"

"She married Kyle."

I shut off the water. "The old roommate?"

"Yep."

I placed the pot on the counter. Opened the cabinet that housed the coffee and filters. Brought them out. Set them next to the carafe. "Wow."

"She is Mrs. Kyle Lewis now. You know, for the next time you send her a copy of Michelle's report card."

I turned to look at Westley, resting my hips against the counter's edge. "Was he there? Did you meet him?"

"I did. And—I gotta say it, Ali—he's a nice guy. I mean, a *really* nice guy. And he looks at Cindie like she's the best thing since sliced bread."

I finished preparing the coffee. Pressed "ON" and then went to sit in the chair nearest my husband. "Well, she *is* beautiful, Westley. I mean, even I can say that with absolute honesty."

"I guess so." He stood as if I'd gotten too close, walked to the cabinet of coffee mugs, and pulled one out.

"I wouldn't mind a cup, too, please."

He looked at me. Blinked. "Oh. Sorry," he said, then pulled another mug from the cabinet. The news of his ex-lover's nuptials had clearly rattled him. I frowned at my own thought. *Ex-lover* was too descriptive for a one-night stand.

I ran my tongue over dry lips. "Wes? Is she wanting—I mean, with the marriage—is she wanting Michelle back? You haven't said."

He shrugged as he stared at the coffeemaker, as though willing it to hurry up and fill the glass pot so he could drink his coffee and move on. But then he said, "I doubt it."

Relief flooded me. Sent me on a cloud of happy I never wanted to return from until I reckoned that Cindie *not* wanting Michelle made little to no sense. Especially now. Didn't she have it all? The education, the job, the husband? Wasn't the only thing missing her daughter? "Why do you doubt it?"

The coffeemaker gurgled to announce the coffee ready, and Westley jerked it by the handle, pouring first one mug, then the other. I stood, went to the refrigerator for milk, and joined him. "Why?" I asked again.

"Because, Ali, for one thing, Michelle is eleven years old. She's not going anywhere this late in the game. For another ... Cindie is pregnant."

"Oh." I set the carton of milk on the counter next to him. We were close enough now that our arms brushed against each other—cotton on cotton. A chill ran through me, but I ignored it. "When is she due?"

"Ah—she didn't say, actually. I'm assuming six, maybe seven, months from now by the looks of her."

"So, she got pregnant *before* she was married." Again. Probably unplanned, too. How was it that some women were able to just think about sex and find themselves pregnant, easily carrying that child to term, while others, like me, could think and do from now to kingdom come and no child would ever be pushed from her womb?

We didn't speak again as we finished preparing our coffee. Westley returned to the table and I followed, this time sitting as far from him as possible. "Was she just letting you know then? About the pregnancy and the marriage? No strings? No demands?"

He took a sip. Swallowed. "I guess so. Just wanted me to know."

My hands quivered; I wrapped them around the heat of the mug. "And you really like this guy? You think he'll be good to Michelle?"

Westley's brow shot up. "What little bit of time he'll see her. Yeah, I do. Seems like a straight-up kind of guy."

I drank from my mug. Set it down, willing my hands to stop shaking. Why were they shaking? What premonition haunted me in the cool of this spring morning? The same one that wove its way through my days? My weeks and months and years? The one that compromised my happiness at every turn? Or was this something new? Something that had nothing to do with Cindie ripping Michelle from my life? "Well, all right then," I said, forcing aside the rush of emotion threatening to overtake me.

Westley stood. My eyes traveled the length of him. As much distance as there seemed to be between us, I still loved him. Wanted him. But more than anything, I needed to know for certain that Westley was right. All was well. Changes were sometimes good, but not always. Sometimes they brought devastation. "Wes?"

"I think I'll go for a ride on my bike," he said. "No sense in wasting this day sitting inside the house."

The words sounded promising. They also held truth. "Can I go with you?"

He seemed surprised by the request, eyes never meeting mine. "Ah—not this time. I'm not steady enough yet."

He reached for his keys and headed out the same door he'd walked through not fifteen minutes before.

"Well, maybe we can do something together later. Go to a movie, maybe? That Matthew Broderick movie looks good." As long as our choices didn't include *She's Having a Baby,* no matter how adorable Kevin Bacon appeared to be in it and how absolutely wonderful DiAnn had reported it to be. "Biloxi Blues?"

"All right," he said. "Dinner first? Henry's?"

Henry's? A dress-up place. Candles flickering on tables covered by linen, their light reflecting on crystal stemware under dimly lit chandeliers. The very notion of Westley wanting to take me there held a promise from a happier time and I smiled. "Who needs a movie if we're going to Henry's?" I asked, hoping he caught the teasing in my voice. I decided I'd wear my black-beaded dress and diamond stud earrings. A gift from Westley in happier days.

He smiled back, but—even from across the room—I could see the force behind it. "Whatever you say." He was halfway out the door.

"I love you," I called out.

"You too," he said as the door closed behind him.

Chapter Thirty-seven

Biff came home for Easter. Unexpectedly. He never arrived announced—a fact that thoroughly aggravated Miss Justine, infuriated Ro-Bay, and tightened a knot inside my soul I could not explain. This man held an attraction I could never be sure of. I only knew that he did and that with things the way they had been of late between Westley and me, Biff's visit could not have come at a worse time.

Ro-Bay met me at the door on Monday with a determined frown and a huff. "He's back," she muttered.

"Who's back?" I asked, knowing the answer. My thoughts went to my appearance. That morning, although the last thing I felt like doing was dressing according to Miss Justine's specifications, I had donned a form-hugging denim skirt with a long-sleeved white with dark-blue pinstripes button-up blouse. Before leaving the house, I grabbed a sweater, which I now shrugged out of and handed over, all the while grateful for the extra care I'd taken.

"That boy of Miss Justine's, that's who. Got her in a dither. Dander riled up." She looked up the staircase. "Still in bed, too. Just like always. Acts like all we've got to do around here is wait on his lazy bones to get up and get moving. Well, if he thinks I'm gonna make another breakfast just for him, he's got another think coming."

"I take it you mean Biff," I remarked as matter-of-factly as I could steady my voice.

Her fist went to her hip. "Who else?"

I glanced up then toward the back of the house. "Where's Miss Justine?"

"Gone already. Had some church ladies circle meeting she couldn't miss."

I started for the library that continued to serve as my office. "Oh, that's right. I remember now. Her Garden Club is meeting with them to talk about their summer show now that the Easter show is over and how they can work together."

Ro-Bay harrumphed. "Every one of them ladies that's in one is in the other. Coffee?"

"I'll come get it shortly," I said.

"Oh no you won't," Ro-Bay said, the thick soles of her shoes sighing against the marble floor. "It's Monday morning. You been here long enough to know that on Monday mornings I mop and wax and nobody, but nobody, is gonna walk across my linoleum till I say so." I smiled as she raised her chin in hopes that her voice would carry up the stairs, something I'd long been watching her do. "I'll bring it like I've done every Monday since you started here."

I found the usual Monday stacks dotting my desk. My shoulders fell as I dropped my purse into an empty drawer. The usual ... everything in my life ... the usual. Ordinary. Scheduled and expected. On Mondays Ro-Bay mopped and waxed and brought me my coffee. On Mondays I looked at the same reports from the previous week and then entered their numbers into a ledger. Every Monday, every Tuesday, every Wednesday through Sunday ... the same. My life had become a Ferris Wheel I could not get off.

I glanced at my watch. Westley had stayed home to wait for Cindie and her new husband to bring Michelle back. "Not sure when she'll be here," he'd said. "And I told her no hurry. After all, she's giving up the whole week so Michelle can stay here." He scooped up a book he'd been reading and headed for the sofa in the family room. "So I just took the day off."

I hadn't wanted to contend that if he had told me he was taking a day, I would have, too. That we could have spent the day relaxing together. Stretched out on opposite sofas, reading or watching a movie on the VCR. I also didn't intend to argue that Cindie hadn't given up anything for anybody except herself. For whatever reason, she hadn't wanted Michelle to come to Atlanta for the week and had chosen to drive down. Perhaps so she could let Westley know about the marriage and/or the baby ... all of which she could have done on the phone.

I shrugged. I'd spent entirely too much time thinking and worrying about it since Saturday morning. Saturday morning and all Saturday afternoon and into the evening, a night which should have been the romantic new beginning I'd prayed for since Westley's heart attack. Instead, I sat across from Westley over an intimate dinner at Henry's debating with myself the issues of Cindie and what a new little brother or sister would mean for Michelle. Not that it mattered; despite the amorous setting of the restaurant, Westley's mind seemed just as preoccupied, a fact that only worsened my concerns. Was he thinking the same I was but not wanting to let on? Protecting me in true Westley fashion?

But I didn't need protecting. I needed the truth and I needed a crystal ball and I needed my husband pulling my body to his and I needed—

"Here you go," Ro-Bay said, interrupting my thoughts. So much so, I jumped. "My, now. What's got you on edge?"

I reached for the cup and saucer. With one look I could see that the coffee had been prepared exactly to my taste. Ro-Bay knew me about as well as anyone, and I smiled as I brought the cup to my lips, remembering our first encounter. I'd been so young then. So frightened. So . . . innocent. But no more. The innocence had been shattered and the woman who had initially invoked fear was now considered a friend.

I swallowed the first sip. "Ro-Bay? Do you mind if I ask you a question?"

"Depends."

Ignoring her, I pressed on. "Is it normal for a man and woman to grow apart from time to time? You know, in marriage?"

Ro-Bay crossed her arms and huffed. "How long you been married now? Just a smidge over ten years?"

"Mm-hm." I placed the cup and saucer close enough to reach but far enough from the stacks of work awaiting me. "Westley says it's the heart attack. The meds." Heat rose in my cheeks and I pressed my fingertips against it. "I cannot believe I'm saying this."

Ro-Bay found an occasional chair and pulled it to the opposite side of the desk. "Now, you listen. I not your mama and I sure not Miss Justine, but I'm a woman and I've been married a good long time. If you're saying what I think you're saying, you need to nip that thing right in the bud."

I wanted to laugh but couldn't find the strength. "Westley says his—his lack of—interest—is from the medication."

"Well, if that's so, my next question would be wondering how long he's gonna be on it."

I shook my head. "I'm hoping that at the six-month mark they'll wean him off." *Wean.* The same word Westley used. Like a baby from her mother's breast.

Ro-Bay appeared to ponder my circumstance before she spoke. "Honey, you listen, now. Marriage is more than what happens between the sheets. And when you spoke those vows some ten years ago you said, 'in sickness and in health.'"

"I know."

"Well, this here is the sickness part. Happened to my husband, too—different reasons—and I don't wonder but what it don't happen to every man once in a while. But don't you worry none. It took some time with mine, but it came back." She chuckled. "And, when it did..." She laughed again. "You just keep on loving your man in all other ways and soon enough it'll be set to rights."

I folded my arms and rested them on the desktop. "It's more than that, Ro-Bay. More than... sex. Westley seems so preoccupied. There's ... something. I don't know what. Something between us and I can't figure it out."

"Another woman?"

"I don't think so."

"No, course not. That boy loves you."

I gave a half smile. "If you say so."

She stood. "Trust me on that one." She returned the chair and headed for the door. "Now on to my mopping and waxing. Something sticky on the floor near the fridge and I bet I know who made the mess."

This time my smile was genuine. "Have fun. And thanks for the coffee."

I had worked a good hour, keeping my ears peeled for the sound of footsteps overhead or coming down the staircase, but hearing nothing but the tick-tock of the old cuckoo on one of the shelves. Then, as though I'd woken from a dream, I felt, rather than saw, Biff leaning against the jamb in that way he had of owning a room without entering it. "I heard you surprised your mother with a visit," I said by way of hello, my stomach quivering enough that I feared he may hear the tremble.

He grinned at me—perfect white teeth showing off his handsome face, making him more attractive than a man his age had a right to be. And, certainly, more alluring than I should have good sense to note, despite my current circumstance. But I couldn't help it; the man simply stirred something inside me ... no matter that he was old enough to be my ... uncle. "Rose Beth, no doubt." He pretended to pout. "Can you believe she won't let me in the kitchen for a cup of coffee?"

"It's Monday morning. She's mopping and waxing. Plus, she says someone dropped something sticky on the floor and she suspects you to be the guilty party."

Biff laughed as he stepped toward me. "Guilty as charged." He stopped flush against the desk, reached across and, with his fingertips, brought my chin up a fraction of an inch. "What's that I see in your eyes? Who has made this little cupcake so sad?"

I pulled back; one light touch affecting me more than it should. A shock vibrated within. A desire. The need I'd felt for weeks—the one I'd suppressed while working and while tending to Michelle—rose up, demanding to be noticed. But not with my husband; with *this* man. A man I was not privy to. A man not Westley. "I don't know what you mean," I whispered.

He strolled to the wingback chairs, opened the drawer of the table between them, then sat back and lit a cigarette. "Care for one?" he asked, one brow cocked.

"No, thank you. I don't smoke, remember?" Although, on occasion, Miss Justine and I indulged as we talked over life's problems, swearing later we'd done no such thing. The smoking. The solving world issues we admitted to.

"Sure?"

No. "Yes."

He chuckled, stood, walked over to me and, as though he had every right, slipped the cigarette between my lips, his fingertips brushing against them, caressing as they curled. "Go ahead, sweet cheeks. I won't tell."

Biff returned to his chair to light another; I followed behind him, found the ashtray, settled it on the table, then sat in the vacant wingback. "I really shouldn't," I said, unsure as to my meaning. Shouldn't smoke? Shouldn't sit next to a man I found so uniquely and strangely attractive, although—oddly enough—I rarely thought of him when he wasn't around. Not even his portrait in the family room raised cause for alarm, perhaps because I'd never been able to catch his true essence. The scent of him. The electrical aura emanating that left me dazzled. Like a schoolgirl awed by her teacher. Or a sixteen-year-old who, once upon a time, had gazed at glossy posters of dreamy idols and imagined being with them. For an hour. Or a day. Or a single blessed night.

I let out a sigh and silently thanked God as the Hoover began buzzing over carpets—the familiar sound of Ro-Bay working in the back of the house. Had I been alone with this man—especially at that moment—I wasn't sure what might happen next. Or how I would justify my actions.

People have affairs all the time, don't they?

But what if only once ... would one time constitute an affair?

If Westley would only—

"So tell me what's going on in your life. Because I can tell something has happened since last I saw you. When was that? Christmas?"

"Yes." He'd brought a leggy beauty with thick brunette tresses to his mother's dinner party and I'd found myself inexplicably jealous. I took a long draw of the cigarette. "I guess you heard that Westley had a heart attack just after the first of January."

He studied me, his eyes primarily on my lips. I chewed at them, then took another draw from the cigarette, noting that the shake in my hand had returned. "I did," he said. "Mother, of course. DiAnn, too. How is he?"

"Fine, thank you. Recovering. It ... it's going to take a while, but ... he's good. He recently bought a motorcycle, which he seems to enjoy. And ... we went skiing in Boone. Well, he and Michelle did ... I sat in the lodge and sipped on mulled hot apple cider and buttered rum."

"Not one for skiing?"

I stubbed out the cigarette and wished I could ask for another. My request would be a telltale giveaway of how he'd set my nerves on fire. I hadn't smoked many cigarettes in my life—Westley would be furious—but when I did, I honestly enjoyed the experience. This had been no different, except for the tension running on a taut wire between Biff and me. So different than chewing the fat with Miss Justine. "I honestly don't know," I answered. "I've never tried it and, well, Westley seemed so intent and in such a hurry to get Michelle on the slopes that I—I guess I just opted for ..."

"Hot cider and rum by a roaring fire in the hotel lobby while people-watching and daydreaming the hours away."

"More or less," I admitted, wondering how he could have possibly known. "I also read a pretty good novel."

"Did you now?" he asked, his eyes hooded. "I get a sense that things are finally waffling in paradise. Seven-year itch? No wait, it's been longer than that. Trust me, I've been counting."

I stood, more aware of where this was heading than before. If I admitted that, yes, our marriage was in trouble—or seemed to be—Biff would suggest that what I needed was a fling on the side. One with a discretionary partner. And then he would suggest himself. I knew the lines by heart; I'd read them in too many books. "I need to get back to work," I said, all the while wanting to play out the script.

Biff crushed his cigarette, then stood and took my hand. The current intensified enough to send warm honey through my veins, set my head spinning, and I inhaled deeply. "If I'd been there, no way would you have been left to your own devices, sitting alone. Hot drinks and good books or not."

"Biff," I whispered, hoping he couldn't feel my resolve nearly giving way, the jerk of my free hand.

"I like the new hair ... your eyes ... You're beautiful, you know that?"

The Hoover shut off, alerting me, and I slid my hand from his. "I'm also Westley's wife. And I love him."

Biff crooked an index finger, brought it to my cheek, and gently rubbed. "More's the pity."

"I don't know what you mean by—"

"Allison," he said, speaking my name with such authority that it forced me to bite down on my lip to stop it from quivering as my hand had. "Let's not play at this. You feel it. You always did."

"No ... I—"

"Stop. I hate games and I refuse to play them, so grow up, cupcake. And when you do, when you can stand it no longer, let me know." He looked first to the door, then to the ashtray where two cigarette butts lay in a tattered sheet of ashes. "Take care of that, will you? I'm going to the kitchen now for a cup of coffee and a bite to eat. Rose Beth can just pitch her hissy fit."

"I will," I whispered, but not until he had left the room.

Miss Justine entered the library/office as the old cuckoo struck two, walked straight for the wingback chairs, and lit a cigarette.

The gaze she shot across the room informed me that I was to join her, which, after I retrieved the ashtray, I did. She offered me a cigarette, but I shook my head. The one I'd had earlier with Biff had left a bad taste in my mouth and a tightness in my chest.

"On this you're wise," Miss Justine said, then drew on her cigarette as though it were an old lover. "On other things, not so much."

Heat coursed through me. Somehow, this woman I carried such respect for, had my number. "What things are we talking about?"

"Rose Beth is worried about you."

A modicum of relief slipped down my spine. "She told you about what we talked about this morning?"

Her sharply penciled-in brow cocked once before she thumped ashes into the ashtray. "No ..."

"Then?"

"She suspects my son is making one of his quintessential moves."

"Quintessential?"

"Darlin' ..." She drew again on her cigarette and, again, thumped the ashes. "Rose Beth has a sixth sense about certain things—could be in her DNA, I don't know—but she has long said—and I quote—she 'don't trust Biff around that sweet chile.'"

I groaned.

"Allow me to rephrase that."

"I wish you would," I said, then reached for the cigarettes.

"She doesn't trust Biff around *any* beautiful woman, but—as she said to me earlier—especially one who seems to be in the middle of ... something. She also said the air crackled in this house this morning."

"I don't know what she means by that," I said, although I most assuredly did. I lit my cigarette before adding, "But Westley and I *are* having issues."

"In the bedroom?"

"And out."

"And my son has finally seen his chance to pounce and he has."

"Gracious, Miss Justine, why in the world would you say such a thing?"

Seriousness shadowed her face. She took the cigarette from my hand and, having put hers out, followed with mine, crushing it against the bottom of the crystal ashtray. "Darlin', I want you to pay attention. One day you *will* grow old. I've crossed into my octogenarian years, so I know."

"You're *not* old." I didn't like to discuss Miss Justine's advanced age; it meant death could come at any time. Life without her in it wasn't conceivable. Not yet.

"That kind of flattery doesn't fit here, and I hate repeating myself. But in this case, I will—you'll grow old and you'll see things as they were. As they really were, which means *as they are. As they really are.*" She pointed an index finger at me, one riddled with arthritic knuckles and decorated, as always, with oversized, ostentatious rings. "And one day … one day … you'll realize that the only enemy you ever really encountered was yourself."

"I don't know what that means."

"You, Allison. Your misconceptions." She blinked once, then closed her eyes against something too ugly to look at with them open. "You believe in storybook marriages and books that teach you how to have one and if yours slips away from that idea—even by an iota—then you are faced with your own weaknesses."

"Miss Justine—I could never—"

"Yes. You could."

I sat stone still. *Yes, I could.* She was more than a little right. And that's what scared me most. I loved Westley. And I believed he loved me. So, surely, we could never—I could never—

"He's right, you know." Her eyes were on mine now. "He's *not* my husband's son. But he *is* his father's." She pressed lips painted deep red together until they trembled. "A man with such charisma I thought I'd die in his presence, in spite of his age—just like you and my son."

I sat back, the air seeping from me as though I'd just drawn and exhaled my last. And I knew, somehow, that the best thing I could do now was listen. Sit and listen and say nothing. So I swallowed hard enough and loudly enough that she caught my invitation to go on.

"It wasn't a heart attack, but my husband had gotten so wrapped up in his business—papers and meetings and trips here and there to seal this deal and that contract—that he forgot about me." She chuckled. "Or maybe he didn't." The fingertips of her right hand fingered the large diamond on her left ring finger. "He'd land some business deal and I'd get jewelry." Her eyes met mine. "He called it good investments and, as far as I know, no other woman was getting anything of any value.

"Then Cheney—that was his name—Cheney came into my life when I wasn't paying attention to the dangers." Her eyes roamed the bookcases as though she were searching for the right title. "When I didn't expect him. He saw a vulnerable woman who thought she was no longer loved by her husband . . . and he made her strong." Miss Justine's head shook slightly. "Not by loving me, mind you, but by *not* loving me when it mattered most."

I waited as her fingers traveled from the diamond to the doily on the small table between us, creating waves within its pattern, then patting it flat. "Once he had his way, Allison ... once he'd finally seduced and conquered, he walked off the victor and left me with a baby inside." Her face returned to mine.

"What did you do?" I whispered, now understanding more about this woman who was, in her own way, an enigma. A puzzle to be put together not in one sitting, but slowly. Over long periods of time.

And time we'd had. Enough that I no longer wondered why she'd been so sure of Westley's devotion to me those first weeks of our marriage. And I no longer questioned her wisdom on forgiving him so quickly.

"My husband and I hadn't shared a bed for weeks by that point. Maybe months."

I certainly understood that and I nodded.

"But I knew what I had to do to keep the tongues from wagging," she continued, "and I did it. Buford was in DC at some convention. I booked a flight as soon as I returned from the doctor's office, then took a taxi to the hotel where I managed to cajole the manager to sneak me into my husband's room." She winked at me. "Told him it was our anniversary and I was there to surprise him. Asked that a magnum of champagne be sent up—and it was. I took a long, hot soak in a tub full of bubbles, dolled myself up as I hadn't done in years, and waited."

"I take it your plan worked."

"It did."

"And he never suspected that Biff wasn't his biological son?"

Miss Justine pulled the drawer open to again reveal the hidden box of cigarettes. "He suspected," she said, removing the box, retrieving a cigarette, and then lighting it. "But I never let on one way or the other."

"And Biff? When did he start to suspect?"

"He didn't need to suspect. He had enough of his father's blood to know and he's let me know it with those eyes of his since he was old enough to understand the way of things."

"But you love him. Surely you love him."

"My loving him has nothing to do with this. Stay away from him, Allison. He'll use you and then discard you like he does all the conquests in his life and you'll be left running toward a hotel room, lying to the manager, ordering up a bottle of champagne."

I sank into the seat. "No worries there, Miss Justine. You and I both know I'll never have to convince Westley as to the paternity of a child."

She drew hard on the cigarette, held her breath, then exhaled. "I'm not talking about paternity, Allison. I'm talking about not believing your marriage is in trouble simply because Westley's head—or maybe his health—is somewhere else right now."

"I've been thinking about this a lot today," I said, deciding quickly what to say and what to leave out, such as, "Cindie's pregnant again. Married."

Instead, I said, "It's more than the medication he's on—our not sleeping together. Westley is so caught up in what he's doing at work—climbing the great financial ladder so he can buy more toys and go on more trips. And his weekends are consumed with Michelle. He thinks—never mind the heart attack—he *still* thinks life is one great big party and that it all works out if you just do the fun things. I think—no, I know—he's forgotten about *me*. About who I really and truly am. To him I'm the woman who raises his child Monday through Friday. I'm the one who makes sure her homework is done and that she makes it to dance class twice a week and Girl Scouts and church. He could have hired someone to do what I do—"

"Not true. He could never pay anyone enough to love that child the way you love her and the way she loves you."

That much was true.

"Allison?" She ground out her cigarette, left the second butt next to the first, both rimmed with the red of her lipstick. "Do you love him?"

"Westley?"

"Of course, Westley. You're not so foolish as to think you love my son."

"Yes." The answer came without hesitation. "I love him very much. And you're right about the other."

"Do you tell him?"

"Of course."

"Then the passion will return."

Maybe ... and maybe I would—could—forget about Biff. About the way he unnerved me. Seemed to read my thoughts and desires. The way he somehow knew me better than I knew myself. Yes, maybe ...

After all, the passion between Wes and me had been nearly astonishing once upon a time. Explosions and starbursts and trumpets and cymbals. Maybe it could be again. "Thank you, Miss Justine."

"Don't let me down," she said as I stood. "And do *not* come back to this house until Wednesday."

"Why Wednesday?"

"Because I'm sending Biff home tomorrow. Whether he likes it or not. This is still my house and I can darn well determine who stays and who doesn't."

I laughed at the notion. "All right." The clock struck, the little bird sticking his head out once, twice, then a third and final time. "I need to go home," I said, then retrieved my purse and started for the door.

"Allison?"

I turned.

"We'll never speak of this again."

I smiled to soften the moment, my eyes roving to the drawer in the little table and the crushed butts in the ashtray. "What cigarettes?"

Miss Justine laughed so hard she fell into a coughing fit. "God love you, baby girl. God love you."

Chapter Thirty-eight

One of the best things about being married to Kyle, in Cindie's mind—besides the fact that he treated her and their son like a queen and a prince, respectively—was Friday nights. Every Friday, after a long week of work, she drove through the torment of Atlanta's typical bumper to bumper traffic to their Tucker home—the same one she'd shared with Kyle when they'd been roommates, the one he had eventually purchased—to find her husband and son waiting. Waiting and ready for pizza.

"To commemorate the night we really got to know each other," Kyle had told her when he began the tradition shortly after their marriage.

Although, in her mind, the evening she'd come home from being with Patterson only to find Kyle stretched out on the sofa—the evening they'd shared their first pizza and their first decent conversation—was *not* the night they'd *really* gotten to know each other. Even five years later, the memory of Kyle walking into her apartment, slipping into her bed, and loving her as if she were the most beautiful woman in the world made her feel warm. Fuzzy.

She loved him. She *loved* him. Kyle Lewis had given her something she'd never thought she'd have—security. Security within family. Within love. And laughter. Lots of laughter. Everything she thought had been meant for everyone but her. The only thing missing was

Michelle, but Kyle had managed to convince her that to take Michelle away from Westley after she'd been with him so long wouldn't have been best for her daughter, her baby who had turned seventeen last November. A junior in high school now. Beautiful and smart and talking about pre-med after graduation. Emory University, she thought. Which would put her in the Atlanta area. Perhaps Michelle would move in with them then. Wouldn't that be a kick in the pants? They'd have all the time in the world. Every day. Every night. And she could talk to her daughter whenever she wanted.

Not that she couldn't now. They talked all the time. They emailed, a somewhat new thing Cindie didn't 100 percent understand but enjoyed. They also spent as many of the holidays together as the courts allowed.

Having their son—hers and Kyle's—helped ease the pain a little—not that one child could ever replace another. The only thing that worried her, truly worried her, was how much Karson looked like Patterson. "Spitting image" as the old saying went. There were times when she wondered if Kyle would see it, too. But then she reminded herself that her husband had only taken one class with Professor Thacker. He hadn't seen the man as often—or in the same way—as she had. He didn't know the line of his face the way she did. The square of his jaw. The line of his brow. The way it rose when he laughed; the way it furrowed when he grew angry.

Cindie sniffed hard as she crawled from one lane of 285 to the next, anticipating her exit. She bristled, bringing her index finger and thumb up to play with the oversized earrings pulling at her lobe. Even after six years, that one inkling of the night she told Patterson about her pregnancy unnerved her. He'd called her the next morning—thankfully while Kyle was in the shower. She answered, heard his voice, and immediately hung up. He called again. She picked up the handset, set it back in its cradle, then took the phone off the hook, grateful that the bedroom's extension wasn't cordless. When Kyle emerged from the bathroom wrapped in a cloud of steam and spied the handset on the bedside table, she convinced him she didn't want their first real morning together to be interrupted by a phone call.

Especially since they'd both decided to "call in sick."

But Patterson had been persistent. Persistent as she was stubborn. By the time he finally caught up to her, a week had passed. A week of being with Kyle every night. A week of learning, in seven short days, what real love felt like. No. Adoration was what it was. And it was nothing like she'd experienced in all the years she'd been with the professor or the one night with Westley.

Patterson had called her name as she stepped out of the car, startling her. But she'd prepared herself. She'd rehearsed exactly what she would say and how she would deliver the words. "Stop right there," she told him, then searched her workplace parking lot for any sign of his car. Finding it at the end of a long line of automobiles, she returned her attention to him.

"Look," he replied, his voice pleading. "I know I said some things—"

"I said stop."

He jerked. She flinched. Then, righting herself, she took in a deep breath and, having exhaled fully, recited her lines. "Patterson, I want you to go back to your car, and then I want you to get in it and drive away. To the college. Or home. Wherever it is you need to be, it's not here." Other cars pulled in and circled in search of their assigned spots. Cindie knew them all. If necessary, she'd ask one of them to call the police.

If necessary.

"Cindie."

"No." She raised her hand. He looked at it, then back to her face. Her eyes. "I do *not* want to have to keep going over this. I'm taking care of ..." She looked down. Back up. "Of all this."

"Does that mean—"

"It means I'm taking care of it. And then I'm taking care of me." Her eyes found his again and held. She was ready now. Ready for the next rehearsed line, whether she felt it or not. "No more victimization, Patterson. I'm done playing that role."

"You?" he asked, nearly laughing. "A victim?"

It was then she caught a whiff of his cologne, one she knew well.

Eternity by Calvin Klein. The irony struck while simultaneously turning her stomach, sending a litany of questions upward. How had she gotten here? What roads, what paths had led her from days of carefree abandon, running freely in her mother and father's home with her sisters and brother to the mess of living without her father? Of being solely raised by Lettie Mae? To that of a grown woman, pregnant for the second time by two different men, both who refused to marry her?

Bile rose from the pit of her belly. Maybe it was the baby. Or maybe this was Patterson sickness. Or sick-and-tired-of-being-used sickness. Whatever it was, she knew then what she wished she'd known years before—that Patterson Thacker was no different, really, than her father. Or her mother. Or Westley. Another user was all he'd been, and she'd been gullible enough—or desperate enough or stupid enough—to allow it. While Kyle ... in spite of the fact that she'd tricked him into her bed, Kyle truly wanted her. Loved her. Treated her with such attention and passion she could hardly believe that what was happening between them was happening between them. To *her*.

She took a step back, pressed herself against her car, mostly to keep any semblance of fear at bay. "Patterson," she said. "Go."

For whatever reason—whether he'd heard some command in her voice or whether he had grown weary of playing *with* the victim—he did. Not that it stopped him from calling her. At least three times a week, always at work. "Just checking up," he'd say. Which meant he wanted to know if she'd aborted their child. But the calls stopped the day she told him that she'd gotten married and that he needed to leave her alone. "No one's the wiser," she said. "You can go on with your life as if I never entered it."

He didn't speak at first. Maybe she'd shocked him, though she couldn't imagine Patterson without retort. "I hope you'll be very happy," he finally muttered. And, with that, he disappeared from her life. Not once in the five years since had she heard from or seen him ... except in the features of the child they'd made together.

She drove now, free of the choking traffic, down the street she called home, an avenue lined with azaleas and dogwoods in full blossom of white and varying shades of pinks and reds and purples. She smiled broadly at the sight of her husband and son standing outside on the driveway, looking down to study something of such vital importance it required mutual concentration. Then, as if on cue, they turned toward her. Karson leapt in place until Kyle scooped him up and deposited him on his broad shoulders. Their son wrapped pudgy hands over his father's high forehead and held on as they made their way onto the grass, sprouting green after the harsh recent winter. Cindie straightened to see what held their attention, then saw the chalked outline of a heart with her name scrawled in its center. She smiled as warmth slid over her. Gosh, how she loved them. Loved them both. Whatever sins she'd committed had been worth the torment of living with the fear of her deceit.

As she stepped out of the car, Kyle returned to the driveway where he leaned forward to release Karson into her arms. She cuddled their son, kissing the warm folds of his neck, then raised her face for a welcome from her husband. He obliged willingly. "Traffic bad?" he asked.

"What do you think?" she asked, nearly wrung out from it. "But I'm home now and ready for pizza."

"Pizza!" Karson exclaimed, throwing himself backward. Cindie nearly stumbled to keep from dropping him.

Kyle moved closer, slipped his hands under Karson's armpits, and drew him away from her before she fell. "I have a surprise for you," he said. "There's a new place that opened up a few weeks ago. A couple of the guys at work say it's some of the best New York-style pizza they've ever had." His eyes widened. Sparkled. "And one of the guys at work is actually *from* New York."

Cindie laughed. "Sounds good." She pointed toward the house. "Just let me get out of these work clothes and into something less professional. I can be ready in fifteen minutes."

Patterson
One of the best things about Friday nights was coming home from

the university, traffic as horrid as it was, to the squeals of his young grandson when he opened the door. "*Papa!*" The four-year-old boy—usually in his grandmother's arms—pushed against Mary Helen to be released. She'd set his feet to the floor and he'd run with every bit of energy given a toddler, straight to his grandfather's extended arms.

"Monty, my boy," he'd tease as he tickled and nuzzled.

"I'm not *your* boy," the child—smarter than any four-year-old he'd ever met—would say. "I'm Mommy and Daddy's boy. I'm your *grandboy!*"

"You are indeed. Every inch my grandboy. And I love you ... oh, let me see if I can remember ... *how* much do I love you?"

"Forever and ever amen," came the answer Patterson had taught him.

A boy. Finally, a boy. Of course, he knew about his biological son, the one with Cindie. She called him the day after she gave birth to inform him of the details. Eight pounds, two ounces. All toes and fingers accounted for. A wisp of blond curls crowning his head. Then she hung up, not waiting for his reply. Not wanting, he surmised, to hear his dismissal or acceptance of a child he'd always hoped to have—a son. Nor had she waited for him to give his own news—that within a few weeks of finding out about Cindie's pregnancy, his oldest daughter Patricia had come home from college with her boyfriend of eight months—or had it been nine—and announced that, having been to a justice of the peace the day before, they were now Mr. and Mrs. Montague Travers Stallard. Mary Helen had burst into tears; she'd already been consumed with hopes of an extravagant wedding. One that would take place in the same downtown Atlanta church where they'd married. Mary Helen would fuss over their daughter in the same bride's room where she had—slightly over two decades before—been fussed over herself.

His wife's plans for their oldest child were not to be thwarted, however. She quickly recovered and declared that they could still have a formal wedding. One that would take a few months to plan, but it would be lovely. "We may," she said after a quick moment's thought, her hands fluttering, "have to forego the teas and showers, but—then again—maybe not. Maybe a few—"

"Mom," Patricia said, interrupting her mother's train of thought as she slipped her slender hand into her new husband's. "Stop." She looked, first to Monty, as everyone called him, then to her father and then, back to her mother. "We're pregnant."

And just like that—once the shock had worn off, which took a good thirty seconds—Mary Helen went from planning bridal showers to baby showers while Patterson stood and, almost robotically, kissed his daughter's cheek, then shook the hand of the young man who had gotten his little girl pregnant.

The thought disturbed him, and he shook it loose to set it free, never to think of it again. A decent father didn't muse over such things. But even in the flurry of the announcements and calling the other girls into the room to fill them in on the latest ... even in the excitement of being told by Helen Leigh—their youngest—that he was an old man now ... reality struck him. In a few months, he'd become both a father again and a grandfather. Not that anyone, other than himself, would know it. Not in this room, at least. But he would know it. And he would have to live with it.

Yet, for all the punishment of living with the knowledge that he had a son, it wasn't too long after that Patricia laid his first grandson in his arms, kissed his cheek, and called him, "Papa." Nothing in this life could have prepared him for the rush of emotion that engulfed him. He had thought before that he'd known love. He loved Mary Helen. She was, after all, his wife. The mother of his children. And, since meeting Nola Edwards, she'd opened herself up to him in ways he could have never begun to expect. Something he still didn't understand but refused to question. He merely accepted and delighted in it.

He also loved his daughters. They could be self-centered—as daughters often were, especially in the teen years—but they were the heart and soul of him.

So, yes, he knew love. *But, this ...*

In that first encounter he held little Monty in such a way that heart touched heart until his own skipped in its rhythm. Perhaps Monty's had, too. Patterson believed they bonded at this exact second. As far as Patterson was concerned, there was no one in the world like this little person. Somewhere out there he had a son, yes. But this was his *grand*son who, wonder of wonders, looked like Patterson had spit him out of his own mouth, a fact proven even more so as the child grew. Life simply couldn't get any better.

"Is the traffic awful?" Mary Helen now asked as she approached him for a kiss.

"The usual," he answered, inhaling her floral aura. "But it's a Friday so I didn't mind it as much."After six months of gracing and blessing their world, Patterson and Mary Helen had gifted little Monty's parents with every Friday night and Saturday all to themselves. Which, of course, wasn't really a gift they gave, but one they stole.

Mary Helen reached toward the kitchen counter where a red-and-white flyer announced the opening of a new pizzeria. "Well, I hope it's not too bad because Patricia brought this." She eyed their grandson who had laid his cheek against Patterson's shoulder, relaxing his body against the strength of his grandfather in the process. "But not before telling you-know-who that we'd take him."

Patterson squeezed the boy. "Do you want pizza tonight, Monty?"

"Pizza, pizza, pizza," came his answer, which made both Patterson and Mary Helen laugh.

Patterson kissed the boy's head. "Let Papa get out of these clothes and into something more comfortable and we'll go, okay?"

"'kay..."

He handed the child back to Mary Helen. "Won't take me five minutes," he said.

"Take your time," she called after him. "We have plenty."

He should have seen her coming. Or at least noticed her when Mary Helen and Monty and he walked into the pizzeria. He should have caught a whiff of her perfume—the scent of her had been ingrained in his memory, after all. He should have heard her laughter, low and throaty. Or seen her hair, waves of it, spilling over her shoulders, framing a face that had grown more beautiful with new motherhood. And marriage.

But he hadn't. He had slid into a booth with his family—his wife, his grandson—and enjoyed a pie and a light beer and the joy of watching young Monty devour first one slice and then another, intermittently swigging down Coke, which, when sucked through a straw, made his nose crinkle and his eyes illuminate.

And he should have guessed when the music overhead changed from Steve Perry's "Foolish Heart" to Lindsey Buckingham's—Lindsey Buckingham of all the artists—"Trouble," that the house of cards he'd so carefully erected since the day he met Little Stevie Nicks was about to topple.

It only took a moment. The recognition by Cindie's husband— "Dr. Thacker! Hello!"—to the exchange of glances—Kyle Lewis to Patterson's wife, the boy, Little Monty—for understanding to take hold. A full moment for Mary Helen to do the same. To see the resemblance in the children. To see Cindie's face change from blush to the whitest shade of pale.

The music stopped. Or perhaps it kept going. "Ohmygosh ..." Mary Helen sighed. "Ohmygosh," she repeated, now looking at him. "Patterson, what have you done?"

Chapter Thirty-nine

Allison

Our daughter had become an old soul. Truth be told, she'd always been. There had been a knowing that grew naturally within her. I couldn't think of a time when she hadn't seemed focused. Hadn't known exactly what she wanted and what steps were necessary to achieve those things.

She had also excelled at everything she put her hands to—she was the star of her jazz dance company, played classical piano as though she were performing at Carnegie Hall, even when she was simply practicing in our living room. Michelle excelled in school—never made lower than an A—and after-school activities. She ran track for the school team, often bringing "fear" to the students from rival schools. If Michelle Houser was running … well. They may as well sit down at the starting line. She and Sylvie—a leggy blonde with a quirky sense of style who cheered for OHS—were both considered leaders in their youth group at church. Neither of them had ever given us or Sylvie's parents a moment's trouble. "Almost too perfect," Nikki once commented with a laugh. "Makes Scott and me nervous to let her go off to college."

Not that everything had been perfect-perfect. There was the time they went out for burgers after a church event but failed to call home first. Nikki and I were on the phone with each other within five minutes of their curfew, nervously remarking that the "girls have never been late before." On the contrary, they typically walked in five to ten minutes *before* curfew, gabbing and giggling, then saying good-bye. Punishment had been ridiculously light—neither girl had been allowed to go out the following weekend—and both were so apologetic that, after church on Sunday, Westley offered an acquittal.

As she aged, Michelle took on more of her mother's look—Stevie Nicks with a little Westley Houser thrown in around the hair color and complexion. Everywhere we went, heads turned, but—while Westley and I were acutely aware of it—Michelle seemed oblivious. Unlike Sylvie—and more especially unlike Cindie—Michelle dressed *down*. Jeans. Tees. Sneakers. All of which she wore like a model strutting the catwalk.

Above all, she loved me. And I adored her. Those who didn't know she was not my biological child wouldn't know. She mimicked me in so many ways, it was as if she and I had been cut from the same cloth. Except that—like Westley—Michelle had no fear. Her athletic abilities—whether on snow or water skis, dancing, swimming, running—were all Westley who cheered her onward and upward.

Everything ... *everything* ... about life seemed good. Worth living. Westley and I were happier than we'd ever been and our daughter was the bloom of that rose. Until that Wednesday evening when our lives forever changed. Michelle dashed in from church by way of the kitchen door at the very moment the phone rang. She jerked the cordless off its charger where it rested next to the copper hammered canister set the moment I entered from the family room.

"Hey, Mom," she panted, then pushed the button to answer. "Hello?" I leaned against the doorjamb, waiting to hear if the call was for me or Westley. "Oh ... hey ... yeah, I just came in from church." Michelle glanced at me, mouthed, "Cindie," then returned to her call. "I love you, too ..."

I returned to the family room.

"That Michelle?" Westley asked from his position on the sofa where he lay supine in a pair of pajama bottoms and a tee, his legs crossed at the ankles.

"Mmm ... Cindie's on the phone."

Westley returned his attention to an episode of *Home Improvement* without comment. I tried to do the same—to focus on Tim and Jill's issues instead of my own. Instead, I became more and more aware of the shuffle of Michelle's feet as she ascended the staircase, the lilt of her voice as it faded into her room, the closing of her bedroom door, the minutes ticking by. It was always like this when Cindie called. I wanted Michelle to have a relationship with her—I did—but their conversations made me uncomfortable. Anxious, as if expecting the worst possible scenario to follow. Even though, most of the time, within an hour or a day, depending on the time of the call, Michelle shared with me their conversation. Leaving me torn in two—part of me wanting to know everything, another part wanting nothing to do with their connection.

Home Improvement ended and Westley changed the channel to watch the last half of a news magazine show starring Tom Brokaw and Katie Couric while I tucked my feet under me and tried to concentrate on the Sue Grafton novel I'd started the night before. I'd just managed to block out the drone of voices from the TV and slip into the world of Kinsey Millhone when Michelle stepped into the room and cleared her throat.

"Dad?"

Westley cast his glance behind him without raising his head. "Yeah."

She looked at me briefly, then back to him. "Can we talk for a minute?"

There was a change in her voice. Something was wrong. I knew it. Instinctively, as though, somehow, every fear I'd ever pushed aside—especially since Michelle had come into my life—now rose to the surface and demanded to be dealt with. "We're here now," they shouted from within me. "We're here and we are far worse than you ever imagined."

"What is it?" I asked.

Michelle tucked a strand of her long almond-blond hair behind an ear, shifted from one foot to the next, then set the cordless on the end table. She jammed her hands into the front pockets of her jeans. Westley sat up then, his fatherly instinct recognizing the ominousness in the moment. "Sit here," he said to her, patting the cushion beside him, then lowered the volume of the television.

And she did. She leaned forward, resting her elbows on her knees. "Cindie just called . . ."

"Your mother told me," he said, glancing at me, concern now drawing lines along a face still handsome and strong. "And?"

"She and Kyle are getting a divorce."

Blood rushed through me, leaving a shiver to race behind.

"Oh," Westley commented. "Wow. Man. That's too bad. He's such a nice guy . . . I thought . . ."

Michelle's eyes welled with tears and she swatted at them.

"Honey . . ." I started to move. To stand and walk across the room. To gather my daughter in my arms and tell her . . . what? That it would be okay? Too cliché, I knew. That this was probably somehow Cindie's doings and that—truth be told—I'd been surprised the marriage lasted as long as it had. Surprised but grateful.

Or was I going to say—to *actually* say—that this wasn't *her* fault. Michelle's. That I understood how she felt, when, clearly, I did not. But Westley's eyes told me without words to stay put. To remain quiet.

"And she—um—she wants me to come live with her," Michelle said, now looking only at her father. She clasped her hands together, cracked her knuckles. "Kyle—um—Kyle took Karson."

"Oh, for crying out loud," Westley moaned. "What has she done?"

Michelle began to sob, her shoulders hunched and shaking. Again, I wanted to go to her and, again, Westley's eyes told me to stay. Instead, he gathered her to himself, kissed the top of her head, and whispered. "I'm sorry. I'm sorry. Sweetheart . . . what did she say to you?"

Our daughter's words became mumbled and messy, leaving me to catch scant few. But by the time she had finished spilling them, I knew only that Cindie was alone. And scared. And that she wanted Michelle to come live with her after junior year. To give her a chance, she said. Because, doesn't every mother, even a bad one, deserve a second chance?

Most shockingly of all, from the sound of her voice, Michelle had taken it all to heart. "She sounded so pitiful," she said. "I mean ... Dad ... you should have heard her. She was crying so hard."

Westley kissed her head again. "Listen to me ... are you listening?" Michelle nodded. "I want you to not worry about this tonight, hear me?" Again, she nodded, and in that single movement, relief slipped through me. Westley wouldn't let this happen. He would never let our daughter just pack up and move. He knew all the things to say. The logical things. Things about school and sports and friends—*Oh, Sylvie!*—and her church group. About senior year and awards that always went to students with a history in the school, and GPAs, which would surely be affected. And he'd speak them with an authority I was no longer sure I had. "I want you to go upstairs and get your shower and get ready for bed. Do you have homework?"

"I did it already. Before youth group."

"Good. Then go get a shower, take some Tylenol, and go to bed. You don't have to answer Cindie right now and we aren't going to make any decisions tonight."

We. Good ... good. This was a *we* decision. Not a *she* decision or a *he* decision. *We* would decide. Two to one, at best. Or at worst ...

"Okay," Michelle whispered. She righted herself from her father's arms, then said, "I've got a lot to pray about, huh?"

"You do," Westley admitted. "But I wouldn't expect the Lord to give you any answers before the sun comes up, so, give him some time to mull it over, too."

Michelle smiled then, wobbly and unsure. But she smiled nonetheless. Stood. Kissed her father followed by me, her lips quaking and lingering longer than usual. Then left the room.

Westley's gaze found mine and held, but he said nothing. Too numb to speak, I closed the book that had remained open throughout the conversation. Then, as soon as Michelle's bedroom door closed, he leaned over and snatched the phone from the table, punched in a number he knew by heart, and waited.

"She's not answering," he said, killing the call.

"Of course she's not," I whispered.

"I'd like to go up there and yank a knot in her," he growled, then stood to pace around the room. "Who does she think she is?"

"Her mother," I said around the knot forming in my chest, because I knew—*I knew*—no matter all I hoped for, that by summer's end, Michelle would move to Tucker permanently. That every plan we'd made for senior year would have been tossed out the window of possibility, leaving only a door of regret. Homecoming. Prom. Graduation. Senior trip ... these would be left for Cindie to enjoy. Applications to colleges—Michelle wanted Emory more than any of the others ... Cindie would pore over these with her. Not us. Cindie. We'd gotten Michelle this far and now Cindie would grab the baton from our hands and run toward the finish line as the victor.

Somehow ... somehow ... I'd known it all along.

And, of course, I'd been right. All along.

November 1993

We fell into a rhythm, my husband and I, as familiar as the one we'd had when Michelle lived at home. Only now, instead of Michelle getting the silverware and placing it on the table—just so, the way I'd taught her—I performed the task. Now, instead of Michelle clearing the table, Westley gathered the dishes and took them into the kitchen where he placed them, gently, beneath soapy water to soak. Later, I came along and transferred them to the dishwasher.

Now, instead of banter about school and friends and church and dance class and track meets and teachers to avoid, our supper conversations were filled with directionless lines about work and what he planned to watch that evening on television and where I was in the latest Sue Grafton alphabet novels.

I'd made it to "J" which meant "as far as they went."

For now.

Westley brought up going to Paul and DiAnn's from time to time, but I nixed the idea before he could even finish the suggestion. "I can't," I said. "Not yet."

The last time, over a Friday morning breakfast, his shoulders rolled forward. "Ali, she's not *dead*. She's living a few hours away, that's all. She would have gone off to Emory in a year, anyway."

I opened my mouth to argue the point that *no*, she wasn't *dead*, and *yes*, I knew that about Emory, but the four hours away may as well have been four states away. To inform him that, unbeknownst to him, I felt as though I'd lost a part of myself. That Cindie and I had been playing some sort of chess game since he and I had married and that she, with all her wrong moves, had me in checkmate. That I only managed to go through the motions at work every day and then, after our supper, I went to the balcony off our bedroom and stared up, wondering if Michelle was looking into the same stars as I, searching for Orion as we'd done every autumn as far back as I could remember. To remind him that we'd not seen her since late July and wouldn't see her again until Thanksgiving, which felt like a million years away rather than two weeks. Instead, I pressed my lips together and said, "I know that, Wes. But ... don't you see? Paul and DiAnn have their children there. And, right now, I cannot bear—" Words caught in my throat. Words I dared not say and barely thought. Words that said *You were a failure as a wife, unable to have children of your own. A failure as a mother, your love unable to compete against Cindie's failures and needs.*

I broke down then, crying hysterically. Sobbing that I simply could not believe Michelle had left us.

"What do you think?" Westley asked me. "That she loves her more than us?"

I nodded between hunched shoulders.

"Come on, Ali," he said, reaching for my hand. "She loves you to bits, you know that. And she loves me, too. Hey now ..." His thumb rubbed over the back of my hand. "Do you know why I'm okay with all this?"

I shook my head, no, my head still down.

"Because I wouldn't be surprised if Michelle doesn't come home for good after the Christmas holidays."

I looked up then, tears and snot dripping from my nose. "Really?"

He handed me a napkin. "Really. Now, how often have I been wrong?"

Chapter Forty

B ut he was wrong. She didn't come home for good. Instead, she returned to Tucker, leaving me with a lovely antique pearl bracelet with a rhinestone fishhook clasp she'd picked out herself at an antique market, along with entirely too much information on the details of the dissolution of Cindie's marriage. Of her long and sordid affair with one of her professors. Her tumultuous divorce from Kyle. Of the custody battle she ultimately lost because she never really fought. Michelle had told me in explicit detail about Patterson—who, according to Michelle, was a nice enough guy who'd managed to salvage his marriage but was back in Cindie's life regardless—of Karson's true paternity, and of how Kyle had threatened to go to the college board with all of this unless he received full custody of the child and a legal obligation never to tell Karson the truth—at least until after his twenty-first birthday. She told me that Karson came every other Wednesday night and alternating weekends. And that she, old soul that she was, couldn't help but feel somehow responsible for this little half-brother.

"She also feels like the odd man out," I told Westley a few days after 1994 had dawned, entering southwest Georgia with its chilly temperatures, days after Michelle had returned to Tucker.

"What do you mean?" He stood at the kitchen counter where he poured himself a cup of early-morning coffee. He glanced at his watch. He'd have to leave within the next forty-five minutes to make it to work on time. I'd have to do the same.

"When Karson comes," I told him, twirling the pearl bracelet around and around my wrist, "Patterson comes. So, even though Karson doesn't know who Patterson really is, it's real father-mother-child ... and Michelle."

Westley crossed into the breakfast nook, then took a seat by me. "How do you know all this?"

"Did Michelle *not* talk to you at all, Wes? When she was here?"

Hurt—or was it disappointment—slid across his features, then disappeared. "Sure, we talked." He shrugged. "Mostly about her new obsession with crooner music—she has a small stack of Sinatra CDs, did you know that? I never thought I could know so much about Frank Sinatra *or* his music."

"Yes, I noticed. At least it's not hip-hop." I waited for Westley to continue, but when he didn't, I asked, "Anything else? Did she talk to you about anything else?"

Again, he shrugged. "Yeah. We also talked about pre-med and how she's learning to drive in Atlanta traffic but will probably live with Cindie one more year before transferring to the dorms."

One more year. I shook my head in disbelief. "Well, apparently Cindie felt the need to tell her *everything*. All about the affair—you know, so 'she won't make the same mistakes.'" I air-quoted the words.

"How long had it been going on? The affair. Did she say?"

"Oh yes ... started nearly as soon as she got to Dekalb."

Westley pointed to me in a siege of victory. "Didn't I tell you? Years ago, didn't I tell you? I knew she was sleeping with a married man. I said it, didn't I?"

I grabbed his finger and squeezed. "I don't quite see why you're so happy about this, Wes. This is not a game or a sporting event where you get to be the winner. Cindie is *not* a good example for her."

"You think I don't know that?"

"Because, what she's telling her by example," I continued, ignoring him, "is that she can sleep with a married man, fool another into thinking a child is his, get married, get a divorce, get the first man back, and somehow, all will work out in the end." I took a breath. "I am genuinely concerned about our daughter."

Westley's brows drew together. "Is that what she did? Fool Kyle into thinking—?"

I sighed in defeat. Apparently, he was missing the point and to shine light on that fact would only aggravate the wound. "That's what she said ... Cindie, I mean. She told Michelle the whole gruesome story in full, cinematic details. I'm surprised she didn't pull out a video diary."

"Ali ..."

I grabbed my coffee mug and took it to the sink. "I know. That's low, even for me."

"Especially for you ... you're better than that."

I turned to him. "Am I? Because right now I want to pick up the phone, call Cindie, and scream every vile thing I'm thinking about her."

"Get in line."

"And so does DiAnn," I added, speaking confidently now of a sister-in-law who had, since March, become my friend. My ally. We talked every day as soon as we got to work. Sometimes in the afternoons as well.

Westley laughed. "I can just bet."

"And don't get me started on Ro-Bay and Miss Justine."

My husband nodded. "I know. Miss Justine offered to pay for any and all legal costs—including investigators—if I'd wanted to fight Cindie over this."

I returned to the table and sat. "You never told me that." And neither had she.

"No point."

"Honestly, Wes ..."

"What good would it have done, Ali? Cindie had guilted Michelle into moving up there. You know it. I know it. Poor pitiful Cindie, lost without her daughter ... her son ... her husband. The only thing she somehow has going for her is her job and, I swear, I don't know how she's doing that. Probably sleeping with the boss there, too."

I'd not thought of that, though, somehow, I doubted it. "If she were, I'm sure she would have told Michelle by now."

Westley stood, leaving his coffee mug on the table. "I've gotta finish getting ready." He squeezed my shoulder. "Allison," he said, using my full name, which startled me. I looked up at him. "We did good with Michelle," he said. "Mostly you. Those seeds you planted didn't fall into unfertile soil. So this much I know—she'll be fine."

I leaned back against the chair, my head resting against my husband's abdomen and his hand moved to cup my face. "From your lips to God's ears ..."

"We've got to trust in that." He tilted my face up. "She'll be fine. If nothing else, a year with Cindie juxtaposed with a childhood spent with us will convince her that she wants to grow up to be like her mother. And I mean you, sweetheart. Her *real* mother."

"Oh, Westley ..."

"Hey," he said, now squatting so that we were at eye level. "There's something I want you to know."

"What?"

"I didn't marry you because of Michelle, Ali. I want you to believe that."

"I know—"

"Because I don't think I ever really, *truly* told you. I married you because I loved you. *Love* you. Stroke of luck for me that you came along, sure, but Michelle or not, I would have proposed to you that day. And I'm sorry—I always have been—that I didn't tell you the truth sooner. That you may have felt like I trapped you. I was young and scared and desperate."

My brow raised.

"Not desperate. Well, maybe a little." He smiled. "But you—you took it—you took *me*—on the chin. Every bit of it and every bit of me. I don't deserve you and I never will, but Michelle did and does and always will. And you've been the best, the absolute best mother." He stood, then leaned down and kissed me, his lips soft and warm. His breath sweet with coffee. "I love you. And I love my daughter and the life we've made here."

"Then why don't you make her come home?" I asked, feeling as warmed by his words as confused by my own desires of loving her and wanting her with us.

"Because the last thing I want for her is to feel pressure from me." His eyes softened. "From us. I won't do that to her. I love her too much."

I stood then. Turned. Wrapped my arms around him, pressing into him, begging for the strength only he could give. "I love you, too." I burrowed my nose into the flesh of his neck, tears burning my eyes. This man... *this man*... whom I'd given so much of my life to. This man who had given so much to me. I'd never understand it, really. What draws one person to another in such a way that we feel we cannot go on, one without the other? From the moment he'd called me on the phone, having looked up my name in the phone book, and asked me out, I had been his and he had been mine. For all his faults—and for all of mine—there had been nothing I wanted in life or out of it that didn't include him.

I squeezed my eyes and kissed his neck. Once. Twice. Thinking, for the briefest of seconds, that the only difference in Cindie and me was that she had fallen into temptation with a married man and that I, a married woman, had nearly done the same with Biff. The very idea made me shudder in both disgust and gratitude that Miss Justine had given me such a good talking to.

Oh, Miss Justine! A woman I could never put in the same category as Cindie, and yet ...

"How is it," I began, then stopped in my unsurety. Did I want to share what was in my heart?

"Hmm?" Westley asked, his voice low and tender.

"How is it that our lives can be so affected by the decisions of others?"

He stepped back. Ran a finger down my nose and allowed it to rest on my lips before I kissed it. "What do you mean?"

"I mean ... do you ever think about it? Cindie decided to sleep with her professor, and then when she found out she was pregnant, and, well, you know ... the whole Kyle thing. And, in the end, her decisions led to us losing Michelle—"

"We haven't *lost* her."

"I know, but ..." I said, my voice now stronger in the light of my grandmother's directive. *Raise your radish, Allison. Raise it high ... This will* not *kick you down.*

There was more, of course. More I couldn't tell him. Would never tell him. We had all made our decisions. Westley's not to marry Cindie. Mine to marry Westley. Cindie and Patterson's to ignore the bonds of the wedding vows he'd spoken with his wife. Hers to drag Kyle into her deception. Even Miss Justine's decision to share with me about her relationship with Biff's father had placed consequences on my own decisions. All of this had left a mark on Westley. But, in his way, he'd gone on about life as though this was just another wave to ski over.

"But?"

I shook my head. No. These were my thoughts and only mine. Not to be shared. Not even to be mulled over. Not too long, anyway. "Nothing," I finally answered, glancing at the digital clock on the stove with a nod. "We've gotta get going."

Westley glanced at his watch as I stepped away from him. "Man ..."

I started out of the kitchen and was nearly to the first step of the staircase when Westley called my name. I turned toward where he stood at the kitchen door, keys dangling from the fingertips of one hand. "Yeah?"

"I *do* love you," he said. "There was never anyone for me but you and never will be—start to finish."

My heart smiled until it reached my face. "I love you, too."

Summer 2006

Westley

A lot had happened to them in a dozen years, him and his wife. Four years ago, they'd celebrated a quarter century together while several of their loved ones surrounded them, raising their glasses in a champagne toast. Michelle—Dr. Hamilton now—had arrived the day before along with her husband, Sturgill, but sans their twins, Charity and Faith, who'd recently turned three. Julie and Dean had come. Paul and DiAnn. Surprising them had been the arrival of his sister Heather and her husband Nathaniel. They'd moved a decade ago to Iowa, of all places, where they bought a farm. Westley kept waiting for Nate to plow up his corn and replace it with a baseball field, but so far, he hadn't.

Friends, such as Trev and Marilyn along with several others they'd acquired over the years, heralded a cheer to the next twenty-five, which left Westley to wonder if they'd live to see it. He doubted it, not with his ticker and his inability to follow much of what the doctor ordered. Medical people were like that; never listening to their doctors or their own bodies. At least he'd quit smoking after they'd married. So, there was that.

Yes, a lot had changed. He owned several of the drugstores that had comprised Miss Justine's empire. Not all of them, but a few, scattered about the towns in their part of the world. Miss Justine had seen to that in her will. Losing her to God, even with its benefits, had been one of the hardest seasons in his life. But she had died at the spry age of ninety-four, he reminded himself. Elderly, but still active and vivacious in her wit. She'd slipped away during the night, her head resting against a satin pillowcase. Ro-Bay had found her first thing on a Monday morning, when the floors needed mopping.

Allison had taken it hard, perhaps harder than when her own mother died a few years later. Unexpectedly, of course—she was only seventy-two—but so much of life tended to come unplanned and unwelcomed, he'd come to realize. Thankfully, both of his parents were still kicking, although they'd slowed down considerably and stopped driving across the state for any reason whatsoever.

The past two years had skipped by. Michelle and Sturgill bought a home in North Carolina after East Coast Medical & Research—a new state-of-the-art center in Wilmington—accepted her application as one of their prestigious research physicians within the field of gynecology. Ali had bemoaned the fact that they were "so far away," but Westley had been grateful that the move had, at the very least, removed Michelle from such proximity to Cindie.

Now, he was at a pharmaceutical convention held in Charlotte, which had given him an excuse to visit his daughter and her family, not to mention to peek at the research center.

"I'm still upset Mom couldn't come," Michelle told him after she met him in the expansive and gleaming lobby where air conditioning brought blessed relief from the oppressive heat outside.

"Me, too," he said with a smile. "But she chose to wait when I told her I was driving to Charlotte instead of flying." He shrugged. "Don't worry. She's staying busy while I'm away."

"Doing?"

"She and Ro-Bay planned to do some canning and—okay—I think your mother wasn't totally upset about having some time to herself."

Michelle laughed. "You don't think she has a boyfriend, do you?"

"Ro-Bay?" he teased. "Nah ..."

"Dad," Michelle said with a laugh, then led him to a group of elevators where she pushed the UP button while Westley studied his daughter.

"You look nice," he said, admiring her.

Michelle blushed. "Dad."

"You do. Very professional. Hair pulled back. Stylish slacks and top. Lab coat with your name stitched in navy blue so nice there ..." He pointed. "Mom will be proud when I tell her."

She shook her head as the door opened and they stepped in. "Y'all are still coming in a couple of months for the girls' birthday, right?" She pushed the floor button and the doors closed.

"We wouldn't miss it. And we want to *thank you* for having the girls so close to *Thanks*giving."

Michelle dropped her hands into her lab coat pockets. "Aren't you funny? Hey, Dad, I was thinking we could go to lunch after I give you the tour. The food here's good but if you want to find a nearby restaurant ..."

Having never had hospital food he liked or enjoyed, he opted for the nearby restaurant.

"I know the perfect place," she told him. "Soul food ..."

"I like it already."

She escorted him down a polished hallway in blinding shades of white to a set of double doors that glided open after she swiped her ID card. The lab was typical, although clearly new. For the next half hour, Westley smiled a lot and shook hands with his daughter's coworkers. Along the way, as they walked through the maze of countertops and medical supplies, Michelle explained the work her team was doing in the field of infertility. "It's exciting stuff, Dad," she said, then slid out of her lab coat and hung it on a hook inside her office.

"I'm impressed," he said, meaning it. He was even more impressed with the number of awards displayed along the bookshelves. Despite her beginnings, his daughter had done well.

"Hey, guys," she told her team as they returned to the lab. "I'll be back in an hour."

He ventured to ask about Cindie over massive plates of fried chicken, mashed potatoes and gravy, and a mound of green beans. "Talk to her much?"

"Rarely," she admitted, then reached for her glass of sweet iced tea.

"Is there a problem?"

"I'm not going to say a problem. But, it's the drama, Dad. Seriously. Now that Karson is eighteen and heading off to Georgia in the fall and Patterson has finally had enough of her, she does nothing but gripe and moan." Michelle waved her fork in the air for effect.

"How is Karson?"

She smiled. "He's good. He figured out about Patterson, which didn't go well. Fortunately, he had good parents in Kyle and his wife. Otherwise ... if it had been only Cindie and Patterson ... gah ..."

"Cindie's a mess. Even when it looked like she wasn't, she was."

"I've tried to talk to her ..."

He stabbed his beans that glistened from being cooked in fat. "About?"

Her eyes widened. "Everything. Her drinking. The dramatics. Finding God, even." She shook her head and her jaw flexed. "To which she replied, 'Why? Is he lost?'"

"Ouch."

"I also suggested seeing a doctor who can *really* help her and not these jokers she's gone to." Michelle's eyes misted, then, with a blink, cleared. "Not to mention her incessant need for a man in her life … seriously, I don't know why you ever …" Michelle reached for her glass again but dropped her hand on the table, eyes wide. "Sorry. That was unkind."

An unaccustomed rush of emotion pushed through him and he bristled. "Michelle," he finally said. "Look … We both know that Cindie is your biological mother and Ali is—"

"My mom."

He nodded. "Your mom. Yes. But, Cindie was—is—a mess, yes, but at one time she was just a little girl whose world got stomped on. A little girl who grew up to be *very* beautiful. You look so much like her, you know."

"I know."

"She just … well, I think her dad leaving the family that way really did a number on her and then, well, you know … Lettie Mae …"

Michelle laughed then. Easily. Freely. "Heavens. Lettie Mae …" She picked up her chicken leg and bit into it, chewed, and swallowed. "That's another thing, Dad. When Lettie Mae died, you'd think Cindie had lost her best friend the way she carried on. You and I both know how it really was."

"Listen, I never wanted you influenced by Cindie, which is why I saw Trev as quickly as I could about getting custody. I wanted Ali and me to raise you. But I also didn't want you to feel sliced down the middle when Cindie brought up living with her, which is why I let you decide. You were wise enough. Always had been. But, I felt that—I still feel that—your mom and I were the better option."

His daughter's brow shot up. "The best."

Westley nodded. "Maybe so."

"Definitely so."

"I'll take that. Anyway, I don't want you to ever think that—even though—and I'm just being honest here—even though Cindie and I were pretty wasted the night you were conceived—"

Michelle feigned shock. "*Dad . . .* you don't mean it."

He chuckled. "Like you didn't know."

She laughed again. "I know. Trust me. Cindie gave me every detail one night when she'd had way too much sake with her Japanese takeout."

He shook his head. "Well ... I want you to know that you were loved. From the get-go. And I also want you to know that Cindie ... she loves you, too, Michelle."

"I get that, Dad. I just can't—there *have* to be boundaries."

"I agree."

"And I have my girls to think about now."

"Yes, you do."

"I cannot have her influence over them at this stage of their lives." She breathed out. "If ever." Their eyes locked—the same eyes, green and intelligent—until she smiled and said, "So. Wait till you see the new skis the hubs bought me recently..."

Westley leaned back, away from the gnawed bones of fried chicken and the remains of mashed potatoes and gravy. Away from his shimmering green beans and sweet iced tea. He leaned back and crossed his legs slowly, listening to his daughter as she talked about the gift Sturgill had surprised her with. He smiled. Nodded a few times for good measure.

A success. His life had been a success. If he died in this moment, at this table, with this half-eaten meal in front of him and the clatter from the open kitchen and dining area nearly drowning out his thoughts and their conversation ... he had accomplished all that he'd wanted. He'd married a beautiful woman whom he loved and who loved him, in spite of it all. Together, they'd raised a daughter—a good and godly girl, decent and kind by nature—and lived to see her married, a mother herself, and now an accomplished research physician. He had worked a job that hardly seemed like work at all. Hadn't that been what he'd always been taught? Find a job you love doing and it won't seem like work at all.

Well, it was true. Indeed. Life had been good. Good, all along.

Chapter Forty-one

Today
Allison

I sn't life funny. For a moment, the briefest of time, one thinks one has it all. One is happy. Content. But one knows—or at least I knew—that if I were so satisfied, then life would suddenly turn, and I would no longer be.

I think—no, I believe—that since the evening Michelle came down the stairs and into the family room to tell us of Cindie's impending divorce, I'd been consciously aware that "happy" and "content" are only temporary emotions. Fickle perhaps. Untrustworthy.

So much since has changed. Evolved. I am a woman in my mid-sixties now, my dark hair streaked with gray, which I pay my hairdresser to color away every six weeks. My body is still fit, if not a little pudgy. I'm a widow, my husband having passed away nearly a decade ago. A heart attack, of course. He could only run from the inevitable for so long, and then, there it was, knocking at the door of his life again. Only, this time, death would not leave without him.

And so, I buried my husband. My wonderful, remarkable, often impetuous Westley. I had already buried my mother and Westley's father and Miss Justine. Since Westley's death, I have also buried my father and Westley's mother, a woman who never quite recovered from her oldest son's death. "Untimely," she called it. But I wondered. Perhaps Westley had beat death once and, this time, he headed toward a wave he couldn't slice into.

It didn't happen all at once, like with Miss Justine. I didn't find my husband in bed, lifeless. Instead, I received a phone call at the downtown office we'd leased for the drugstores after Miss Justine's passing. The available thousand-square-foot space with exposed-brick-and-plaster walls and scarred, unpolished wood flooring had, at one time, been a candy- and ice-cream shop where children gathered after school, the younger ones with their parents, the older ones without. *Miss Penelope's* had been an iconic Odenville site until Miss Penelope, an old spinster with a knack for bringing joy to everyone around her, passed on to her heavenly reward. Without heirs, the shop closed and remained that way until Westley had the idea to turn it into the office/storage space for the drugstores.

"We'll add a few walls," he suggested. "Make a boardroom where local groups can hold their meetings."

"What kind of groups?" I asked as we walked through the dust-laden space.

He slipped his arm around my shoulder and drew me close. "You know, sweetheart. Book clubs. Women's meetings. Men's clubs. They can go across the street to Mama Jean's, grab a cup of coffee and some donuts ... whatever ... and then come here. We'll be *the* spot for this kind of thing."

"But what will we *get* out of it? Do we charge?"

He squeezed my shoulder. "No, baby. We're giving back to the community. That's all."

Westley had been right. What the good citizens of Odenville dubbed *the drugstore office* became *the* hub for club meetings, but it also offered me a chance to get to see how Westley's work at the pharmacy had touched so many. *Everyone* loved Westley. Through the years, I'd become so enmeshed in raising Michelle—her schooling, her socializing—and my work at Miss Justine's that I had failed to realize his influence on our small section of the world.

Now, I knew.

It was here, while a book club gathered in the boardroom early one afternoon as the summer's heat gave way to autumn's promise, that I sat at my desk, entering numbers into the computer as I had once entered into a ledger, that my phone rang and an anxious pharmacy tech told me to "come quick."

And so, to the pharmacy I went. Just as I'd done that afternoon when I had a sore throat all those years ago. Only this time, I ran. Because, this time—unlike the day I followed Michelle's dictate that her father needed me behind the house—this time, I understood. This time, I knew.

No, Westley wouldn't dare leave the world in a snap. Instead, he lingered twelve days. Long hours upon hours where, every day, I sat by his bed where he lay comatose under a DNR sign. In a room where machines pumped and whirred, blinked numbers and codes, sending fluids in, drawing fluids out ... keeping his heart beating and his lungs breathing. I stroked his arm, held his hand, worked his fingers when they curled inward as if in some wild attempt to hold on to a life that wanted him to let go. I spoke reassurances to him, telling him I knew he could beat this. That he had to stick around to see our grandchildren grow up and do all the great things we'd dreamed of. I reminded him how he'd planned to teach them to ski ... and ride bikes—to enjoy life. I pressed into him the memory of how much we loved him—all of us—and that he had been the best husband I could have ever dreamed of having. The best father for Michelle ...

Michelle, who had come down right away, leaving her work behind. Then, ten days after his heart attack, she and I made the godawful decision to end all life support. Michelle's arm slid around my shoulder as my shaking hand scrawled my name on a solid line I barely could see ... the final okay to bring our marriage to a close.

"It won't happen right away," his doctor told us. "Could be days. His heart is weak, but his lungs are still in good shape." And then he left us.

"I have killed your father," I whispered to Michelle when the door closed behind him.

"No," she said, her voice choking. "You've merely allowed *God* to make the final decision."

From then on, the only time I dared leave Westley, whether to get a cup of coffee or stretch my legs, was when Michelle insisted, saying she'd call immediately if anything changed. So, on those rare occasions, I kept my phone in my hand as I stepped down the now-familiar corridors, or entered the noisy cafeteria for coffee, and even as I sat in the tiny hospital chapel with its nondescript stained glass window and icons and books welcoming anyone of any faith to come in, to reflect, or pray.

Although I was able to sit quietly and draw strength from the words of those who had prayed there previously, I found saying my own impossible. Perhaps, I mused, their words lingered in this room of low lights and padded pews. Perhaps they rested on the heavy silver candlesticks or along the table near the front where a scattering of meditative books and pamphlets lay. Or, maybe, they skipped along the measures and bars of the almost imperceptible piped-in music. I don't know; I only know that they were there, and it was upon a padded pew that I sat when the phone vibrated with a text message from Michelle. "Come quick," it read.

I bounded up. Ran out. Dashed down hallways and up the staircase, not wanting to wait for the elevator. "Please, God," I said over and over. "Please God ..."

I cannot tell you, even now, what I was asking God for. Please don't let my husband die *ever*? Please don't let him die without me beside him? Please let him, by some miracle, be okay? But I can say, with the greatest marvel, that as I bounded toward his room, a memory crossed my mind. A flash of the night we stood outside my parents' home—my childhood home—standing toe to toe in our first real battle. Westley was leaving me to live in Odenville for the two months preceding our wedding. But, as he'd always been able to do, he'd won the skirmish and had pulled me into his arms, almost without a fight from me. And there we'd spoken the words that now seemed to reverberate between the narrowing hospital walls, the precisely placed opened and closed and half-closed doors of the patients' rooms.

"I don't like the idea of you not being here," I'd said. *"With me. Always."*

"Me either. But it's just a little while, sweetheart. Not forever. Never forever."

I ran into Westley's room to see two nurses working, although I could not register what the work of their hands entailed. Michelle stood next to her father, her hand on his chest, her arm stretched out as though she were casting some type of healing spell on him. I didn't know what it meant, but I did the same—I pressed my left hand against the blue-and-white hospital gown, watched my wedding set rise and fall in the rhythm of the ever-slowing heartbeat of my husband, my life partner. His breathing had become more labored than before and the monitor's beep-beep-beep slowed to vast spans of time between.

One of the nurses said something—I don't know what—and left the room, then reentered. I looked up at Michelle whose eyes spilled tears but without her sobbing. "What?" I asked her. "Why aren't they doing something?"

Michelle glanced at the DNR, telling me without words that there was nothing they *could*, by law, do. Westley had a directive, as did I. We'd signed them together. Only, I never thought we'd need them. Somehow, I'd believed we'd live forever ... never truly growing old, never really growing tired. That, even though we'd buried our loved ones, Westley and I would carry on and death would never separate us.

The beating under our hands thumped in finality. His breath came in puffs. Once ... twice ... three times. Finally, a fourth intake of air—a last gasp of our time together—followed by a long sigh, and it was over. Westley's life. *My* life. "Oh, Wes," I cried, my knees buckling, my hands gripping the siderails of the bed.

Michelle came around, gathered me up and helped me to the chair I'd let out to sleep in every night, then slid in beside me. Together, we sobbed until our own breathing became normal again. Michelle whispered, "Mom, we need to let the nurses take care of things."

I nodded and we rose to leave the room, but not before I gave Westley a final kiss. While his lips were still warm. While his spirit still hovered. While he could—*oh, surely he could*—how much I would always love him.

An hour later, Michelle and I left the hospital to plan a funeral. To make the necessary calls to family and friends. To somehow ... *somehow* ... begin a new normal.

Southern women are strong by nature, my grandmother once told me. *We are the true Scarlett O'Haras. We raise our radishes into the air and declare that, "as God is my witness we shall never go hungry again." Remember that ...*

And so I stayed in Odenville and continued to run the drugstores. I joined one of the book clubs. For a while, I became active in a Single & Over Fifty group at our church, which too often was made up of men looking for "a nurse or a purse," or women who wanted to man bash. I wanted neither. I would never marry again; this much was for sure. I'd had too many years of wonderful to ever settle for anything less. Perfect? No. But wonderful. Always easy? Definitely not. But ... wonderful. I wouldn't trade a moment of the bad with Westley for a second of the best with someone else.

Westley never fully left me. I sensed his presence. I caught the trail of his cologne as I walked within the rooms of our home. I talked out loud to him, then "heard" his retorts.

Your favorite movie is coming on TV this weekend ...

Which favorite movie...

When Harry Met Sally ...

Ali ... that's your favorite movie ... Mine is, and always will be, Black Hawk Down.

I laugh. *No, Westley ...* When Harry Met Sally *is yours. Remember? I want what she's having ...*

Oh, yeah ... Let me see your best Meg Ryan ...

Each night I held his pillow close to my breast and imagined kissing him goodnight. Then, as my eyes closed and I slipped into dreamland, I felt the heat of his arms coming around me. The strength of them. "I love you," I whispered into the dark of every night. This sustained me.

During those first years, for the most part, I filled my days with work, which didn't seem like work at all. Westley had always told Michelle: find something you love to do and then figure out a way to make money doing it. Well, I had. I wasn't changing and touching lives like Westley had or my old friend Elaine continued to do, and I missed my time with Miss Justine and Ro-Bay, but I enjoyed my days. Routine days at times, but I knew I could count on them.

Routine days include routines. Each morning I woke at the sound of an alarm, put my feet on the floor, tossed the covers back over the bed, then padded into the bathroom. Minutes later, I slipped downstairs and into the kitchen where I made my morning coffee, sat at the breakfast table, opened my iPad, answered emails, then played Spider Solitaire to help wake my brain along with the caffeine. Then I headed back upstairs for my shower. I dressed, then went to the downtown office. Every day, the same thing. Except Saturdays and Sundays.

Saturdays I slept in. During the day I took care of things around the house, did my shopping, took in a movie ... that sort of thing.

Sundays I slept in and went to church, then came home, grabbed a book, curled up in my chair, and read until I fell into the best sleep ever—a Sunday afternoon nap.

But routines can be interrupted and so it was that one Thursday morning as I took my shower, life's minutes slowed to a stop. I sucked in my breath as I glided the loofa sponge over my right breast and felt the abnormality. A lump.

I dropped the sponge, pressed my fingers against the area. Raised my arm and rubbed in circles. Yes ... a lump. Small, but it was there.

As soon as I got out of the shower, I found my phone and, while sitting on the edge of the bed, called Michelle and explained what I had felt.

"How big?" she asked me.

"Like a pea?" I said as though unsure.

"Hard or soft?"

"Soft."

"Painful?"

"No. Not at all. Is that good or bad?"

"Does it move?" she asked, not answering my question.

"No. Michelle?" I said, my radish raised and my voice remarkably strong. "Is all this good or bad?"

"Mom, I can't say. I mean, my gut tells me that your first step is to call your doctor and get in to see him as soon as you can. When was your last mammo?"

"Six months ago, I think. Wait ... yes. Six months. Maybe seven."

"But within the last year."

"Yes."

"Okay. Call and get an appointment. They'll probably want to do another mammo."

"I'll call when I get to the office."

"Do *not* get distracted. Call."

"I will. I promise. But ... Michelle, what do you think?"

"It's probably nothing, Mom."

Chapter Forty-two

I was right.

Not initially, because life, and its complications, comes in stages.

"The doctor said it's nothing but that we'll watch it," I told Michelle a little over two weeks and a mammogram later.

"Let's get a second opinion," she suggested.

But I nixed the idea. "I'm sure it's nothing, Michelle," I said, because that's what I wanted it to be. Nothing.

Over the next year, however, as the world dealt with a pandemic and civil unrest, the lump grew from a pea to a grape. Still unmoving. Still painless. But growing. I spent those months lying to my daughter, telling her everything was okay. That nothing had changed. When I finally admitted the truth, she immediately took time off from work and drove down to be with me through the next round of office visits. The new doctor. The next mammo. The sonogram. The biopsy followed by gene testing. And Michelle sat beside me in the new doctor's office when she pronounced the diagnosis—invasive ductal carcinoma, Stage II, Type II—and listened while the discussion of lumpectomy versus mastectomy was beat nearly to death.

"I want you to come back to Wilmington with me," Michelle told me as soon as we'd settled in her car but before she pushed the Start button. "I mean it. I won't take no for an answer."

"Michelle," I said, pulling the safety belt over me and locking it. "I'm sure that—"

"I swear, Mom. I will pack your bags myself and throw you into this car. Hear me?"

"Lord-a-mercy, you sound like your father."

"Dad would want you to come back to Wilmington with me. Especially these days." She paused long enough to give me her best I'm-a-doctor-I-know-what-I'm-talking-about smile. "I guess a global pandemic wasn't enough for you, huh?"

"You know me," I returned. "I don't do anything halfway." I also smiled, but inside my heart squeezed. She had played the "Dad" card. Thing is, I knew she was right—Westley wouldn't ask me to go, he would demand it.

And so, I went, hopeful I would hear a completely different conclusion to the tests. But the diagnosis was the same. However, this new doctor gave me a third choice: double mastectomy. "To avoid future issues," he said.

I allowed myself days to decide, finally settling on having both breasts removed. After all, I wasn't planning to marry again—or date for that matter—and I surely wasn't going to nurse a baby.

And so the deed was done. Afterward, the doctor placed me on oral chemo along with a clean slate and orders to return for regular checkups.

"Mom," Michelle said one evening after dinner had been cleared away and Sturgill began the process of putting the twins to bed. "Stu and I want to talk with you about moving in. Permanently."

I curled my feet under me in the family room chair I'd taken up residency in and breathed out her name. "What? No ..." I had already mentally packed my bags and pointed the car toward southwest Georgia.

"Mom, I'm serious," she said from the sofa. "Our guest suite has everything you need including a private entrance. We can bring some of your things up to make it more like your home and—"

"And, what about my job? I love my work, Michelle."

"Sell the stores, Mom. I know you love your work, but you don't need the cash flow and—if you do this—you can enjoy your life a little."

"But I *do* enjoy my life," I protested. "I've always worked, you know that. And I've always enjoyed it."

"I know that, but, Mom … *Be* with us … be with Faith and Charity. I promise we won't get in your way. We won't expect you to babysit every time you turn around. You can come and go as you like. Besides your best doctor is here."

I started to say that I would love nothing more than to babysit my grandchildren, but Michelle interrupted with, "Look." She leaned toward me. "You're my mother. I want you *here* with us."

For the silliest moment, I delighted in her words. *I* was her mother. Without Michelle, I would have never heard that declaration. Ever. And without Westley, I would have never had Michelle. Without Westley …

Would the spirit of him come with me or stay in Odenville? Or did the spirit of him live within me because I had felt the beat of it in his last moments dancing around my wedding set to trail up my left arm and reside within my own heart? I wondered about the first question; I believed I knew the answer to the last.

"All right," I said.

Her mouth formed a silent "o" as if she'd expected to fight harder for what she wanted. "Seriously?" she asked, her eyes wide. Michelle clapped like a teenager, then leapt up, crossed the room, and gathered me in her arms, kissing my cheek repeatedly. "Thank you, thank you, thank you! I love you to bits."

I laughed with abandonment. "I love you, too, baby girl. To bits."

I brought our bedroom furniture.

I brought my favorite chair and the sofa Westley stretched out on nearly every evening after dinner. I brought odds and ends. The day before I left, I drove out to see Ro-Bay who, thanks to Miss Justine, had invested well. She and her husband now lived in a quiet neighborhood of sprawling brick homes surrounded by tended gardens and made up of spacious rooms with thick carpets so "walking isn't so hard on these old bones."

After our last visit, she kissed my cheek soundly and said she would miss me "something awful."

"I'll call you every Sunday night," I told her. "Without fail. Eight sharp."

"You best."

I held her amazingly unwrinkled face in my hands and stared into eyes that had grown cloudy with time but still held all the wisdom of the ages. "Promise me you'll take care of yourself."

"Haven't I always?"

I released her, allowed my hands to travel down her arms, less muscular than they'd once been. Fleshier. Tears bit at the rims of my eyes, threatening. "We sure had ourselves a time, didn't we?"

She chuckled. "Lawd, I remember that little girl who walked through the door with our sweet Westley that Sunday afternoon..."

"I didn't have a clue."

Her cool fingers cupped my chin. "But you had love."

"I did have that," I said, swallowing past the memory of how I'd almost thrown it away after Westley told me about Michelle, and then again with Biff, a man now retired and living in Key West doing, as Ro-Bay once put it, "God only knows what."

But that near infraction was something only Ro-Bay and I knew about. Ro-Bay and God and me. Ro-Bay, I hoped, had forgotten. God, I prayed, had forgiven. But as for me, I would simply have to live with the truth of my own weaknesses. Although, as the years had passed, I'd finally been able to nearly convince myself that if I'd had more male attention as a teenager—as Elaine once argued—perhaps the second man in my life to show such attention wouldn't have been able to turn my head with sugar-laced words and butterfly-wing touches.

"Go on, now," Ro-Bay told me, bringing me back to the moment. "I got things to do and you got miles to go."

We hugged a final time and then... I walked away from my dearest friend.

I sold off the things I would not take, then put the house Wes and I had raised Michelle in on the market. The movers loaded a truck with the items I kept, then hoisted themselves into their seats and drove away after assuring me, again, of their ETA. I took a final look around the rooms—cavernous and echoing in the absence of that which had given them life—allowing myself a precious memory from each room. Something to savor.

Michelle waited in the car—my car—with the garage door up in anticipation of our departure. Finally, when I knew I could wait no longer, I retrieved my purse from the kitchen counter, walked out the door into the garage, and locked it behind me. After I settled in the passenger's seat and Michelle backed the car out, she pushed the remote to close the garage door. It jostled to life, then edged its way down until, with a shudder, it hit the cement.

My heart burst; the dam holding back my tears went with it. "Mom," Michelle said, wrapping her arms around me. "It's okay."

"I know it is," I said between sobs. "It's just that ... it's my *life*, Michelle. And so much of it was here. Right here."

"But you have so much more life to live," she reminded me, her tone that of her father's.

I reached for one of the brown Dunkin Donuts napkins I kept in the console, then dabbed at my eyes and blew my nose. "I know." But something nagged at me. A puzzle with missing pieces. Something I couldn't quite put my finger on. Yet it was there all the same, hovering under the surface of my soul.

It wasn't until we reached Wilmington, and, in my unpacking, I found the box of small photos that I began to find a few of those pieces. Pieces that revealed their precisely cut edges as I arranged the silver frames atop a marble and mahogany occasional table and stared at the faces of the women within them.

There was *Hillie* ... with her sleepy eyes and wispy head of hair piled atop her head.

Miss Justine ... with her bangles and jewels, her arched brows and bright, painted-on smile.

And *Grand* ... who, even after all the years since her passing, spoke to my heart from time to time. I felt her spirit, strong and resolute, remembering my mother's words concerning her. "Something rose up in your grandmother that day," Mama told me time and again, speaking of the day Grand found my grandfather dead on the side of the road. "Something strong and powerful. She's never lost it." Well, I knew what it was, even if Mama didn't. A fist holding a radish. Like Scarlett.

There was a childhood photo of me and Elaine ... who, with her husband, had won countless awards and accolades for their work with Native American children, and who declared that she'd stop working when God snatched her last breath from her lungs.

And, *Ro-Bay* ... who had family of her own, but who had made Miss Justine's—and mine—as much hers as those who shared her bloodline.

Mama ... who frustrated me often but comforted me more. Just her presence in a room brought all that it should.

Julie ... a grandmother five times over. She and Dean remained in Nashville, Dean now retired, Julie still the quintessential and contented homemaker. She'd sure lived a happy life for someone who married a "bum."

DiAnn ... brilliant businesswoman who had become my unlikely ally. My sister-in-law in the truest sense. My friend, even more so.

And *Michelle* ... my daughter. My world. My unique and special gift. From Westley.

And so it was that, sometime many days and weeks and months later, Michelle found me sitting in the silence of an afternoon made gray with rain. I'd been listening earlier to one of my Pandora radio stations—Simon and Garfunkel—but had since turned it off, wrapped so tightly in a memory I almost couldn't breathe.

That's the thing about music; it evokes both the brightest and darkest of emotions tied to the happiest and saddest of times.

"Hey ... what are you doing?" she asked, flipping on a table lamp. "Did you forget how to turn on a light?"

I shook my head, knowing the telltale signs of my tears would give away the state of my unusual mood. Since reaching an older, hopefully wiser, age, I'd not been one to dwell too much on the negative, but today I allowed myself the luxury of it.

"Mom? Hey—this isn't like you."

I blinked. Looked up to the concern on her face. "Sorry, sweet pea. Just ... I heard a song earlier and ..."

She walked around my chair—she was still dressed in her work clothes, her hair still pulled up in a messy bun—and took a seat across from me. "Did the song get you to missing Dad? Is that it?"

My smile wobbled. "Something like that."

Michelle rested her elbows on her knees, her keys dangled from her fingers until she clasped them in her palm. "Want to tell me about it?"

I shrugged. Did I? At her young age, would she understand what I had to say? Did *I* even have a grasp on the cascade of sentiments flooding over me? Through me?

"Okay, how about I help you out ... what was the name of the song?" she asked, encouraging.

"Dust," I began, then swallowed and glanced at the floor. "'Dust in the Wind.'"

"Oh, yeah. Yeah. I know that song. Kansas. Mid-to-late seventies."

Startled, I looked across the room and caught her gaze. "*You* know Kansas?"

She chuckled. "I lived with Cindie for a while, remember?"

I nodded, no longer bristling at the mention of a name so tightly wound with my past and the man I had married. "What does she have to do with it?"

"Patterson. The man knew everything about music and musicians. He also thought he had to teach everyone what he knew. So, thanks in part to him, I learned about everything from classics to country, rock to the great jazz musicians." Her green eyes widened. "Ask me

anything about Mozart. Or the Grand Ole Opry. Or Hank Garland."
She pointed toward me. "Or *Dylan*. Lord help us, that man loved
Dylan." Her eyes rolled. "He also played a *lot* of Sinatra, which I still
love, and Fleetwood Mac and, well, Kansas."

Her attempt at humor only mildly consoled me. I said nothing.

"Sorry," she finally said. "So ... 'Dust in the Wind.'"

I would tell her, I decided. I would share this special moment in
my life she had not been privy to. "Your father and I were on our way
from Uncle Paul and Aunt DiAnn's to Miss Justine's for the first time.
We were in his old Caprice convertible—"

"I remember that car. Blood red. He had that until I turned—
what—about eight?"

I laughed lightly. "Yes. About that." I took a breath. Worked my
fingers, picking at a cuticle until it turned red with anger, then moved
my hand over the pearl bracelet I'd worn since Michelle gave it to me
as a teenager. "That song came on the radio and ... I remember asking
your father if he thought that it was true. About us only being dust in
the wind."

"And what did he say?"

I chuckled at the memory. "He quoted from the Bible."

"For dust you are and to dust you will return."

Again, she surprised me. "How did you know?"

"Well, I didn't think it would have anything to do with sackcloth
and ashes," she answered with a grin. "Or offspring being as numerous
as the dust of the earth. That sort of thing."

I could only stare in wonder. "How did you get to be so smart?"

Her smile curled naturally. "I had two pretty sharp parents." Then
she waited, but when I said nothing, she continued. "So, the song made
you think about that day with Dad?"

"No," I answered honestly. "That song made me think about me.
Question my worth. My value. My purpose for having ever been born.
I honestly—I honestly don't think I ever knew ..." A pitiful chuckle
escaped me. "...what I wanted to be when I grew up."

"Mom ..."

The tears threatened again. "I'm sorry, Michelle. But I—I've just been thinking, is all. I mean, maybe losing your dad ... and then my breasts ... and the gamut of emotions that goes along with that ... and the move here ... and ... and getting old and then everything we all went through when the country shut down and all that happened afterward ... just everything. I mean, *what* will I leave behind when I die? I'm certainly too old to do any great, monumental thing now. And I keep thinking that all anyone will ever be able to say about me, other than that I was a fairly decent person, is that I married Westley, moved across Georgia to Odenville, and entered some numbers into ledgers day in and day out until I entered them into computer spreadsheets and then I sold a business and moved to North Carolina." I stood. Started for my bedroom.

"Where are you going?" Michelle called after me.

"I have *no* idea," I said, returning on nearly the same footprints as I'd left.

"So, looking back, what would you have been ... if you could have been anything?"

I blinked. "That's just it. I still have no idea. I only wanted to be Westley's wife and your mother."

She stood before me, my daughter, arms crossed, lips drawn into a thin line. Her hip was cocked, one foot rested slightly above the other. Then, after a tap of one low-heeled pump, she jiggled her keys and said, "You're coming with me." She waved her arm in the direction of the door. "Come on."

I followed, not knowing why, only knowing that to do so was important to her. "Where are we going?"

"Come on."

"Just like your father," I breathed out in frustration. I was hurting, for crying out loud. *Let me hurt. No more radishes brandished high! Let me hurt!*

After a nearly silent half-hour ride in her car, we pulled up to the research center where she worked. "I want to show you something," she said as she popped the car door open and stepped out.

We walked without speaking, first into the lobby, then—with a wave of a security badge—into the area of the building where she spent her days, so cold, my breath formed puffs of air around my face.

"You get used to it," she said in response to my shiver.

"I suppose you do but remind me to buy you mittens for Christmas."

"Cute. Now, then. Do you see all this?" she asked, pointing to the countertops filled with equipment I couldn't begin to understand, much less title.

"Of course."

"Good." She took another step, then looked over her shoulder. "Please follow ..."

I started to grin at this daughter of mine with her authoritative voice, then thought better of it. I wasn't sure I liked the way the tables had turned but was equally sure that I did.

Michelle led me into her office, which was almost as sterile as the rest of the lab. A desk neatly stacked with papers and files. A black leather executive's chair. Two occasional chairs made of chrome and white leather. A white Ikea-purchased bookcase filled with books separated by plaques and awards dominated the largest wall. It was to this wall, she took me. "Do you see all these?"

I nodded. "Yes."

"Whose name do you see?"

I blinked toward them, then back at her. "Yours."

She took one of the wood-and-brass plaques from the shelf. Wiped it with her hand to scatter the dust that had gathered there. The irony played with my heart and I nodded into a half-smile. "What does it say here?" she asked, now handing me the award.

I peered down and read: "This award is presented to Dr. Michelle H. Hamilton in recognition for her outstanding work in the area of obstetrics and gynecology, most especially ..." My words caught, my eyes having read the words ahead. ". . . most especially in the field of infertility."

Gently, Michelle took the plaque from me. She placed it back on the shelf, then led me to one of the chairs before sitting in the other. "Mom, do you know how many women have been able to have children because of the work we do here? Women who otherwise would never know the joy of carrying a child in the womb? Of feeling it kick or hiccup?"

I swallowed. Looked at her. Looked fully at her, seeing the passion she felt toward her job and the compassion she had for me. "No."

"Me either," she whispered, then smiled. "There are too many to count." She straightened slightly before adding, "Do you know *why* I chose this field?"

I crossed one leg over the other. "You told me once it was something you were just interested in."

"Well, then I lied. I wasn't just *interested,* Mom. I saw—my whole life—I saw what not being able to carry a child did to you." She reached over and touched my bracelet. Rubbed one pearl between her fingers. Lovingly. Tenderly. "I *know* how much I mean to you, how much you love me, but I also know that you would have done anything to have given birth to a baby of your own." She looked around the room, then over her shoulder toward the door leading to the austere laboratory. "I did all this because of your influence, Mom. I did this—all of this— because you were willing to take in a little girl who was a stranger and make her your own, the surprise daughter of your husband and some flaky girl he had a one-night stand with—"

"Michelle," I breathed out, pleading with her to stop, hardly able to see now for the tears. Nearly unable to breathe from the knot in my throat that matched the one forming in my chest.

My daughter's fingers played with themselves, then stilled. "Can you even imagine what my life would have been like—how I might have turned out—if Cindie had raised me?"

"I've considered it." Because I had. How could I not. Westley had been right. His methods may have been questionable, but he'd been right to fight for her.

"Well, I have, too. During the time I lived with her, she made it more than a little clear that, while she loved me in her own sweet way, I was not about to be her first concern. She had enough of Lettie Mae in her, trust me. Getting me to live with her was only to keep from being alone. And then Patterson came back and her focus in life was him because—and this is probably me being a little Dr. Phil here—I think she needed that father figure." She paused. "So, no matter how much they tried to make me a part of their little duo or trio, it really was all about *her*. Her and him. Her being my mother was only by genetics."

"But, Michelle, I always knew she was your *real* mother. Genetics or not."

"Mom," she answered firmly. "No. You." She caught my eyes with hers—hers and her father's. "*You*. And if you think you'll leave nothing behind, if you think that nothing matters but the dust our bones return to, then look again. There are a lot of mothers out there with *you* to thank." She glanced toward the shelf again. "Your name should be on those plaques. Those awards."

For long moments we said nothing, the only sound in the room a steady tick-tick-tick coming from the wall clock, counting away the seconds. "Well, well..." I finally said as a lone tear slid down my cheek. "What do you know about that..."

We sat in silence a few minutes until Michelle cleared her throat and said, "Kerry Livgren wrote 'Dust in the Wind.'"

"What?"

"That song. Kerry Livgren wrote it."

I raised my chin a little. "Did Patterson teach you that, too?"

"Well, he got me interested enough to know who wrote that and 'Carry On Wayward Son'—Patterson was big into the 70s—and then I did my own research." She shrugged. "I like music and, obviously, I like research."

"I remember when you were big into the 70s."

"Yeah, well, that was also Patterson's influence." She scooted forward in her chair. "Thanks to him, I fell in love with all types of music and I learned to research the stories behind the songs, the groups, the singers. That kind of thing."

My daughter's love for music—an interest that had grown during her senior year in high school—resonated in her telling. "I remember you playing Sinatra at Christmas."

Her face lit. "Ah, yes. Francis Albert Sinatra. They don't make 'em like that anymore." She stood and indicated I should do the same. We were leaving. We were going home.

"You know, I told your father a long time ago—well, I may not get this quite right—but I told him that all the people in our lives touch us. They leave a fingerprint. Some for a moment, some for a lifetime." Michelle flipped off the light as I continued. "Some of those people we never even meet."

"We are influenced by all sorts of people," she said, her voice playful. Philosophical. Dr. Phil again. "No doubt about it. Even those who ended up having a negative effect can leave positive breadcrumbs along the way."

"You don't say..."

Her arm looped with mine as the elevator door opened and, in unison, we stepped inside.

"He saw them in concert once."

"Who?"

"Your daddy. He saw Kansas in concert."

"Wow," she said as though she were contemplating her father at a rock concert. "He never told me that." Then she laughed. "Do you know, for the longest time, I thought they were singing, 'Kerry, you're my wayward son.'"

"What?"

"Seriously." And then she sang the words. *"Kerry, you're my wayward so-on..."*

The elevator doors slid shut to capture the echo of our laughter.

And somewhere, somehow, I thought I caught the rhythm of Westley laughing with us.

After

When I think back on it, I realize I never received a formal proposal of marriage. Not really, anyway. Westley never got down on one knee, never presented me with a diamond ring sparkling above a blanket of black velvet, prisms shooting out in the moonlight. There was no sweet scent of honeysuckle wafting from my mother's garden. No violins playing in a quiet Italian restaurant while candles flickered atop checkered tablecloths. He never said the words women—especially those reared in the South—dream of. Never said, "Will you marry me" or "Will you make me the happiest man in the world and be my bride" or "my wife" or any of the phrases that accompany dreams.

Westley never promised me a perfect life. He never promised me forever.

What he said—if I remember the words clearly after all these years—was "Well, that sounds good."

And I suppose it was.

The End

CHRISTMAS FICTION FROM EVA MARIE EVERSON

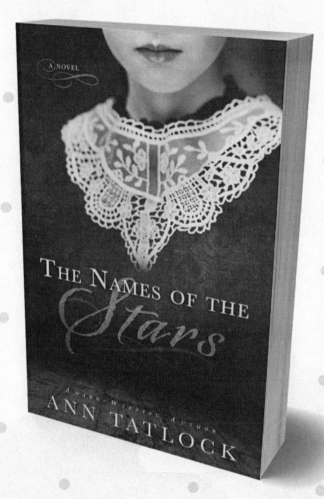

Where her journey ends, the lake begins.